THE LIFELINE

Deborah Swift

SAPERE
BOOKS

THE LIFELINE

Published by Sapere Books.

20 Windermere Drive, Leeds, LS17 7UZ,

United Kingdom

saperebooks.com

ISBN: 978-1-80055-147-3

For Phil,
artist, boat builder, theatre designer and all-round good dad

ACKNOWLEDGEMENTS

My thanks go to novelist Heidi Eljarbo from Norway who advised me on accuracy in the Norwegian sections, and to Maxine Linnell for her excellent suggestions. As always, I'm indebted to editor Amy Durant and the team at Sapere Books. But most of all, I'm really grateful to all the readers who have chosen and bought my books. The best way to help readers find authors like me is to leave a review, and I'm truly grateful for each one.

*'We must be willing to let go of the life we have planned,
so as to have the life that is waiting for us.'*
E. M. Forster

CHAPTER 1

Nazi-occupied Norway
January, 1942

Astrid skied rapidly downhill, heart pumping. It was a risk coming all this way alone, where there was always the possibility she might meet up with some Germans. If she was perfectly honest, it terrified her. A woman on her own was asking for trouble. But Jørgen had been kingpin in the ski club and she'd plucked up enough courage to pretend to be the kind of intrepid girl she thought he'd like, even though it made her stomach crease with nerves.

She brought her watch up to her eyes and squinted at it. Saturday at four o'clock, he'd said. No earlier, as he'd still be at work, and Jørgen was always very precise with things like being on time. Astrid knew her way to the mountain hut though, and she was going to get there first. She'd surprise him, and get the place ready; the fire lit, and a hot dinner bubbling on the stove. She hitched her rucksack further on her shoulders, glancing nervously behind. Carrying a rucksack was forbidden; they were all supposed to have been handed in to the Germans. Pointless Nazi rules; everyone kept their rucksacks anyway.

Still spooked that someone else might be out there watching, she slowed her slalom and scanned the horizon. Nothing. Just crisp white snow flowing into the few patches of Norwegian spruce. Relieved, she wheeled to a stop, admiring the view now she was away from the oppressive streets of Oslo. The snow gave off plenty of reflected light though the sky was already dimming, at only three. That was winter in Norway for you, long and dark.

Almost there. She was looking forward to Jørgen's expression when he found her there, and everything ready. She sped onward with only the few early stars dotted above, and the chill wind making her cheeks ache with cold. At the next fold in the hills, the familiar roof of the hut made a sharp angle against the white.

A sting of disappointment. Damn, he was there before her after all.

A trickle of grey smoke was spiralling from the chimney, and a rectangle of light bled from the window, where the blackout blind was too short.

She looked to the other ridge, to where a single pair of ski-tracks led down.

His, probably. He must have finished work early.

She let out a sigh of frustration. So much for surprising him. But then she pushed off with her poles, whooshing silently downhill, stomach tight with both nerves and the new thrill and anticipation of seeing him again.

Maybe she could still sneak up on him though. She slipped off her skis and waded through the drift to the window, bending down until she could see him through the crack beneath the blackout blind.

Astrid paused, breath steaming the glass. What was he doing? An oil lamp lit the room, and as she squinted in, she could see he was sitting at the table, wearing earphones. A box with a bunch of wires coming out of it was attached to a battery in an open suitcase. She cupped a hand over the glass and stared as he tapped a forefinger onto a black button. Open by the side of him was a notebook. He glanced at it, and continued to tap. He was sending a message by morse code.

Should she interrupt him? She knocked. A quiet rap.

He didn't hear. She knocked louder and he leapt up, startled. The earphones were yanked off his head by his movement, his hand shot to his pocket, and before she could make a sound, a gun was pointing directly at the window.

Astrid threw herself flat on the ground into the soft pile of snow. A moment later and the hut door banged back against the wall. A torch beam skewed wildly side to side.

'Jørgen, no!' she cried, holding up her hands. 'Don't shoot! It's me. Astrid.'

'What the hell...?'

She sat up, brushing snow from her jacket. Her voice came out more tearful than she expected. 'I wanted to surprise you.'

'You idiot. We said four o'clock.' He was shoving the gun back in his pocket. 'I could have killed you.'

'How was I to know? Who gave you that gun?'

'Come inside, I can explain there.'

Astrid was wary; fear had made her jittery.

'It's all right,' Jørgen said. 'It's just I wasn't expecting you. You made me jump. I can explain. But I need to finish sending my message first, or they'll think something bad's happened to me.'

'Who? What are you doing?'

'I didn't want you to know. It's too much of a risk.' He sighed heavily. 'But ... oh, just sit quietly a moment, and let me finish, then I'll explain. It's important. Norwegian lives depend on it, and this time slot's critical.'

Astrid perched on the hard wooden bench on the opposite side of the table. In her canvas rucksack she had some pork belly that she'd queued for hours to get, and a small flask of brandy she'd been saving for tonight. She unscrewed the bottle and took a large swig. She needed it. Her legs were trembling, whether from cold or shock, she was uncertain. *Only Nazis had guns.*

Jørgen put the earphones back on over his thick fair hair, and tuned in the box in front of him with a few twists of a dial. After a few moments his face lit up, and he made a few taps in morse, and then a few more, faster. In this light, the white scar on his eyebrow where he'd slalomed into a tree, stood out like a slash, but his eyes were fixed only on the notebook in front of him, his shoulders hunched and tight. She might as well not have existed.

It lasted less than thirty seconds before he turned everything off and packed it all back into the suitcase in a business-like way. He stood on the table, heaved the case up, and slid open a panel in the ceiling. Once it was stowed away, he pulled the panel back, and vaulted easily to the ground. The notebook went into his trouser pocket.

'Oh Lord, Astrid. I'm sorry.'

He tried to take her hand, but she wanted answers. 'What's going on? You could have killed me with that thing.'

'I'm sorry.' Jørgen shook his head as if to shake the whole situation away. 'You didn't see any of that,' he said. A look at his face showed he was deadly serious.

'Okay,' Astrid said. 'But before I tell you I saw nothing, I have to know. I saw you transmitting something, but who are you doing this for?'

Jørgen's eyes widened. 'You really have ask?' He sat down opposite her and leaned his elbows on the table. 'The Milorg. The Resistance.'

Relief flooded through Astrid. Of course. He'd been a bit of a communist sympathizer at their university — always protesting about something, always arranging marches and handing out flyers, whereas she'd always been inclined to run a mile at the first sign of trouble.

'I know it's a lot to swallow, but I can't tell you exactly what I'm doing,' Jørgen continued. 'If I get caught, and they find out we've been seeing each other, the Gestapo will interrogate you.'

Astrid blinked, trying to take it in. Even the word, Gestapo, turned her mouth dry. Now, so much made sense. Why he was always so evasive; why they had to always meet where no-one else could see. 'I thought we had to meet out here because you had someone else. I thought you might be married or something.'

'Married?' Jørgen let out a bark of a laugh. 'I'm married all right. To the SOE.'

'The what?'

'You remember after university I went to England in a hurry? When the Nazis came?'

'Vaguely. What's that got to do with it?'

'The Special Operations Executive. The English organization that's helping Norway hit back against the Nazis. I went to get training. They help us with intelligence gathering, arms supply — you name it, we couldn't do anything without them. The Germans have a stranglehold on every factory, every communications hub. For any resistance to happen at all, there have to be men like me.'

'It's dangerous, then.' Astrid was trying to make sense of the gun, and there was still a tension in the air.

Jørgen leaned towards her and took her hand. His grip was firm and warm. 'Remember when we first met, when we both skied to this hut by mistake?'

'And we decided to share it for a few hours, and the hours turned into days, you mean?'

Jørgen smiled, but then his smile faded. 'I was looking for a place to transmit from. I wasn't just skiing, and the university's hut seemed ideal. They've hardly ever used it since the Nazis came. But then there you were, and I'd always liked you, right from when we met.'

Astrid remembered. She'd joined the ski club at university, like she'd joined every other club she could join. Trying to find a place she'd fit in. Jørgen stoked her thumb with his, and a frisson of excitement made her catch her breath.

'I'd always thought you attractive,' he said, 'and besides —' he grinned — 'you ski well.'

'Thanks to my father. He loved the great outdoors.'

'Astrid?' Jørgen let go of her hand, leaned towards her. 'This is serious. I shouldn't be getting involved. That's why I left so abruptly that first morning after we got together.'

'And here was I, thinking you'd had second thoughts, and then when you didn't contact me —'

'I wanted to. But it was hard to find a place to meet where the Germans wouldn't see us, and I couldn't risk anyone else being involved.' He let out a groan. 'Why was I so stupid? I should never have used this place for my Resistance work.'

'I won't tell anyone.' Astrid had the impression the words just slid off him, like they meant nothing.

'I know,' he said. 'It's not that.'

'I'd no idea. I thought it must be another woman, and that's why you blew so hot and cold, why you could never commit to dates or times, why you'd never tell me any personal stuff about yourself.'

'There's not much to know.' Jørgen paused and gave a slight shake of his head. 'But a wireless operator's life is often short. Months, sometimes, at best. I've had a fair run, so it worries me that the odds are getting shorter. If they catch up with me, they'll look for all my contacts and interrogate them. If you know what's good for you, you should turn around now and ski away.'

There was a moment's silence whilst he held her gaze. His eyes were hard, uncompromising.

Astrid got up and walked around the table to squeeze his tense shoulders through his plaid shirt, before wrapping her arms around him. 'Fool. I'm not going to do that. I'm staying right here. Whatever you're doing, if it helps get rid of the Nazis from Norway, then I'm right behind you all the way.'

Jørgen turned and swung his long legs over the bench, pulling her onto his knee, and into an embrace. 'You don't get it,' he said. His eyes were troubled as they looked into hers. 'I need to know you've really understood the risk.'

'I've understood. But I also understand that for Norway to survive, to remain as the place I know from the old sagas, for us to honour our culture of fjords and fish, mountains and glaciers, someone has to fight for it. I'm glad it's you. And actually, I'm rather glad it's not me.' She laughed. 'I could never be that brave.'

'You don't need to be,' he said. 'I'll do it for both of us.' He ran his forefinger down her cheek before he lowered his lips gently to hers. 'You taste of brandy,' he said.

'There's only one way to remedy that,' she said, and passed him the bottle.

The next kiss was much longer.

CHAPTER 2

After returning from the mountains on Sunday evening, Jørgen was keen to get back to his house, and to get a good night's sleep before he had to go to work at the engineering office at the State Gas Company the next day. All the way home he'd thought of Astrid, and his blood had run cold at the thought of what could have happened.

How was he to know she'd turn up early? And how stupid he was to go for the gun. But he'd been jumpy lately — kept thinking someone was following him. And he had some Class 1 information to get to the British about German submarines in the U-boat bunker in Bergen, which he'd discovered was codenamed *Bruno*. Last night he hadn't had time to send it.

There was still snow on the streets of his suburb, so Jørgen skied down the middle of the road in the darkening light, listening for traffic, or patrols, and ready to jump sideways if anything came. The whole journey he'd worried about the risk he was putting people under by his work for Milorg.

When he was in England, they'd trained them thoroughly to calculate risk. He hadn't seen his family in months, not since he got back from training. Not that they'd want to see him anyway. But Astrid had just been too tempting.

Jørgen's street was in darkness; most of his sensible neighbours had pulled the blackout blinds down so only the odd slit of light remained. He pulled off his skis by the front door, leaving them propped there in his ski-sack with his poles. As he opened the door he caught a glint of something. He hesitated.

Puddles of snow-melt gleamed on the stairs in the darkness.

He was instantly alert. He never went upstairs in his boots. No home-owner ever did. So instead of going inside, he carefully pushed the door shut again, just short of the latch. He was fairly sure whoever was upstairs would have heard him approach; heard him stamp his boots on the doorstep, heard his key in the door.

He might gain precious seconds to run, if the door was shut.

Quietly, he picked up his ski-sack, careful that the skis didn't clank, and slung it over his shoulder, then sauntered back towards the pavement, patting his pockets as if he'd forgotten something, and walked hurriedly down his neighbour's drive as if he might go inside. He'd already spotted the car parked just off the main street, its engine idling. His heart had begun to race. Only Germans had cars these days.

At the last minute, he dodged down the side of the house and across an expanse of thick snow which in summer passed as a lawn, and towards a snow-laden hedge. A shot whipped the snow in a powder trail just in front of him.

Shit. They'd seen him. Heart thudding, Jørgen pushed himself through the hedge's springy branches and into the alley beyond. Immediately, he heard shouts, and the noise of an engine roaring into life.

He ran, pelting down the dark streets, grateful for his strong boots and water-resistant oiled trousers. Behind him he heard the blundering steps of men running. He was fit from skiing in the mountains, so he went where no cars could go; dodging down through gardens, skittering down the back of a fish-paste factory, towards the harbour. Another shot whistled past him and embedded itself in the wall, but he kept on going. He paused an instant to catch his breath, before ploughing on, the ski-sack bumping against his back.

The harbour below was full of Nazi warships and troops, a bad choice of direction. He'd need to change tack.

Thinking quickly, Jørgen doubled back, making for the steep hill towards the city. Behind him he heard men shout again. Panting, he forced himself into a run up the hill.

A third shot, too close for comfort. No pain. He risked a glance back. Only one man, the other had given up.

Jørgen pushed himself upwards, legs pumping, glad of his mountain training. He gambled that the German would be hampered by his bulky clothes and his rifle, which added more weight than his lightweight skis. The Wehrmacht here had a soft city life; they wouldn't be as fit as him. Another shot, and a woman who was passing by screeched and cowered against the wall, hugging her basket to her chest. Jørgen hurtled past her.

At the top of the hill he dived into a side street and then twisted and turned his way into Lakkegata. It had been cleared of snow and there were many boot prints in the slush. Thank God. Into another side street. In the shadows was a float of the sort used by milk delivery men; one with a charcoal-burner to fire the engine. He crouched down, thrust his ski-sack under it and crawled into its shadows on his belly. He wriggled the pistol out from the pocket of his trousers and waited. With luck, he could pick this German off and give himself more time.

A few moments later, ears straining, he heard the German pause at the crossroads; a silence as the footsteps stopped and he wondered which way to go. A few tentative steps down his street. From this position Jørgen could clearly see his shiny boots, the dark serge of his flapping coat. The German took a few steps down the alley, breathing hard.

Jørgen levelled his pistol quietly at his kneecap. But the man didn't see him and turned away. A minute later he went back the way he'd come, his thudding boots moving quicker now he was going downhill.

Jørgen exhaled. He didn't have to shoot. It would only've made things worse. Then it really would be a manhunt.

Obviously he couldn't stay in Norway now his cover was blown. He'd have to make for Sweden.

He wondered what had gone wrong, how they'd found him.

Astrid? No. She'd never make a spy. The chances of it being her were more than remote. But radio operators rarely lasted long. Even though he'd moved the transmitter every week, someone must have seen his comings and goings to the mountain hut and alerted the police.

He missed the friendly Norwegian police of his childhood, the ones you used to go to if you were in trouble. Now, the police themselves were the trouble; the ones he remembered had all been replaced with the ruthless men in dark blue, the traitor Vidkun Quisling's police. Even Falk, his old professor from the university had joined them.

Jørgen crawled out from under the truck, and paused to light a cigarette. Mostly he didn't smoke; the cigarettes were in his pack only for barter. But his nerves were jangling, and beneath that a deep sense of disappointment festered. He had failed somehow.

He took another drag of the cigarette, grateful for the warmth and the calming effect on his body. He'd have to get transport to Sweden, go across country. That'd be the quickest way out of this mess.

Then of course there was Astrid. He'd have to get word to her.

Damn, damn, damn. Just when he'd found a girl he really liked, the Occupation had ruined it all. Of course she'd be all right without him, she had so many interests; he'd never met anyone who seemed to be in so many clubs. It was one of the things he found attractive about her; she never crowded him. She was so independent, belonged to so many things. But he'd have to warn her somehow, that his cover had been blown, and hope to hell no-one had seen them together.

He didn't dare go to her house, it wasn't worth the risk.

Keeping to the shadows he started to walk back towards the city, aware that to break curfew would mean he would be stopped, and then it would be the end. There was a route he'd heard of, one which went to the southern tip of the country, where a narrow fjord divided Sweden from Norway, close to the Swedish border. An insurance man, Bjørn Lind, had set up a Jewish refugee route that way, by train out of Oslo to the border town of Halden. If he could get to Lind's office unseen, he might get help. He had no radio, so he couldn't contact anyone, and besides, he couldn't go home.

His clothes were suspicious too, for a city man. He was dressed for the mountains, in jersey and cap, to blend in there, not for the world of suits and ties.

One last drag and he finished his cigarette and stubbed it out. He heard sirens and car horns below, and knew they'd be hunting for him as soon as that German could get help.

Quickly, he turned and wove his way back to the city centre, listening for patrols all the way. In this unfamiliar territory, and in the dark, it was a good hour later by the time he located the street where Lind's insurance office was, close to Carl Berners Plass. The name of his firm was painted on the glass window at street level, but he knew the man lived above. He knocked, using the morse 'V' for Victory, followed by a short pause and

'N' for Norway. There was no answer, and the windows remained blacked out. Unsure what to do, he tried again. As he glanced up, he was sure he saw movement at the corner of one of the blinds. Insistently, he repeated the knock, more softly so it wouldn't wake the neighbours.

A few moments later the door opened a tiny fraction, and a man with receding hair and wire glasses peered anxiously out. He looked to be in his thirties, at a guess, and was wearing a baggy knitted jumper which made him look more like a fisherman than an insurance agent.

'I'm Knut Henrikson,' Jørgen said, giving his Resistance name. 'I need help.'

Something in Jørgen's face, and how he was dressed, must have looked desperate enough for Lind to open the door and beckon him in. 'What is it?'

Jørgen explained he was radio operator for Milorg, and that his cover had been blown. 'I don't know how they became suspicious, but there were men waiting for me at home.'

'Do they have the transmitter?'

'I don't know. I left it concealed in the roof void at the mountain hut. If I'd known I was under surveillance, I would have destroyed it. But I have the book. There's not much in it, just a few coded keywords only I could understand.'

'Good,' Lind said. One of the main fears was that a German would find the radio and logbook and start to transmit to England as a Norwegian. 'You weren't followed?'

'No.'

'Thank God. Then come upstairs and I'll get you a drink, but I've not much time.'

Lind padded upstairs and into a parlour which still bore some heat from a settling fire. A small haversack and strong leather boots stood next to it, alongside a pair of old-fashioned-looking skis. 'Your book,' he said, pointing to the fire. 'Destroy it. I've just burned all my papers too.'

Jørgen took it from his pocket and they watched as the papers crackled and flared. 'What's going on? Are you going somewhere?'

Lind poured a small shot of aquavit into a glass and passed it to him. 'I've bad news, I'm afraid.'

'What?' Jørgen took a gulp of the pale liquid, and felt it hit the back of his throat with its fire.

'The last group failed. At the railway station in Halden. My brother was waiting to guide a group of Jews to the border. Unexpectedly a pass control was carried out on the train by a quisling policeman. When things got sticky, my brother lost his nerve and shot the bastard.'

Jørgen sucked in his breath.

'I know. A bad move,' Lind said. 'Two of the refugees, Jacob Bauer and his wife, jumped off the train. But it was no use — it prompted a full scale alarm. Hundreds of soldiers and men with dogs were sent into the area. They soon found the two Jewish refugees, poor devils. Apparently the remaining group on the train were arrested before they could even get off at Halden.

'My brother was travelling under an assumed name, but to cut a long story short, they caught up with him, and I guess he broke under torture. Two days later the Gestapo searched his home in Trøgstad and arrested my father and my elder brother too. I don't know where they've taken them.' Lind's voice cracked, showing signs of strain. 'I thought you were the Gestapo coming for me. Until I saw your face.'

'Sheesh.' What could he say? He stood awkwardly silent. As well as feeling bad for Lind, it was a blow. He'd been banking on that route out. After a pause, he said, 'I'm sorry. It's awful timing, me turning up now.'

'It doesn't matter. Looks like we're both on the run.'

'What will you do?'

'I can't do much here. If I show my face anywhere, I'll be hauled in like the rest of my family.' Lind paused. His eyes had gone glassy. 'Sorry. I'm not much use, am I?'

'Where are you going? I can see you're going somewhere.'

'I'm not trained for Resistance fighting, so I thought I might try and hide out somewhere in the mountains. I should have left already. I was about to put my boots on.' Lind poured himself a second shot. 'Just needed a bit more courage to get on the road.' He downed it in one. '*Skol*. At one point I thought I might have a go at joining a unit in England and fight the bastards from there. Pilot training, but it just seems a crazy idea now, when I'm scared to go out of the front door.'

'Well, why not?' Jørgen said. 'It's better than being sitting ducks here.' Like most of the other radio operators he'd been trained in London. He'd come back into Norway by fishing boat from the Shetland Isles. 'We could try to make it to England. Through the Northern waters to Shetland.'

'Is it possible to still get out that way?'

Jørgen shrugged. 'I came in that way about six months ago. Got to be a better chance than being shot at the Swedish border.'

'You're right. Since the last fiasco, they'll have stepped up border controls by now.'

'I'm game if you are.' Jørgen saw the doubt cross Lind's face. He knew two men were more conspicuous than one, and the Germans weren't keen on groups gathering. 'I have a pistol and I'm not too bad a shot,' he continued. 'One of us can always cover the other. Have you got a gun?'

'No. But then again, a career in insurance doesn't exactly equip a man for armed combat.' He smiled in a self-deprecating way. 'And I never used to like the idea of hunting. Deer are so beautiful. I've never been much of a sportsman, too skinny. But I guess it would be better to go together.'

Jørgen's heart sank. Perhaps it wasn't such a good idea to travel with him, but leaving him behind would be unthinkable when he was grieving for his family like this. 'Do you have maps?' he asked. 'I have some basic idea of the route, but I'd rather scout out the terrain on a map.'

'I can't shoot, but I used to be a keen hiker. Maps I have.'

'Show me.'

Just before dawn Jørgen watched Lind turn the key in the lock.

'Can't believe I'm saying goodbye to this,' Lind said. 'Who knows when I might see it again?'

'When the war is over, you'll be back,' Jørgen said, shouldering his pack.

Lind had supplied him with a grey canvas rucksack, and a change of clothes, a smarter set for daytime wear, in case they had to be in a town. They'd be tight and too small for him, but they'd have to do. A swift call from the public telephone to one of Lind's friends had already secured him new false papers, but they needed to fetch them from a safe house near the outskirts of town.

Jørgen examined the maps, and they decided to go straight out of the city by tram, up the Holmenkollen Line, then up into the mountains working their way northwards, skirting Lillehammer where there was a big Wehrmacht presence, and aiming for the inlets around Ålesund where they hoped to pick up a boat to Shetland.

Lind had been daunted by the route. 'It's a hell of a long way,' he said. 'Climbing those mountains will be tough.'

'If we go up, we have to come down. Half of it will be skiing downhill,' Jørgen said. He grinned and slapped him reassuringly on the shoulder.

Jørgen kept watch from the end of the street, as Lind went to collect their false papers from the safe house he obviously knew well. He watched Lind walk up the path as if the path itself might bite him, his head swivelling to check for patrols the whole time. The place was in darkness, but Lind had no trouble gaining admittance. It was a contact he had used before, for the Jewish refugees still intent on leaving Norway. Many Jews had heard reports from other countries, and were taking no chances, fearful of what might come next in Norway under Nazi rule.

Jørgen trod from foot to foot, restless. What he hadn't expected was that this place would be so close to the street where Astrid lived. Only a few hundred yards away. She'd be sleeping right now, her blonde hair spread on her smooth naked back, unaware that Jørgen was so close.

It wouldn't be much out of their way to say goodbye.

He weighed it up. He'd never wanted to drag her into any sort of danger, but at the same time, after what they'd done last weekend it would be bad to just disappear from her life without a word.

A shaft of torchlight alerted him to a patrol, walking past in the next street. Just what they didn't need. Spotting a wood store in a garden, he crept towards it. It was empty, but shelved and too small to get inside. Just in time, he wedged himself behind it, as the patrol turned the corner and came down the street towards him. Two men. He was relieved they had no dogs. They were chatting, talking in German about the women they had got to know. Jørgen's German was passable, but not as good as his English, since he'd trained in England. He willed Lind to stay inside the house as the swinging flashlight beam came nearer.

His fingers felt for the cyanide capsule in his pocket. If caught, he was supposed to swallow it rather than die a traitor's death. Could he actually do it? He shuddered, then held his breath. The men passed by less than a car-length from him, but they were intent on their conversation. So much so, that when Lind came out of the house he froze at the sight of their retreating backs.

To his credit, Lind was motionless, as if welded to the doorstep. When the men had turned the corner again Jørgen saw Lind look frantically from side to side, searching for him. He put his hand up and waved it, and Lind had the common sense to wait another five minutes before they both emerged.

'Christ, that was close,' Lind said. 'We're in luck. Christina had a contact in Ålesund for the Shetland Bus. I've got the name written down. We have to memorize it, then destroy the paper.'

'Good work. Are these my papers?' He took the folded pass Lind held out.

'Yes; you are now a naturalist called Olaf Stensen. You studied entomology at Oslo University, and you are in the mountains to study rare bees. It was a cover we'd intended for someone else, but he never needed it.' Lind's expression told Jørgen the other man was already dead.

'Bees? In February?'

'Best we could come up with.'

'And who are you?'

'I'm luckier. I'm Otto Ramundsen, a shoe repairer.'

Jørgen laughed. 'After trekking five hundred miles, we might need you.'

'Except that I haven't the first clue how to repair a shoe. Come on, let's get out of here. We'll head for the mountain hut. What shall I call you?'

'It's Jørgen. But best stick to Olaf.'

'Okay Olaf.' Lind gave a lopsided grin.

'Olaf and Otto. Good grief. Sounds like a double act.'

Lind mimed doing a tap dance, but then set off walking. They'd agreed the route the night before, and now they began to make their way northwards, eyes peeled for anyone on the streets.

They had only gone a few hundred yards when Jørgen stopped. 'I just need to do something on the way,' he said. 'I won't be long.'

'What?' Lind's eyes were instantly wary.

'There's someone I need to see, that's all.'

'Who?'

'Just a friend.'

'Are you crazy? Whoever this friend is, they could tell someone they've seen you, and then who knows what might happen.' Lind's eyes were fearful behind his glasses.

'You told Christina.'

'She's been part of the Milorg since the beginning. She knows to keep her mouth shut. Who is this mysterious friend?' When Jørgen he didn't answer, Lind said, 'Oh no. Don't tell me. It's a woman, isn't it? Do the Nazis know she's your girlfriend?'

Jørgen shook his head. 'It won't take long. I won't even go inside. I just want to leave her a message.'

Lind's hand came on his shoulder. 'She'll keep it, and then if they question her and find it, it will go badly for her.'

'It won't be that kind of message.' Jørgen set off at a loping run. He hoped Lind would keep watch, and not go off on his own. They didn't know each other well enough to be certain of each other's loyalties.

Astrid's street was still in darkness, though the light was beginning to pale over the horizon behind. He looked up at the window, behind which he knew she would be sleeping. It seemed so strange to think of her breathing there, only a few yards from where he stood, his own breath steaming in the winter air. Near the front gate was a letterbox on the picket fence. Jørgen slipped his hand in his pocket and felt the cold weight of the brass compass. It used to belong to Astrid's father, and had been a gift from her last time they'd skied together. With a swift movement, he pushed it through the slot. It landed with a loud clunk, and immediately he ran for cover behind a neighbour's shed.

Nothing moved. A blackbird began its piercing song, heralding the dawn.

With regret he hurried back to where Lind waited, shifting from foot to foot and blowing on his hands to warm them. 'You're an idiot,' Lind said.

'Nobody saw. It's fine.'

'Maybe, but knowing I'm on the run with someone who'll take unnecessary risks isn't exactly reassuring.'

'Stop beefing, and let's get moving before someone sees us. We need to be out of here before first light.'

CHAPTER 3

On Monday morning, Sveitfører Falk of the quisling police, drove out to the hill above the suburb where Astrid Dahl lived, and parked in a quiet layby at the edge of the road. He pulled off his warm fleece-lined gloves and took out a pair of binoculars from their black leather case. Within a few moments he had focussed them on Filestredet 14, Astrid Dahl's house. He knew that Jørgen Nystrøm and Astrid Dahl had been close friends at university, along with a group of several other young men and women. All of them were under suspicion of being sympathetic to the Resistance, and all were being watched now in case Nystrøm went there.

Nystrøm had been too cocky as usual. He'd sent signals once too often from his mountain location, and they'd tracked it down, and guessed it was him from the ski club records. One of his men had got a shot at him, but just missed him on his return. The fact he'd run, made it certain it was him.

W/T operators were the bane of Falk's life. Somehow it was always his fault if Norwegian Resistance did something to upset the Nazis, just because he was Norwegian, and so by implication, suspect. The Kommandant had given Nystrøm's capture the highest priority, and if he, Falk, could bring him in, then it would grease the wheels with Nazi command, and move him up the ranks of the quisling police, the *Hird*. Of course, he had the advantage in that he actually knew what Nystrøm looked like from his time teaching him at the university.

Falk pressed the binoculars to his eyes and scanned the street for movement, but could see nothing amiss. He thought back to his days in front of the blackboard, teaching engineering. He knew his lectures were dull, because of the ripple of amusement when he turned his back, and the pellets of spit-covered paper that mysteriously surrounded his feet at the end of every lecture.

And Nystrøm had been a cocky student, one of the worst offenders; too clever for his own good, and far too handsome. Students like Nystrøm, the popular ones, set off a feeling of resentment so intense it hurt. He remembered being a student himself, and the girls flocking to men like Nystrøm, leaving Falk in the shade. He'd always been awkward around girls. Too short, too tubby, and without the good looks that made men like Nystrøm's life so easy.

For Falk, his survival depended on him being in the right place at the right time, and ready to offer something the other person wanted. At parties, he'd get invited because he had a bottle of good wine, or because he drove a car. He knew he had to buy his invitations, because once at the party he was roundly ignored. He saw other men his age were the life and soul of the party with no extra effort on their part whatsoever, just because of their looks. He remembered that awful feeling of exclusion, of sitting in the corner alone, nursing a drink and pretending it didn't matter.

But now, with the Nazis in power, he saw that his bargaining skills could be useful. Good looks wouldn't help you if you were on the wrong side, and Falk had learnt early that being on the right side was essential for survival in this new Norway.

He took his Swiss lighter from his pocket and lit it to warm his fingers, cupping one hand in turn around the flame until the metal case got too hot to hold. The street was beginning to come to life now. At number seventeen a housewife let out a small yappy dog into the garden, and a man further up the road set off in overcoat and cap in the direction of the fish canning factory. Blinds came up, and he saw a couple of Wehrmacht men come out of their lodgings and stomp off towards their car.

After another hour he was getting agitated and cold, despite his fur-lined gloves and the earflaps on his hat. He rubbed at his nose which was crystalline with his frozen breath. Clapping his hands together in his gloves he stamped his feet in the well of the car, before rubbing another clear patch into the steamed-up window.

He looked at his watch. Seven thirty, and the postman was just making his way along the street with his heavy sack. He watched him drop off the letters, glad to have something to watch. He swung the binoculars up and down the street and adjusted them. The door to number fourteen had opened and Astrid Dahl was outside on the path. Tall and slim, she had the blonde, willowy good looks favoured by the Nazis. She was dressed in a skirt and tight-fitting knitted jersey in the local style. She unlocked the mail box and took out a letter. Then she paused, took out something else and stared at it. Something in her sudden stillness was odd.

Falk adjusted the binoculars, trying to bring them into closer focus. From here, the object looked like a stone. Maybe something to hold the letters down. Whatever it was, it made her scan the street and look up and down as if searching for something. Her glance came his way and her face looked straight at him. He dropped the binoculars down, feeling guilty.

Foolish! Of course she couldn't see him, not all the way up here. But her expression had been worried. After another half an hour he spied her leave the house, dressed in hat, coat and boots, with a briefcase in her hand. She would be going to the school. The dossier on his front seat told him she was an elementary school teacher. She was one of those bluestockings who'd studied languages at university, including English and German. He decided to go down to the house; it was just too cold to sit here any longer. She would soon be out of a job anyway. More schools in Oslo were to close because of the shortage of coal, and the premises taken over as billets for the army, or as hospitals for Nazi wounded.

With a cough and a splutter, the engine turned over, and he drove down the hill until he could turn into her street.

Astrid was unaware of the man with binoculars as she reached into the mail box for the letters.

What was this? Her hand touched something cold. She curled her hand around it and withdrew it.

Her father's brass compass.

Its presence made her heart leap because there was only one explanation. Jørgen must have left it there. Was he still somewhere close by?

She glanced up and down the street before locking the box. The compass had belonged to her father. He used to keep it as a paperweight on his desk and she had given it to Jørgen as a gift about a month ago. He knew it had great sentimental value to her, and the fact that he hadn't knocked at the door, or come inside to return it in person tugged at her heart. Did it mean he no longer wanted to see her? Or did it mean something had happened and he was trying to tell her something? The fact he was in the Milorg still hadn't quite sunk in, and the very thought of it made adrenaline race round her veins.

She gave an involuntary shiver, aware of a prickling sensation; a feeling, as if someone was watching her. It could be Jørgen, or it could be … she ran back up the path and in through the front door, shutting it firmly behind her. Jørgen had said his work was dangerous.

No time to think too much, or she'd be late for the tram. She put on her coat and buttoned it up to the neck, jammed on her hat, and slipped the compass into her pocket. Negotiating the ruts of ice, she speeded her step, following some other women with shopping bags who were headed towards the city.

Mondays. Always the worst for crowded trams. She clambered aboard, stamping the snow off her boots, and looking round for an empty seat. She swayed down the carriage as it moved off, and sat down, well away from the men in dark blue uniforms that had taken most of the seats at the back. They were the quisling police, the Norwegian supporters of the fascist government that had sprung into action the minute the king evacuated to England. And they were everywhere.

From the outside, they looked like every other Norwegian, but they were Nazis in their hearts. She had learnt to ignore them if she wanted a quiet life.

She stood her briefcase by her feet and rubbed the misty windowpane for a better view, still mulling over the mystery of the compass. As usual, the streets were full of people queuing in front of almost empty shop windows. Norway had been under German occupation for more than eighteen months, and every now and then she'd pass a building with a slash of red and black, the Nazi flag — the only garish colour in the leached out streets.

The bell dinged as another passenger got on, a tall, muscular man in German Wehrmacht uniform. He saw the empty seat next to her and swung down the moving aisle. Automatically, she stood up, ready to move. Norwegians had a tacit agreement that they would not share a seat with these interlopers, the German occupying forces, or with their supporters, the quislings.

'No need to move for me,' the man said smiling disarmingly. His accent was thick, but his Norwegian practised.

'I'm getting off anyway at the next stop,' she said, anxious to avoid a direct confrontation.

'Keep your seat until then,' he said, still smiling, but a steely determination in his voice. 'I'll stand for you when it's necessary.'

'No, really,' she protested. The arrogance of the man. She thrust the briefcase ahead of her along the bench to prevent him sitting, then struggled out of the narrow seat and into the aisle.

The man shrugged and sat down. 'Your loss,' he said.

She gave a tight-lipped smile back. Of course she wasn't getting off at the next stop. Instead she clung to the metal pole, her face going pinker as he continued to stare, and the stops came and went. Ignore him, she thought. But she couldn't help but watch him from the side of her eyes as she kept her eyes open for her stop. He was straight-nosed, with light sandy-coloured hair under his peaked cap, and the sort of chiselled jaw favoured by movie stars.

'Where are you going?' he called.

She pretended not to hear. The tram slowed and she hurried to the door, desperate to get off. At the next stop she jumped out, staggering slightly as the tram hadn't quite stopped.

Damn him. Damn them all. Now she'd have a long walk, because it wasn't her stop.

As the tram sped by, throwing up slush, his face was still staring at her from the window. How did it feel to be him; to be able to intimidate just on the basis of his uniform? So certain, so self-satisfied. So convinced that the Norwegians were just like him under the skin, simply more Aryans who just needed to see the light of the Nazi ideals.

At the school gates she bumped into her friend Sonja, who taught at the same elementary school. Her round pink face and her big grin, instantly dispelled the morning's awkwardness.

'Who've you got this morning?' Sonja asked, as they crowded in through the main door. The building was cold and dilapidated; the new school with its spacious rooms and special facilities for woodwork and chemistry had been taken over by the Germans for billeting their forces. So they were back in this old draughty barn of a place.

'4B,' Astrid answered. 'You?'

Sonja shook her long fair plait from her knitted hood. 'Geography with the first form. But I've got to teach them all about German rivers. Ugh.' She unclipped a paperclip from her coat lapel. Paperclips were worn by Norwegians as a symbol of unity against the Occupation. 'Better take this off. Mr Pedersen's more quisling than Quisling himself.' Sonja said. 'I wish we still had Mr Kristiansen.'

'I never wear my paperclip now,' Astrid replied, 'it's just asking for trouble.' She thought of the man on the tram. 'Mrs Bakke got stopped just for wearing a red knitted bobble hat. They told her wearing such Norwegian folk-art was banned. Poor woman was only trying to keep warm.'

'Talk of the devil,' Sonja whispered. Mrs Bakke, a short, stout woman with her hair in a hairnet marched by, ringing a hand-bell. The clanging stopped their conversation and the corridors instantly filled with rushing children.

'See you later,' Astrid called, as she followed the stream of jostling children down the corridor.

Later that day Astrid shrugged her way into her fur-lined coat and put on her knitted hat before picking up the pile of exercise books from the staffroom table and pushing them into her briefcase. Twenty-five essays to mark tonight, but she'd still make time to stop off with Sonja. Sonja had taken her under her wing when she was new to the school and made her feel like she belonged. And after a day at the chalkboard, a hot chocolate in the little café on Drammensveien always hit the spot. Though these days it was more water than chocolate, and sugar was something she could only dream of. Besides, it was always better to walk together; some women on their own had been the victims of what people euphemistically called 'Nazi Chivalry'. The sort of chivalry that couldn't be refused.

As she stood on the threshold of the school turning up her collar against the biting cold, the children rushed past — all flapping coats and earflaps, satchels slung over their shoulders, excited smiles lighting up their faces, the smiles that had been mysteriously absent in her arithmetic lessons.

'Hey!' Sonja's hand came on her shoulder. 'Café?"

'You bet,' Astrid said.

They walked briskly down the pavement in their winter boots avoiding the edges where the snow was heaped and set solid into ridges. As they approached the turn off, they had to dodge a tram rattling around the corner, but as they did so they saw the little street off Drammensveien was already full of people.

They stopped abruptly at the sight of the uniforms, immediately wary. So many grey-green Wehrmacht uniforms always spelled trouble. A second glance showed them that many of the Germans were armed and moving people forward down the road. Two men were being hustled from the café, their hands on their heads, by quisling police.

'Let's go,' Astrid whispered, tugging hard at Sonja's sleeve., 'It's not worth it.' She turned to walk away.

'Halt!'

Astrid felt Sonja stop and stiffen. She turned and looked back to see what the hold-up was.

A German soldier holding a rifle was right in front of her, and with him, the German from the tram.

'So you lied to me,' the man from the tram said, his eyes finding Astrid's. 'You said you were only going one more stop.' He grabbed her by her coat lapel, then pulled, trying to drag her away.

Wait!' Sonja protested. 'What are you doing? This is crazy! What's she supposed to have done?' The words came out as a torrent. Astrid could feel Sonja's fingers clutching her arm.

'She insulted me,' he said.

'Let go,' his soldier friend said, in thickly-accented Norwegian, pushing Sonja away. 'Let go, or I take you too.'

But Sonja didn't let go. Astrid was dragged by the collar, stumbling, down the street, with Sonja still clinging to her elbow.

'Leave me,' Astrid tried to call to Sonja. 'It's okay.'

'Quick, walk.' The man from the tram dragged her forward as you might a dog, determination in the set of his mouth. The snow had begun to fall again, and her boots skidded on the slippery surface.

'Let her go! Where are you taking her?' Sonja was still following, objecting,

'*Jezt, ein mehr!*' shouted another German Wehrmacht officer, a shorter man with a face raw and ruddy from cold. He waved his rifle, corralling people into the cul-de-sac at the end of the road.

One more. Astrid's German was good enough to understand, and it struck dread into her.

In an instant, the red-faced Wehrmacht man grabbed Sonja roughly by her long plait and pulled her away.

'No! Not her. This one,' said the German from the tram, trying to stop him and pushing Astrid forward.

'What's it matter, Schmitt? Any woman will do,' the red-faced man said.

'Stop!' Astrid cried. But she had no time to ponder further because a blinding blow hit her across the eyes as he swiped hard at her face with a gloved hand. The shock was enough to make her let go, and bend double, clutching at the smarting pain.

When she stood, cheek throbbing, eyes streaming, she found she was holding Sonja's school bag that had been over her shoulder. Through eyes blurred with water, ice already forming on her lashes, she saw the soldier drag Sonja to the wooden palisade at the end of the street that fronted the railway line behind. A crowd of people were already there, ashen-faced, held there by a rank of men with machine guns. Sonja looked dazed, eyes fixed on the men in front. As Astrid watched, she started to tuck her fair plait back inside her hat in a familiar nervous gesture

Before Sonja's hand could drop, the men opened fire.

The noise ricocheted over and over around the walls as if it would go on forever.

Astrid's mouth opened, and a gasp of cold air entered her lungs, choking her. She couldn't even blink.

In the moments afterwards there was not a single sound. If there was birdsong, their ears couldn't hear it. The whole city seemed to have stopped.

An older, heavy-set German in a long leather greatcoat and peaked cap stepped forward. Some big noise in the Wehrmacht, bristling with gold buttons and insignia. He ignored the crumpled people, slumped on top of one another like sandbags against the red-spattered wall.

'Forty Norwegians will be shot for every German man lost,' he said. His Norwegian was understandable, but guttural. 'You knew that. Better you tell your comrades to behave themselves, hey?'

As he went, the rest of the Germans followed. One of the last to go was Schmitt, the man from the tram. He turned and looked over his shoulder at her. His slight smile was knowing and triumphant. Then he walked away towards a parked truck filled with other Germans. His long rangy stride was leisurely, as if he were taking an afternoon stroll.

A lorry came, and some prisoners of war climbed out, in their thin ragged clothes. They piled the bodies in the lorry and drove away. Still nobody moved. She had the impression that somehow Sonja and the other people were still there, ghostly presences still waiting by the wall.

An elderly woman in a fur hat began to whisper the words to the Norwegian anthem, 'Ja, vi elsker dette landet.'

'Yes, we love this country, and the saga-night that lays dreams upon our earth.'

Astrid joined in with of the rest of the Norwegians on the street, as the snow fell thicker now from a leaden sky. Nobody sang, just this low mutter under the breath. When it was done, they were reluctant to leave, the feeling of being a witness to the atrocity was so strong. But finally the piercing blast of a train whistle behind the wall broke the spell.

It had been so quick. One minute she was about to enjoy hot chocolate with Sonja; the next Sonja was dead and no trace of her remained, except the red stain, which even now, was being covered by the gently falling snow.

She turned to a man behind her. 'What was it about? Why did they do this?'

He stabbed at a newspaper. 'The Resistance. It's their fault. Bastards. They blew up a German train. A German was killed.'

Astrid shook her head, thought of Jørgen. 'They're just good Norwegians, who want Norway back. Just like us.'

'Not like us,' he said bitterly. 'Those scum are not like us. They risk our lives, good Norwegian lives, for their own glory. What good does it do, I ask you? What good?'

Jørgen used to be so popular at university. Now he was reviled; one of these Resistance men in the Milorg that they were blaming for this.

It could have been Jørgen who'd blown up the train.

No. No use to blame anyone. Only herself. That German, Schmitt, was going to take her, because she hadn't sat next to him on the tram. But somehow they'd taken Sonja instead, and she should have stopped them.

When Astrid got home the shock had set in and she was shaking. The winter cold had numbed her feet through the soles of her boots, but inside she was frozen, as if her emotions too had become encased in ice. So it was, she thought, with all the citizens of Norway, who had seen their country torn from them and their king exiled. But worst of all was that they had to just walk away from atrocities like these and go home as if nothing had happened.

She still had Sonja's school bag. She didn't open it; she couldn't bear to; she knew what it would contain — 4B's Geography homework books and the tin which Sonja had taken with her containing her *matpakke* for lunch. Instead she warmed her fingers over the gas, and when the kettle hissed on the hob, she turned it off and went to the window. It should have been her against that wall. Schmitt had chosen her because she'd refused to sit next to him on the tram; he'd have put her to death for something so small. It seemed unbelievable. She remembered the feeling of Sonja clinging to her arm, sticking by her side as she always did.

If only she could turn the clock back. She remembered skiing with Sonja before the war — the dazzling sun on their faces, the snow a pristine white tablecloth over the land. The random senselessness of her death made her so angry she thumped her fist down on the sill.

Outside, her street looked as it always had. Planked houses, the eaves decorated with carved fretwork finials, neatly cleared paths. Yet this disease was in their midst, one that killed without warning. She had the intense urge to tell someone what had happened, but who could she tell? She wished Jørgen were here. He ought to know that his Resistance work had repercussions. But she knew he wouldn't want to think about that; it was far easier to pretend such things didn't exist.

CHAPTER 4

The next day Astrid decided not to get the tram to work. She was self-conscious about her bruised face, which was now turning into a black eye, and she didn't want to risk getting into a carriage with another man like Schmitt. So she walked quickly for she had three miles to cover, and needed to keep warm. She saw a car turn the corner into her street and a stout man in a fur cap drive by. He slowed as he passed her but didn't stop.

Just the sight of it made her shrink inside. Saloon cars like those were only owned by Nazis and their sympathisers now. As she strode along, she worried all the more, wondering what it meant, it being on her street.

She dodged around a queue to the butchers, where about twenty women stood in line. Poor things. They'd probably end up with only a small piece of sausage meat anyway. Past the empty bakery window which had a sign pasted on the front, 'No flour today'. At the school gates though, groups of schoolchildren hung around, chattering in the usual way. She wondered who would cover Sonja's classes; what Mr Pedersen the head, might say.

She passed Mr Feinberg, thrusting a package wrapped in greased paper at his daughter. Astrid had taught ten year-old Sara Feinberg last term, and found her a vivacious and sharp-witted child, always keen to learn. Of course she knew they were German, and Jewish, and had fled their own country when the Nazis refused to withdraw from Poland. They'd seen what was coming.

'Morning Miss Dahl,' Sara chanted, grabbing the package from her father and cramming it in her satchel. Within a minute she was gone, her brown plaits lost amongst those of her fair-haired friends.

'She's settled in well,' Astrid said, one hand hiding the bruise.

'I know,' Mr Feinberg said. 'It seems a shame to have to move her again.'

'You're moving again?' Astrid asked. 'Do you have to go?'

He grimaced. 'You know how it is. At first, they said it would be a peaceful occupation, but I see now that they want to Nazify the whole country, with their so-called "enlightenment" films and propaganda.' He looked away, watching the bigger children go by. 'Someone threw a stone at us just last week.'

Astrid thought of Sonja but said nothing. She didn't want to scare the children.

'It breaks my heart,' Mr Feinberg said. 'Sara wanted to know why everyone hates us, why we are always hiding and running away. What can I tell her? Pretty soon, my bookshop will be targeted. We've seen it before in Frankfurt, that's why we came here.' He saw her eye, where her hand had fallen away, and stared a little too long. 'I see it's started here. The bullying.'

She shook her head emphatically. 'If the children ask, I've walked into a lamp-post.'

He frowned at her a moment, curious. 'See now why I want Sara out of here. I'm just waiting for some advice; to decide where's best, and we'll be off.'

'Where will you go?'

'I thought Sweden, but some friends of ours were trying to get out of here that way, and they got stopped before the border and deported to a camp somewhere.'

'That's awful. And Sara's so bright; all this change can't be doing her education any good.'

Mr Feinberg looked at her with his intense brown eyes as if she were a crazy person. 'School's not important. I don't care if she never passes a single test, or is the biggest dunce in the class, as long as she's alive and safe, and we can be together.'

She'd offended him. 'If there's anything I can do to help...' Astrid said, tailing off, knowing that there would probably be nothing, but feeling like there ought to be something. She had never seen a sign of a mother, or any woman. They were a lone pair, Mr Feinberg and Sara.

She watched him go. A man in a threadbare overcoat, who would be tall, but for his slightly stooped walk, as if he was bowed down with worry.

The morning assembly made no mention of Sonja at all and she found out in the staff room that a student teacher had been drafted in to cover Sonja's classes. Should she say something to the others? She couldn't get the scene out of her mind, and felt tearful at the thought nothing was being done about it.

The bell rang for lessons to begin and she was still worrying what to do. Instead, she did the next thing, which was to open the door to her classroom and place her pile of books on the table.

'Before you ask,' she told the class, 'I had a bit of an argument with a lamp-post.'

Giggles and whispers from the girls. She'd barely picked up her chalk when the door opened and Mr Pedersen, the head, came in, carrying a thick pile of documents. He was an untidy, balding man who always sported a university gown over his shabby tweed suit, and talked as if the words in his mouth were in danger of escaping — with his mouth almost completely shut. It gave a whiny quality to his voice.

She waited as the class stood and greeted him. 'Sit down, class,' he said, pushing his heavy square glasses back up his nose. He placed a sheaf of typewritten paper on the desk in front of her. 'Guidance from President-Minister Quisling. Physical education is to be replaced today by activities suitable for the new regime. All class members will join the *Undomsfylking*.'

Astrid stared at him. The *Undomsfylking* was the equivalent of Hitler's Youth organisation.

'It's all in there,' Mr Pedersen said, tapping the top sheet with a fingernail. 'And you will need to join the National Teachers League, the *Norges Laerersamband*. Those that do not, will be deployed elsewhere. It goes without saying that it is in your best interests to join.'

'They're changing the curriculum today? With no notice at all?' Astrid asked. 'What about the girls' gymnastics? Will they still need their kit?'

'I'm sure it's all spelled out in the documents, Miss Dahl,' Mr Pedersen said, with a thin smile. 'I've taken up enough of your class time, so I'll leave you to get on.'

With that, he was out of the door, no doubt to deliver the same news to every other teacher. She thought of Sonja. The school had not even acknowledged her death. Mr Pedersen had said not a word in assembly, and not a word to her class about where she'd gone. It was as if she had never existed.

'Quiet. Quiet!' she said, frowning. The class were whispering among themselves.

'I'm not joining their Youth group, Miss,' one of the girls in the front row said. 'Our neighbour's boy joined. It's all things against King Haakon and saying that Germany is better than Norway. They can't make us, can they?'

'I don't know, Ingrid. Give me time to read it, and we'll see what it says.'

'Oh, Miss —' A chorus of disapproval.

'Get out your geometry books and we'll come back to it later.'

A banging of desk lids as they reluctantly got out their books. Geometry couldn't compete with the idea of rebellion against the new rules, so it was a somewhat rocky lesson. At lunchtime she had the chance to sit in the staff room and read the paper, along with all the other disgruntled staff. It made depressing reading.

One of her colleagues, science teacher Ulf Johanssen waved a page at her. 'It says those that teach "in improper conditions" whatever that means, will be subject to severe punishment. Apparently the Nazi Head of Church and Education will give us more guidelines as to "improper conditions" soon.

'Anyone who doesn't toe the Nazi party line will be slammed in prison, it means,' said Karen Baum, the girls' history teacher.

'There won't be room,' Ulf said. 'The prisons are filled to capacity with Norwegian objectors to the Nazis. Intelligence is; they're putting six of our men into a one-man cell. Even Grini detention camp is overcrowded. They say there are more than six hundred of us in there.'

'Don't. It's too depressing.' Astrid put her papers down. 'How am I supposed to explain all the changes to the girls of 3C? Or explain it to the parents? I've a good mind to refuse. I'll write to the education minister and tell him so.'

'You wouldn't really.' Karen looked at her with wide eyes.

'Well why not?' Astrid was suddenly impatient with them. Why should they just knuckle under and follow like sheep? 'If we explain why in a reasonable tone it might delay it, even if they still try to push it through.'

'Delaying it might work,' Ulf said. 'It'd have to be a letter we can all sign. And all the other teachers. We'll send it round all the schools.'

'Who'll draft it?' Mrs Bakke asked. 'Astrid?'

Everyone looked round. Nobody wanted to volunteer.

'Where's Sonja?' Mrs Bakke asked. 'She's usually good at this sort of thing.'

Astrid was trying to find the words to reply, but the question was never answered. All fell guiltily silent because Mr Pedersen suddenly appeared, clutching his copy of the quisling newspaper. His appearance was deliberate, thought Astrid, because of the new rules. He wants to make sure we don't have time to complain. Normally he'd just sit in his office and never come near them.

After the bell went for the end of school, Ulf caught up with her just outside the school gates.

'Do you mean it, about the letter?' he said. His earnest face searched hers.

'I just feel we should do something. These new regulations are forcing propaganda down children's throats. They betray everything I've ever believed in teaching. All this "superior" race stuff … it's discrimination on a huge scale.'

'If we do it, it might provoke … recriminations.'

She drew back her shoulders. 'I know what it might do. I saw them pull Sonja off the street and shoot her. For no reason at all.'

Ulf searched her face. Her expression must have told him she was serious. 'Shit. I didn't know,' he said. He stood awkwardly, twisting his long scarf in his hands. 'You saw it?'

She nodded. A lump had risen in her throat and she couldn't trust herself to speak.

'Is she…?'

Silence.

'All the more reason,' Ulf said finally. 'We can't be party to that. Can I come back with you now and we'll draft the letter together? Better to do it behind closed doors I think, and I've no coal or wood at my place.'

She let out her breath. 'Come on then. But we'll have to walk. I don't travel on the trams anymore.'

'Well I hope my shoes will hold up. They're more hole than shoe, and I can't get a new pair for love nor money. All leather shoes have gone to the Germans. They're saying they're bringing in paper shoes, with wood soles. Still cost the same number of coupons on our ration cards though.'

She looked down at his shoes, where the sole had separated from the upper. In fact now she looked, she realized he looked like a pauper, even though he was one of the most respected senior teachers in the school. His face had the care-worn appearance of someone who'd been very ill, and his greying hair was lank and needed cutting. All the teachers looked this way, she realised. Thin, worried, and with a haunted look around the eyes.

At her kitchen table they talked about Sonja. It felt good to unburden herself on someone who would listen. Someone who knew what Sonja meant to her. He watched silently as she cried, passing her his grubby handkerchief. Afterwards, they read through the papers Mr Pedersen had given out which told them all teachers were to join Quisling's new Teacher's League. Together they drafted a short response to the quisling Minister for Church and Educational Affairs, Ragnar Skancke, which said that their initial contract as teachers forbade them from indoctrinating the students and they would not be participating in the new League. It was short and sharp and had a space for a signature with the teacher's name and address.

I cannot participate in the upbringing of Norwegian youth according to the guidelines of the Nazi Youth League (NSUF) because it is against my conscience. Since membership in Norges Lærersamband makes me obliged to contribute to such upbringing, and because membership also puts other obligations on me which are against the conditions on which I was employed, I hereby declare that I do not consider myself a member of Norges Lærersamband.

'D'you think they'll all sign?' she asked. 'We could be fired. Or worse.'

Ulf shrugged. 'We just have to hope they will.'

Astrid typed it up. 'We'll send it via the existing teacher's union,' she said, unrolling it from the typewriter bar with a flourish. 'If we get more to sign it, so much the better. And if we all refuse to make the children join their Nazi Youth enterprise, they won't be able to make us do it. We'll just all stick together.'

'I've a friend who'll print it,' Ulf said. 'He has a hidden linotype machine. We can get everyone's address from the register and get it out there by the end of the week. We want to make sure every single teacher in Norway gets one and signs it. Though we'll have to be careful no-one knows it came from us.'

When they had finished she made him a cup of what passed for coffee — ground acorn, with no milk. She had queued for the milk ration but hadn't been in time to get any. Ulf looked like he needed building up, his neck was scrawny where it stuck out of his frayed shirt collar. 'Do you live on your own?' she asked him.

'Yes. In a boarding house. I'm the only Norwegian left there now, apart from the landlady — the rest are Nazi officers billeted on her. Poor woman had no choice. It's not very comfortable, and it makes me feel like I'm going into enemy territory every time I go home. But I've nowhere else, so I just make do.' He took a gulp of coffee. 'Hey, not bad.'

'It's terrible. You don't need to be polite.'

They laughed. 'I'll drink it anyway,' Ulf said. 'Can't waste anything. Actually, sending round this letter will give me great pleasure — to rebel right under their noses.'

'It feels good to be doing something, doesn't it,' Astrid said. 'I never thought I was patriotic, but resisting them only seems to make me want to use the same sort of fatuous phrases that the Nazis use. Suddenly, I'm "safeguarding the youth of Norway".'

'Yes, me too. You can't help it. War's divisive; it's what it does. Now the Germans are just "the enemy", instead of actual people.'

'I don't know how to teach the children without showing that I hate them all, and ending up peddling hate just like they do.'

'Yep. There's love of your country, and then there's downright bloody jingoism.' Ulf's mouth curled in disgust. 'Specially when they shove their propaganda right in our faces.'

'The hardest part will be the physical sending out of the letters. I've no more coupons for stamps, have you?'

'No. But maybe my friend ... the printer, maybe he'll have an idea. If this takes hold, I can see the Milorg wanting to help us out.'

'So are we bona fide Resistance fighters then?' Astrid joked.

'Safer than setting fire to munitions factories anyway. Three people were shot for that last week.'

They sat a moment more in silence as they realised that this too was a risky operation.

'We're going to be in deep trouble if this gets out to the *Hird*, aren't we?'

Ulf picked up the typed letter and put it in his pocket. 'We just have to trust each other,' he said.

They exchanged glances.

'Right,' Astrid said, 'Let's hope it works. That part in the document about the children being put "into service" for the Reich made my blood run cold.'

Ulf wrapped his scarf around his neck again, and took a deep breath before heading out into the cold. Her stomach suddenly full of nerves, she waved to him as he went. He looked so vulnerable, hunched against the sleet in his shabby clothes and worn-out shoes.

At the end of the street, Falk, who'd been on watch, saw the man come out of Astrid Dahl's house and trudge towards the city centre. He followed him in the car, the wipers squeaking, but once he had turned the corner, he pulled over to the kerb, got out of the driver's seat and stood in his path. He'd soon find out if he knew anything about Jørgen Nystrøm. He flashed his police identity card. 'Papers please.'

The man produced them and Falk looked at the name and address. 'Johanssen? You're a long way from home. What are you doing here at this time of night?'

Johanssen frowned, obviously annoyed to have been stopped. 'I was doing some preparation with another teacher from my school,' he said. 'We were going through the new regulations together. It's not a crime, is it? It's before curfew and I'm going home now.'

'Open your briefcase.' Falk made a mental note to remember the name. *Ulf Johanssen.*

Falk watched as, disgruntled, Johanssen unclipped the briefcase and opened it up, leaving it standing open on the pavement. It was stuffed with exercise books and a thick bundle of papers.

Falk bent down and drew out the bunch of typed foolscap. It was the new school regulations, just as Johanssen'd said. He flipped through them, hoping to find evidence of some subversive activity. Whilst he was looking at them, Johanssen was tying his shoelace. His shoes looked like they were only fit for a tramp. 'Stand up,' Falk said, irritably. 'Empty your pockets.'

Johanssen blinked at him through his heavy-rimmed glasses but turned out his pockets. They were empty except for a fountain pen, an elastic band, and a few stubs of chalk.

'Trousers?'

He obliged, and handed over his travel pass, a bunch of keys, and a few kroner. Nothing in the contents of his pockets seemed unusual and Falk, feeling faintly foolish, was obliged to give them back.

'Do you know Astrid Dahl well?'

Johanssen shrugged, but evaded his gaze. 'She's just a teacher at my school. We're colleagues, that's all.'

Falk narrowed his eyes. The man's manner was defensive. Perhaps there was more to the relationship with the Dahl woman than he was telling him. 'Did she ever mention a man called Nystrøm? Jørgen Nystrøm? He used to be in the engineering faculty at the university.'

'No. The name's not familiar.' Johanssen rubbed at his glasses with his sleeve.

'He's a friend of hers.' Falk paused. 'Probably more than a friend,.' He probed, hoping for some reaction. There was none. He sighed. He was getting nowhere and it was too damned cold to be standing out here all night. 'If you hear her mention this man, Jørgen Nystrøm, you must come to me, understand? Ask for Falk in the *Hird* office on Victoria Terrasse.' He glanced down at the man's feet. 'I see you need new shoes. If you hear any information about Jørgen Nystrøm you will be well-rewarded.'

'She's never mentioned him.' Johanssen's expression remained stony.

Falk sensed the resistance in him. 'Remember,' he said over his shoulder, as he walked to his car. 'Falk at the *Hird* office.'

He drove away dissatisfied. He'd look up the records of this Ulf Johanssen. He had a nose for subversion, and he had an inkling there was something about him and this Astrid Dahl that smacked of treason to Quisling's regime.

The next morning, Ulf caught up with Astrid in the school corridor.

'Hey, Astrid.' She paused for him, pressing to the side of the wall so the children could get by. 'I got stopped last night on my way home,' he said in a low voice.

Her stomach gave an unpleasant lurch. 'What happened?'

'It's all right. I hid the letter in my sock. A police officer made me turn out my pockets but he didn't look there, thank God. It got a bit creased, that's all, but I'll tell you it was a close thing. I'll deliver it tonight. As long as you haven't had second thoughts, I mean.'

Astrid slumped against the wall. 'You nearly gave me a heart attack. But no, I'm still happy to do it.'

'It's just … he was asking questions — about someone called Nystrøm. He was trying to bribe me to tell him what I knew about him. I just thought you should know —'

'Move along there. What's the hold-up?' Mr Pedersen strode up behind them. They were forced to go to their separate classes, Ulf to the boys, and Astrid to the girls.

Astrid worried about it all morning at class. At break time, she managed to find Ulf again and he told her more details. It didn't make her feel any easier. Though she trusted Ulf, she knew coming to the attention of the quisling police was never good. One slip-up could cost someone their life.

What had happened to Jørgen? They must be trying to track him down, and it was pretty clear that they'd set a watch on her house, all of which was terrifying, now she had started actively disobeying Nazi orders.

She put it from her mind and headed down the corridor, but speeded her step when she heard the hubbub at the classroom.

One look told her what had happened. Even from the door she could see that all the usual pictures had gone and been replaced by Nazi propaganda. Gone was the lovely Victorian print of girls by a fjord, painted by Hans Dahl, her namesake, and gone was Sohlberg's *Sommernatt*. A large poster of the NSUF, complete with brown uniformed boy and girl marching to a drum, now occupied one wall, and a *Nasjonal Samling* poster the other. Above her desk, to add insult to injury, the map of Norway had been replaced with a map of Germany with the cities all marked in German.

She ignored it all and told the class to settle down, threatening detention to anyone who would make another comment. Then she took the register as usual, and noticed that Sara Feinberg was absent. Only a few days ago Jews had been ordered by the government to complete a questionnaire, and she remembered Mr Feinberg telling her they'd have to leave. Had they already gone? Where would they go? It seemed like everywhere people were on the move, fleeing the Nazi regime.

None of her clubs were allowed to meet now; not the university ski club, not the English conversation group, nor the Norwegian folklore society. Not even the chess club. The only club you could belong to these days was the Nazis.

CHAPTER 5

Jørgen and Lind had spent a night at a mountain hut, and after waiting out of sight of German police near the train sidings, had managed to get on the late train heading to the mountain area of Frognerseteren. They were about halfway there when the old teak carriage squeaked to a halt. Jørgen peered out into the darkness, to see why they'd stopped. He squinted to read the sign.

Engerjordet. A disused station, trains hadn't stopped there for at least five years.

All he could see were spindly pines and telegraph wires, behind an empty platform. But parked next to the station were two German army vehicles, and he made out helmets and the blink of flashlights heading towards the carriage.

'Trouble,' he whispered urgently, rousing Lind. They retrieved their bags and skis hurriedly from the overhead racks and put them close by.

'Shall we try to run for it?' Lind asked.

'No. They're too close. Stay calm and sit separately,' Jørgen said. 'It'll be safer.'

Jørgen moved to the very back of the carriage, to where an old man was shifting side to side, nose pressed to the glass, as he tried to see through the window.

'What's the matter,' the man asked him, 'have we broken down?'

The door opened suddenly and four German officers got on at Jørgen's end of the carriage, two of them heavily armed with machine guns. 'Papers,' they said, in Norwegian. Two took one side of the carriage, two the other.

They filled the aisle with their bulk and the fusty smell of their damp uniforms. Jørgen didn't dare turn to look at Lind, he just felt in his pocket for his *Reisepass*.

The elderly gentleman handed over his papers. 'I'm going to visit my daughter,' he said. 'She works in the café, the one with the dragon roof. Lovely view of the fjord from there. You should try it.'

The German who had the old man's papers in his hand smiled in a polite way. 'You stay long?' he asked. His friend, the armed one, stood guard.

'Just until the weekend. Then she'll be too busy. But I like to see my grandson. He grows so quickly, he's almost up to my waist, and —' He continued to talk, but the German passed his papers back and held out his hand for Jørgen's, turning his back on him. He glanced at the ski-sack. 'You ski?' he asked Jørgen as he took up his papers and flipped it open.

'Yes. I'm a naturalist. I work for the university.' Too much information. His nerves were showing.

The German was poring over his papers. 'Olaf Stensen?' He was comparing Jørgen with the photograph, which was of a man with a much broader face.

'Terrible photograph,' Jørgen said. 'University photographer. I've lost a lot of weight since then.'

The main's eyebrows shot up as he read the pass. 'You are *entomologe*?' In German the word was obviously the same. His face split into a smile of delight. He prodded himself in the chest. 'Me, I am *zoologe*!' His eyes were suddenly alive with interest. 'Before army, I work for Zoological Society in Berlin. What you study?'

Jørgen swallowed. This must be the only German Officer in Oslo who actually had a clue about naturalists. What were the chances? 'Study of insects, bees, in my case. I'm looking into how to increase the bee population. Very important in Norway now we can't get sugar.' He was making it up on the spot. He hadn't even had the chance to consult an encyclopaedia.

'Are there many beekeepers in Norway?' the German asked. His face was open and friendly.

'Oh yes,' Jørgen said, with an attempt at authority. 'I want to see how the bees are overwintering, because if the farmers don't feed them properly the queens will die. The best thing to use is a sugar solution, but —'

'Hey, Gunther!' His friend with the gun was hustling him on.

'Maybe we can…' The German looked like he would like to say something, but thought better of it. There was an awkward pause. Before the war they could have been friends. His eyes showed the same wistful regret that Jørgen felt. He cleared his throat. 'Good luck then with your bees, have good trip.' He smiled and snapped the pass shut, handed it back without a word, and moved down the carriage.

Jørgen's pulse rate began to subside and he took a few long, slow breaths. As soon as the men had moved further down the carriage, he went to sit on the opposite seat next to the old gent so he could see them as they went towards Lind.

Lind looked terrified, his face white. He watched him wipe a hand over his balding brow. *Easy, Lind.* He wanted to tell him to calm down, to relax. When they got to his seat, Lind opened his pass too quickly and held it up, and the armed German who'd been with Gunther plucked it from his hand and scrutinized it. He pursed his lips, examining Lind's face, then glanced down. 'All right, Mr Ramundssen. You will come with us.'

'Why? What's the matter?' Lind looked wild-eyed from one to the other. 'My papers are in order.'

'You say you are a shoe-repairer. Well, I don't believe you. Look at your shoes.'

Gunther looked at Lind's feet in their worn-out shoes and let out a laugh. 'Business is bad, eh?'

'D'you think this is Nystrøm, the man we're looking for?' said the other.

'This man in the foolish shoes?'

Jørgen jolted, as if electrified, at his own name. He couldn't do a thing, but watch and wait.

'Don't know,' said the other. 'But I suspect he's not who he says he is. We'll take him in, get the Gestapo to question him, no harm in that.'

No. They mustn't take Lind. They've got the wrong man. Jørgen stood up, in a desperate bid to distract them. 'Excuse me,' he called.

Meanwhile the other Germans had nearly finished their side of the carriage, and when he called out, Gunther turned to look. In an instant Lind was out of his seat. He flung open the nearest carriage door in a panic and leapt onto the track.

Jørgen attempted to distract Gunther, but one of the others had seen Lind jump and yelled, 'Halt!'

All four whipped round and rushed to the open door.

The two armed men got there first and opened fire. The blast of noise made everyone cower in their seats. The old man next to him clung to Jørgen's coat. He gripped his arm in some sort of desperate show of solidarity.

'Did you hit him?' called Gunther in German.

'Yes, he's down.'

Jørgen felt the blow deep in his solar plexus.

Gunther said something in German that sounded like, 'Looks like our work here's done, then.'

The two armed men climbed down followed by the third, who took Lind's bags from the seat opposite. No doubt the bags would be searched. In his mind Jørgen frantically went through what was in Lind's bag. Was there anything that could lead to him? The fourth German, the man called Gunther, turned back, and caught Jørgen's eye as if he might exchange a pleasantry, but then, seeming to realise the inappropriateness of it, given they'd just shot a man in plain sight, he pressed his lips together, pulled himself up stiffly, and got off the train.

Moments later the train rattled on its way.

Jørgen caught a glimpse of Lind as they passed. A snap-shot. A man with limbs twisted, writhing in agony on the ground. The four men stood over him, their flashlights catching him like a fly in a web.

The picture was gone.

The man on Jørgen's right let go of his arm, and stared out into the dark. Jørgen noticed the man's legs were trembling. 'You all right?' he asked.

A silent nod.

No-one in the rest of the carriage spoke. These days it was always better to pretend it had nothing to do with you. You never knew who the quislings were, and any sympathy could land you in jail.

Jørgen cursed himself, twisting the cuff of his jersey. He went over and over the situation, replaying it with different outcomes. And the journey ahead had just become more daunting. He'd thought he would be travelling with a friend, and now he was alone. His guts cramped, and every time the tram creaked to a halt he broke into a sweat, fearing the worst.

He spent most of the journey on the edge of his seat ready to run.

At the end of the line he disembarked in a daze, and headed into the town with the straggling queue of passengers. Under his assumed name of Olaf Stensen, he checked himself into the only hotel, a log-built cabin-type affair, with moose antlers hung from the walls.

When he got to his room he turned the key in the door and simply sat on the bed, picking tufts from the candlewick and staring at the pine floorboards. Was Lind dead or alive by now? He'd no way of knowing. All he knew was, he'd been hit and was down. If he was still alive, he'd have to assume that they might drag him in to question him, and then he might break under pressure and tell the Gestapo where he was heading. It was pretty clear it was him, Nystrom, they were looking for on the tram routes out of Oslo.

He unpacked his rucksack and unfolded the map. What luck the map was in his pack, and not in Lind's. Though Lind had been carrying all the food, and they'd soon guess he hadn't been travelling alone. Damn.

And he'd need a new route. One that he hadn't discussed with Lind. Trouble was, there were not many options. There were a few mountain huts, and then a safe house on an isolated farm that they'd dismissed as too difficult a route before, when he was travelling with Lind.

It would have to be that way. And he'd have to pray that Lind was either dead, or didn't talk.

He shook his head at himself. Of course he didn't wish Lind dead; it was just the scared man in him talking. He'd thought he was so clever; that this would never happen to him, that he would be one of the lucky few radio operators that survived the war, but Lind was a stark reminder that these days, nothing was certain. He'd been over-confident, it had all seemed like a game. But now his shaking hands reminded him he was only mortal like everyone else.

He reset his mind. At least he was alive right now, though he'd have to keep going; have to get out of Norway. He'd seen what they would do to 'Nystrom' when they caught up with him, and it didn't look pretty.

Jørgen slept little, and awoke ragged, but the next morning he borrowed paper and an envelope and wrote a brief note to Astrid. He couldn't say much, and didn't sign it. *'I'm thinking of you,'* he wrote. *'I can't tell you where I'm going, but you're in my thoughts. Stay well, stay safe. Thank God for your life. We'll meet again when Norway is free.'*

He pictured her in her red Norwegian sweater and ski pants and wondered about what she thought when she saw her father's compass. He couldn't write to his parents. They would take him in willingly, but want to try to make him live their kind of life; one where nobody took risks, everybody did the 'sensible' thing. Which in their case was to knuckle down under the Nazis. He loved them, of course he did, but their way of life was stultifying. Two days spent with them, and he always felt he couldn't breathe.

At the post office, which was also a general store and bakery, he posted the letter, replenished his food stocks and then set off on skis into the mountains, at first on well-worn trails, and then making his way through open countryside to the first of the more remote mountain huts.

For almost a week he travelled this way, following reindeer trails and seeing no-one except for a pine marten that scooted away as soon as he appeared between the trees. The skiing was hard, with many miles of cross-country, and steep sided mountains to navigate. Fortunately, there was a light wind, and only moderate snowfall. His legs ached, and his skin burned with cold, despite his growing beard.

But though the hardship kept his mind off Lind, in this white landscape, far from human troubles, he began to feel as if this whole venture was unreal; as if he were the last man on earth. The only thing that kept him moving forward was the thought that every push took him closer to Shetland and freedom.

CHAPTER 6

After travelling five weeks, and not seeing a single German, Jørgen arrived by the less-travelled route at the small hamlet of Tessand. From above, the houses just looked like toys — a collection of wooden boxes roofed with snow, fronting a glassy fjord. He had the safe house circled on the map, so that he could find the place. He skied easily downhill, and unclipped his skis, stamping his boots to release the snow. When he knocked on the door, the farmer greeted him like a long-lost friend. 'You'll be one of us, then,' he said, eyes bright and lively under bushy brows.

'Olaf,' Jørgen said. 'Olaf Stensen.'

'Good a name as any. Don't suppose it's your own, anyway.' He grinned a gap-toothed welcome. 'Gustav Hovda,' he said. 'Call me Gus.' He was a small wiry man with a big bushy moustache. 'Come in, come in! I've got reindeer sausage and bread. And you can join me in a Carlsberg.' He led the way indoors and patted the seat next to the table.

Jørgen barely had time to struggle out his thanks before Gus was off again, talking nineteen to the dozen as he fetched tin plates and bottles of beer. Jørgen made a rapid assessment of the house. It was clean but chilly; dried fish and meat hung from a beam near the unlit fire. There were no pictures or books, nothing that wasn't utilitarian. A roll of twine hung from a nail, and behind the door were stacked a pick-axe and a sledgehammer, and a roll of wire for fencing. A pile of split logs teetered in the corner. The radio and telephone were the only luxuries, taking pride of place on a sideboard crammed with tools and chipped crockery.

It seemed Gus lived alone. By the time Jørgen had finished his bread and sausage he'd had Gus's whole life history. About how his wife had died three years back, and he had two daughters both of whom were now in Trondheim with children of their own. 'They don't come home often,' Gus said, his lined face creasing in regret. 'I'd like to see their little ones, but no. They don't come often. Summer afore last, was when I last saw Hilde.'

Jørgen listened. He was dog-tired, and it was a relief not to have to speak. At the same time, he knew that Gus needed to talk. He was a man who needed an audience, living all alone, tending his few cattle.

'How many head of cattle do you have?' Jørgen managed to get in a word.

'Sixteen cows for milk plus I try to keep a few bulls for beef, and I've twenty sheep, for slaughter or for wool. Keeps me busy. Always glad to have a hand if one comes by.'

'I don't mind helping with the milking,' Jørgen said, 'but I'll need to be moving on, as soon as I can tomorrow.'

'I know that. They always do. Here, have another beer, Olaf lad.'

Gus continued to talk until Jørgen felt his eyes droop. The beer had taken its toll, and it was all he could do to stagger to the small room that Gus pointed to, next to the toilet. The room had once been a child's bedroom, but now was stacked with copies of the farmer's newspaper, tubs of cow nuts, and a laundry basket full to overflowing with rough shirts and woollen vests. The bed had a good thick quilt, and two old stiff sheepskins thrown on it. He didn't even bother to undress, just threw his skis and his bundle under the bed and fell into oblivion.

The light came early, with the crow of a rooster from the farm next door, and as he shaved, he heard Gus clanking about the kitchen making coffee. He flung open the door, inhaling the cold crisp air. The snow was still hard around the house, and icicles hung like teeth on the eaves. The cattle were turned out in a low pasture where the sun had begun to thaw the ground away from the trees, and he helped Gus bring them up for milking.

To Jørgen's surprise, the milking was not done by machine. 'I don't hold with these modern methods,' Gus said. 'Of course Hilde used to help me with the milking, and she'd take the cows up to the summer farm, leaving me to fish and string up the hay for drying.'

They brought the herd into the cattle shed and began milking, the milk steaming in the pails. When it was done, he helped Gus fill the churns and stand them by the gate for collection by the co-op men, who took the milk from all the neighbouring farms.

It was good to do physical work. He'd been so tense that he'd forgotten the pure pleasure of farming the land. This was what he was fighting for, he realised. For men like Gus, keeping the traditional Norwegian way of life alive. Gus never asked him about what he was running from, or to. Simply told him to shut the gate as they watched the cows roam back to their pasture.

They went back into the house and Gus brought out the salt cod, and a box of soft brown goat's cheese. He peeled off a few strips of cheese for Jørgen to have with his bread, and packed more for his onward journey. The taste of home.

He was reluctant to leave, he liked Gus, and he'd been so hospitable. He felt bad leaving him there again with no-one to talk to.

'Who helps you get the cows up to the summer farm when it's time?' he asked Gus.

'My neighbour, if I give him a few fish. Keeps trying to persuade me to sell my grazing land to him, but even though it don't profit me much, I want to keep it. I like the cows, see? They're company. Thing is, I'm better at fishing than him; but he's better at farming. Anyway, we rub each other's backs. He's not much of a talker though, keeps himself to himself. And I don't like the way he hunts.'

'Why's that?'

'He'll take a deer, even with fawns. Shoot anything that moves, he will. Reads too many Westerns. I reckon he's trigger-crazy.' Gus shrugged; grinned under his moustache. 'Comes of living way up here; I guess we're all kinda weird.'

Jørgen strapped his skis and poles to his pack. Gus was right. All humans were their own country inside. They had their own borders, their own rules, their own idea of how the world should work, and how to defend their view of it. He was no different himself. For him now, it was about always moving on. If he didn't, he might have to look back, and that he didn't want to do.

'Take you. You don't look like an agent,' Gus continued. 'You look like a lumberjack. Last man who came through here looked that white I thought he can never have seen the outdoors.'

Jørgen heaved up his pack and eased his way into it, but he didn't answer. Best not to encourage talk about what he did. Better for Gus not to know about German U-boats or their plans for Bergen harbour.

Gus seemed to understand his reticence, and walked him down to the boat by the ramshackle jetty. Gus climbed in and Jørgen gave it a push before joining him, and they slid away from the shore with just a slight tinkle of ice as the bow broke the surface. For an old man, Gus was a fast rower; his sinewy arms pulling rhythmically on the oars, his breath steaming in the morning light. Across the narrow strip of water towards the soaring mountains behind, dark near the base, but rising to snow-topped peaks.

Jørgen glanced up and down the fjord. The only other sign of life was a kestrel hovering over the hillside, and another fisherman way down the fjord. Here, it was as if the Nazis had never existed. He sighed, let his stomach relax, before taking the map from his trouser pocket and examining it. Only another hundred miles to go, but hard going through rugged terrain. He'd have to avoid the towns and cities, and food and shelter would be hard to come by.

'Thanks Gus,' he said, as the boat scraped onto the shingle at the shore. 'You've no idea how welcome it was to spend a night on your farm. Thanks again for your hospitality.'

'Happy to oblige. Can't stand that Quisling fellow. Nearly throw a brick at the wireless when he comes on. And good luck. Hope you get to where you're going.'

They shook hands. As he walked away and up into the pines and the snow line, he turned to see Gus still watching him. He waved, and Gus waved back like an old friend.

By the time he had reached the ridge, he saw the boat was almost back to the other side. From here, he could also see the grey shadows of Nazi submarines further up the fjord near the passage out to sea. Resolutely he strapped on his skis, turned away from the coast and headed up the pass.

Gus was sad to see the young man go. Olaf, he said he was called, but that was probably an alias. He looked like he'd stand more of a chance than the last one. Last one'd been shot in

Lillehammer when he tried to get food. How they'd tracked him there, he'd no idea. You had to be careful who you spoke to.

A knock on the door, and it swung open. 'You got help?' It was his stringy neighbour, Hemming. Hemming pushed his cloth cap back on his head, and leaned against the doorway. 'Saw you bringing your cattle in.'

'My cousin's boy,' Gus said. 'Just passing through.'

'Didn't know you had no cousins,' Hemming said.

Gus rubbed his moustache as Hemming looked about for evidence of his visitor. He knew Hemming had seen the other boy, the thin bookish one, only a few weeks ago, when Hemming called in to borrow a hacksaw. Then he'd told him it was a man come to talk about buying a cow. Afterwards he knew it had been a feeble excuse. Anyone could see the boy didn't know a cow from his elbow. He'd driven that boy to the town in his Packard; which in itself was suspicious — he hardly ever used it, even though he'd fitted it with a charcoal burner at the back. The last time he'd used it was to take a sheep carcase to market before the winter set in.

'He's on his way to Trondheim,' he said, uncomfortable, corralling his thoughts into order.

'You taking him in your wagon?'

'Nope. He's already gone.' Anxious to avoid any more questions, he went to the big barrel of dried salted cod, and took off the wooden lid. 'How many fish d'you want?'

'Two,' he said. 'Or maybe four. Just in case I get guests too.' He placed an unpleasant emphasis on the word 'guests.'

Gus was flustered. There was some sort of threat in Hemming's words. Had he imagined it, or not? Hurriedly, he took out four of the stiff, flat fish and wrapped them in a piece of brown paper.

'You've a telephone here, haven't you?' Hemming said. 'To talk to your daughters.'

Gus nodded, wondering where this was leading.

'Me too. Ever wondered why we're the only two places for miles around with a telephone?'

Gus was silent.

'While we're talking cousins, the head of the *Hird* in Trondheim is my cousin. He thought I should have a telephone fitted, didn't like me living here alone. Could be dangerous, he thought.'

This was something Gus didn't know. He licked his lips; his mouth had gone dry.

Hemming's eyes were sly. 'He'd be interested to hear how my neighbour's got so many visitors, this time of year when the snows are hardly gone.'

Gus swallowed. 'Don't see how it's any business but my own, Hemming,' he said.

'Except that it's against regulations to help known Resistance men, isn't that right? You know, we could still negotiate a good price for your land, and then I could pretend I'd never seen any visitors at all.'

CHAPTER 7

The day Jørgen started his journey out of Oslo, Ulf told Astrid he had passed the letter to his printer friend, and over the first week of February, after getting the Teachers Union dossier of addresses, they met at his tiny apartment to address all the mail. It was a risk of course, but finally it was all done. Ulf took it by several bicycle trips to another friend, a member of the Resistance who worked in the Post Office, who agreed to get it all sent out. Then all they could do was wait.

After two more weeks they had still heard nothing. Astrid passed Ulf in the corridor, and he shook his head. The other thing that worried her was that she had heard nothing more of Sara Feinberg. She called at Mr Pedersen's office to ask if she had been withdrawn from school.

'The *Nasjonal Samling* has decided to open special schools for Jews,' Mr Pedersen said, with an offhand wave. 'I expect she'll have gone there. In any case, our education plans for the future would not have suited someone like her.'

'Can you let me have her address? I'd like to check she's attending school somewhere.'

'I'll look it out later. I'm too busy right now.' His lips tightened. He stood up and held open the door for her to go. 'And you'd do best to focus on the rest of your class, rather than this girl. She was never going to amount to anything.'

He was wrong. Sara was easily the most hard-working in the class, despite the fact she had to cope with yet another language since her flight from Germany. Pedersen's short-sighted dismissal of Sara Feinberg seemed to epitomize everything that was wrong with the new Nazi regime. It made her angry inside, the injustice of it.

The next morning, she waited until Pedersen had gone into Assembly, and then hurried along to his office. She knew where the files were kept, in the green metal filing cabinet behind the door. In the distance she heard the children singing the old Lutheran hymn, 'Lord God, thy Wondrous Name' to Mrs Bakke's strident piano accompaniment.

She slid the drawer open, and fingered her way through all the 'F's until she got to 'Feinberg'. Bingo. There it was. Hastily she copied the address on the inside of her arm with her fountain pen, and pulled her sleeve down to hide it.

Suddenly the door banged into her arm, and she was confronted by Mrs Helland, the headmaster's secretary.

'Oh! You didn't half make me jump!' she said, clutching a register to her chest. Mrs Helland was young and flighty, and reminded Astrid of a startled owl.

Astrid pulled her sleeve hastily over her arm. 'I was just getting out last year's exam results. I needed to check something. I've finished now.' She gave a radiant, confident smile and hurried away. When she glanced back, Mrs Helland was staring after her in a bemused way.

Gosh, that was close. Astrid prayed she wouldn't tell Pedersen. To be caught pilfering in the headmaster's office would be hard to explain. She slipped into the back of the Assembly as everyone had eyes closed for the Lord's Prayer, and took a place next to Ulf. His presence was reassuring.

Class continued as it had for the last few weeks, in uncomfortable friction with the Nazi rules. Today she was supposed to be setting the class a series of problems from a new textbook. All the old textbooks had gone, and new ones had appeared in their place. One of the arithmetic problems read, 'What is the cost of the hereditary sick?' It showed pictures comparing one group of people in hospital with another, and claiming that sick people cost the State too much to maintain. The inference was clear; that these people were a drain on Norwegian society, and that only productive, healthy people mattered.

At lunchtime, the weather was blowing a bitter gale, so she kept watch whilst Ulf hurriedly retrieved some of the old textbooks from the rubbish wagon that had appeared at the back of the school and crammed them into an empty locker.

Ulf shivered in his suit as they padlocked the locker. 'We'll have to smuggle these out somehow,' he said.

'I'll take some home,' she said to him. 'I never thought I'd live to see the day when they banned perfectly harmless books.'

'I'd like to ban theirs. I flipped through the official science book for twelve-year olds this morning, and it had an exercise referring to "thieving Jews". They're putting value judgements on everyone.'

She thought of Sara Feinberg, glad she didn't have to read these. It made her all the more determined to find out what had happened to her. Sara reminded her of herself; and her heart had gone out to her on her first day when she was standing all alone in the playground. She almost cheered when Sophie Hermansdatter went to ask her to play.

By the end of the afternoon the trash wagon had gone, taking with it their long-cherished copies of science primers, and Norwegian novels that were now banned.

After school, she put some of the banned books in her briefcase, rolled up her sleeve, and deciphered the Feinbergs' rather smudged address. A rudimentary map at the bus terminal, designed for Germans who didn't know the city, showed her where the street was. The weather was still bitter, and the pavements slick with ice, so she wrapped her scarf further around her nose and mouth as she battled her way against the icy wind.

The house was in fact a shop, Feinberg's International Bookshop the sign said, although the shop itself was closed, a lopsided blind pulled down over the window. The whole street was grey and bleak, except that someone had painted a six-sided star on the Feinbergs' window in dripping grey paint. As soon as she saw this, she realised that just to knock on the door would probably cause the family great alarm. There was a letterbox on the door, so she scribbled a note on a page ripped from a notebook, saying she was from the school, and enquiring after Sara's health, and that if they were there, she would wait across the road by the tram stop. She didn't sign it. Instead she knocked hard on the door and pushed the note through, letting the letterbox slam hard.

She waited across the road, eyes fixed on the building. Had they gone already? If so, her note might be found and cause trouble. A few minutes went by, but there was no sign of life. She was about to go home when she saw a small twitch at the upstairs curtain. She smiled up at the window and lifted her hand. So they were still in Oslo. Hopefully, she crossed the street, and just as she got to the shop door, it opened and Mr Feinberg beckoned her in, locking the door securely after him with two bolts.

'Sara's upstairs,' he said.

Today he was dressed in a threadbare dark suit. She'd never seen him without his overcoat before. She followed him up to a cramped sitting room where Sara was doing a wooden jigsaw puzzle at a table by the window. The floor was piled with books in different languages.

'Sorry about the mess. I had to salvage these. They took everything from the shop that wasn't in German, but I managed to save a few.'

A few. More like a few thousand.

Sara stood up shyly to greet her. 'Hello, Miss Dahl.'

'I couldn't let her go to school any more,' Mr Feinberg said defensively. 'I was worried they'd take her to one of their institutions.'

'Pappa says we must stay together,' Sara said.

'I understand. It's just, I was worried when you didn't come. I wondered why you weren't in class.' She turned to Mr Feinberg. 'When I last talked to you, you said you might be leaving. I thought you might have gone already but I wanted to wish you well, and tell Sara how well she's doing.'

Sara looked shyly at the ground, but Astrid could tell she was pleased.

'We can't get out of Oslo,' Mr Feinberg said. 'I keep trying friends and neighbours, but no-one can help us.' He looked away, embarrassed. 'Nobody knows what to do. Going to the train station is too much of a risk. So we just sit here day after day, contacting friends, writing letters, hoping a solution will come. We never thought the Nazis would want Norway.'

'Nor us,' Astrid said. 'We've new regulations at the school, and to be frank, the Head, Pedersen, is just a puppet of the Nazis. None of the staff know how to oppose him without losing their jobs. It's like mass intimidation.'

'So, you Norwegians see now, how it is for us,' Mr Feinberg said. 'I am one man. I can't fight them, much as I'd like to. All I can do is try to keep Sara safe.'

Sara leaned on the back of her father's chair. 'I like it here with Pappa, but I miss school.'

'I've brought you some school textbooks,' Astrid said. 'Though I see that you have rather a large collection already.'

A flicker of a smile from Mr Feinberg.

She held them out. 'Some of the old ones they've banned. I took them from the rubbish bin at the back of the school. No-one will miss them and it will help you keep up.' She put the books on the corner of the table and opened up the arithmetic textbook. She pointed. 'We were here — Exercise 11. If you do the next four exercises, I'll call in next week and mark them for you — that's if it's all right with your father?'

Sara nodded, blushing pink. 'Thank you, Miss Dahl.'

Mr Feinberg looked doubtful. 'She can take the books, as you can see, a few more will make no difference. But we don't like people to know we're still here, that's why our lights are off. And you've done enough. We're grateful you came, and I know you mean well, but we'd rather be left on our own.'

'I'm sorry, I didn't mean to interfere. I was only —'

'We don't want to draw attention to ourselves,' he said. 'It's too dangerous. So if you don't mind, it's better if you don't come again.' He looked as if it had pained him to say the words because his eyes shifted away. There was an aura of loneliness about him that set off the same ache in her.

Uncomfortable, Astrid took a few steps towards the door. 'Of course. I didn't mean to be a nuisance. But if you change your mind, and would like Sara to have some tuition, you can write to me at home.' She wrote down the address on a piece of paper and handed it to him. 'It must be hard for Sara cooped up without her friends.'

'We manage,' Mr Feinberg said, stiffly.

She realised it must sound like a criticism. With horror, she realised she had offended him again, and fumbled for the door. 'Goodbye Sara.'

Sara looked up from the books on the table. 'Could you please tell Sophie that I'm thinking of her, and I miss playing two-ball?'

Astrid's chest contracted. Sophie was Sara's best friend. It must be hard for them both to be separated like this. 'I'll tell her,' she said.

Five minutes later she was outside the house, hearing Mr Feinberg shunt home the bolts on the front door. As she came out she almost ran smack bang into a patrol on the opposite side of the street.

One of the men turned to stare, and she saw it was Schmitt, the man who had been there when Sonja was executed. Even the sight of him made her legs turn to water. She pretended not to have seen him, but hurried on up the street. When she risked a look back, he was prowling the front of the Feinbergs' shop.

She kept walking, her heart almost in her throat, hearing the crunch, crunch of her boots on the icy pavement.

CHAPTER 8

One morning a few days later Astrid got to the school gates to find Ulf, in a moth-eaten fur hat, waiting for her. He was almost leaping out of his shoes with excitement. 'It's working. One of my Resistance friends stopped me on my way here. More than eight thousand teachers have signed. Can you believe it?'

His nose was red with cold, but his eyes were bright.

'No? That many?'

He pulled her over the side of the school, out of view of the headmaster's office and the secretary. 'We can ignore their crazy curriculum. We'll damn well teach what we want to, even with no books. Quisling can do nothing about it.'

'You mean we did it?'

His face was enough to tell her. She whooped and grinned.

'What's all the fuss?' asked Mrs Bakke, coming up behind them.

'Eight thousand teachers have sent letters,' she whispered.

Mrs Bakke's eyes widened. She was one of the first to agree to send the letter to the government. 'That many?'

'Sssh,' Ulf cautioned. 'We don't know who might have joined us, and who hasn't.'

By the time they got to Assembly, the news had spread, and many of the teachers were exchanging gleeful glances.

Pedersen swept up onto the podium to make the day's announcements from the lectern as he usually did. Today his expression was even grimmer than usual. He glared round the room, his eyes coming to rest on Astrid and Ulf. 'Due to the unfortunate actions of some misguided staff, this whole school is to suffer,' he said. 'From today, the government has ordered all schools will be shut. They will remain so, until such time as sufficient teachers decide to join the *Nasjonal Samling* Teachers' League.'

The children erupted into a cacophony of excited noise.

'Quiet!' He thumped a fist on the lectern. 'Furthermore, no teacher will receive pay or coupons during this time.'

Gasps, quickly stifled.

'No lessons will be taught today until we are sure those lessons fulfil the required standard of our Minister-President's advice. Students will read one of the prescribed texts until such time as they can go home or be collected. Please proceed to your classrooms and remain there until further notice. I will visit each class in turn to ensure order is maintained.'

Nobody spoke. Nobody knew what to say. This was Quisling's government stamping its foot down hard. It was bad enough existing on coupons, but if those stopped, how would they manage? It just wouldn't sink in, that this could be happening.

By the time Astrid got to her classroom, there was already uproar. She had no sooner gone through the door when Pedersen arrived with a sheaf of forms.

'Miss Dahl,' he said. 'You'll be needing one of these, when you decide to return to work.'

Before she could object, he'd thrust one into her hand. She glanced down. It was the *Nasjonal Samling* Teachers League Membership Form.

'No,' she said. 'We teach our children not to be bullied, and to stand up for each other if bullies should try to force them to do something they don't want to do. The time has come for teachers to practice what they preach, Mr Pedersen.' She tore the form in two, and placed the two halves on the desk. 'I won't be needing this form, no matter how much you bully me.'

'That was a mistake. You cannot see what's good for our nation because you lack vision, Miss Dahl. It is probably why you are so mediocre at your job. You need to educate yourself. Perhaps this time away from school will enable you to do just that.'

'I will never educate myself in the Nazi way,' she said, her words growing more heated. 'One of your best teachers was shot for no reason, and you simply brush it under the carpet as if she never existed. Do you wonder why we rebel?'

He raised his chin, and tapped the rest of the papers in his hand. 'You'll change your tune when you're hungry and can't afford food or fuel. No teacher will work unless they join the League. Minister-President Quisling's orders. The form will be available at reception when you decide to sign.' With that he strode away.

At lunchtime she approached the staffroom with trepidation. Would the others have signed? She put her head through the door and was met with a sea of enquiring faces. 'I didn't sign,' she said.

A cheer.

'Then that's all of us,' Ulf said. 'We're all going home now. I refuse to watch some poor child reading their skewed propaganda.'

Everyone stood and went to get their coats from the hooks, and put on their outdoor boots.

'What about the pupils?' Astrid asked. 'I'm supposed to be supervising Class 4.'

'Leave them,' Mrs Bakke said. 'Let Pedersen sort it out. It was his idea the school should shut, and if I'm not being paid, I'm not staying.'

'And let's take those textbooks from the locker; the old ones,' Ulf said. 'It will remind us what we're fighting for.'

Fifteen minutes later the staff had all collected their belongings from their desks, and crammed the old textbooks into their briefcases. They were just about to leave when Pedersen shot out of the secretary's office near the front door.

'What d'you think you're doing?'

'Leaving,' Ulf said. 'As your school no longer trusts our experience, we will go and teach elsewhere. Besides, you told us the school is shut.'

'You can't do that. Not until tomorrow! I'll report you to Sveitfører Falk, the district police commissioner. He'll have something to say about this.'

'We aren't your pupils, Mr Pedersen,' Astrid said. She turned her back on him and walked away, immediately followed by the rest of the teachers.

Behind them she heard Pedersen shout, 'Staff! Come back at once.'

It gave her great pleasure to carry on walking.

The next day Ulf called in, to tell her that news of their solidarity against Quisling's regime was all over Oslo, and he wouldn't be surprised if it hadn't spread all over the country. Every school was shut. The capital was in chaos. People were late for work, parents had to suddenly mind their own children, and feed them, which was no small task in these days of reduced imports and rationing.

'It's working to our advantage,' he said, 'rather than theirs. If we can just hold out a few weeks; it will really affect all the Nazi factories if the women aren't able to work.'

'As long as we can survive without pay or coupons. But I had an idea; we can do a barter system, any teacher with anything spare can offer to swap it. And I thought we could each do some private tuition somehow. We could see if the churches would let us use their community halls.'

'Good idea, let's write it all down, get a proper plan. I'll get the word out, and we'll see what we can do.'

A week later, one of many ramshackle classes had established itself in St Luke's tiny community hall. All churches were closed already because the Lutheran Bishops refused to sanction the new Nazi service. Churches had been almost universally supportive of their campaign, and Reverend Foss was no exception. Like all the clergy, he was keen to do what he could to foster community spirit against the Nazis, and his hall hadn't been requisitioned like some of the bigger ones. Astrid told children to come separately, and at different times, partly because of lack of space and partly so as not to arouse suspicion from the quisling authorities, who would almost certainly shut it down if they knew it existed.

To her delight, Astrid was able to drop a note to Sara Feinberg, who was able to walk to the hall and be reunited with her friend Sophie. It pleased her greatly to see the two girls sitting side by side on the hall chairs, sharing the same textbook.

Being inside the church grounds itself led to a feeling of protection, with the high stained glass windows of the neighbouring church visible through their iron-framed windows, and shielding them from the road, and the plain white walls giving natural light. Of course it was cold, and there was no heating. Some children brought heated bricks wrapped in a blanket, and all were muffled against the cold with knitted balaclavas, scarves and mittens.

The children treated it like an adventure in a book, and the teachers themselves found new friendship in their efforts to do the best for their classes. They met often, many of them overlapping, for with only one classroom, they had to make do with what they could.

Of course only parents they could trust were told of the school. It was too risky to expose it to anyone they felt might report it. Ulf told Astrid it was going on all over Norway. Schools were in every available space, in shop basements, in private houses, and in halls like this one, and they both took pride in the fact they were part of a National revolt against Nazi indoctrination. But every day felt like a pressure building, and she knew the Nazis would be planning some other political move that would force them to their way.

CHAPTER 9

In the Police Headquarters on Victoria Terasse, Falk was pacing his office floor, thinking. The man they'd brought in from the tram more than a month ago turned out to be a man called Bjørn Lind, whose brother had shot a Nazi officer on the Swedish border. Not Nystrøm at all. They'd executed Lind, of course. But now, after no trace of Nystrøm for over five weeks, they'd finally got some intelligence, and he, Falk, must decide what to do about it.

An informant on a farm at Tessand in the Frisvoll area, had sent in a report that his neighbour had taken in a lone skier late at night. He'd seen the stranger help his neighbour with the cows before he'd gone on by boat across the fjord in the direction of Geiranger. This was the fourth stranger he'd seen at his neighbour's farm; all had been young men, and all had stayed only one night. It had all the hallmarks of a safe house.

When he had asked for a description of the skier, there was no doubt it was Nystrøm. The man had watched him through binoculars and seen the scar on his eyebrow. He asked his aide, Blix, to assess the time it would take to get there — one man on skis, and the time tallied, give or take a day or two for bad weather.

The location had surprised him though. He had expected Nystrøm to head for Sweden, but it seemed he was headed for the coast, and probably then back to England. He got on the telephone straight away to his secretary.

'Selma, I need an excellent long-distance skier. Not just a good skier, but one who can cover many miles quickly. And I need him now. Ask around; see if there's anyone in the ranks who'll do. He needs to be self-sufficient and to be able to handle himself in a fight.'

'Shall I make a shortlist?'

'No time. Just find the best there is, and send him up to me. He needs to be on the road to Lillehammer as soon as we can get him there.'

By the evening, nobody had appeared, so he got onto Selma again.

'Yes sir,' she said. 'Someone's on his way, but he's coming by train from Bergen. I think you'll be pleased. The man's an Olympic skier. Got a reputation as a bit of a daredevil. He was supposed be on our team for Helsinki, but as you know, everything was cancelled when war came.'

'I don't need a sport skier. I need a man with a brain; a tough man, who won't give up.'

'Sorry sir, but it was all we could find, within our police ranks. He's been vetted and he should be all right. His father was President of the Norwegian Fatherland League. '

Ah. The Fatherland League was an organisation seeking racial purity for Norway, and favoured by Hitler. 'What's his name?'

'Karl Brevik.' She placed a photograph on his desk.

He'd heard of him, so his name must have been in the papers. He sighed. The last thing he needed; some kind of celebrity. He pulled the photograph of the man towards him. A man in an advertisement for cigarettes, handsome, urbane, smiling out at the camera. The only distinguishing mark was a small mole just above his upper lip.

He stared at the picture weighing it up. Nystrøm was getting nearer and nearer his target, and the information he had about his contacts was getting further and further away.

'He'll be here tomorrow sir,' Selma said.

The next morning, though he was early, he was surprised to see a man already waiting for him outside his office. He took up most of the space in the lobby; he must be about six foot five inches tall, with broad shoulders like an American footballer.

'Mr Falk? Karl Brevik.' He held out a hand and they shook. Brevik's grip was firm.

Falk led him through to the office, slightly annoyed he'd not even had time to order coffee.

'I need a man good on skis,' he said, as Brevik slid himself into the seat opposite, and pulled off his ski cap to reveal thick, light-brown hair.

'Didn't they give you my resumé?' Brevik asked. He had an intent look about the face.

Falk nodded. 'The man you'll be chasing is an agent, Jørgen Nystrøm, trained in England, who survived eighteen months as a W/T. So he's no fool. Not only that, but he's a mountain man, with excellent snow skills. Now he's on his way back to England, but we need him tailed. We need to know every contact he has, every single thing he does, and we need you to follow him to England if necessary. '

Brevik leaned in, eyes sparked with interest. 'Where is he now?'

'Heading for the coast. Ålesund. But we think this is a pursuit better done by one man, someone who can track him, befriend him, and get the names not only of his contacts here in Norway, but of his whole network that are in training in England. It goes without saying, we want to eliminate the safe houses if possible, and prevent others following in his tracks. Nystrøm likes to operate alone, and out of range of our men, out on the *vidda*. Our city men can't get near him.'

'That won't be a problem for me.' His expression was matter-of-fact. 'I was practically born on skis. And I can handle most situations.'

Falk didn't doubt it. The man in front of his desk was powerfully built, and oozed a lazy self-confidence. 'You'll have back-up of course. I'll arrange a chauffeur to drive you to Lillehammer, and we'll give you maps with Nyström's last tracked location. After that, it's up to you.'

'You said I'd to follow him to England. Then what?'

'We suspect he'll try to take a fishing boat from the coast. The British are well-organised at ferrying Norwegian refugees to the Shetland Islands, and he's familiar with their methods. We know he trained in England. So you'll tail him there, just like another refugee, and find out all you can about this operation. We'll supply you with a transmitter.'

'It's not the usual police work, then, is it? Leaving Norway, I mean.'

'Are you a bad sailor?'

He laughed. 'No. But I know a risk when I see one. And it's people, not the sea. I'll need your assurance it will just be one trip. Repeating any spying activity triples the risk.'

So, Brevik was not just a sportsman after all; he sounded very knowledgeable about undercover police work. 'Of course,' Falk replied. 'You have my word. One trip — out and back. And gather as much intelligence as you can.'

'What about a cover story?'

'Yes, there's a man working on it now. It'll be watertight.' He made a mental note to get Blix to do the leg-work and devise something.

'So what's it worth to you?' Brevik asked.

'What d'you mean?' The question caught Falk short. He had assumed that Brevik would do it for the good of the party, or for promotion.

Brevik leaned back in his chair, obviously prepared to wait. He looked down at his fingernails, before speaking. 'Ten thousand kroner might make it more worth my while.'

Falk smiled faintly. He was caught over a barrel and he knew it. He didn't want to pay anybody. Quisling might think it a waste of resources to spend that amount on pursuing one man and his contacts. Yet the very thought of giving that self-satisfied bastard Nyström a lesson decided him. 'Ten percent now and the rest when he's brought in — when you've brought him back to this side of the North Sea.'

A lazy shake of the head. 'Half now, and half when I've done the job. And new papers and anonymity afterwards.'

My God, he was on the ball. 'I'll see what can be arranged.'

'Good,' Brevik said. And in a single word, Falk realised that it was he who had been interviewed by Brevik, not the other way around. And the thought rankled, along with the feeling that here was another man who had bested him simply through his good looks and physical prowess.

Later that afternoon after telling Blix to supply a plausible cover story, Falk peered into the small office where he'd left Brevik poring over the most detailed maps he could supply. They showed the farm communes and villages in detail and all the mountain huts or goatherd's shelters on the overland route from Lillehammer. He'd get there in a few days with express driving, unlike the weeks it had taken Nyström to go overland through the mountains in winter conditions. Now he saw it on the map, he realised what he was asking the man to do, and it looked insane. Only a desperate man like Nyström would attempt it. Or one who'd just been offered ten thousand kroner, he thought to himself.

Brevik though, seemed enthused by the task. 'Here's the farm where your intelligence says Nystrøm was last seen,' Brevik said, pointing to a series of dots he'd marked in red pen, 'and here's his probable route. He would have to go this way, via this valley here. So his only stop for shelter after the farm would be here — at this mountain hut, I guess he'll make for that.' He stabbed a finger down on the spot. 'And then if I was him, here and here.' He pointed to two more.

Falk nodded. 'We've made you a pack — weapons, maps, and an up-to-the-minute transmitter to contact us. The best skis available.'

'No thanks to the skis. I'll use my own.'

'As you wish. Overkonstabel Berg is waiting downstairs to show you how to use the transmitter and the pistol. Sorry you only get such short training, but we need you on the trail this evening if possible.'

Brevik smiled. 'Always the same in war, isn't it? Proper training goes out of the window. Still, I expect I'll pick it up. I've done a fair amount of undercover work. Can't be much different, can it? What time's my car?'

'Six o'clock.' He paused, fearing that he'd lose control once this man was out of his office. What if he just took the money and ran? He began to run through it all again. 'To recap; the aim is to discover Nystrøm's contacts in England that enable this so-called Shetland Bus, so unless there's no other way, don't kill him; the Stapo will do that later once he's back here and we can interrogate him. The safe houses here — try to put those out. We don't want any more Nystrøms heading for the —'

'I'm on it,' said Brevik, cutting him off.

CHAPTER 10

Four days after the man that he called Olaf left, Gus was surprised to see another man ski down from the ridge from his window. He wouldn't have paid him much attention, except for the fact he stowed his skis and his pack in the trees, and walked down on foot, He was glancing side to side, scouting out the landscape. It was the way these agents behaved. Yet nobody had telephoned him to expect another agent so soon after the first, and he was a little annoyed. The one called Olaf had caused him no end of trouble with his neighbour, and he had vowed never to take another agent again. It was just getting too dangerous.

Though he'd liked Olaf. He'd have him in his house again — he'd been a good listener.

He watched this new chap covertly as he approached, a tall man in a thick pullover and oilskin jerkin. His dark wool hat was pulled down to his eyebrows. He'd have to turn him away, no matter how far he'd come. Now Hemming had turned nasty, he daren't risk it. Probably better to just pretend to be out.

When the rap came he didn't answer it, but hid in the bathroom where there were no windows. He heard the crunch of footsteps in snow walking round the yard, but then silence. He peered out behind the shutters. The man had gone to Hemming's and was knocking on the door there.

'You've got the wrong house,' he said to himself. He wrestled with his conscience. If the newcomer was another Milorg agent, he'd just sent the poor chap to a man who'd probably report him to his cousin in the *Hird*.

There seemed to be no answer at Hemming's though, and Gus exhaled. Where was Hemming? Probably down by the shoreline, with his fishing rod, the lazy oaf.

He was about to turn away when the man glanced furtively around the yard, and seeing no-one, smashed his way through a downstairs window with a single heavy blow of his forearm. The noise of the glass shattering made hairs stand up on his neck. If this was an agent, he was a desperate one. More likely a burglar, a man thinking to take advantage of a lonely community like here in Tessand.

He picked up the telephone, wondering whether to call the police, but the line was dead. Blast the thing. It didn't surprise him. Since the Germans had taken over, private lines were often shut down or intermittent, electricity came and went at their whim. What to do? He was not feeling very charitable towards Hemming, but he felt it his duty to do something. He crept out of the door and hurried down the path to the shore. The least he could do was to tell him.

Hemming was sitting in his boat about a stone's throw from the shore, his line out.

Gus beckoned to him furiously, until he shouted, 'What?'

'Quick,' he said in a half-whisper; 'someone's broken into your house. Smashed through the window.'

Hemming frowned, but rowed back, stowed his oars and climbed out. 'What's the problem?'

Gus told him what he'd seen.

'My house, you say?' Hemming's mouth fell open but he fired into action like a lit fuse. 'Just wait till I get the bastard.' He ran to the barn and grabbed a rifle off the hook, began to frantically load it.

'No,' Gus said, putting a hand on his arm. 'Don't take the gun. We don't want it to turn bad, what if I'm mistaken and it's someone you know?'

'And he'd break into my house?'

'Just leave the gun, okay?'

'No. Bastard could be armed.' Hemming ran up to the house and unlocked the front door. 'Come out,' he yelled. 'I know you're in there.'

Gus stood well back. He didn't want to get involved.

No answer. Hemming opened the front door warily, his shotgun pointing the way. The man must have been waiting for him, for all Gus could see was black shapes flailing, and then the crack as Hemming's shotgun went off. The door was kicked shut in his face.

There was no way to phone, no way to fetch anyone else. He was the only person who could help. He hurried home, skidding on the slippery drive, and took down his old hunting gun. He couldn't leave Hemming fighting on his own.

Round the back, ducking down. A cautious peek in through the window, to see what was happening. The man was pressing a gun to Hemming's chest. He seemed to be questioning him. Hemming was pressed backwards into his armchair, his arms and legs spread-eagled as if thrown there, his eyes white-rimmed with terror, as he garbled something back at his attacker.

What was he saying? Gus couldn't hear Hemming's words, but he saw the man shake his head in disgust and move away, slinking like a cat towards the door. Gus was about to run when he saw the man turn, coolly aim the gun and pull the trigger.

There was no noise. No gunshot. But Hemming's forehead now showed a dark red hole, and the force was enough to jolt the chair backwards on the floor. Confused, Gus ran.

He couldn't go into the house. What if the man came there? He was a professional killer. The silencer had told him that.

Adrenaline made him clumsy. He slipped and stumbled down towards the boat. Got to get away. Row down the fjord. Fetch help. He had a hand on the mooring rope when he felt his left leg swept from under him, and he crashed down onto the jetty.

A glance at his ankle. It was a mass of blood. He'd been shot with the silent gun. He looked back fearfully over his shoulder in time to see the big man almost upon him.

'Don't move,' the man said calmly, pointing the gun. His voice was a Norwegian one, no accent.

'What is it? What have we done?'

The man crouched down over him, the gun still held before him. He wasn't even out of breath. 'Now, you don't want to go the same way as your friend, do you?' Pale blue eyes bored into his. 'So I want the truth. Your friend next door says you've been helping Milorg . Specifically, that you helped Jørgen Nystrøm.'

'No,' Gus said. 'I don't know anything.'

'But your neighbour says you had a man stay with you who matched the description of Nystrøm. A tall man — young, fit, a scar across his eyebrow? Remember yet? The finger tightened on the trigger. 'Where did he go after he left here?'

'Maybe. I don't know. I didn't see where he went.'

'You want to lose the other ankle, bleed to death?' A nudge with the gun. 'Your telephones are both out, you know that. I cut the lines.'

Gus thought quickly, though his mind was skittering, clinging to one thought then the next. 'I rowed him downstream. Down towards Garmo. He was going to catch a train … a train to Bergen.' He tried to keep certainty in his voice, and maintain eye contact; hoped it sounded convincing.

'You're a liar. Your friend watched you row him straight across and wave to him on the ridge. Liars are no use to me.'

The man raised the gun and for a moment Gus just saw the shiny silver ring of it. The man's eyes narrowed fractionally, the irises flaring black. Gus thought of his daughters' faces. And then he saw nothing more.

CHAPTER 11

Astrid was about to leave for the makeshift school when she found a letter in her mail box. It wasn't signed, but she knew straight away who it was from — Jørgen. The sight of his handwriting on the envelope jolted her. It had taken a long time to reach her, like all wartime correspondence it had been through the censor and by the look of it, many hands. She hoped it didn't say anything incriminating; it seemed so long since he'd been gone and so much had happened at school since then.

From the postcode, he seemed to be in the mountains to the North. She guessed something must have happened to blow his cover, and he'd been forced to get away from the city. She was just thinking of him, and wishing she had a return address so she could write, when she noticed a familiar car. It had been parked near her house in the week that Jørgen disappeared, but she hadn't seen it since. Now it was back. Cars like that meant you were being watched by the *Statspolitiet*. The thought of that produced an involuntary shiver. She stuffed his letter hurriedly in her pocket. She'd read it later.

She took a shortcut to the church by veering left down a narrow alley. When she emerged at the other end, the car was already idling at the kerb. So the man was watching her. She had the impression of a man with some bulk, though it was hard to see through the steamed up windscreen, and he was muffled in a fur hat pulled down low to his nose. Straight away, she knew she couldn't risk leading him to the church, so she decided to lead him a dance around Oslo. First she hopped on a tram, then two stops later got off. She'd take no chances.

He was still there. Cars were easy to spot, as they were all driven by Germans or quislings. Uneasy, she went and queued for meat, which took at least an hour for just a few offcuts of pork belly, and when she walked back down the street, the same car was there. He was persistent, this man. She took a long walk back to her house, and went indoors having been nowhere near the school.

Only then did she read Jørgen's letter. It was short and sweet, but at least he was alive. *'Thank God for your life. We'll meet again when Norway is free.'* His words were strange. She'd never thought of him as a religious man. She sent him her silent good wishes, but wondered where he was now; probably heading back to England where he'd done his training. It hurt, the thought that she might not see him again.

Ulf arrived that night to ask her where she'd been all day. The children were worried; they'd missed her, especially the younger ones. He pulled out a kitchen chair with a scrape and sat down.

She peered out of the curtain. The same car was across the street about a hundred yards down. 'You shouldn't have come,' she said. 'I'm being followed by the Stapo.'

'Why? Do you think they know about the school? Or is it that they're after that Nystrøm chap again?'

'I don't know. It could be. I had a letter from him today.'

'Were you close?'

'I suppose so. But this invasion pulled us apart. He was doing something in the Milorg. I can't say what. He's ... he's on the run.'

'He must have been a big fish if they're tailing you.'

She shrugged. 'Maybe it's because of Jørgen, or maybe it's about the school. I'm frightened that if I come to the church hall tomorrow, the Stapo will follow me and then we'll be shut down.'

'Damn,' Ulf said. 'You could be right. When you didn't come in today, I thought you might be ill. I never thought they'd be onto us. If it's the same man, he'll make me empty my pockets again, so I'd better empty them here.' When he'd emptied them onto the table, handkerchief, keys, pass — the only incriminating thing was a stub of chalk, so he stuffed everything else back.

'What if he follows you home?'

'Then he'll find that I live in a house full of Nazi officers. I never leave anything there. Everything's always at my printer friend's house.'

'Has he got a name, this printer friend?'

Ulf rubbed a finger back and forth on the table top, obviously reluctant to tell her. 'His name's Herman,' he said, reddening. 'That's all you need to know for now. But if anything should happen; I mean if I was to be arrested, would you let him know? You'll find him here.' He scribbled an address on the back of a tram ticket. 'Best if you memorise this, then burn it.'

'Gosh, it sounds like a spy film.'

'That's what we've come to, I'm afraid.' He pinned her with a frank gaze. 'I'm serious. If anything happens to me, you'll tell him, won't you?'

Falk saw the young man come out of Astrid Dahl's house, the same down-at-heel man he'd searched before. There'd been reports of illegal schools, so he was determined to rout these out. The schools had been closed for three weeks and Minister-President Quisling was infuriated to the point where irate memos about schools came every day. Both Astrid Dahl and Ulf Johanssen were teachers, he knew that, and he remembered Johanssen's address from his pass. It had stuck in his mind, the way useful information did. You never knew when it might be used to your advantage. But it was in Frogner district. He didn't fancy getting out of his warm car and following on foot. It was a job for a lesser officer than him. He'd find out if one of his men lived close by and ask them to instigate surveillance.

He drove back to his office round the back of the Statspolitiet Headquarters in Victoria Terrasse, the big white apartment block in the centre of the city. It was a grand building, made even more stately by the banners of red and black swastikas undulating in the breeze.

Up the three punishing flights of stairs to his office, where his aide, Blix, was typing up replies to harassed parents. They'd had more than seven thousand letters of complaint through this office alone, and it was really getting up his nose.

'Blix,' he snapped. 'Find out which officers live in Frogner district. I want a man to tail someone for me. Ulf Johanssen, probably a member of Milorg.'

Twenty minutes later and Blix came back from the filing room with a buff folder. 'Fifteenth Division,' he said. 'They're nearest. Four of them live in the same apartment. I'd go for Schmitt, sir. He's the one in the next door apartment to the man you're tailing, and he'll hear when your man leaves. Also, he's got a brain on him, sir.'

'Very good. Get him on the telephone and give him instructions to follow Johanssen. We suspect he's running an illicit school. Close it down, and take the names of everyone attending. They have links to other members of the Resistance, so don't let any of them slip away before we get intelligence on them.'

CHAPTER 12

The next morning Astrid was teaching in the hall, battling the fact that the March weather was even worse, with a below zero chill that made sitting still in an unheated building almost impossible. About twenty children of mixed ages, including Sara Feinberg and her friend Sophie, were shivering in the hall, their breath forming clouds around their heads.

When the children became fractious she made them stand up and do jumping jacks for ten minutes until they felt warmer, and then to pummel their legs with their fists to bring the blood back to their hands and feet.

She sat them down again and began to explain long division with the aid of a piece of plywood painted black and leaned against the wall — a makeshift blackboard supplied by Reverend Foss, who pretended he wasn't involved, but did all he could to help. Many of the children had no paper because it was scarce, and hoarded for fires or insulation against the cold, rather than for writing on, so she set them practical problems involving counting the panes in the windows, or number games with playing cards that they'd managed to glean from helpful parents.

She had them busy with the cards when the big oak door creaked open and Ulf arrived at the back of the room. She gave him a brief smile, but continued what she was doing. He was going to take the children next for science, though these days that seemed to cover all manner of different things, like nature study, making a crystal radio and how to make charcoal from burnt wood.

He looked thinner, she realised, and more anxious, and signalled at her that he wanted to speak with her.

'I think I was followed this morning,' he said. 'There was a car outside my house, and a couple of times, I've spotted the same uniformed Nazi whenever I go in or out. He lives in my building, but he seems to be appearing too often by coincidence in my hallway.'

'What shall we —?' She paused. The noise of some sort of disturbance outside. It sounded like feet on the pavement and voices.

They exchanged glances.

'Get the children,' Ulf said, but there was no time to do it.

The door flew open and a group of armed soldiers burst in, rifles held before them.

'*Hände hoch!*'

Ulf put his hands on his head.

'Get down!' Astrid tried to press down the heads of the children nearest to her, who were dazed and staring. Outside the windows she saw more helmets and rifles.

'You. Hands up.' It was Schmitt, the man from the tram.

She held her hands high.

'What are these children doing here?' he asked. 'School is *zu*. Closed. You understand?'

'But we're doing no harm,' she said. 'By doing this, we allow the parents to work.'

'No. All the children must leave. But first you will give me your names. Bring me your identity cards.'

She delved into her coat pocket and brought out her pass. He took it from her and handed it to another uniformed soldier who wrote down all the particulars in a notebook. 'You seem to be wherever there is trouble, Fraulein Dahl,' he said. 'If you wish to teach, then you may join the Teachers League and you will be assigned a school. If not, I can find better work for you to do in one of the factories in Germany.'

She said nothing. He stared at her with a grim air of satisfaction. He turned towards Ulf . 'Your documents,' he said. Ulf obliged. 'Another troublemaker. We will remember your name Herr Johanssen. Now clear the building. Everyone out.'

They hustled them into the cold and closed the door posting two armed guards outside.

'What now? Ulf whispered.

'We wait,' she said. 'Nothing else we can do. We keep the children busy on the street until the parents can come for them.' She turned to Schmitt. 'I take it you will have no objection if we continue our lesson out here.'

He ignored her, so she began a round of the song; '*Ro, ro til fiskeskjær*' with the children joining in all the actions of rowing to the fishing reef, and shouting out a different name of a child each time at the end of the verse. At least it kept them warm, but not for long. The sky was an ominous grey, and as she suspected it might, the cloud began to release its weight of snow in ever heavier flakes.

'Please,' she said to Schmitt, as the children huddled together, teeth chattering, their shoulders growing whiter by the minute, 'let us wait inside. The children will be frozen to death in this snow.'

'It's your fault, if they do,' he said. 'You knew you were breaking the law with your illegal school.'

It was all right for him, in his thick leather gloves and warm wool greatcoat. She bet his boots were fur-lined too. 'It would be a kindness,' she persisted. 'Some of them are not dressed for so long outdoors.'

He approached her then, too close, so he was looming over her. 'Look Fraulein, there is a way.' He took hold of a strand of her hair, fingered it with his glove. A shiver of fear rippled up her spine. 'I'll tell you what; we go in first, have a little time alone. He gave a suggestive smirk. 'Then later, if you please me, maybe I'll let the children inside.'

She could not reply. Everything inside had hardened to stone. She turned her face away.

'Ha! So you cannot really care about the welfare of these children. You are a fraud, Fraulein Dahl.' He came up behind her so she felt his breath on her neck.

She stayed immobile, as the sound of his boots receded again. Ulf, who had witnessed the conversation, but was too far away to hear, came over. 'What did he say?'

'Nothing,' she said, folding her arms and gripping her trembling hands under her armpits. 'Only another half hour to go. Let's keep the children moving or they'll freeze.'

Another round of forced gaiety as they sang the farmyard song, and did a version of a traditional dance which was soon stopped by Schmitt for being pro-Norway. Finally, thank God, a few parents began to arrive. The Germans insisted on taking everyone's names and addresses. When Mr Feinberg arrived, he was grim-faced at the sight of the armed soldiers. He pulled Sara into a fierce embrace and tried to hustle her away.

'You,' Schmitt called. 'Wait. I need your name and address.'

Mr Feinberg stopped, his expression blank. He took out his pass and handed it over.

'Jew hey? Who else lives at your address?'

'No-one. Just us.' To Astrid it looked like Mr Feinberg was shrinking into his shoes.

'What do you say we send someone to check?' Schmitt said. 'The SS would have something to say if you've lied to us. Who else lives there?'

Astrid saw the flicker of panic in his eyes. 'Just me and Sara.'

'Never trust a Jew,' Schmitt said to his colleagues. 'They bled Germany dry with their lies and double-dealing.' He turned back to Mr Feinberg. 'Names?'

'Isaak Feinberg.'

'And this is?' He pointed to Sara.

'Sara,' Astrid said.

She had drawn his attention. 'How many Jews do you have, in this so-called school?'

'I don't know. We don't differentiate between religions or races in Norway, Herr Schmitt.'

Had she gone too far? His eyes narrowed as he heard her use his name. She saw his frown as he tried to work out how she knew it, but she didn't flinch. She kept herself erect and defiant, until he turned away.

By now, more parents had arrived that needed his attention and his men to record their names. When she looked around Isaak Feinberg and Sara had disappeared, ghostly shapes fleeing into the flurrying snow. When all the children had gone, she realised Schmitt still had her identity card. With trepidation, she approached him and asked him to return it.

He juggled it in his hand. 'So, *Astrid*,' he said, emphasising her first name. 'You think you can defy your government and the orders of the Fuhrer? You are setting a bad example. I would not want such a person teaching the youth of tomorrow.'

'Then it is fortunate you are not in charge of Norway's teachers,' Ulf said, appearing beside her.

'I have both your names,' Schmitt said, pulling back his shoulders, 'and your addresses. There are punishments for disobeying the orders of the State. Do not be surprised to hear the night-time knock on your door.' With that, he summoned his men and they strolled away, like tourists in a seaside town.

'Don't let him scare you,' Ulf said. 'He would have arrested you then, if he'd had the power.'

Nonetheless, that night she double-checked all the windows and doors, and with the wind moaning in the trees, she could not sleep easy.

CHAPTER 13

When no more letters from Jørgen came, Astrid scoured the papers every day for further news of him, though she dreaded reading his name in the paper for it would mean he was certain to be dead. The Nazis revelled in showing the punishments of saboteurs, radio operatives and rebels, and in executing random Norwegians if any Resistance men escaped.

So it was with surprise when one morning over her acorn coffee, she saw the headline that schools were to reopen. Did this mean their protest had won? No. Unlikely. The Quisling administration must have realised it was causing too much disruption to keep them shut. They needed all hands in the factories to manufacture what the Nazis needed for the Russian offensive, and school closures were blocking people getting back to work. It was pragmatic, designed to get the Norwegian arms-machine working efficiently for the Nazis again.

She closed the paper, took a gulp of her coffee, now cold and bitter. In one way returning to school would be good, for she missed her familiar classroom, and her colleagues, but in another she was apprehensive. If she knew Pedersen, a man she now viewed with a kind of repressed loathing, he'd apply more pressure on them all to teach the Nazi ideology.

The official letter informing them of the reopening arrived the next day, complete with its horrible Nazi crest, so by the following day she was back at school. She couldn't afford not to work. Pedersen behaved as if they'd never been away, despite the over-excitement of the children. The joining of the League was not mentioned again, but nor were the old textbooks replaced, and there was no sign of Sara Feinberg in her class, or of any other Jewish child.

The staff in the staff room were subdued, for even though it was some kind of victory, being back at school under the reality of the Occupation — the repression, the rationing, and an unforgiving winter which seemed never to burst into spring, was beginning to get to them all.

It was a week later when Pedersen threw open the door of Astrid's classroom and announced, 'All staff to report to the school gymnasium, now.' At her frown, he reiterated, 'Now!'

'Get on with your work, class, whilst I'm gone,' she said, in as calm a voice as she could muster, though inside she was in a turmoil.

What now? Was it an air-raid? It must be something serious to summon them all like this. She flew down the corridor, heels tapping on the linoleum floors, passing other members of staff also hurrying there. A glimpse through the corridor window showed the school was surrounded by armed soldiers. A sense of dread made her swallow, pull her cardigan more tightly across her chest as she pushed through the double doors into the hall.

A group of armed soldiers were waiting on the stage, surrounding a huddle of quisling officials. She recognised one of them, Sveitfører Falk, a jowly, thick-set individual, from his photograph in the paper. She stared. The set of his shoulders was familiar. Was he the one who had been watching her house?

The group of teachers gravitated nervously to the centre of the hall, like birds flocked together in the huge space. Pedersen arrived shortly after, his gown flapping, with a few more teachers, including Ulf, in tow. She threw Ulf a glance as if to say, 'What is all this?' but his slight shake of the head told her he was no wiser than she was.

But then she saw his eyes fix on the stage as if something had caught his attention.

'What?' she whispered.

'That man. He's the one who's watching your house.'

So she was right. The wire-like tension in her stomach increased.

'Quiet!' Falk raised a hand.

Silence fell as Pedersen mounted the steps to the stage. He was sweating and white-faced, his usual arrogant demeanour gone. The visitors had obviously rattled him.

'Is that all of them?' Falk asked.

'Yes.' Pedersen gave the teachers a cursory glance. 'All here.'

Falk took out a piece of paper. 'These men are to stand to one side. Gustav Hansen. Bo Baum. Ulf Johanssen.'

Nobody moved, but the men looked to each other.

'Stand to one side, or we will fetch you.'

Reluctantly the three men moved to the spot Falk was indicating. Immediately they were surrounded by armed soldiers. The sight of them being held at gunpoint elicited gasps from the women, especially Karen Baum who was married to Bo, the biology teacher.

Falk moved forward on the stage to address them all. 'These men will be imprisoned until such time as teachers in Norway come to their senses and decide to join the official Teachers League and teach the curriculum that is best for Norway and its allies. If everyone in this school signs, the men will be released. Papers are available on the desks by the door.'

'No. Don't sign!' Ulf shouted.

His response was quickly taken up by the other two. 'Don't sign!'

'*Alt for Norge!*' Gustav yelled.

'*Alt for Norge!*' All for Norway, Astrid took up the rallying cry.

Karen Baum was silent. Her face was white as her husband was forced to move and the men were hustled from the room at gunpoint.

'Don't give in!' shouted Ulf as he was taken away.

'Mrs Baum,' Pedersen said. 'Don't you want to sign?'

Karen Baum gripped Astrid by the arm. 'We stand together. I'll never sign. Bo would never want me to sign.'

One by one the remaining teachers linked arms. 'We won't be bullied,' Astrid said.

Falk narrowed his eyes. 'You don't recognise what is good for you,' he said. 'But you will, in time.' With that, he clomped heavily down the stairs from the stage. No-one moved as the tread of Falk's entourage faded into the foyer.

At the bang of the door, everyone rushed to the windows. Outside, Nazi soldiers hustled the men at rifle-point into a truck.

'Where are they taking them?' Karen turned on Pedersen.

'Prison, or the camp at Grini, I should think,' he said. 'I warned you what would happen, but none of you wanted to listen.'

'They're inhuman,' Mrs Bakke said. 'The Nazis are like a different species.'

'They are not so different from us,' Pedersen said. 'We have the same Norse roots. In history there've always been raids and occupations. Look at the Vikings. We were the same as the Nazis when we raided England. We all sail by the same wind. The power just shifts back and forth. Best sail with it, I say. I wish you'd see, that by making all this trouble, you're only hurting yourselves.'

'Rubbish. They are betraying their roots,' Mrs Bakke said, her face red with outrage.

'It is a waste of energy to complain or resist. They have might on their side and they're bound to win in the end.'

'They can't imprison us all,' said Astrid, holding tight to Karen's arm.

Pedersen shook his head. 'You think not? I think they'll do whatever they need to do to make sure we follow their rules.' For a moment he was almost contrite. But then his expression hardened again. 'Thanks to difficult members of staff like you, I've three more classes to get cover for, so you'd best get back to your class while I decide who will take them. Unless of course, you want to be unemployed.'

CHAPTER 14

The mountain passes were hard in winter, and battling the weather took most of Jørgen's energy. He didn't sleep well at night; he kept having nightmares of men chasing after him whilst his feet were trapped in the snow. It was a week later when he turned to look back and glimpsed another figure in the distance. A lone figure, just cresting the hill.

No. His mind was playing tricks, he had to be hallucinating.

The figure had disappeared into a dip. Or maybe he'd never been there at all.

Until he reappeared. A dark stick-like figure moving closer.

Jørgen squinted against the blowing snow; definitely another person. A bolt of fear streaked up his spine.

He shot into a brake of trees, took out his binoculars and focussed them. They were Swiss binoculars, with a powerful magnification, and what he saw filled him with deep unease.

The man was tall and well-built, wearing goggles against the light, a black hat, and a dark scarf over his nose and mouth, so he couldn't see his face. He was examining Jørgen's ski tracks, and he saw him dig in his poles and swoop off to follow them, arcing around the trees in smooth curves. Of course, he could just be a sportsman having fun in the mountains, but the likelihood of that in the middle of winter was what? Close to zero.

He'd need to gain distance. He took advantage of the downhill to pick up speed, but it was tough going up the steep side of the mountain and his thighs burned with every step. The weather was closing in too, a thick saddle of cloud hung low over the pines, with the occasional eddy of snow. A glance back.

Unbelievable. The man was gaining on him, doggedly marching uphill. Jørgen redoubled his efforts and headed for a denser forested area. He'd be able to take off his skis there and disguise his tracks. The snow, which was increasing, would cover them too. With any luck, then he'd be able to double back on himself and come back the way he'd come in.

The other man wasn't in any kind of uniform, but that meant nothing. He still didn't want to take any chances.

He took off his skis and jammed them into his backpack to run dodging through the trees away from the obvious cleared routes made by deer or cattle. Underfoot, the ground crackled and spat with pine needles, and when he was a little way into the dark of the forest he scraped at the ground and buried his pack and skis under some snow and fallen branches, the skis'd be a hindrance for what he planned. He spotted a tree which had branches close to the ground that would make good footholds and climbed until he had a view of the man coming up the hill towards him.

Wedging himself in the branches, he focussed his binoculars again on the man coming up.

From the movements of his pursuer, he could see he was an experienced skier on the latest skis. He moved powerfully and fluidly in the modern style. At the edge of the forest he paused where Jørgen's tracks had disappeared. Jørgen stayed motionless, legs wrapped around a high branch, watching, not daring to move. The wind whistled in the branches now, an eerie moan. Snow was blowing horizontal, making it difficult to see.

The man took a few steps into the forest, boots crunching on hard-packed snow, before coming out again and systematically working his way around the edge looking for tracks. He took off his goggles again and lowered his scarf as he squatted to examine the ground which was being rapidly covered by snow.

Jørgen wiped the lenses of the binoculars and zoomed in on his face. Hard cheekbones, strong jaw. He was clean-shaven, and fair-haired, judging by his eyebrows under that black hat. He searched him over with the viewer and made a quick assessment — bigger and more muscular than him. Worrying.

Black hat took off his skis and began to creep through the forest on foot. He was about seventy-five yards away — too far away for Jørgen to pick him off. If he took a pot shot and missed, he'd be a sitting target for this man, whoever he was, and he could be armed.

He waited until the man had gone deeper in, before slowly easing himself downwards. It was always harder going down, and the trunk and branches were rough, scraping his hands and banging his knees.

The snow was whirling thicker now and settling on the branches. Losing his grip with one boot, he fell out of the tree. He listened a moment but could hear no sounds except the wind and his own laboured breath. He pulled his scarf over his nose and mouth and dug frantically where he thought he'd left his skis, but the snow had blown in from the edge of the forest and buried them.

He was still searching when he heard a noise from within the forest. Whipping off a glove, he scrabbled in the snow, until his fingers found the end of a pole and dragged it out. The rest of his gear was there too. Hurriedly, he gloved up, and strapped on his skis.

Shit. The man was coming back, he could see him moving from tree to tree, retracing his steps. Every sensible thought said it was better to stay in the shelter of the forest, but his urge to get away from this unknown pursuer over-rode everything.

He'd have to break cover.

He dived out of the shadow of the trees and straight into the storm. The wind was whirling snow like soup around him, as he pushed off into the white void. But the wind direction was against him and soon plastered a thick layer of snow over his front, but he didn't stop, burning a trail down through the white.

He looked back over his shoulder. Snow stung his cheeks. He crouched, a blizzard blowing freezing into his eyeballs, pellets of icy snow stinging his cheeks. He renewed his push, his poles digging into the snow, over and over.

Now he was in the centre of the storm, with only a vague sense of direction, his skis cutting swathes into the snow as he veered into the side of the mountain, and then away. A glance back.

He'd lost him. Whoever he was, he'd had a narrow escape.

For a few more days Jørgen skied onwards, eating up the miles, and seeing not a soul. The weather was still squally, but he was used to dealing with it, and made the most of the times when the fierce wind was behind him. He wondered about the other skier, whether he'd dreamt him. He was low on food. He'd eked what he'd had from Gus, but he'd have to start trapping food soon, and that would slow him down. Though he was hardened to the weather, skiing on such low rations made him permanently exhausted, so his mind veered in all sorts of strange directions. Back to the past, when he and Astrid were at university. Back before all this madness, before the Nazis came to Norway.

He paused to catch his breath, relieved to have spotted his next target, a mountain hut half-buried in a snowdrift. Thank God. Although it wasn't dark yet, he'd be able to rest for a few hours before moving on.

Gratefully, he let gravity float him downhill. Once outside the hut, he had to dig out a path before he could open the door. He cleared it as best he could by using a ski as a shovel, and just hoped he wouldn't be snowed in by the morning. Once in, he left his skis just inside the door.

The hut was basic. A plank-constructed shed with a fixed table and bench and a sleeping platform with bunk above. There was a stone constructed hearth with an iron chimney through the roof, but it was winter, so there was no wood, nor any hope of getting any. There was a hurricane lamp on the mantel which still had paraffin in it, so he used one of his precious matches to light it.

Still, at least it was dry, and he cupped his numb hands around the lamp. He was on the last of his rations. Gus had given him dried salt cod and bread which though old was still just about edible. He chomped on it. Foul. But at least there'd be some nourishment in it.

He lay down fully dressed on the sleeping bench, dragged his sleeping bag up over his clothes, pummelled a rolled-up jersey for a pillow and put his pistol under it. Outside, the wind groaned and the snow on the roof creaked.

The next thing he knew he was woken by a blast of cold wind as the door flew open.

He sat up, disorientated. A flashlight shone in his face.

'Sorry, I didn't know there was anyone here,' a voice said. A male Norwegian voice.

Jørgen fumbled for his gun. His thoughts tumbled over one another. The man on the mountain. The storm. 'Stay back,' he shouted, as his fingers finally found the cold metal of the gun. 'I'm armed.'

'Whoa! I don't mean you any harm. I just want a place to sleep.'

The light flashed into his eyes as the man raised his hands above his head.

'Don't move,' Jørgen shouted. 'Or I'll shoot. And turn that bloody light off.'

'Okay, okay.' The flashlight died.

'Don't move.' Jørgen struggled out of his sleeping bag, keeping the gun aimed at his chest.

'Hey, hey!' The man raised his hands above his head. 'I'm on your side. Easy now.'

'Put your weapons on the table,' Jørgen said. 'Slowly.'

'What? This?' The man stretched out a long arm to put a fish-gutting knife on the table.

'And the gun.'

He caught a glimmer of surprise on the man's face, but he reached slowly inside his jacket with his gloved hand and placed a pistol on the table.

So he *was* armed. He turned up the lamp to get a better look at the intruder. The tall man with a strong jaw he'd seen a few days before. 'You were following me. Why?'

'The hell! I thought you were following me. I saw tracks and didn't know who they belonged to. I thought it might be Germans who'd caught up with me. So I went to take a look.'

'What are you doing out here?'

'I might ask you the same thing. Except I'm not pointing a gun at you. Can't you put it down? It makes me nervous.'

'Not until I know who you are and what you want.'

'I don't want anything. Except a good night's sleep. My name's Karl Brevik. I'm on my way to the coast. I want to get out of Norway, and preferably without any Nazi blowing my brains out.'

Jørgen frowned. The name had a familiar ring. Where had he heard it before?

'Now it's your turn,' Brevik said. When Jørgen was still silent, he said, 'Look. I didn't know there was going to be anyone here, ok? But if it's a big problem, I'll just ski on to the next place. But don't shoot me, right?'

Jørgen weighed it all up. He was suspicious. Before he'd been convinced the man was following him. He should have shot him on sight, by rights. But what if, like he said, he was just another man like himself? He raised the gun again. 'Why didn't you go by train or bus? Why go through the mountains?'

'The Germans are after my blood. I was working with the Milorg in Bremen, but they found out I'd instigated a sabotage attack on the steelworks.' Brevik shrugged. 'So I had to get out quick. Besides, people know my name. They know they couldn't catch me this way.' He paused. 'I'm a pretty good skier. A downhill champion.'

That was it. Karl Brevik. He'd seen him in the papers. 'Good Lord, you're *that* Brevik. Weren't you on the Norwegian Olympic team?'

He looked pleased. 'Still would be if it wasn't for the Nazi invasion. Look, can I lower my hands now?' He lowered them anyway.

Jørgen sat down, but kept the gun pointed at him. 'That must be tough. All that training gone for nothing.'

'Four bloody years,' he said, bitterly. 'At first, I wanted to punch someone. I'd worked myself to the bone to reach peak performance, sacrificed friendships, social life, everything. And what happens? It's all wiped out like that.' He snapped his gloved fingers.

'There's always next time —'

'Too old by then. And don't bother with the sympathy. I've got over it now, found other things to do. You have to move on.'

He was impressed. Judging by how he skied, there was no way this man couldn't be who he said he was, and he saw no reason to hide his identity as the other man hadn't. He slid the safety catch back on the gun, and pushed it back in his pocket so he could shake hands with him.

Karl slid off his gloves and his hand was solid when he reached for Jørgen's in return.

He couldn't help being elated to see a friendly face after so long. 'Jørgen Nystrøm,' he introduced himself, 'wireless operator on the run. Also headed for the coast.'

Karl grinned and sat down on the bench opposite. 'You had me then. I thought you were going to blow my head off. I wouldn't even have come in if I'd seen your skis outside. I thought it was empty.'

'You gave me the shock of my life.'

'And all the time we're on the same side. D'you mind if we share shelter? Only I'd feel more comfortable if we left our weapons on the table.' He pulled out another gun, complete with silencer, laid it on the table in front of him next to the knife.

Jørgen stared. It was a model he'd never seen before. 'Sheesh. Where'd you get that?'

119

'Stole it from a German soldier. He was dead when I got it. We blew their truck off the road. Haven't had chance to use it yet though.'

'Don't suppose you've got any food, or drink with you?'

'As it happens, I have.' Karl heaved off his pack and rummaged in one of the side pockets. 'Here, aquavit.' He offered Jørgen a flat glass flask.

The first taste of it, its herby fumes immediately revived him. 'By God, that hit the spot.'

'Food wise,' Karl said, rummaging in his pack, 'I've got some tinned fruit, and dried biscuits, and some goat's cheese from a farm in the last valley.'

'Did you get to Tessand? Did you have a night with Gus?'

'Yes. What a great guy. Took me over the fjord in his boat.'

'You didn't have trouble with the neighbour then? Gus seemed worried about him.'

'Didn't see a neighbour,' he said, turning away. And he took the flask back and took a swig.

They shared the biscuits and cheese, and after a while Karl said, 'You got maps? Which way you headed?'

Jørgen brought out his much-thumbed map, and they stood to lean over and study it by the light of the lamp. 'I thought this way,' Jørgen said, tracing a route to Ålesund with his finger.

'I was thinking the same route,' Karl agreed. 'We can't go this way because it's too steep, and this glacier's unstable. Only here I'd go that way.' He indicated the new route. 'There's a village here, I was thinking to restock with food, make contact with Milorg,' he said, 'always supposing the locals are friendly. We could travel together.'

Jørgen hesitated. The picture of Lind's scared face rose up in his mind, so different from this new man. What happened with Lind still made him shudder. At the same time, the long punishing trek across country had been harder than he'd expected. Having an expert skier like Brevik with him could be a bonus, and he was impressed; keen to see him ski close-up. 'Have you got a contact with the Shetland Bus to get you out?' Jørgen asked.

'Not yet,' Karl said. I had to leave in a hurry. I've got a crystal set with me though, so once we get nearer I can try to make contact with them.'

'You've got a wireless?' Jørgen was so surprised he sat down.

'It's not great. Home-made kit. But I've long wire for an aerial, and good sensitive headphones.'

'Aquavit *and* a transmitter! You certainly travel in style.'

Karl shrugged. 'We were warned things were getting sticky, and you know how it is, it's best to be prepared.'

The transmitter would be a bonus. It made his mind up. 'Yeah. Seems best we travel together,' he said. 'Two heads are always better than one.'

Karl smiled a pleased sort of smile. 'What do you say we get some sleep?' he said. 'I've had a long day, and I thought I'd never reach this hut.'

Jørgen watched him take off his boots and wriggle into a sleeping bag near the unlit stove. The sight of Karl's large leather boots next to his own reassured him. He couldn't go outside without his boots. Nevertheless, Jørgen couldn't sleep. Partly he was thinking about how he'd tell his friends he'd travelled with *The* Karl Brevik, Olympic champion. Partly it was unease that they had somehow ended up in this one tiny spot out of all the vast expanse of snowy *vidda*. He kept looking at the guns on the table, and something inside him couldn't rest.

When he heard Karl's breathing slow into a steady rhythm, he studied him as he slept, the fair, wavy hair, his slightly open mouth with the mole on his upper lip. Karl's sinewy hands gripped the top of his sleeping bag with some sort of animal tension.

All the staring did not answer his doubts. He was still on edge. Despite all the reassurances and the evidence, the fact another man had appeared here in the middle of nowhere was just a weird coincidence that didn't feel comfortable. When he was sure Karl was deeply asleep, he crept out of his bag and very carefully prised open the toggle at the top of Karl's rucksack.

Inside, an oilskin sack held the component parts for the transmitter, a board with coil and wire. He probed past this to find the tins of food, the squelchy pack of cheese. At the bottom he unearthed a large detailed map of folded silk. It had been marked in red with a route through the mountains. Now the lamp was out, couldn't figure out the detail, but it looked like the route only started from the farm at Tessand, near Gus's place, not at Bremen.

That was odd. He took it to the window to get reflected moonlight from the snow outside. Yes. The route had all the mountain huts including this one dotted out in red. It was far more comprehensive than his own map. The area of coast around Ålesund had been outlined in red too.

'Found what you're looking for?'

He whipped round. Karl was sitting up. He fixed Jørgen with an amused smile.

'Sorry. I have to be careful.'

122

'Go on, have a good look. But watch out for last week's socks; they're pretty lethal. You could get gassed.'

Jørgen laughed. The tension dissolved. 'Standard procedure for a Resistance man,' he said. 'Nothing personal.'

'You can show me your dirty socks tomorrow,' Karl said, and turned over.

Jørgen told himself to calm down. Karl hadn't tried to do anything. His gun was right there on the table. He was unarmed and entirely vulnerable to him. There were few resting places on this route, and it wasn't beyond the bounds of possibility they'd found the same one. Still, the map was odd. Maybe Brevik just knew the earlier terrain too well to bother. After all, this was the most unmarked part of the route. He told himself that if Karl Brevik had wanted to kill him, he would have done it already.

With that, he fell into a fitful sleep.

The next day he woke to find Karl already up and packed, despite the winter darkness, and keen to be moving on. With minimal small talk, they strapped on their skis and set off together. Karl was a superb craftsman on skis and he soon took the lead. To be honest it was a relief to follow in the wake of him for a while, to not have to decide about the best route, to not have to assess the snow quality, and just to follow the curved tracery of his ski tracks through the snow, with the steep peaks rising either side into the grey of the mist and sky.

He'd estimated the next mountain hut was about fifty miles distant, and they should make it by the evening as long as the weather held. Last night there'd been heavy snowfall, but when they got further up the slopes he noticed some slides and some instability in the snowpack.

He called out to Karl who was schussing ahead.

Karl wheeled to a halt, turned, and raised his goggles.

'Snow feels a bit hollow on this slope,' he called.

Karl waited until he pulled up alongside. 'Problem?'

'See these cracks?'

'Don't worry, I've seen worse,' he said, putting his goggles down and poling off.

Jørgen followed, hard pressed to keep up. They were facing downwind now, scooting through a sparse brake of trees. All went well until late in the afternoon.

When an avalanche comes; there's no warning.

The noise was something he was barely aware of. A soft 'whump' from the side of the mountain. He glanced to the right to see what looked like a white unrolling cloud rising from halfway up the slope. 'Avalanche!' he yelled, but the word was unfinished as a ton of snow hit like concrete from the side and he tumbled and rolled.

A roaring in his ears.

Eyes flashing: white, black, white. The small voice in his head said, 'swim!'— the thing they'd always been taught in school. But the world was spinning and he didn't know which way was up. He flailed arms. Legs wrenched from under him.

When the movement stopped he could hear a rumbling vibration like thunder, and the snow near his ears creaking and groaning, but he couldn't move. One hand was free enough to make an air pocket near his face and clear the snow from his mouth and nose. Frantically he jabbed at the snow with a hand, the rest of him was set, as if in plaster.

His eyes were jammed shut with snow. He rubbed them clear to see what looked like dense layers of cloud. 'Here!' he yelled.

Where was Karl? Had he seen? Had he been overtaken too?

He must conserve air. He knew the survival rate was low if you weren't found straight away. Be calm. Work slowly. He dug again with his free hand. Nothing.

Must stay conscious. The odds that Karl had taken the hit too were about fifty-fifty. Not good.

He kept digging but now his fingers were frozen. It must be five minutes. His chances were decreasing by the second.

Was he going to die here? Would Karl come? He couldn't feel his legs.

Each breath was like sucking through a straw. He saw the faces of his mother and father, of a childhood Christmas at home; of a fir tree and his parents lighting a candle every night of December. He was starting to drift. He made one last stupendous effort to scrabble up to the surface, but he was too weak. He let himself go. Closed his eyes, fell into the haze of white.

CHAPTER 15

A sudden gaping black hole. A man's face. Black-gloved hands clawing at the snow.

Jørgen took great gasps of icy air.

'Hang on there,' Karl said. 'I'm going to get you out.'

The sight of the sky brought tears to his eyes . *I'm alive*, he thought. *Thank Christ.*

'Your pole was sticking out,' Karl said, through the muffle of snow, 'or I'd never have found you. I have to get you out in case there's another.'

He coughed, still trying to get enough air into his lungs to speak. The world looked grainy and he wasn't sure if it was lack of oxygen or relief that made him light-headed. Finally he managed to free his other arm as Karl dug and scraped at the snow to try to free his pack and get him out.

After about fifteen minutes he was able to grapple his way to the top of the pile, and collapse breathless on the surface.

'Anything broken?'

'Don't know. Don't think so. A bit battered maybe.' Jørgen didn't say that his knee was aching like the devil.

'Lucky there were no trees.'

'Or rocks.'

'I thought you were a goner,' Karl said, puffing. He was rubbing at Jørgen's legs to get the circulation moving. 'Rub your arms,' he said. 'Keep moving. Hypothermia sets in real quick.'

'Christ. I would have been dead, but for you. I could never have dug myself out.'

Karl paused in his rubbing. 'I've got to get you to the coast,' he said.

Jørgen looked up at the big man working away on his frozen legs. The blood returning hurt with the pain of a thousand needles. 'Karl?' He looked up at the use of his Christian name. 'Thanks.'

'Don't thank me.' He sounded angry. 'But I need to know if you can walk, and where your skis are. We'll get nowhere without them.'

More digging unearthed one ski, but the other was nowhere to be found. Probably buried under six foot of snow.

'You take mine,' Karl said. 'I'll ski on one. It will be slower, but it's the only way. And we'll have to take the risk and try for the village I showed you. You'll need to rest, get seen by a medic.'

'What if there are Germans there?' But when he stood up, shock had made his legs weak as cotton. He almost stumbled, but Karl held him up. Suddenly enormously grateful he tried to give Karl a hug.

Karl moved away from his embrace. 'Pass me your ski.'

Soon he was equipped with Karl's skis and poles, whilst Karl managed with one ski and one pole, alternating, like punting down a river. After they'd gone a couple of miles Karl found a group of pines and managed to fashion another improvised pole.

Jørgen watched in awe. He'd thought he was fit, but this man was a machine. He barely slowed, even though one foot was taking all the pressure.

It was dusk by the time they reached the village. There was little snow on the slopes downward, so they had to take off skis and walk. By now Jørgen was barely awake on his feet, everything ached, his legs were trembling, his feet like lumps of lead.

Karl explained to a middle-aged woman in an apron that they had been caught in an avalanche and Jørgen had lost a ski. His handsome face and polite manner smoothed the way, and she took them inside and made them sit before the fire.

'You can have the spare bedroom,' she said, smiling kindly. 'My son is away from home.' She didn't ask questions; but she called on an older neighbour to come and look them over. He made a face, said something about 'young fools', but he soon went away again.

The next few hours were a blur as Karl insisted he should go upstairs and rest. The bed felt so soft after so many nights on the mountain that it must have been only moments before he fell asleep.

When Jørgen woke it was already light, and at first he heard what he thought was a ticking clock. Too irregular for that. A soft tap, tap. He sat up in bed to see Karl, headphones on, cross-legged on the floor sending a message through the transmitter by morse code. Unable to resist, Jørgen couldn't help trying to translate what he was hearing. Damn. In code, so he could make out nothing. Only the name of this village, Bøverdalen. A notebook was by his side with some words written down. He craned to see what was written. All of a sudden Karl turned and, startled, slapped the notebook shut.

'You're awake,' he said. He didn't look pleased.

'What are you doing?'

'Just sending a message.' His good humour had returned.

'I thought you weren't in contact with anyone at Milorg yet?'

'Just a friend. A friend from Sivorg. He can get word to someone in Milorg. At least I hope he can. Thought I'd better tell him where we are.'

'Did you tell them about us meeting up, or about the avalanche?'

'No. Too complicated.'

'I'd like to get word to my op at the SOE,' Jørgen said. 'I left Oslo in rather a hurry and haven't radioed since. They won't know where I am.'

'There's a lot of interference. It was hard enough to even hear a signal. Like listening through static. And that's with the aerial up that tree out there.' Karl rose to his feet and indicated a pine standing close to the window.

'You'd better get that back inside. If anyone sees it, we'll be done for.'

'Relax,' Karl said. 'No-one can see. Give it a go; try to reach your contact. But you have to persist through the static. And while you're at it, you'll need to send a message to arrange for our pick up. We're only a few days away now. You can do it now, whilst the transmitter's out.'

'Could be a risk. We were always told to make our messages short — to stop them finding our location.'

'Don't sweat it. I was on for less than a minute.'

Jørgen crouched down to put on the headphones. 'Jesus, you're right about the signal. It's like soup.' He fiddled to try to find the frequency and finally managed to tap out a signal.

He waited, but he was signalling at the wrong time of day, and no-one would be listening out for him. Since he'd been on the run, he'd had no contact and they must all fear the worst. After a while he shook his head and pulled off the phones. 'No joy,' he said. 'Best if I try at 1400 hours. That's when they expect me.'

Karl frowned. Reluctantly, he climbed out of the window anyway and began to reel in the wire.

Jørgen stood up to help, but winced. He stretched. 'Gosh, I'm stiff.'

'You got pretty bashed up, but we won't need to ski from now on,' Karl said, still winding. 'I've arranged for us to get a lift.'

'How? Who with?'

'Turns out that neighbour who came in yesterday has a pony and trap.'

'What? You're not serious.'

'I buttered him up a bit and he's offered to take us down to the coast. We'll be able to get passage on a boat. That Shetland Bus you were talking about.'

'Sounds good. How the heck did you get him to agree?'

'Oh, I'm very persuasive.' He grinned.

I bet you are, Jørgen thought. Though Karl Brevik had rescued him from certain death, there was still something about him he couldn't quite warm to. He pondered it in his mind. Was it just that he was jealous because he was such an impressive athlete? Was it something about the lack of small-talk? He hardly knew anything about him. He decided he must make an effort to get to know him better.

'What will you do in England, Karl? Have you thought?'

The question seemed to take him aback. 'No. I didn't think further than getting out. But I'd like to go back to Norway, be of some help against the Nazis. Work the boats. If the Resistance will take me.'

'They'll take you. You're fit enough.' A pause. 'Did you leave anyone at home when you had to run?'

'No. No-one. Professional sport doesn't leave time for dating.'

Again Karl had closed off the conversation. Yet something was itching at the back of Jørgen's mind. Hadn't he read somewhere in the papers about Karl Brevik's girlfriend? He wracked his brains but couldn't bring it back.

Falk was in his office when Selma, his secretary knocked. 'Come,' he said.

'Intelligence has picked up a message on Brevik's frequency,' she said, handing him the typewritten sheet.

She waited expectantly.

'All right, Selma.' It was a dismissal.

He scanned it quickly. A few random letters, and his tag, but then two coherent sentences. 'The salmon has been caught. Salmon is on my line. Taking to market now.'

It could only mean one thing. Brevik had caught up with Nyström and was following him somehow to the Shetland Bus. Falk sat back in his chair, and rubbed a hand over his brow. He was sweating. He hadn't been this excited since his first boy had been born. 'Salmon is on my line.' What did that mean?

Of course. 'On my line'. Nyström would be sending from the same location.

He pulled open the door. 'Selma! Get that location tracked. Where Brevik was sending from. Pull in any messages from the same location, track who they're sending to.'

Where were they now, he wondered? Of course there'd been reports a week ago of two men killed at that farm where Nyström had first been seen. When the reports had come in, he hadn't been sure if it was Nyström or his man who was responsible, so he hadn't claimed responsibility. Besides, the Stapo were annoyed because they should have been questioned before they were killed. He took it as a good sign. It meant

Brevik was on Nystrøm's tail, and their information was worth the sacrifice.

Besides, what could those farmers know, stuck out there? Whereas he was aiming for the whole network. He had bigger fish to fry. This thought, in combination with Brevik's message made him laugh out loud. Salmon. Fish. He guffawed, but stifled it with a hand over his mouth, in case anyone should hear him and wonder at such odd behaviour.

This called for a celebration. Unable to remain still, he stood up and took out a flask from his drawer. With relish, he unscrewed it, took a large gulp and felt the brandy wash down his throat in a warming stream. 'Ahh.'

He had the insane desire to tell everybody, but he knew he couldn't. It was imperative to keep a lid on this if he was to keep the final success of it himself.

Instead, he sat down to write a confidential report. He tried hard not to gloat at the thought that his agent was now privy to all the secrets of the Shetland Bus operation. But he couldn't help feeling smug, and it was such an unusual feeling for him, that he rang up his wife. 'I'll take you out for dinner,' he said, expansively. 'Anywhere you like. The best.'

CHAPTER 16

Astrid struggled on, teaching like the rest of her colleagues, with the least possible adherence to the Nazi line. She missed Ulf, and the school was sadly diminished with the best of its male staff missing. Early one morning before school began, and careful not to be followed, she took the address Ulf had given her and went to see his friend, Herman — the one with the printing press. She wanted to know if he'd heard any news of Ulf.

Herman almost seemed to be expecting her, for when she gave her name he beckoned her in without a word, and pointed to a collapsed-looking sofa, where she took a seat. Herman was a short, skinny man with thin blond hair and eyes that were never still. He moved from place to place like a nervous cat, never settling anywhere, even though his apartment was a one-roomed basement flat, very cramped, with barely room for the printing press beside his single bed. The walls were plastered with printed poems, and playbills for plays popular before the Nazi invasion. He smoked incessantly and the room stank of cheap Russian cigarettes.

'So you heard it too,' he said.

'What?'

'Isn't that why you've come? The news about the teachers?'

'No. What? I came to see if you've heard from Ulf.'

'That's just it. It's not good news. They're moving some of the prisoners on,' he said. 'The teachers. I'm worried Ulf's amongst them.' He took another drag on his cigarette. The long stick of ash dropped onto the carpet and he scrubbed at it with his shoe. 'If you ask me, the move's been leaked to the papers on purpose — a deliberate act, meant to horrify the schools and make all the rest of teachers think again.'

'Well we won't budge, that's the whole point. Where are they moving them to?'

'A concentration camp near Kirkenes, in the arctic. It'll be minus thirty. Inhumane conditions, and they'll be put to hard labour.' He stabbed out the words, as he paced.

'My God,' Astrid said. 'Ulf won't survive that; he's not built for it.'

'Crap. He might be skinny, but he's tougher than you think,' he flashed. 'But I don't know what to do. I feel so useless. And I can't bear to think of it.'

'How long have you known him?'

'About nine months. We met at a bar. We just sort of hit it off. We've seen each other most days since.'

He was talking as if he was his … oh. Wait a minute. She felt herself grow crimson.

He saw her discomfort, but stuck up his chin. 'He's the best thing that happened to me. The only good thing about this bloody occupation is that I met Ulf.'

She waited for her face to cool, and for him to stub out his cigarette in the overflowing ashtray before speaking again. 'When are they taking them?'

'Not until next week. They're allowing time for the news to spread, hoping it will make teachers everywhere cave in.'

'It would be a betrayal if we did, you know that. So what else can we do?'

'Not a damn thing. We can't blow up the train; too risky, and all the teachers I've spoken to insist all protests must be peaceful, or it undermines their entire message. Ulf would agree, I know he would.'

'We could get some support for them though, couldn't we? The Church?'

He shook his head moodily. 'God no. Ulf hates the church; calls them all hypocrites. And anyway, the bishops who support the Resistance have all been sacked.'

'Can't we get up some sort of petition or demonstration? Come out in solidarity?'

'If we gather together, they'll shoot us. You know gatherings aren't allowed.'

'How about if we line the track? Stay a few miles apart? If you were being sent somewhere, wouldn't you want to know you're not on your own? Men like Ulf shouldn't think we've forgotten about them. Maybe we can give them some cheer, as they pass, make them realise we are all behind them?'

Herman stared at her. 'You know what, you might be on to something. We won't actually be a gathering if we keep our distance. It will give our men a boost, and enrage the Nazis.' He lit another cigarette. 'If Ulf's on that train, I'm going to be there. To tell him we're fighting for him; not to give up. Now, pass me that map.'

On the day the train carrying the teachers was due to leave Oslo, Astrid caught a tram out to the suburbs. On the same tram were Mrs Bakke and Karen Baum. They were all dressed warmly against the spring wind which cut like a knife, despite the pale sun. What would Mr Pedersen do when he found they were all missing? Of course he'd suspect something, and there would be recriminations. The thought of it made her grip the handle of her string bag tighter, winding it round her fingers. She caught sight of herself in the window of the tram, her pale distorted face looked a hundred years old.

Mrs Bakke got off a few stops before her. '*Alt for Norge!*' she whispered to Astrid as she passed, her red knitted bobble hat pulled down to keep her ears warm. Astrid felt a surge of affection for this little mole-like woman who had backed her all the way.

Fifteen minutes after it was the turn of Karen Baum. Karen made a grave sort of smile and gave Astrid the thumbs up. Astrid hoped Bo, her husband, was not on the train. Karen had got thinner and more lacklustre over the past few weeks, and the strain was obviously taking its toll. Karen had a basket of home-cooked food over her arm covered in a cloth. Astrid had spent the long dark evenings in the last week knitting socks and gloves, and these were sewn together in pairs, in her string bag.

Not until she got off the tram and walked out of the suburbs to the train line, did she realise that there were hundreds of teachers lining the route. Small groups of people stretched for a mile down the line, little blobs of colour against the grey. A few wild flowers poked through the few remaining inches of snow-melt.

Where she was, near a road crossing, there were two other men, who grinned at her and asked her which school she was from, before moving further down the track. They were suited, but in warm jackets and one of them had a wolfskin hat with earflaps tied under his chin. She kept glancing their way, as they waited.

She thought of Herman, who would be waiting even further down the line, for a glimpse of Ulf, and how Ulf had once told her to let Herman know if anything ever happened to him.

Half an hour passed but no train appeared. An hour. Just as her feet were turning numb, one of the men returned to speak to her. She looked down at her watch. An hour and twenty minutes late.

'What d'you think's happening?' the man in the wolfskin hat asked her. 'D'you think the Germans have changed their mind?'

'Who knows? But I'll wait a little longer. One of my friends was arrested. He might be on that train, and I owe it to him.'

'They took five from our school. Bastards.' He looked up the track again. 'Maybe the schedule's changed,' he said. 'Wouldn't surprise me. Someone must have told them we were here. What a bloody stupid idea. Whoever arranged this needs his head examining.' He stomped off down the track, back to his friend.

Astrid felt immediately guilty. What if he was right? All these people would have had a wasted journey. She stamped her feet and rubbed her arms against the wind which bit through her coat and whipped strands of hair round her face.

Just when she was losing hope, there was a sound. Faint, from up the line.

Not the train, but people cheering. It must be coming! Her relief was tempered with trepidation. The line of people began to move forward. The men nearest her, further up the line, pulled out Norwegian flags and flapped them in a frantic flurry of red, white and blue.

'*Alt for Norge!*' they shouted.

The noise of the train was deafening, the steam, the crank of the wheels. It was only when it was close that she realized. It wasn't a passenger train after all, but cattle wagons, their long narrow slatted windows open to the elements.

Herman must have known. That was why he'd asked her to bring things for the men; food and warm gloves. She was shocked they were expected to travel like animals, with the icy wind blowing through, and here was only the mild part of the journey. What would it be like in the frozen north?

Further down, the man in the wolfskin hat and his friend were jumping up and down waving their arms like crazy men. The front of the train bristled with Wehrmacht in helmets, their rifles at their shoulders. As soon as the engine passed, Astrid ran forward towards the wagons, stumbling along the track beside the train in the wake of the steam. From inside the train, the teachers reached out their hands to take whatever they could. A thin, cold hand reached out to her, and she thrust the whole string bag at him. The bag disappeared inside the narrow slit.

'Thank you!' came a shout.

'Don't give up hope!' she shouted. 'We're all with you! *Alt for Norge!*'

A barrage of machine gun fire. Astrid dropped to her knees in the snow. But the bullets went over their heads, and anyway they were too late, the train had passed and was clanking its way onwards.

'You all right?' The teacher in the wolfskin hat ran up.

'Fine,' she said, brushing snow off her knees. She turned her head away, so he couldn't see the wet in her eyes.

'It was a warning fire only,' his friend said, arriving at his side. 'They weren't officers so they wouldn't have the authority to shoot us.'

'My word, that felt good,' the wolfskin hat teacher said. 'Just to let the anger out of my lungs. Just to do something. Whoever thought up the idea needs a medal.'

Collar up against the blustery wind, Astrid walked to the school the next day with mixed feelings. On the one hand, she was elated they had achieved their objective, but on the other, the thought of Ulf and the other teachers, freezing somewhere in that cattle truck, made her so angry that, now she had time to think about it, she could barely breathe. They were good, kind men who had never done anyone any harm, and her headmaster, who should be proud of them, was condoning this ugly Nazi regime.

At the door, she handed in a sick note to Pedersen's secretary, claiming she'd been ill with a stomach complaint. It was what they all had planned to do. Pretend an outbreak of a virus. Of course they'd know it was nonsense, but they had to all agree the same story. She'd no doubt that Pedersen would have something to say to them all when he received it. Would she be dismissed?

In the morning assembly she exchanged anxious looks with Mrs Bakke and Mrs Baum, but Pedersen said nothing during assembly, and she got back in the classroom without a word being said.

Was he just going to let it pass? She felt the cold weight of the compass in her pocket, thought of Jørgen, and all the other Milorg agents, and their silent patriotism. The squirmy sensation in her stomach lasted all morning, until finally, just as she was collecting in the textbooks at the end of the lesson, the door opened, and Pedersen summoned her with a crooked finger.

'Fetch your coat, Miss Dahl.'

The words were like a cold sluice over her. She turned to the nearest girl. 'Helga, collect in the books for me please. And please everyone, don't forget to put on your outdoor shoes before break.'

She dragged her coat from the back of her chair, grabbed her handbag and gloves, and followed Pedersen's flapping figure down the corridor to his office. Before she even got inside, she could see police uniforms through the open door. She slowed as one of them, a thick-set man in plain clothes, turned at the sound of them coming.

'This is Sveitfører Falk,' Pedersen said.

'Ah, Miss Dahl.' Falk raised his chin to peer at her; for she was taller than him. 'We have one or two questions we need to ask you about your whereabouts yesterday. I'm afraid I must escort you to the station.'

'I was sick. This isn't a matter for the police. I handed a note to the secretary this morning. Mr Pedersen has it. A stomach upset.'

Pedersen said nothing.

Falk smiled. 'Yes, we've seen the note. And those of your colleagues. Nevertheless, those are our orders. I suggest you come without fuss. We will be interviewing your friends in due course, so there is no point in resisting.'

'Eight years I've been teaching, and now you want to arrest me because I was off sick? Mr Kristiansen would never have treated people this way.'

'Mr Kristiansen was old and incompetent,' Pedersen said. 'He was due for retirement anyway.'

'You mean, you pushed him out,' she said bitterly.

'Miss Dahl, our car is waiting outside.' Falk's hand was on her arm.

'Don't you touch me.' She whipped away. 'I'm going.' She marched out of the door. 'And I resign. If I can't teach the way I think I should, then you know what you can do with your school.'

By the time she shrugged on her coat and reached the front steps of the school, the two uniformed policemen were at her side. A car waited at the kerb, and they opened the back door for her to climb in. The car was upholstered in leather, and heated. It stank of aftershave, and just travelling in it made her even more resentful. No real Norwegian travelled in this comfort any more.

At the police station she was made to fill out her name and address and next of kin. She always hated this; the writing of 'None' in the box for next of kin. It made her feel small and incredibly alone. She wondered where Jørgen was, whether he'd made it out of Norway to England, and where he was now.

They led her into a small interview room that was just a box with a high window and a bare lightbulb dangling above her head.

Falk told her to sit, and sat down at the table opposite, whilst two policemen guarded the door.

'I'd like to see a lawyer,' she said. It was what people said on the movies. It was all she could think of to do.

He ignored it. 'Tell me where you were yesterday.'

'I told you. Sick.'

'So you had nothing to do with a group of people interfering with the progress of a train?'

'No.' She crossed her arms over her chest.

'Are you aware that four other people from your school were all absent with the same excuse?'

Again she was silent.

He sighed. He stared up at the high window a moment, even though there was no view. 'Why do you do it?' he asked. 'Why do you want to make life harder for yourself? You had a perfectly good job, and I saw you throw it away just now. Like

141

it was trash.' He rubbed his forehead as if trying to understand. 'You're pretty, you have a university education. You hung around with Nystrøm and the others in the popular set. Before I took this job, I taught hundreds like you.'

Jørgen's name jolted her onto high alert, and she suddenly realised where she'd seen him before. 'You were at the university?'

'Taught there twenty years, until they made me redundant. But the Nazis, they recognise intelligence when they see it. People like you think you're so entitled. You rant about your fine beliefs, about what should and shouldn't happen. You can afford them, that's why. But what about the rest of us?'

She shifted back in chair. He was angry now, she could feel the bristle in the atmosphere.

He stood up and prodded a finger down on the desk in front of her. 'You're like all the rest of the college kids. You've obviously never known what it's like to have to wonder where the next meal is coming from.' He strode away, but then turned and leaned towards her over the desk. 'Think you're better than us, don't you? Because you get to choose not to obey the Germans.'

She still didn't speak.

He leaned in again until his face was close to hers. 'You were on that protest against the transportation, and you think your stupid sick note is a little joke, that it's funny.' He leaned in, so his spittle flew in her face. 'Think you're so bloody clever. Well, a night in the cells should get rid of that idea. And I'll show you how clever you'll be feeling when you're on the list for transportation to Germany, or to a labour camp like your friend Ulf Johanssen.'

A shiver ran through her, but she stayed still.

'He will be in the north of Norway now, learning how to work hard for a living, and be grateful just to be alive.'

She wouldn't let him see her fear. The fact Ulf had been on the train made the knot of anger inside her condense into cold iron. What had happened to Ulf could happen to her.

'So you've nothing to say.' He glared at her a moment longer while she looked past him to the wall behind. 'Then you will be charged and a trial date arranged. I suggest you plead guilty and ask for leniency. If you join the Teachers' Union then you might avoid transportation. Take her down,' he said to his men by the door.

As she stood up, Falk loomed over her again. 'You think you're so much better than me, don't you? You and Nyström. Well, if you don't heed my warning, you'll just be dirt, hear me? Dirt.'

CHAPTER 17

In the back of the farmer's cart, Jørgen stretched out his bruised leg and rubbed his twisted knee. It was swollen and he guessed he'd torn ligaments when his skis were taken in the avalanche. Every jolt of the cart hurt, and even today, he still felt shaky, but he wasn't going to let Karl see how rattled he was. And he was grateful for the lift. The farmer was a cheerful soul, and the journey by horse and trap to the edge of the fjord made up in speed what it lacked in comfort.

Jørgen and Karl got off at a small village close to Ålesund, a cluster of houses around a stone jetty. Their farmer was delivering bales of hay to a farm close to the shore, and there, under shelter of an outside barn, Jørgen was at last able to transmit at the proper time to his contacts in the SOE.

It was a relief to hear the familiar tapping of his contact in England. The precision soothed him. Astonishingly, he could recognize the pace of her transmissions and it was like hearing an old friend. His coded transmission told them back at base in England there would be two people needing to travel.

'Two?' came her coded reply. 'Supply details.'

'Friend,' he tapped.

'Name?'

'Karl Brevik.'

The next time he checked in, there was an address and code word, and they soon found Jan Balstrud, the fisherman that was their contact, in the herring-smoking hut by the edge of the water. He was a toothless old man of about eighty, but still seemed to be working the boats.

'You'll be all right up here,' he said, pointing to a rickety ladder.

He put them up in a cramped attic under the turf roof of his house. The rafters stank of the linseed oil used to keep out the wet, and the place had to be accessed by the lethal-looking ladder, but it was dry, and warmed by the smoky heat from the peat fire downstairs.

His next radio contact informed him the boat would be with them in three days.

'Three days?' Karl seemed unimpressed they couldn't be quicker.

'It's rough water, and the weather could be bad.'

During the three days they had to wait for the boat to Shetland, Karl was restless, and kept disappearing for long walks, taking his rucksack with him. He never left it unattended. The third time he did it, Jørgen found himself getting irritated. Didn't Karl trust him? Why had he taken the pack? He didn't need it for just a stroll around the harbour, surely.

When Karl returned, still wearing the rucksack, Jørgen asked him, 'Where'd you go?'

'Just along the shoreline. Not far.'

'With all that stuff?'

Karl's eyes blanked for a moment. Then he smiled. 'Thought I'd better keep fit. No use getting out of condition. Never know when you might need to run, or carry weight.'

Jørgen looked at him a moment longer. Something about it didn't ring true. He realised he still didn't really like the man. He'd tried to, but something about him just rubbed him up the wrong way. I suppose you can't like everyone, he thought. But it was something to do with the fact that Karl never let down his guard. Their conversations were always on the surface, like he never got to penetrate beyond acquaintance.

The day before the boat was due, Jørgen sat down to write to Astrid. He might not get another chance; once they were in England the mail to Norway would be censored.

Karl was sitting on the horsehair mattress in his corner of the attic, examining a map of Shetland he'd found in the old man's kitchen.

'Hey, Karl?' Jørgen said. 'Have you a paper and pen? I thought I'd write to Astrid before we leave.'

Karl sat up and pulled the notebook from his rucksack, and carefully tore out two pieces of paper, before pushing the notebook back in to the pocket.

Again, Jorgen was annoyed at this small act of meanness; that he hadn't handed over the whole book, but he said nothing. He kept reminding himself he wouldn't even be alive if it wasn't for Karl.

He uncapped the pen and focussed on what he wanted to say.

Dear Astrid,

By the time you get this, I'll be out of Norway. Sometime, I'll come back home and when I do, I'll look you up. You are a special part of my life. In the meantime, don't forget to enjoy yourself, and I will understand if you meet someone else. I don't want you to feel you have to have any ties to me. The Occupation in Norway makes it hard for me to have any certainties about the future. There is much more I'd like to say, but I'll only say this, I'm not running away, only going where I can be most useful. And the fight goes on, not just for me, or for you, but for all Norwegians.

'What are you telling her?' Karl asked.

'Nothing. Nothing that'll bother the SOE, anyway. Just keeping in touch.' Again, Jørgen did not sign it. He asked their elderly fisherman friend, Jan Balstrud, if he had an envelope, and whether he could get it passed through Sivorg, the civilian Resistance. Jan agreed to pass it on.

The rest of the day was a strange limbo time, whilst they waited for enough dark to be rowed out to the rendezvous point on a smaller island out in the mouth of the fjord.

As he and Karl put their bags aboard the big fishing vessel that would take them across the North Sea, Jørgen took a last look back at Norway. His feelings about it were complex. The land he loved and knew had been tainted by bombs and shootings and blood. He didn't like to abandon it, this way, it made him feel like a traitor.

But the Nazis had given him no choice. He'd have to fight for Norway from Shetland instead.

Laughter made him turn. It was Karl, already aboard and having a joke with two of the crew. In less than five minutes he'd made himself popular, become the centre of attention, with an exaggerated tale of how they'd crossed Norway to get to the boat. Jørgen sucked in a huge breath of salty, sea air. The fact that other people could now take on the burden of Karl Brevik made his heart rise, and when he heard the chug of the engine and the slap of the waves, he stumbled to the prow and turned his face into the wind. He was unsurprised to see Karl was a natural sailor, though on more than one occasion, Jørgen's heart was in his mouth, as the boat plunged into the trough of the waves and Karl gripped the rail, feet floating in mid-air.

Jørgen was more cautious. Spying had taught him to always calculate risk, and it was a hard habit to break. When the wind ceased to howl through the rigging, he managed to sleep. At dawn he went to the prow to try to catch the first sight of land.

Summer would soon be coming and over there, somewhere, lay Shetland; a place of peace, pure air and wide open spaces — an island still free.

CHAPTER 18

The boat arrived by the eastern shore of the Shetland Islands at night, and the shouts from the crew on deck brought Jørgen to the rail to peer out into the black, where a faint hump of darker black bled into the horizon. Frustratingly, because of sea defences designed to trap the enemy, they had to wait till the pale light of morning before they could motor round to the harbour.

The new centre of operations for the Shetland Bus was in Scalloway, the ancient capital of the islands. To Jørgen's surprise, the village was on the Atlantic side of the island, facing away from Norway. Unlike the few houses he'd expected, Scalloway was a working village, clustered under the ruins of a tumbledown seventeenth century castle.

A British army captain, Harcourt, greeted them. He was a short, stout man, looking like he'd been shoe-horned into his uniform, but he spoke good Norwegian, which was a relief. With him was the female secretary to the Norwegian Consul, Morag Airdrie, who spoke Norwegian like a native. Jørgen found her warm smile immediately endearing.

'I'm afraid I have to ask you to hand over your bags,' Morag said. 'And I'll need all your documents too.' They led them into across the main harbour road to a garage-like shed with a long trestle table.

Jørgen knew from instinct that Karl would hate protocol or any kind of paperwork. He was a man who preferred action to talking; he could never be still for long, and was always pacing or on the move. Now, he was hurriedly taking things out of his pack and stuffing his pockets.

'No,' Morag said, sharply. 'Leave everything inside. And empty your pockets.'

'What's your name?' Karl asked her, in English, giving her a dazzling smile. It was the first time Jørgen had heard him speak English, and he sounded confident.

'Morag,' she said, but continued in Norwegian. 'Sorry this is necessary, but all incomers have to be searched and vetted.'

'It's a pretty name,' Karl said, again in English. 'Mine's Karl. Karl Brevik.'

If he's been hoping for a reaction, he got none. She gave a brief smile, but Harcourt then stepped in to watch as Karl emptied his pockets, and Jørgen shrugged off his pack.

'You can't keep any of it,' Harcourt said.

'Nothing?' Karl asked, disgruntled.

'No, don't worry, we'll issue you with everything you need. We'll drive you to the Mission for debriefing,' Harcourt said, after they'd handed everything over.

'The Catholic Mission,' Morag explained. 'It's a big old house. We'll need to drive.'

They piled into the back seat of a rusty old Morris car. Morag did the driving, and Harcourt filled them in on the SOE from the front seat. Apparently the Shetland Bus wasn't the only wartime operation from Scalloway — there were also engineering works, an RAF station and a military hospital, though there was little sign of them today for the landscape was almost invisible in the early morning mist and populated only by scattered sheep. The Catholic Mission proved to be dilapidated, draughty stone-built house a few miles up a deserted track. Jørgen's first impression was that it had been built at some time in the Victorian era, by someone with zero architectural taste.

Jørgen got out of the car, and after being at sea he swayed slightly as Morag led them both up the steps and into the hall. One good thing though, in the main living room, an enormous urn was on the boil with a vast teapot for dispensing tea, along with plates full of hard, dry oat biscuits. At one side was a billiard table and scoreboard, presumably for off-duty games.

He was relieved when Karl was taken into the interview room first. It gave him time to recover. He helped himself to tea and a biscuit, and for the first time in a month he was still, and it was as though his heart dropped down a gear.

A big bay window had a view over the harsh landscape of fell and heather. The land was devoid of trees, and the wind was clearing the mist and blowing the grass in undulating waves. He gazed into the distance where a few more hardy sheep grazed, their backs to the prevailing wind.

So this was Scalloway. Last time he left Shetland was after he'd done his training in the Highlands, and he'd left from Lunna, an even more remote part of the island. This place looked equally dour and grey.

He suppressed a pang of homesickness for Norway; for blue fjords and snow-capped peaks. He told himself not to be so stupid. He'd go back, one day, when Norway was free.

'Glad to be here?' a soft voice said in Norwegian. It was Morag, the girl who was part of the Norwegian consulate.

'I still haven't really landed,' he said.

'Yes. It takes most of the refugees that way. Partly it's just being safe; having got here at all.'

He turned to get a better look at her. She was dressed in a plaid skirt and a knitted jumper in traditional Scottish style; nothing showy. Her face was pleasant and open, a few freckles across the nose, her brown hair brushed to a shine. She was gazing at him enquiringly.

'You speak good Norwegian.'

'My mother was Norwegian,' she said. 'Father brought her back here when they got married. But she died before the war. Of T.B. It's why I do this; for her. To help her countrymen. She was from Trondheim. Where are you from?'

'Oslo. Are there many other refugees here?'

'Hundreds have passed through, I've lost count. Most go on to London, so I don't see much of them. Just arrange their transport. One or two of the Norwegian men stay though, and work here for the Shetland Bus. They like to be close to home, and to feel like they're still helping.' She raised an eyebrow at him, challenging.

He gave a brief nod. He wondered if she approached all the Norwegians in this way; with a gentle hint. He turned to glance at the door to the office where Karl was being interviewed.

'He's being a long time,' she said. 'Usually it's a quick in and out.'

'Maybe they've got onto skiing. He's an Olympic skier, you know.'

'Really? He'll find it hard on Shetland then. More rain and wind than snow.'

Just then the door opened, and Karl emerged. His eyes fixed on Morag straight away, smiled and asked her, 'Any more of that tea?'

'Of course.' She led him over to the tea table. Jørgen noticed Karl's blue eyes were twinkling in a way he hadn't seen before. It took him aback; he hadn't realised what Karl would be like with women.

'Jørgen Nystrøm?'

Jørgen tore his eyes away from where Karl was charming Morag. Captain Harcourt was holding the door open for him, so he hurried through and sat in the worn leather chair opposite the desk. Another younger man, a sergeant in English army uniform, was there at a side table to take notes in shorthand. The room smelled of leather and damp carpets.

He couldn't help recce-ing the room. A glance at the bookshelf showed mostly Christian books and books on the Catholic Church. The only thing that showed they were at war was a Mark III 'Tinker Box', the long-range wireless combo which he recognised from his training.

Captain Harcourt saw him appraising his surroundings. 'Take no notice of the background. We borrow the office from the chaplaincy.' He offered him a cigarette but Jørgen waved it away. 'You were a W/T operator, code name The Whale?'

Jørgen nodded. The Whale had been loosely based on his name Jørgen, like Jonah in the Bible. Usually people were named after mice, or other small burrowing animals. It was the Norwegian idea of a joke to give him something so enormous. He briefly outlined all the information about the U-boat base at Bergen. So many miles he'd travelled, hugging this information to his chest, that to see the Sergeant write it all down gave him almost a feeling of euphoria.

When he'd finished Harcourt asked him; 'So, just tell us in your own words how you came to get passage on the Shetland Bus.'

He detailed his journey, how he met Karl Brevik.

'Ah, yes. Brevik. What do you know about him?'

It was then that he realised he knew virtually nothing. 'We didn't have much time for small-talk,' he said. 'But he saved my life.'

Captain Harcourt nodded. 'So he said. He dug you out of an avalanche. Must have been pretty frightening.'

'I'd be dead, if it wasn't for him. My pack was stuck in the drift. And I'd never have made it to the coast unless he gave me his skis.'

'Did he speak to you about his parents, or his family?'

'No. It was a hard journey, and not much time for talk.' Was this about Brevik or him? Jørgen squirmed. He felt lacking somehow, that he didn't know more.

'Shame. Still, we got onto SOE by telephone last night and researched his background, as we did yours. His father, Anton Brevik was a big mover in something called the Fatherland League. It has something in common with Hitler's ideals for his country, but that was in the past, and thankfully there's no sign at all of the son following in his father's footsteps. Brevik's police career seems to have been exemplary. Citations for bravery too.'

He was trying to catch up. They'd researched him, and Karl? He glanced round to see Harris, the young sergeant scribbling away in shorthand.

'Brevik's obviously a bit of a well-known sportsman,' Captain Harcourt said, 'won all sorts of medals for Norway. We noticed there were a few things in his pack that were a bit unusual though. Did he tell you where he got the map? It's not like the ones we issue.'

'I was wary when he turned up out of the blue, so I took a look in his pack,' Jørgen said. 'There was a transmitter, and I saw the maps. He said he was working for Milorg.'

'Yes, that checks out. A failed sabotage of some steelworks in Bremen set him on the run. He gave us names of the men he'd been working with.'

'What did they say?'

'Unfortunately nothing. They were men who'd been caught by the Gestapo and executed.'

Jørgen weighed the thought a moment before speaking. 'I don't want to sound suspicious sir, but it was odd the way Brevik just appeared in the middle of nowhere. And now you're telling me he didn't give you the name of a single contact that's still alive?"

'I thought you were friends? Are you telling me the man's not trustworthy?'

'I don't know. I just think we should keep an open mind.'

'I understand you've been through a lot, Nystrøm. And that wireless operators live on their nerves. It could be that you're seeing phantoms where none exist.' Harcourt tapped his fingers on the desk, ruminating. 'Of course it will all be checked out. Now we've talked to you, perhaps we need to make further calls to the SOE.'

'If there is something … what are you going to do about him?'

'Nothing for now,' Captain Harcourt said, fiddling with the button on his cuff. 'We find this a lot, with men who've been on the run. A kind of over-sensitivity. All Brevik's credentials check out, and obviously he's a well-known figure, so he's rather been in the public eye.'

Over sensitivity? Jørgen felt rage mount within him. He was doing his job; that was all. Raising valid concerns when he thought it right to do so. But here was Harcourt treating him like some kind of nervous wreck. He suspected even Harcourt had been dazzled by Brevik, by his good looks and charm and the fact he was a kind of celebrity.

Harcourt was still talking. 'We've billeted you together at the barracks. And we need to know your plans — whether you'll be moving on — separately or alone, so we can make provision for further appropriate training. I take it you wish to further the cause against Hitler?'

'Yes, sir, of course.'

'Obviously we don't want to rush you into anything,' Harcourt said. 'There's a price on both your heads and we won't be sending either you back to Norway for a while. Now the light's increasing, it's more of a risk. And anyway, we wouldn't send you until it's calmed down.'

'About Karl Brevik —'

'You can leave him to us. Over the next few days the SOE will be checking him out,' Harcourt said impatiently. 'And in the meantime we'll be double-checking your logbook, so we can tally your broadcast times against ours, okay?'

'Yes, sir.'

'Oh, and Nystrøm, Welcome to Scotland.'

When Jørgen got out of the room a sense of disorientation had taken hold. Maybe Harcourt was right. Karl had saved his life, and he was treating him like the enemy. War did odd things to people, and perhaps the strain of his flight across the *vidda* and the whole business of Lind and the avalanche had got to him more than he thought it had.

Two close shaves. He thought of Lind, lying by the side of the tracks. Probably dead by now because they thought Lind was him. He supposed that kind of responsibility was enough to bother anyone.

He glanced over to where Karl was seated, over by the window, one long leg crossed easily over the other. He had a cup and saucer in his hand, and was obviously still attempting to hold Morag Airdrie in his thrall.

'Ah, Jørgen,' Karl said, gesturing him over. 'Let you stay, have they?'

'Well they've given me a billet number, so I guess so.'

'Good show,' Morag said. 'Your bags should be ready for collection, and I'll drive you both down to the barracks. Captain Harcourt will take his own car; he's got to go to Lerwick before he goes back to base.'

They climbed aboard the creaking Morris, and Morag drove, bumping down the rutted tracks. It felt odd to be driven by a woman, but she was obviously a capable driver, despite Karl's attempts to win her over from the front passenger seat.

'Where do you live?' he was asking. And, 'Where can you get a decent Norwegian beer?'

Jørgen was uneasy. Was this just chat-up, or was it intelligence gathering? He chided himself. He was being over-suspicious again. Trouble was, once you thought like a spy, it was hard to change your thinking. He told himself to relax.

Karl's charming smile persisted throughout, and Jørgen had to admit, he was a handsome man. Just the type to knock the socks off a girl like Morag.

Morag however, seemed to be holding her own. 'Beer? In Scotland? An absolute travesty! You need a good old dose of Scottish whisky. Something warming.'

No flies on that one, Jørgen thought, with admiration. Probably all the guys tried it on with her.

They drew up at Lerwick, at some long low buildings. 'Here you go,' Morag said. 'You'll be billeted here with ten others, when they eventually arrive. Used to be the sardine canning factory, but now it's our camp for refugees. It's only temporary, until we know where you'll be going on to.'

'Back to Norway, I hope,' Karl said. 'To get a few more of us out.'

She seemed surprised. 'The journey out didn't put you off then?' She let down the tailgate of the boot.

'It wasn't that rough. I've seen worse.' Karl slung an arm around Jørgen's shoulders. 'And Jørgen and I want to serve Norway the best we can.'

Jørgen flinched surprised at Karl's sudden chummy behaviour. Probably for Morag's benefit.

'Then I'll be seeing you both back at Scalloway soon,' she said, as she heaved their new kitbags out of the boot. 'You're in room 3. Beds 7 and 8. Cheerio.'

She was in the car and trundling away in a spatter of mud from the tyres before they could even wave.

The billets were as they'd expected; spartan. Iron bedstead, wooden locker, grey army blankets, lumpy pillow. Each bed was supplied with a metal torch for going out to the toilet block, and a rudimentary printed map of Shetland.

'How did the grilling go?' Karl asked, as Jørgen tried to shove his whole kitbag into the locker.

'Okay. Standard stuff. You?' As Jørgen sat on the bed to ease off his boots, the springs gave an ominous creak.

'Same. Volunteered for the Shetland Bus crew though. Think I'd like to get back out there, now I've seen what it entails. I could be crew, easy, even if not skipper a boat. Used to sail a lot when I was a kid.'

'I was thinking of it,' Jørgen said. 'Harcourt seems to think we need time to recover, spend a bit of time on dry land before we put to sea again.'

'Tosh. He means they don't put out in the summer. Too risky — could be spotted by enemy planes, and the nights are not long enough anymore. The "simmer dim" I've heard the Shetlanders call it — endless daylight. So I guess it'll be four more months before they send anyone.'

'Then I might look for a job in the office. Decoding, or clerical work. I've the skills for that.'

'You're not serious about staying stuck in an office? You'll be crewing for them, soon as you can, won't you?' Karl asked.

Jørgen lay back on the pillow. Harcourt's mistrust of his judgement had disturbed him. 'I'll think about it,' he said.

Karl shoved Jørgen's feet to one side and sat down on the end of his bed. 'They need good W/T operators back in Norway. Are you really saying you'll sit out the war here? I never thought you one for giving up.'

Jørgen didn't know what he thought any more, except he didn't like being pressured by Karl. 'Let's talk later. I'm all in,' he said. 'I'm going to take a nap.'

He felt the rise of the springs as Karl moved away, and the noise of him taking off his boots and unpacking. In the distance seabirds squawked and sheep bleated. The wind rattled the iron-framed windows in impatient gusts.

Later Karl said, 'I'm going to find a beer. Coming?'

'No. You go,' Jørgen said. 'I'm going to doze a bit longer.' He felt odd, as if half of him was still on the other side of the sea. He thought of Astrid, and life going on in Oslo without him, and of the long nights he'd spent alone in mountain huts. He wondered how he'd been rumbled, how he hadn't known the Germans were onto him, until it was too late. It had knocked his confidence.

And then he thought of Karl. He didn't want to admit to himself he was losing his judgement. He weighed the probabilities that Karl Brevik was an enemy agent. There was no evidence at all, so the risk was maybe less than one percent. After all he'd met Astrid by chance at a mountain hut, hadn't he? He'd have to get over this suspicion; leave Harcourt to investigate. He chafed against the idea that people thought he was suffering from some sort of war fatigue.

Finally, rocked by his own not-yet-stable-on-land stomach, he slept.

The next morning, he woke to find a heavy hand on his shoulder, pressing him down. 'No!' he yelled, lashing out.

'Calm down,' said Karl.

'What? What's going on?' He sat bolt upright, his heart pounding, his mind full of confused images of Nazis burrowing like ants as he tried to escape through tunnels of snow.

'You were having a nightmare, moaning and calling out. I didn't want you to wake the others.'

He looked around. Most of the other beds were occupied now. Another boat must have come in in the night, and they were surrounded by a bunch of ragged refugees snoring in the early morning light. 'Sorry,' he said, feeling foolish.

'I can smell toast,' Karl said. 'See you at breakfast.'

After he'd washed and dressed Jørgen began to feel more normal. A little investigation found him a draughty dining hall where a big vat of oatmeal was on the boil, with toast, butter, and a red paste proclaiming itself to be jam, though there seemed to be no fruit in it that he could discern.

He tucked in, hungry now his stomach had settled. He joined Karl at one of the trestle tables. Today, Karl seemed less threatening, and more like just a guy having breakfast. Jørgen relaxed.

After breakfast Morag appeared in the old Morris banger again and said Captain Harcourt had asked to see them over at Scalloway, and she was to drive them there for a guided tour.

'Does that mean we've been accepted?' Karl was keen.

'Too early to say. You'll need to do on-shore duties with the rest of us, if you're staying,' she said. 'Mind you, you've picked a good day for it.'

She was right. The sky had cleared into a pale blue with clouds scudding by, and as they drove down towards the bay at Scalloway the sea sparkled, topped by runnels of miniature white horses. Karl had leapt in the front seat next to Morag, and left Jørgen to ride in the back.

'Wouldn't mind a swim in that sea,' Karl said.

'As long as you don't care about being blown to smithereens,' she said. 'It's mined.'

That was them firmly put in place.

Morag caught Jørgen's eye in her rear-view mirror and grinned. Suddenly, his cares evaporated.

When they got out of the car, the wind had whipped up and spray was blowing up onto the slipway. Shouting over the wind, Morag told them it had recently been built so that the Shetland Bus boats could be hauled in for repair after every trip. A couple of boats were already resting there in dry dock, the decks being scrubbed by men in oilskins and boots.

A garage was the next port of call, where some smaller motorboats were being housed. 'They're for when agents need to get between islands,' Morag said. 'They never come back, so we need a lot of them.'

'What do you mean, never come back?' Jørgen asked.

'Oh sorry, I meant the boats, not the men! The Germans are onto us now, how we get our agents in or out, and how we do our weapon drops. It's getting too risky for the big fishing boats to go right into a fjord or harbour, so we thought we'd provide these. The agent zips where he wants to go, and then just dumps the boat.'

'Meaning you can get to places the Germans would never think you could get to,' Karl said.

Karl continued to stare at the motorboats until Morag pulled her mackintosh closer round her chest and said, 'Come on, let's get out of this wind. There's work to do.'

She took them into a small joinery workshop. 'Those boats we just saw? They need their engines protecting for the journey over,' she said to Karl. 'The deck often gets swamped, so we make housings for them, to keep the sea out. The boats are no earthly use if the engine's flooded.'

Another of the men moved aside from the bench where he was sawing, so Jørgen could take a look.

It wasn't a bodge job, like he expected, but well thought through. The engine was securely mounted in a plywood box, and the propeller shafts stuck out of the box via a watertight membrane, all neat and workman-like. The petrol and water pipes were mounted on a brass plate, and there was an insertion hole for the starter handle that could be sealed with a plug.

'We need six more of these making,' Morag said. 'Jacobsen, will you show these two the ropes?'

Jacobsen, an older man with a bristly walrus-like moustache and rheumy eyes, handed them two brown twill aprons and soon got them working. Jørgen was glad to be busy with his hands doing something practical.

Karl was watching Morag go. 'She's not a bad looker,' he said. 'A bit stiff though. Might try to take her out for a few drinks, loosen her up.'

'She probably has to be that way,' Jørgen said. 'After all, there aren't many women here at base, are there? Except the ones somewhere behind the serving hatch in the canteen or hidden away in the laundry.'

Karl leaned in to him and whispered, 'What d'you say we take one of those motorboats out one day, explore a bit?'

'Too risky. You heard what Morag said. Don't want to blow ourselves up.'

'Aw. Where's your Viking sense of adventure? Are you a norseman or not?'

'There's adventure,' Jørgen said, 'and then there's rank stupidity.'

Karl laughed. 'Yeah. You could be right. Probably best to try to stay alive now we've actually got here.' He turned back to measuring his sheet of ply.

Jørgen was relieved. He'd had to quash the idea that Karl could well have an alternative interest in looking at the coast. Now he let go of it. Harcourt was right, he must try to calm down and not be looking for trouble everywhere he went.

A month went by with work in the woodwork shop, and the repairing and repainting of the fishing boats that would go out to Norway next winter season. Jørgen was under a boat with his paintbrush when Morag came to tell him he was wanted at the Mission again. 'Captain Harcourt wants a word,' she said.

He wiped his palms down his overalls and hopped into the front seat of the battered old Morris while she drove him over to Lerwick, over rugged brown hillsides dotted with crumbling rock, past abandoned crofts and pylons.

'Have you always lived in Shetland?' he asked her. And then cringed, he was sounding like Karl.

She didn't seem to notice. 'Yes,' she said, changing gear, 'except I went to school in Aberdeen. It's the nearest place with a school that does Higher School Certificate. I learnt to get rid of my Scottish accent there.'

'So what made you come back?'

'Aberdeen's all right. But I missed the island, and I've always felt more Norwegian than English because of my mother. They say Bergen's nearer Shetland than Aberdeen.'

'Doesn't seem like it,' he said. 'The journey over seemed long enough.'

She laughed. 'Rough, was it?'

'You could say that. I think my stomach's still in Norway.'

They were coming over the hill now and going down. A mizzle of grey rain had started up again and she put the wiper on.

'All this must have changed since the war.' He gestured at the town laid out before them.'

'Yes. It was much quieter. I used to work in the Post Office here, that's where I heard about a post in Scalloway as a general factotum. They needed someone fluent in Norwegian, and I thought, why not? And I've been with Larsen's outfit ever since.'

'Must be interesting.'

'Hard though, when you send a boat out and it doesn't come back.'

'Does that happen often?'

She pulled up. They'd arrived. She turned and looked him in the eye. 'It's the weather, more than the Germans. The North Sea in winter's a cruel master. Our men risk their lives in the biggest seas you could imagine. Sometimes I can't sleep, thinking of them out there. It's the thought of them drowning; the thought of falling into those towering waves, of sinking in icy seas and what they must think of in those last desperate moments. Knowing no rescue will ever come.'

'You're not being a very good advertisement for it, are you?'

'Sorry.' She made a face. Then smiled. 'You're right, I shouldn't have opened my big mouth. I hope I haven't put you off. Lord knows, we need men who are prepared to do it, even when they know the risks.'

Jørgen found himself about to volunteer, just to see Morag Airdrie smile again. When she smiled, her whole face became mischievously alive. He reminded himself of Astrid, back home in Norway. Get a grip, he told himself. Don't let yourself be de-railed by the first pretty face you see.

At the Mission Morag showed him into Harcourt's Office. Today Harcourt was alone, staring gloomily out into the rain. Even though it was summer, the rain still blew across the island in sheets. 'We've had the report back on Karl Brevik,' Harcourt said, without turning. 'We've found nothing.'

'Thank God,' Jørgen said. He let out his breath.

Now Harcourt came to sit down. 'It was a thorough investigation. His contacts were all double-checked.' He frowned, shrugged. 'It could happen, you know, Nyström. He could be the only one who got away. And there's no evidence of him having been anything other than a good police officer before the war. No affiliation to any political party or organisation. And we talked to the Olympic committee; he's a model athlete. No drugs, nothing like that.'

'Sounds too good to be true.'

'Not quite. There was a girlfriend; she claimed he'd blacked her eye, roughed her up. But he said she was making it up, that she was just wanting to get attention from someone with celebrity status. And I can see that might be a possibility with a "name" like him. It had quite a spread in the papers until the Athletic Board had it hushed up. They needed him to be clean for their team.'

So that was it. 'I thought I'd read something about that.'

'So now what do *you* think? You've seen more of him than the rest of us. Is he a man you can trust?'

Jørgen squeezed his hands into fists. 'It should be an easy question, I know, but it isn't. Karl dug me out of an avalanche when he could have left me to die. Yet I've never really warmed to him. We rub along all right, but…'

'Your instinct is, that he's not one of us?'

'No. I can't just say that, because I don't particularly like him. He's never done anything to me, and he's always been perfectly polite to everyone else. There are plenty of people I don't exactly hit it off with, but it doesn't mean they're all spies. I guess there's just something I don't trust.'

'We noted your reservations, but I'm afraid we feel they may be unfounded. But I suppose it's best we err on the side of caution since you obviously feel so strongly. Because of that, we can't send Brevik to SOE for training, but nor would it be wise to keep him here. Yet the man could be entirely innocent.' He stood up and paced across the room staring into space. 'An awkward little conundrum.'

Was Harcourt blaming him? He didn't want to be responsible for holding Karl back from training because of some unproven feeling he had. 'I'm sorry, sir.'

'Best thing would be to get him back to Norway, get them to deal with him.'

Pass the buck, in other words. 'He told me he wants to join your operations,' Jørgen said, 'and was talking about getting on the next boat back. That much I can be sure of, he fancies crewing for the Shetland Bus, and if you're right and I'm wrong I don't want to hold him back.'

'What about you? Will you join us on the operations? They tell me you're handy on board ship. You have good radio skills but I feel you're not ready for another W/T job just yet.'

What did he mean? Did he still think of him as too shot with nerves for the job? 'I did wonder about The Shetland Bus,'

Jørgen said guardedly. 'You're right, they'd be looking for me if I went straight back to Norway as a W/T op, so it would have to be an out and return job. Crew or something.' He didn't want the man to know how afraid he was of going back.

'My thoughts exactly,' Harcourt said. 'Could be, you're still not ready. Best take a few weeks to think it over, and let me know your decision at the end of the month.'

Jørgen swallowed. He was ready. As ready as he'd ever be to go back to a place where they shot people like him on sight. But he didn't want to look like he was ignoring Harcourt's advice. 'I'll think it over,' he said.

CHAPTER 19

Astrid had been released from prison after a night in the cell, with instructions to report to Falk the following week and every week for the foreseeable future until the trial came. 'Disobeying State Orders' was the charge, and who knew what sort of sentence she could expect for that? She'd have to be careful about seeing Herman, and about where she went. She hated this new restriction, and her stomach contracted at the thought of having to see Falk again. She'd sensed suppressed anger in him, and the thought it could blow up at any moment scared her.

What was her life to become, now? She couldn't go to school, not while Pedersen was still in charge. She'd never go back on her resignation. If there was one thing she was, it was stubborn, and teaching was all she ever wanted to do.

All the way home she looked over her shoulder. Every man behind her became a threat, every curious glance something more sinister.

At the gate, she opened the mailbox to find two letters there. The top one was from Jørgen; she knew his handwriting. Thank goodness; he was still alive. With a quick glance behind, she took the letters indoors, and without even taking off her coat, ripped open the letter.

The few words did nothing to cheer her. So he'd left Norway after all. He'd be in Scotland by now, with the North Sea between them. And from his tone, it sounded as though he wouldn't be coming back any time soon.

I don't want you to feel you have to have any ties to me. The Occupation in Norway makes it hard for me to have any certainties about the future.

A hollow feeling in her chest made her put the letter to one side. Of course she felt ties to him. This bloody occupation.

She pulled the other letter towards her. After reading it, she sat down and raked her fingers through her long fair hair, wondering what on earth to do. The landlord wanted her to vacate the house by the end of the month. A German Kommandant had agreed to take on the tenancy from the first of July, and his rent would be paid by the army.

She gave a groan of frustration. Hadn't she any rights left? She suspected they couldn't legally do this, throw her out with so little notice, but now she was in a predicament. She'd already got on the wrong side of Falk, the chief of the quisling police, and now she'd no job, no means of paying rent, and a trial in the offing. Arguing with the landlord would do no good, and she hadn't the money for a lawsuit, even if she had the grounds for one.

Yet the thought of moving on filled her with dread. Where could she go? With no job, she couldn't afford anything. The thought of crawling back to Pedersen and signing his teacher's contract was unthinkable.

She'd have to get some sort of work. Up until now she'd used her savings whilst she kept applying for teacher's posts, but it was just as she expected. No school would take her without the new union card. She pulled over the newspaper but hadn't the heart to even look at the 'Situations Vacant' column again. The only thing she could think of was private tutoring, but for that she'd need a place to live.

In desperation she wrote to all her teacher colleagues, copying the same letter over and over, explaining her situation. Did any of them know of a room, somewhere cheap, that she could rent?

In the weeks while she waited for replies, Astrid packed up her books and personal possessions. How had she acquired so much stuff? Boxes or crates were scarce these days because people used them for firewood, so she struggled to tie her few essential belongings into bundles using spare bedsheets. She took a long time agonising over Pappa's stamp collections, an heirloom that she decided in the end not to sell.

But as the month wore on, and the only replies were apologies, she began to feel desperate. Every week as she signed the attendance form at the Police Headquarters, there was a Teachers Union form in front of her on the desk, and every week she studiously ignored it, but it got harder and harder to do so with no work. She took more unwanted clutter to the market, and sold off what she didn't need. The Occupation meant almost everything was in demand. Simple things like paper, string, or thread for sewing.

Daily she crossed her fingers as she opened the letterbox, hoping not to see the official letter with the trial date. Instead, more replies from her teacher friends, all saying they couldn't help. No, they were all struggling. They knew nowhere.

Only three days left to find somewhere. Surely it was impossible.

Until finally on the day the trial letter came, she opened a letter from Mrs Bakke.

She had to read it twice before she could take it in.

It's not much but my sister has a small apartment in a block in the city. She's got TB and has gone to a sanatorium, in the country. She will be away a few weeks at least. I can give you the key. But obviously, you'll have to move out when she comes home, and my mother is paying the rent, so might have to stop if it the disease gets worse and goes on too long. But you're welcome, until you find something else.

Mrs Bakke gave a telephone number and within a few moments Astrid was standing in the red telephone box by the corner of the street and asking the switchboard to get her the number.

Mrs Bakke sounded exactly the same. 'I left, you know, when you did,' she said. 'Good thing my Dagrun's working. They can't lay off the dockworkers' office or we'd all starve.' She talked a while about the others at the school, who'd stayed and who'd left, as Astrid fed in her precious coins. Karen Baum had told the quisling police that Astrid had helped to organize the petition, in exchange for getting Bo out of the camps. Of course it hadn't worked. Bo was still there. But at least it explained why Falk'd singled her out.

Eventually Astrid interrupted, 'I need to be out in a few days, can I collect the key today?'

'Soon as you like,' Mrs Bakke said. 'It'll be good to have someone to collect the post and keep the place warm.'

Back home, Astrid looked at the court summons with the eagle and swastika on the heading, and slowly, deliberately, tore it into pieces.

Two days later, she surveyed her new apartment. Actually, it was more like a rabbit hutch than an apartment, but at least the odious Falk wouldn't have her address. She lugged her belongings up to the third floor and plonked them down. A glance out of the only window revealed a rickety iron fire escape and a backyard full of dustbins where mangy cats prowled looking for scraps. The fire escape backed onto a concrete tunnel used as a shelter, but pray God there would be no air raids, as rushing down those stairs in the dark would be lethal.

The next day she scoured the telephone directory for her pupils' parents, and careful who she approached, wrote more letters offering to give lessons in English, or basic tuition in mathematics, history and geography. She even wrote to Mr Feinberg, but she didn't expect a reply; she remembered all too clearly he'd asked her to leave them alone.

After a week she had gleaned just two hours a week teaching. Hardly enough to feed herself, now her coupons would be stopping. She was in hiding now, and things would be more difficult. She sat on the floor of the apartment and sighed. People just couldn't afford to pay for out-of-school tuition. School had been free, and in wartime nobody had money to spare. Not even for their children's education. It made her angry. The children would be held back without new work to do, new challenges, and a whole generation would be losing out because of this damn war.

It was then she thought of it. If they wouldn't come to her, then perhaps she could go to them. What if she could prepare some free learning materials, exercises and so on, that children could do at home? She had some of the old textbooks. She could do a series of worksheets, with some resources attached. More fun than the stuff that was in the usual textbooks. For geography, she could include maps, and suggest walks around the city.

The idea took hold. Within a few minutes she was pulling books from Enge's bookcase and frantically looking for paper to scribble notes. Of course it would be forbidden, unless it was part of the Nazi curriculum, so it would all have to be done in secret, and she couldn't think of a way to make it pay. And where would she get paper? But still, she was determined to do it.

She remembered Herman, and his printing press. Would it be possible?

A week later, and Astrid had her first batch of learning materials. They were printed on newsprint, and the only way she had been able to persuade Herman to help her was by agreeing to deliver anti-Nazi propaganda with each batch. He'd wanted the Milorg advertising printed on the same sheet, but she'd flatly refused. She'd argued long and hard with him about this, as she felt that giving children any kind of propaganda was wrong.

'Ulf wouldn't like it,' she said. 'You know he wouldn't.' And the thought of Ulf in arctic conditions, breaking rocks or building roads silenced them both.

They had compromised in the end, but it did mean that delivering the educational materials was going to be a lot riskier. After all, she had now unwittingly joined Sivorg, the civilian Resistance.

So today she was going door to door with a batch of the new educational papers hidden under her shopping. The sun was shining and she felt optimistic for the first time in weeks. Summer had come at last and the sky was blue, with a sharp bright sun. Falk and the trial seemed a long way away. Herman's recruitment flyers about joining the Milorg were in her pocket and she had to put one of each through the doors where she was delivering. He had supplied her with a little cash for using the tram, and she was able to criss-cross the city that way.

After the first day she was tired, but had got rid of a hundred of her worksheets.

When she got home, she immediately started preparing the next, though she had no idea if the sheets would be used, or if they would be thrown away. On this next one she had the idea to put in a few jokes, the sort a child might enjoy, and a drawing with 'Spot the Difference' and a simple crossword with answers relating to Norway's history.

When she went to collect them from Herman, he said, 'I think these will be popular. They're good. The drawings are lovely, and it's nice to have something cheerful.'

She flushed. 'Thank you, I enjoyed doing it.'

'You realise it's propaganda, though, don't you?'

'What d'you mean?'

'It sells a particular point of view. That everyone should be free to choose.'

'That's not propaganda! It's human rights.'

'Just be careful, though. Nothing's ever neutral. Everything has an agenda. Yours is anti-Nazi.'

She thought of his words often over the next few months as she continued to invent new materials, agonising over each one. The Sivorg had found the funds to supply the paper, and it gave her great pleasure to think of the children in homes all over Oslo colouring in her drawings and doing her educational puzzles. In all this time she kept a low profile, and didn't go near the police station. What had happened when she didn't turn up for trial? She'd no idea. Though every day she worried that she might bump into Falk, or one of the policemen that had arrested her, and living with that degree of fear made her lose weight and bite her fingernails to the quick.

To keep Herman safe she varied her route each day, in case of attracting German attention. Over time she was surprised to find the children came to recognise her as 'The Puzzle Lady', and many of them watched for her and came to the door excited for the next week's batch of puzzles and exercises.

By the end of the summer the demand for the children's paper had become so great that it was hard to hide the papers in her basket. Herman often asked her to deliver messages or propaganda, but she always kept strictly to her principles and kept the Milorg business separate, although by now it was no use pretending she wasn't actually working for the Resistance.

Coming out of Herman's house one autumn day with her usual heavy basket, she caught sight of a man further down the road loitering on the corner by the tobacconist's, lighting a cigarette. She ignored him, and paused to pull on her beret and scarf, but as she set off up the road towards the tram stop he set off too in the same direction. At first she was not unduly alarmed. Probably just on his way to work.

He got on the same tram and walked past her to sit a few seats behind. She caught a whiff of aftershave, a pungent, slightly bitter smell as he passed. A thin-faced man in a raincoat, wearing a felt hat with a brim. Something about the way he avoided her eye made her wary. If he was following her, she'd have to lose him. She waited until the tram was about to pull up at the next stop, then made a sudden run for it.

As she suspected, he dived after her. So she was being tailed. She ran across the street and in through the revolving door of Steen & Strøm department store, haring up the escalators, pushing past the crowds to the fourth floor, where she hid herself behind a shoe display of expensive leather shoes.

She crouched down, trying to calm her breath, pretending to admire the shoes on display. Of course all the other women in the store must be rich, or in cahoots with the Nazis. She watched their legs go by, clad in sheer stockings that most ordinary Norwegians couldn't afford. Had she lost him?

She picked up a pair of high-heeled shoes. It was so hot in here. A bead of sweat trickled from her hairline. She pulled off her beret and scarf and tucked them in the basket. The beret was a rusty brown colour. Without it, maybe he wouldn't spot her.

After about fifteen minutes the man hadn't appeared, and the female shop assistant was staring at her. Probably thought she was after stealing something. Hastily, she put the shoes back on the shelf.

Astrid turned to leave. What would she do if she was him? Wait outside. She'd be easier to spot by those revolving doors. She'd have to go out some other way. Was there a back entrance? A hanging sign said 'Stairs' so she hurried down to the next floor where she knew there was a Ladies Powder Room.

A cubicle was vacant so she hurried in and bolted the door. She dragged the Milorg recruitment leaflets from her pocket. They were dynamite. She thrust the whole batch in the toilet and pulled the flush chain. But what to do with the children's paper? It was too bulky, there were too many sheets; it would never flush down.

And it was so much work. She hesitated. She didn't want to leave it behind.

No choice. The man had followed her from Herman's, and she didn't want the paper to be linked to him or it might never get printed again. Carefully, she emptied the basket of her purse and keys, and her identity cards, and pushed her scarf and beret in with the papers. A loss she'd have to bear.

She came out of the toilet to find a woman in a fox fur stole waiting, so she hurried away, guiltily, knowing the pan was clogged with paper. Down the stairs to another floor. Here she abandoned the basket on the landing before going down again.

At the ground floor she scanned the crowded shop for the man who was following her. No sign of him.

She headed for the side door further down the street, and followed close behind a young couple. There he was, waiting near the main entrance.

Across the road was the tram stop. A tram was just approaching with a squeak of wheels. She made a dash for the tram, leapt on, and saw him spot her just too late.

Heart thumping, she ignored him as he ran alongside, praying that the tram wouldn't stop again. She only rode a few stops before changing trams once more, and this time heading for the Ekeberg Line, nowhere near her apartment. The more changes she made, the less chance he'd catch her.

Nobody must know where she lived. The official resident of her apartment was still Mrs Bakke's sister, Enge. As far as the authorities were concerned, Astrid Dahl had just disappeared. There was always the faint chance that one of the parents might tell, but she didn't think it likely, as she used a false name on the worksheet, Aunty Nora. So she made as certain as she could that she wasn't still under surveillance when she went home.

She'd have to get word to Herman though, that his house was being watched. But how?

In the end she did nothing. She didn't dare risk it. Besides, she knew he'd wonder why she hadn't brought the next week's sheet for printing, and guess something was wrong, and make a calculated guess that she was keeping away from him for his own good.

The following week Astrid was on her knees on the rug, creating another worksheet, when she heard an unfamiliar buzzing sound.

With shock she realised it was the doorbell from the street below.

Warily, she put the door on the latch and went down the three flights. 'Who is it?' she asked from behind the locked door.

'Herman.'

She opened it. 'How the hell did you know where I live?'

He pushed his way into the lobby. 'Surprising what we know. We have to be careful who we trust.'

'Come up. I live on the third floor.' She set off up the stairs. 'You weren't followed?' she turned to whisper at him.

He rolled his eyes.

'Sorry. I had to ask. Someone was following me. That's why I didn't make the drop offs last week. I had to dump everything at Steen & Strøm's.' She pushed her way into her apartment, and closed the door after him.

'I knew something was up,' Herman said, sitting down and lighting up without asking her permission. 'So we have to be careful. You're not to come near me, or make any contact from now on, understand?'

'But what about my children's paper?' She pushed an ashtray on the table towards him.

'Not important. It was a nice thing, and a good cover for our recruitment campaign, but —'

She was outraged. 'Is that all you saw it as? Just cover for your campaign?'

'It was useful to us, but you're getting too popular, too easy to trace.'

'It was a vital service for those children,' she flashed. 'For them it reminded them of normal life, gave their parents a few hours to themselves —'

He put on a soothing voice. 'Oh, I'm not saying it wasn't valuable in its way, just not to us. So we won't be printing any more, and I'll ask you to stay away from my house.'

Now she was livid. 'So that's it? You're dismissing me, now I've risked my life delivering your damn leaflets?'

'Now look, Astrid, I know you think a lot of your teaching, and I admire that, but your time with us was always going to be limited. A woman who looks like you is bound to attract German attention. Just be thankful you're alive.' He tapped his ash into the ashtray.

She walked to the door and opened it. 'How dare you. It's time for you to leave. You've made your point and it works both ways. You had your uses to me, but now I no longer need you.'

'Aw, Astrid, don't be like that.' He stood up, tried to put a hand on her arm. 'Ulf wouldn't like it if we weren't friends.'

'Don't dare to bring him into this! Get out of here before I lose my temper.'

'You can't just resign, you know. Once you're in, you're in for life. Think about it some more because Milorg won't hesitate to remove people who threaten their networks.'

'Get. Out.'

He went, trying to swagger, but failing, and leaving a cloud of cigarette smoke in his wake.

When she'd calmed down she opened the window to get rid of the smell, and made some chicory tea. So she was trapped in the Milorg now, was she? Threatened by the Germans and now threatened by her own people.

Herman was wrong, her children's paper was important. Children's minds were important.

She hugged herself, trying to come to terms with the loss of the activity that had kept her sane in this mad world. The loss of the paper meant she was once more a person with nothing to offer. It made her redundant again, as if she had no value.

Who needed her now? No-one. She was expendable to her own country. It was an odd sensation, as if she had become invisible. A citizen of nowhere.

CHAPTER 20

Karl crept out of his bed and dressed silently. He carried his boots downstairs, listening for the creak of bedsprings that meant he'd woken Jørgen in the room next to his. There was no sound, so he took himself out into the wild dark, closing the door by turning the handle gently so the latch made no noise.

Outside, he blew out through his mouth, a sigh of relief, and paused to put his boots on before heading down towards the harbour. The wind whipped around him, but he moved stealthily, quick and cat-like in the dark. God, how he loved this. He thought he'd die if he didn't get out to some action soon. Jørgen stuck to him like a limpet, always watching him with those assessing eyes. But Jørgen wouldn't give him much trouble; he was already showing cracks.

Karl smiled in satisfaction. He'd always been good at brazening things out. He'd got Harcourt on side at least; he knew how to charm the men that were influential.

And the women for that matter.

The harbour was full of the noise of the wind, the buzz-clank of metal wires, the slap of waves and the thud of wood against rubber as the boats bumped into the tyres that protected them from the harbour wall. He grabbed a pair of oars from a rowing boat and headed out to one of the small motorboats bobbing at the end of the quay.

He untied the mooring rope and jumped in. He'd row out until he was out of sight, and earshot. He grasped the oars and pulled strongly away from the shore. The wind blew in his face and the waves were steep but it felt good to use his arm muscles like this. Like they needed some heavy work, not the fiddling and tinkering he'd been doing in the workshop.

The village was quiet, no lights and nobody around. Not a guard, nothing.

Once he'd rounded the corner, out of sight of the harbour, he threw the oars inside the boat, and cranked the handle hard to get the engine going. He was rewarded with a throaty roar. The sound made him grin. Now he'd really let rip.

A second later he opened the throttle, feeling the little boat power away. He stood up by the wheel as the boat shot out towards the islands, bounding over the waves.

Thank God for old Hard-core. He'd a map in his office showing all the mined areas. A dead straight course would keep him out of their way. Though their presence did add extra excitement to this joyride. He half-wished one would go up. Though not with him above it, of course.

The wind was at his back as the boat sped through the dark. He made a roaring pass around the first island, cutting a swathe of white wash and narrowly avoiding a pinnacle of rock. He had about twenty minutes of exhilarating speed, before he slowed down to come back closer to shore.

He'd done this twice before. The other times he'd gone round the main island to get what intelligence he could. Tonight, he just felt like it. He had to get rid of his pent-up energy somehow. It used to be skiing, but Shetland was a useless, bald rock of a place.

Now he cut the engine, and rubbed his hands through his salty hair. It was harder rowing back with an offshore breeze, but he enjoyed the effort, the chance to pit himself against the tide. His sporting muscles missed their exercise. He missed the feeling of besting someone or something.

Soon the boat was moored back where it had been before. Time to go up to Harcourt's office.

Keeping to the dark shadows of the buildings, he pushed himself to head rapidly uphill toward the Mission in long, loping strides. A dog yapped and came snarling to a gate as he passed, but he ignored it. The Mission itself was open. Shetlanders were stupidly un-aware of security, considering they were at war. At least the building was blacked out; no lights showed. He walked straight in, up the front steps. Harcourt and Harris were billeted there, but the stone building had thick walls and their rooms were on the other side of the building from the office.

In the dark, he skirted the billiard table, feeling his way around its edge, and along the wall to Harcourt's office. It was locked of course, but the police force had taught him basic lock-picking. Actually, he'd never used it much before. More fun to break down the door.

But here, he needed the quiet way in. He slipped his homemade picks from his pocket. The inside of a fountain pen, a wire from a boat, a paperclip and a broken knife. The paperclip and knife should do it, like last week.

Footsteps creaked above, and he stopped. Listened.

He took a few hurried moments to rake the lock, listening for the sound of the pins dropping before opening the door, and he was in. Better shut the door.

He drew the blind and pulled the curtains across slowly, minimising the rattle of the hooks. Wouldn't do for someone to see him in there. Now he switched on the torch they'd been issued with and headed for the radio. Within a few minutes he'd got set up.

He smiled at the idea that Harcourt was asleep somewhere upstairs whilst he made full use of his office. After a lot of hiss and crackle he finally got through to Norway and Falk's W/T operator. The girl on the other end was slow, and he had to keep repeating. Some country hick, probably. Didn't she know the risks he took to even get the message out to her?

He was just repeating information about the make-up of boats and crew when he heard a noise outside.

A shaft of light flashed under the door. Instantly, he logged off, switched off the torch and replaced everything as best he could by feel.

Just in time. The door swung open, and the room was suddenly flooded with electric light.

'Who's that?' Harcourt was in a paisley dressing gown and slippers, his squinting face without his glasses was wrinkled and bald. 'What's going on?'

'Sorry, Sir, it's Brevik. I came up for a game of billiards, and saw your door was wide open. I came in to see if —'

'Billiards? At this time of night?'

'Couldn't sleep, sir. Thought it might relax me, a bit of practice. I've got a bet on, with one of the other lads.'

'And my door was open?'

'Probably the wind, sir. Could have blown it open when I came in the front door. It's a real bluster out there. But when I saw it open, I thought I'd better look in to check all was well. But it's all right, there's nobody else here, as you can see, just the wind. The blind and curtains were open too, so I've closed them to keep out the draught.'

'Thank you, Brevik. I could have sworn I locked it. I couldn't sleep either. Something woke me up; I kept imagining I was hearing an engine and that the Germans were invading. Ridiculous, eh? The things you think of when you're half-asleep.'

'Sorry if I disturbed you. I'll let you get back to bed.'

'Well, as we're both awake now, d'you fancy a game?'

Karl blinked. He didn't. But he smiled in a relaxed way. 'Sure. I didn't know you played.'

'I was the one who got the table installed. Used to be a bit of an expert in my youth.'

'You can put me through my paces then, sir.' Karl led the way out of the office and strolled to the billiard table. Under his jersey, his armpits were damp, his heart too loud, but it would soon settle. The dangerous part was over. Police work had taught him the sooner you moved on from the flashpoint, back to ordinary life, the better. People forget so easily.

Within half an hour, Harcourt was lecturing him on the importance of angles and slide-shots, and had even got out the brandy for a nightcap.

As June turned to July, and July turned to August, Jørgen continued to watch Karl. He simply couldn't help himself, and yet it was impossible to do this without becoming his friend. They'd spent so much time together in the last few months he began to feel like there was something missing if he couldn't see him out of the corner of his eye. Karl, on the other hand, seemed to be doing everything possible to get away from him.

The nights were light now, like a permanent dusk, and Jørgen was a light sleeper. They'd been moved from the refugee camp and had use of an old crofter's cottage, close to Scalloway harbour. A room each, thinly partitioned by a stud wall, over the one room below that served as kitchen-cum-living room. On several nights he'd heard Karl go out at night. Lying awake now, unable to sleep, he heard Karl moving about in the room next door, and a light, creeping tread on the wooden stairs as he went down.

Jørgen got up and went to the landing. 'Couldn't you sleep?' he asked, leaning over the bannister in his pyjamas.

Karl turned, boots in hand, a flash of annoyance on his face. 'It's this time of year. It always makes me restless, even at home. Like I should be up and doing something.' He continued to go downstairs.

'Where are you going?' Jørgen followed him down into the gloom. The blackout blinds were still down in there.

'Just out. For a walk round.'

'Mind if I come? If you just give me a few minutes to get —'

'No. What is it with you? Can't a man get any peace?'

'Okay, okay, sorry I even asked.' Jørgen couldn't keep the sarcasm from his voice.

Karl's face hardened. In this light it was all sharp angles. 'Look, I know you're watching me. It's bloody obvious. I can't move an inch without you being at my elbow. I'm not sure what you think I'm up to, but I'm sick of having you trailing me like a dog everywhere I go.'

'I'm not,' he said. 'I don't know what you mean.' Even to his ears it sounded thin.

'Who put you up to it?' Karl said. 'Harcourt?'

'Nobody. Calm down. You're imagining it.'

Karl stared at him pityingly a moment longer, and then swung on his kitbag and barged out of the door, leaving it swinging behind him.

Jørgen didn't follow. Damn, damn, damn. He thought he'd been subtle, but of course he couldn't be. Shetland was a tiny place, everyone knew everyone else; you couldn't move an inch without somebody seeing. And he felt bad. Like he'd hurt a friend. The fact they'd been on that journey together across the *vidda* had given him a respect for Karl. For his sheer physical prowess, for his quick-thinking when they'd been in danger, and for the fact he'd inspired him to keep going when his own legs would barely move. Without Karl he probably would still be out there in a drift, one more soul lost to the wind and snow.

Jørgen was summoned to Harcourt's office the next day. Morag came for him in the car. Karl had apparently been in earlier to ask Harcourt why he'd been put under surveillance.

'It won't do, Nystrøm,' Harcourt said. 'We work here as a team. What has Brevik done that means you must be on his back like that? Poor chap was quite upset by the whole thing.'

'It was just a silly argument. We're both a bit stir crazy, wanting to do something to help Norway. It gets a bit intense when we share a billet.'

'You need to find a way to let off steam. You're a good man, Nystrøm, but you need to calm down.'

Calm down? He was already calm, or at least he was before he was in Harcourt's office.

'I'll make sure you and Brevik are billeted separately now,' Harcourt said. 'Take the pressure off him a bit. How's that sound?'

Jørgen gritted his teeth. He had to nod and agree, even though the conversation with Harcourt made him uncomfortable. It made him feel he was letting the side down.

Harcourt got out a folder and began to talk about the next few missions on the Shetland Bus, but Jørgen hardly heard him, just kept agreeing. It seemed important to look to be on his side rather than someone who was always throwing a spanner in the works.

He was glad to see Morag waiting for him in the lobby when he came out. She seemed to read his mood. 'How about we go the long way back, whilst we've got a few minutes breathing space. Give you an idea of the coast.'

Anything to take his mind off the fact that Harcourt thought he was some sort of headcase. 'Sounds good,' he said.

She set off through the intermittent rain, the wiper making a rhythmic squeak. 'Keep it quiet though, won't you? Petrol's rationed, so we'll have to freewheel down the hills.'

He was amazed to see that she knew exactly how to do this and had obviously done it many times before. It was an odd feeling to be bowling downhill with no engine — like floating. It eased his agitation and his anger.

She let him gaze out of the windows, as he trawled back through his conversation with Harcourt. Against his better judgement, he'd finally agreed to crew on the Shetland Bus. He wanted to make amends and prove willing, now he'd been accused of spying on Karl.

He was pondering this, and so it was a moment or two before he realised they'd stopped. They were overlooking a bay, and the horizon was peppered with small islands. The sun streaked through the clouds, lighting up the folds of the hills and the green of the sea. It was breath-taking.

'Whiteness,' she said. 'My favourite place. It's where I always come if I need space from life at base.'

'It's beautiful,' he said. 'The grass is so green here.'

'It's limestone underneath — hence the name. Here,' she reached to the seat behind and dragged over a bag. 'I've got coffee. Not the real thing, obviously, but it's hot and wet.'

They opened the doors and climbed out, and he followed her to a rocky ledge of limestone that acted as a seat.

As Morag poured the coffee from the thermos he took in a great deep breath, staring out at the sea and the layers of islands fading into the distance, savouring the sharp sunlight on his face, and the wind ruffling his hair. This was it, he thought. Forget Karl and Harcourt. This view was a taste of freedom. The first time he'd felt free since joining Milorg in the winter of 1940.

And yet he'd just given all this up again for possible arrest and execution by the Nazis, crossing the sea back to Norway again. What an idiot.

Morag handed him a tin mug. The coffee was hot and bitter and reviving.

'I think I just volunteered for the Shetland Bus,' he said.

'I thought you might,' she said. 'You struck me as the type to give something back.' She twisted her head towards him and smiled.

Her eyes were brown, the colour of chestnuts. Her gaze made something tug in his heart.

From then on, whenever Morag had to drive him somewhere, they would go the long way round. She always had the thermos, and they would stop somewhere different and spend a few moments talking and admiring the view, and slapping away the midges that always seemed to form a cloud around their heads.

It never went any further than that. She was aware he would be going out with the next run of boats to Norway, and that he might not return, and that he was still in some way attached to a woman in Norway. He told her about Astrid, and about his parents, about how he was the youngest of three brothers and always had to use cunning to avoid being blamed for everything. In turn she told him about her childhood in Shetland, the only daughter of older parents who doted on her.

'I was stifled by them, even though I loved them,' she said. 'The wild coast was my escape.'

She knew every inch of the island, and all the best views. She was modest about how much organisation it took to funnel the refugees from the boats. 'No. To tell you the truth, I'm more comfortable with puffins and otters than people.'

'Just treat me like a puffin or an otter then,' he said.

'OK. Next time, forget the coffee, I'll just throw you a fish!'

In the weeks after that, Jørgen found himself thinking of Morag often, looking out for her at lunchtimes, hoping to see her windswept figure with the wild brown hair, hurrying towards the boatyard from the car park. She was always ready to share a joke and had a sense of humour that was both sharp and dry.

He spent the rest of the summer fitting out the boat he was to sail in — a fifty-foot open clinker-built fishing vessel called the *Vidar*. She had a diesel engine, and was in every way indistinguishable from the other fishing vessels you might see, hugging the Norwegian coastline with their creels and pots and nets piled on deck. The only difference was, this one was going right across the North Sea and back, and needed to be armed, carry vast amounts of fuel and water, and enough food to sustain the crew for several weeks at sea.

Larsen, who ran the whole Shetland Bus operation, told them to take the *Vidar* out fishing to dirty her up a bit more, and make sure she smelled of fish, in case the Nazis should come nosing around when they got back to Norwegian Waters. Another 'Bus' crew, headed by an ex-military man, Clausen, was to do the same.

To Jørgen's surprise, Karl managed to get himself taken on as part of the crew of the *Vidar* for this 'dirtying' trip, and it was the first time Jørgen'd had any close contact with him for more than a month. After their argument, Harcourt had moved Jørgen in with the rest of the Norwegians, into a former net loft jokingly nick-named 'Norway House'.

Another Norwegian, a stout fisherman called Anders, had been billeted with Karl. How did Anders get along with Karl? Best not to ask. Karl seemed to be Harcourt's golden boy.

A little of the discomfort in Jørgen's chest ebbed away when Karl greeted him in a friendly-enough manner, and offered him a smoke. He accepted, just to ease the awkwardness, and they puffed away together until Jacobsen the skipper gave them the orders to cast off. The seas were light today, with a fresh easterly breeze that meant they had to have full throttle to get out to sea. Once out from the shore, Shetland lost its beauty; it looked a forbidding place — wind-scoured and uninteresting, no dramatic, soaring peaks like Norway. They cruised around the coast, navigating well away from the shore to avoid mines, and past steep-angled cliffs full of raucous kittiwakes who'd painted the cliffs white with droppings. A few of the inlets had rocks where seals basked in the thin sunlight.

As they passed out towards the open sea, they caught sight of Clausen's boat further out, and another genuine fishing boat coming in after their catch, thronged by a blizzard of gulls.

When the mainland was a blur on the horizon, they likewise cast out their nets and trawled in their haul of silver shimmering fish.

'Like home,' Karl said, as they hauled together.

'Did you know Shetland was once part of Norway, five hundred years ago?' Jørgen said. 'Morag told me.'

'Is that so? Now it seems to belong to the English. Better if we could take it back.'

'Scottish,' Jørgen said. 'It's Scottish.'

They didn't speak again as they helped the rest of the crew slice the heads of the fish, drawing another crowd of marauding screeching gulls. The ship certainly stank now, of blood and fish. He was mesmerised by Karl's hands as he sliced through the fish, twice as fast as he could manage.

'I saw you were out with Morag last week,' Karl said. 'Saw you drive past in that old car.'

'Had to go and see Harcourt. Report on how this old girl's doing.' Jørgen slapped a hand affectionately on the side of the boat. Though the boat was called *Vidar* which meant 'warrior', from long habit he still thought of all boats as 'she'.

'You were a long time.'

He shrugged, but he knew what Karl was getting at.

'You said you'd got a girl back home in Norway?'

'Astrid? Yes, but obviously I haven't seen her for a long time. I don't know what she's doing any more.' The niggle of guilt made him defensive. 'Anyway, she could have found someone else, for all I know.'

'You've asked Morag out then?'

'No. We just...' What? There was something there, but it was too new to talk of. 'She just takes me round the island, to see a bit more of it.'

'Would you mind if I asked her?' Karl heaved up the crate of fish-heads and tossed them into the sea. The resultant screeching and dive-bombing of gulls prevented further conversation, but not the stab of feeling in Jørgen's heart.

'No,' he said, ''Course not.' Though he did mind, terribly.

When they got back, there was a truck waiting to take the fish to the gutting sheds to be salted. From there it would go to the rest of Scotland. 'Before the war it used to go as far as Italy,' Jacobsen told them. 'The war's decimated our —' He paused as a group of men were making their way to the harbour.

'What's up?' Jørgen asked.

A big-wig welcoming committee was heading down the slope, holding their hats to their chests to stop them blowing away; Harcourt and a few other officers, along with Larsen.

'Sorry men, you need to come to the marine supply shop,' Harcourt said. 'We've urgent instructions.' His expression was grim.

They trudged there in their boots and oilskins, like children about to be told off by the headmaster.

'What d'you think we've done?' Karl whispered.

'Dunno,' Jørgen said. 'They told us to go fishing, so it can't be that.'

Harcourt waited until they had all filed in and were silent before speaking. 'I'm sorry to have to tell you, but we lost the *Fiskegutt* last night, and five of the crew have been taken by the Nazis. One managed to swim ashore and radio back to us, but the others tried to get away in one of our motorboats. Sad to say, the engine-housing for the motorboat was faulty, the thing wouldn't start, and none of our men, including the agent we'd taken months to train, could get away.'

Jørgen glanced around at the other men. They looked as horrified as he felt.

'The housings were watertight,' Jacobsen said. 'I made sure of it.'

Harcourt sighed. 'I know, Jacobsen. It isn't your fault; we don't know what went wrong between here and Norway. And it was foolish to send them at this time of year. But we needed that updated intelligence, and observations are easier in good weather. Now we've learnt our lesson the hard way. We've lost a good boat, but worse, five of our men. We realize now we sent them too early and we can't risk it again.' He raked his gaze around the assembled crew. 'But you must do your part too; we must be certain every single one of those engine housings are checked and double-checked. Men's lives depend on it. I don't need to tell you that you will all be in their position in a months' time.'

It was a sobering thought. Jørgen thought back to the housings he'd made. He'd double checked every single one.

'So no reconnaissance about the German defences has come back?' Karl asked. As well as dropping in a trained W/T op, the *Fiskegutt* had been sent try to update the SOE's information about Nazi positions on the coast — where watch posts and patrol vessels might be operating, what the new Nazi shipping regulations might be since last winter.

'Unfortunately not much,' Harcourt replied. 'Anders had to swim for his life. They didn't have time to complete their mission, which means our first few trips to Norway in the season will be running blind.'

It was a blow. Jørgen looked over to Karl, but his face was impassive, blank. He remembered Anders had been billeted with Karl. Karl didn't ask where he was now, or how he'd get home. Jørgen frowned. A memory had just surfaced — of the day he went over to Karl's bench to tell him he hadn't quite plugged the hole for the starter handle properly. Karl had thanked him, and Jørgen just assumed Karl would have done it again until it was watertight.

But it made him wonder. Had it been just a beginner's mistake, or had Karl been sabotaging the housings? He shook his head to free himself of these thoughts. He'd washed his hands of Karl; there was no way he could go and report this to Harcourt. Harcourt would just tell him he was being neurotic.

'Our first forays will begin on the first of September,' Harcourt continued. 'Briefings will take place next week. We've a lot of advance preparation to do for the first few missions, and we need to adapt and re-arm the boats. The first boat out will be crewed by Haraldsen, Barlie and Nystrøm. The rest of the crew is yet to be assigned.'

Though he had known it was coming, Jørgen startled. This was it. Harcourt had said he needed action, and was obviously as good as his word. He was actually going to be going home.

It was sooner than he thought, and he was apprehensive. Every mission was a risk, and of course there was no way he could stay there until the heat had cooled and they'd forgotten him. He wondered if he'd get the time to look up Astrid. But then he thrust the thought away. Morag Airdrie had occupied his thoughts for so long that he found himself torn. He'd never thought of himself as a philanderer, but now Morag would keep trespassing into his thoughts.

'Don't be a fool,' he thought to himself. 'Don't get sidetracked. There's no time for shenanigans now, it's hard enough without that. Just do your job.'

CHAPTER 21

Falk took another cigar and lit it. He was impatient for results but had to keep away from the W/T room now because the women had got tired of him hanging over their shoulders. Apparently Brevik's transmissions were difficult to decipher. They always came in the early hours of the morning when most people were sleeping, so he suspected he had to 'borrow' a transmitter from the base on Shetland. His equipment was good; but he'd had no formal training, and he was apt to fire messages into the ether instead of waiting for the time agreed. Also, they were often hurried and he forgot to sign off properly. This was a danger because they never knew if someone else had infiltrated his cover.

Of course in the summer the Shetland Bus operations were less, because they couldn't use the cover of darkness. It bothered him that Brevik was taking ten thousand kroner of State funds that he, Falk, must account for, and right now there was with little activity to show for it. To produce at least something for the record, a month ago Falk had sent instructions to Brevik to sabotage anything that wouldn't endanger his position. At first the message didn't get a reply. Karl was ignoring him despite repeated requests. He suspected Brevik was having a nice little holiday at the Fuhrer's expense.

But then, a reply. *For five hundred kroner more, I will nobble the horse.*

He'd almost been amused. But the man had at least made it to Shetland, so he'd felt he could not refuse him. He had to keep him sweet, or perhaps he'd turn informer. 'Offer him four hundred,' he'd told the girl who was decoding.

After a week of radio silence he'd relented, and sent the message 'five hundred'. As he did it, he couldn't help feeling he was being played. But what could he do about it? After that, the messages started flowing more easily again and he breathed a sigh of relief. And so far, so good. A little unorthodoxy hurt no-one.

That morning he was expecting a visit from Fehlis, head of the Gestapo in Oslo. A man he'd met before and found somewhat intimidating, despite the fact he was never in uniform. He arrived on the dot of ten, as arranged, and walked in without knocking, wafting away Falk's cigar smoke with a frown. Falk reluctantly stubbed the cigar out.

Fehlis was a tall, thin individual in a carefully tailored suit. He had one of those faces that looked as if he'd just tasted something unpleasant. He crossed his legs easily, and his pale grey eyes took in the room. 'Nice office,' he said. He managed to make it sound like a criticism.

Falk gave a nervous laugh. 'Serves me well enough. Near the hub of things,' he said.

'As you advised, Wehrmacht command have increased the defences around Ålesund.'

'Good, good.' The location of the British agent pick-ups at Ålesund had come from Karl Brevik. Even now it was hard to imagine that Brevik was actually there, in Scotland, and that he, Falk, had a direct line into the special operations of the British forces.

'And we have a report just in from our patrol boat near Ålesund. The enemy vessel the *Fiskegutt* has been boarded and all the crew, bar one, are drowned or in captivity, transferred to Bredtveit Prison.'

'Congratulations, sir,' Falk said. 'And according to my contact, the *Fiskegutt* was the reconnaissance boat, and the

British were relying on it for their intelligence for future runs, so good news all round from our man. He will be on the next boat back to Norway.'

'I'm afraid not. We are anxious that Karl Brevik should stay where he is and not attempt to return to Norway for the time being.'

So they knew who he was. Someone must have talked. One of the girls? 'I see. He won't like that. He was expecting to make only one trip to Shetland and then to return.'

'They tell me he's being paid for his services.'

Who? Who had told the Gestapo that? Falk shuffled in his chair. 'Yes. That's correct.'

'So his allegiance has been bought. He is not a natural advocate for the party.'

'I disagree. His father had great sympathies for the Fuhrer's ideas, and my impression of Brevik is that he likes adventure. Extreme competition skiing can no longer scratch that itch, so he was looking for a challenge. Money was just … just the icing on the cake.'

'Still, I see no reason why we should bring him back,' Fehlis said. 'If he stays there, not only does it give us vital intelligence, but it will save us money, heh?' He gave a tight smile.

'But I gave him my word. A single trip, I said, and new papers afterwards.'

'Circumstances have changed. Your promise cannot be upheld, you must see that. Anyway, what would we do with him when he returned? He would have to be eliminated then anyway. No, your task is to keep him dangling there as long as possible. Make promises if necessary, but keep him there.'

'And if I can't?'

'There is no such word as can't, as far as Herr Hitler is concerned.'

CHAPTER 22

Astrid was mending a blouse by the light of an oil lamp. The electricity had gone off again, as it often did, so she was used to doing things in this half-light. It was a quiet occupation, so when there was a buzz at the door, she startled and stabbed herself with the needle.

She sucked at her finger. Her immediate thought was that Falk and his men had somehow tracked her down. But a quick lift of the blind showed no sign of any activity outside in the back yard. No soldiers or Germans.

Should she answer it? Maybe it was Herman, or Mrs Bakke, or worse, her sister Enge, who owned the apartment, wanting it back. Her mind ran through the possibilities. None of them good.

The buzz again. Her feet were moving before she could stop them. Down the stairs, gripping the banister in the blackness. There was no glass in the door, so she couldn't see who was there.

'Who is it?' she called, heart almost in her throat.

'Isaak Feinberg,' came the whisper.

Feinberg? What was he doing here?

She opened up and Isaak Feinberg's white face was right up close to the door. He was holding tight to Sara's hand, and in the other he held a battered suitcase. Sara was loaded down with a big bundle that looked like bedding. And books.

Astrid swung the door wider and ushered them in. 'Have you walked?' She led the way up the three dark flights of stairs. 'Sorry there's no light, we've no electric. Come in where it's warm.'

Feinberg's taut expression was enough to tell her something was wrong.

'Sara,' she said, 'go to the bookshelf in the bedroom. Take the lamp. You'll find a set of encyclopaedias there that are really interesting to look at.' When Sara was out of earshot, she asked, 'What's going on?'

'Sorry to come here. I didn't know where else Sara would be safe. The police came for my neighbours last night.' There was a stark anger in the way he spoke. 'They've rounded up all the Jewish men. More than two hundred, we think. I escaped the round-up because I'd taken Sara to look for coal. In the old railway sidings.'

She gestured to him to sit in the only chair. In the dark, his face was gaunt, with deep shadows under the cheekbones. 'What happened?'

'When I got home, my neighbour's house was full of women weeping. They just took the men away at gunpoint. All the husbands. All the sons.'

'Oh my heaven. Where are they taking them?'

'A camp? Deportation? Who knows? They wouldn't let the women go with them, and wouldn't let them take anything, only one suitcase. Aaron couldn't get to the bank, couldn't leave any instructions what to do. Poor Aaron. They kept shouting at him, like he was stupid. "Hurry up," they said. "Move, Move!" And I've never seen Mary cry before. But she told me to get out of Oslo. Leave everything and get out. "They'll come for you, too," she said. "And then what would Sara do?"'

There was no answer to that. With a flicker, the electricity came on, the bulb above her head flaring into a too-bright light. 'Thank goodness,' she said. 'Look, there's an electric ring so I can make hot tea, and you can stay here for the night, whilst we work something out. I have friends who might be able to help you, but we'll have to be careful. The police have me on their list, and I have to keep a low profile.'

Later that night, Astrid heard Sara crying, and the soft soothing tones of Isaak comforting her. She couldn't hear the words, but sensed they were laced with an undertone of anguish.

After a restless night, wondering what on earth she could do to help, Astrid woke early and after they'd taken turns to wash at the kitchen tap, got out some food. It was only vegetable broth and bread smeared with a little whale fat, but she salted it to try to disguise its foul smell. Butter was so scarce now, any sort of dripping was better than nothing. They devoured it hungrily.

She watched them with a sense of deep unease. She had to do something, but what? They couldn't stay, that was obvious, but at the same time she knew she'd never hand them in to the police.

'Jewish children are supposed to report daily,' Isaak said. 'We reckon it's so that they can take them next, but my friend Berthe says there are rumours the women and children go somewhere different from the men.'

It didn't bear thinking about, that Sara and her father should be split up. The only person Astrid knew who was in touch with the Sivorg and the Milorg was Herman. He had to be worth a try, but she knew it was a risk to them both if she was discovered going there, and besides Herman wasn't exactly her friend any more. He'd been pretty clear she wasn't to go to his house.

'Don't go outside,' she said to Isaak, 'and don't answer the door. I'm going to go to a friend to see if he can find a way to get you out of Norway. I'll be a couple of hours, okay? See if you can get Sara to do some school work, whilst I'm gone.'

'Is he trustworthy, this friend?' Isaak asked.

Was anyone? 'Don't worry. I'll be back soon.' Her best chance was to get to Herman before he went to work. Going at night was too risky, the Germans were much stricter after curfew.

She wound her hair up under a woollen cap, and walked briskly with a few strides of a run every now and then, holding up her umbrella against the rain. By the time she got to Herman's she was breathless. He came as soon as she pressed the bell, his beaky face peering in suspicion from the door. 'What is it? Some news about Ulf?'

'No. Sorry.' She shook her umbrella and went inside. 'I need help. I've a family of Jews at my house. A man and his daughter. They need to get out of Norway.'

He sighed. 'You as well? I thought this might happen. My doorbell's never stopped. Well, it's not my problem, you can't come running to me now. The rest of the family was taken, I suppose?'

'No. I think it's just the two of them. There's no mother, as far as I know. Can you help? They're desperate.'

'Maybe. But the route to Sweden is risky and much in demand. The best I can offer is something in a month's time.' He was putting on a jacket as he spoke. 'But you'll have to do deliveries again —'

'A month? I can't last that long. I've got quisling neighbours, and the police know me. I'm never sure if I'm under surveillance.'

'Look, we can't work miracles. Everything needs meticulous planning. And I can't have your lost Jews cocking up my operations to supply arms for the Resistance.'

'Sara's only ten years old, Herman. We have to help.'

He glanced irritably at his watch. 'Sorry, but I haven't got time for this now. I'll see what I can do. I'll need to contact some safe houses.' He searched for his scarf and gloves. 'There's a chance we can get them out before the next round of deportations, but you have to be prepared for the answer being no.'

'You mean the Nazis will take the women and children too?'

'I shouldn't even be saying this. But intelligence suggests they'll round up the women and children in a few weeks.' He slapped his gloves against his palm. 'There's a boat already been commissioned, the *Donau*. A cargo ship. Chances are we'll be too late to get your family out.'

'But what would I do then? I can't send them back home. They'll be picked up and deported.'

He was putting on his thick tweed overcoat and hat, and picking up his keys. 'You'd best get them out of your house. The Jews aren't your problem. The Nazis don't take kindly to people who collaborate with them. They're apt to deport them too.'

'Please, Herman. Do what you can.' She followed him to the door. 'It's what Ulf would have wanted, isn't it? To resist in any way we can? Well, this is my way.'

He paused as he put the key in the lock, closed his eyes and shook his head. 'We're trying to win a war here, not rescue every waif and stray. If I can do it, it's only because of Ulf, because he was so full of idealism, and because you were friends. But don't come here again, hear me? It's too risky. Not just for me, but for dozens of other Milorg men who rely on me. I'll contact you if I can help.'

A week went by and Astrid heard nothing. She began to despair. Mr Feinberg and Sara grew argumentative, what with the strain and being cooped up in the house. Even in the day she had to keep the window blind down in case anyone in the yard should catch a glimpse of them. It was also odd to have a man in the house, to have to be careful about when and where she dressed or used the bath. They moved around each other warily, giving each other a lot of space.

To ease the tension, Astrid spent the days bartering for potatoes, turnips and carrots from the council flowerbeds which had now been turned into allotments. Of course Isaak and Sara dare not use their ration cards, in case they got caught, and she couldn't use hers, so food was tight.

The barley stew she made that night was meagre, but she couldn't help noticing how Isaak gave most of his portion to Sara. Afterwards, whilst they washed the dishes, she took him to task. 'Isaak, you must eat. You'll be no use to her if you are weak from hunger.'

'I can't bear to see her hungry. That hopeful look on her face when her eyes follow the plate round to see if there's a scraping left.' He rubbed frantically at a plate with the drying cloth. 'I hate the way her ribs are showing through their skin, and her shoulders are like scrawny chicken wings. And I think of my father, her grandfather, and wonder where he is, and know it would break his heart to see her like this.'

'Is he still in Germany, your father?'

'I don't know. We can't get word to him, but I hope he got out.'

'And Sara's mother…?' She let the question hang.

'She left us. She became a Nazi party member. Didn't want to be shackled to what she called "bad blood".' His bitter tone told her it still hurt.

'I'm sorry.'

'Don't be. She was a bitch. What sort of mother would walk out on a five-year-old girl?'

Astrid spent the next day washing and mending, and worrying about how to help them. All her clothes were threadbare now, her cardigans through at the elbows. Sara's were even worse, and there was still no news from Herman. She daren't go back to him and risk endangering the network, but she was desperate for some sort of answer. She put Sara's cardigan aside. She needed more darning wool and would need to swap one of her precious books again. Not that anyone read them anymore; they were used for lighting fires or writing letters.

Later though, as she was returning from the shops, the precious card of darning wool in her pocket, she heard footsteps fall in behind her. Startled, she turned, to see who had suddenly come up so close behind. Thank God, not Falk or Schmitt. But the man who'd been following her at the department store.

She was about to run when he took hold of her sleeve. 'Astrid Dahl? I'm a friend of Herman,' the man said, from under a flat cap and muffler. 'Head for the toy shop of the corner of Josefine's Gate. The door will be open.'

So he was not a Nazi spy after all, but a Milorg man.

He overtook her and carried on, his head down against the wind, his overcoat flapping.

Astrid hesitated, but did as he asked. The shop was run-down, there were only a few second-hand toys in the window. A worn-looking spinning top, some building bricks, a train set. When she got inside, shaking the wet from her mackintosh, an old man in a threadbare green cardigan over another pullover was there to greet her. He looked as if he'd come from another century.

'Upstairs,' he said, 'in the stock room.'

She followed his gesture up a set of narrow lino stairs and through a brown-painted door into a room that was mostly empty except for faded cardboard boxes that looked like they'd once been packaging, and a few wooden chairs around a rough trestle table that had seen better days. A bare lightbulb dangled from a ceiling rose, and yellowing wallpaper was peeling from the walls.

A rasp of metal as the door below was locked, and she heard men's voices, before footsteps followed her up. Astrid swallowed to quell her nerves.

'Sit down,' the old man said, dragging a chair up over the bare boards.

'Where's Herman?' she asked.

'This is Mr Grieg,' the man who had followed her said, 'and I am Mr Kloster.' Kloster pulled off his flat cap to reveal a balding head, pink with cold. 'Herman is … not available.'

'Miss Dahl,' Grieg said, 'we've found a way out for you and your … visitors.' He held up a hand to prevent her thanks. 'But it will mean you leaving the day after tomorrow if you're to get to the transport.'

'Me? I'm not leaving. Just Mr Feinberg and his daughter.'

Grieg exchanged a glance with Kloster. 'We think it advisable for you to leave.'

'Why? I'm not Jewish.'

'Herman was arrested last night for running an illegal printing press.'

They watched her closely as this news sunk in.

The fact of it was like a slap on the face. 'How did they know?'

'It's not clear,' Kloster said. 'Perhaps a neighbour? The point is, the Nazis have their methods, and they already suspect you were responsible for the countrywide school strike, and the demonstration at the railway line. You distributed leaflets for the Milorg too.'

'You know?'

Grieg shrugged. 'Herman told us. It's our business to know. And we also know you skipped trial and there's a warrant out for your arrest. For that reason you are advised to leave for a destination you choose, rather than wait for the Nazis to choose one for you.'

'When did you say I must leave?' She was still trying to take it in.

'The day after tomorrow,' Grieg said. 'There's a well-organised route to Sweden, but it's not without its dangers. Because of this, the cost will be six thousand Norwegian kroner in cash for each person.'

'What?' The amount seemed staggering. 'Where will they get that sort of money?'

'Where there's a will…'

'Even Sara? She's only a child. She doesn't take up much room.'

'Your choice. What cost your life? Besides, a place is a place. Other people could go in their stead. You have to appreciate it's dangerous for all concerned, and the time and effort in organising it is immense.'

'Is there no other way? I don't know if they have the money, and a day is hardly enough time to raise it.'

'So you are refusing our offer? You know they'll deport you to a camp? The child too.'

'No ... no. I suppose I'll have to help them find it somehow.' After all, it was better to be poor and alive, than dead in some Nazi camp.

'So how many?' Grieg lifted his pen ready to write it down.

'Three.'

'Very well. You will be the contact for this group?'

She nodded.

'Write the names here.' He pushed the paper over to her. 'Your refugees will need false papers. These refugees, do they look like Jews?'

She bristled. 'What do you think Jews look like?' Her anger evaporated. Grieg was only trying to help. 'No. They look like anyone. Brown hair, brown eyes.'

'Good. Then we can get papers ready. Could you be a family? It will be a rush to get something that will hold up. Write down the Feinbergs' ages, descriptions and any distinguishing marks here.' He passed over a notebook. 'Your own too.'

She scratched down the Feinbergs' details with his fountain pen, which didn't like accommodating itself to her writing. It felt odd describing herself from the outside — as if she'd stepped into someone else's life already. She gazed down at her own description, blonde hair, blue eyes. It could be anyone.

'What must we do next?' Her question sounded calm, but inside she was still in shock.

'Pack one small bag each with warm clothing and any necessities. And I mean necessities. Food, medicine, soap. Put the money in individual bags for counting. The meeting place is at the pharmacy near the tram stop just down the street from here. I suggest you behave as if you are family travelling together.'

'What about the papers?'

Grieg shrugged. 'You'll need to leave yours so they can be amended. The others'll be rushed, so they won't hold up to much scrutiny,' he said, 'but you can collect them from here tomorrow afternoon. Oh, and you'll need to bring a thousand kroner for each of you as a mark of good faith. An advance, if you like.'

She nodded, though the whole thing seemed impossible, as if she'd fallen into some sort of fantasy.

'One more thing. Herman could talk. So make sure you're not followed tomorrow when you come here.'

'I haven't got that kind of money,' Isaak said when Astrid returned. 'I have no bank account. I closed it down; it was just too risky. We kind of ... live under the radar. Now we just have what we brought with us.'

'I guess that's that, then.'

He drooped. Then slowly he took off his jacket, and felt along the seams of the sleeve. 'Have you scissors?'

Astrid got some from the kitchen drawer and watched as he slit the lining and emptied something onto the table.

Gold glittered in the kerosene lamp. A rope necklace of gold links, a diamond brooch and two rings, set with precious stones. 'This is all my mother's jewellery,' he said. 'My mother's wedding and engagement rings. She died before Sara was born, and I kept them for her as an inheritance until she was older. So they came with me when we fled Frankfurt. Like an insurance policy. It's all we have. If I give this up, we'll have nothing but what we stand up in when we arrive in Sweden.'

Astrid watched him spread it out on the table. It didn't look much.

'I don't know what it's worth,' he said. 'Do you think it's enough, for both of us? I don't really want to sell it, but if it's the only way…'

'I don't want it, Pappa,' Sara said, firmly. 'It's pretty but if it helps us get away, somewhere safe, then sell it.'

He hugged her tight. 'I'll buy you lots of nice things, one day.'

Later, when he was alone with Astrid, he said, 'Trouble is, I don't know how I can turn it into cash without arousing suspicion. I bet there are no jewellers left open, in the whole of Oslo.' He shook his head sadly. 'They were all Jewish.'

'There's Edvard's,' said Astrid. 'They were still open when I passed last week. I'll take the jewellery for you, see what price I can get, then we'll see.'

The next day, Astrid hurried over to Edvard's. The shop had a window full of glittering necklaces and earrings on stands, but the plate glass window was criss-crossed with a blue-painted iron grill to deter thieves, and the glass was taped in case of bombs.

She placed Isaak's items on the counter, and watched as Edvard, a man with carefully coiffured hair, prodded at them with his manicured finger. 'Beautiful. Excellent quality, they have some value, but they're all very old-fashioned. Not the glitz the Nazis favour.' He sighed, looked up at her with a kind expression. 'I can give you four thousand for the necklace and brooch, and two thousand five hundred each for the rings. Say nine thousand for the lot. Were they your mother's?'

'No. A friend's.'

'Ah. This friend, they must trust you, hey?'

She felt her cheeks grow hot.

'So, as it is for a friend, a friend who is in some sort of trouble —' he raised his eyebrows in a knowing way — 'we must help each other, and though it breaks me, I think I can give you nine thousand. But that's my best offer. It's more than they're worth.'

She felt her eyes fill with tears. He was trying to help, but it wasn't enough. She swallowed. She didn't know how to tell Isaak. He couldn't go without Sara.

It took a moment before she could compose herself. 'All right,' she said. 'I'll take it … and thanks.' She would have to find the rest of the money somehow.

She watched him pull the objects into his palm and put them in a drawer. A moment later he opened the till and brought out the notes. 'I'm sorry it cannot be more,' he said. 'This occupation hurts us all.'

It seemed a travesty that she should have to let go of these treasured items that would mean so much to Sara in future years. She had no such items herself. Her parents had both been drowned in a boating accident, when she was ten years old, and their bodies had never been found. They had pulled her out of the freezing water but Mamma and Pappa were still at the bottom of Sognefjord somewhere.

She used to imagine they were still alive, in some frozen wonderland under the water, but by the time she was twelve she'd grown out of such fantasies. They would not come back. And she had lost count of the number of times she was glad they didn't have to witness the Nazi occupation of their homeland.

She pulled her scarf more closely around her neck. So much to do in so little time. She'd have to give Isaak a loan. Her next call was the bank.

'Wait a minute,' the cashier said, and came back with a ledger. She was a neat, middle-aged woman with a heavily made-up face. Her face furrowed. 'That account is closed,' she said. 'The balance is zero.'

'Closed? Why? I don't understand —'

'The account belongs to a missing person. There's a note on it to say that should the person try to claim any money from this account they should be referred to the *Staatspolitiet*. Are you Astrid Dahl?'

She was aghast. 'No. No, she's a friend,' she faltered. 'It doesn't matter.'

'I'll just fetch the manager, he'll —'

Astrid didn't wait. She blundered out into the street, putting as much distance between her and the bank as she could.

Her savings were gone. The thought of the empty account gave her a pain she hadn't anticipated, and left her feeling strangely vulnerable. This was it. She was really on her own. She knew now how Isaak must feel. And only a few hours left to raise the money for herself too. Was there anything at all she could sell?

She fingered the compass in her pocket. She didn't want to lose this last link with her father, and besides, it was old and only made of brass. Worth shillings, if that.

But it gave her an idea. She remembered her father's collection of stamps from all over the world. Mr Rask, who used to be her father's neighbour, had been trying to persuade her to sell them for years, but she never would. He was so proud of his collection, and used it to teach her about other countries and other languages. She thought of Pappa's craggy face, his blue eyes behind his tortoiseshell glasses. When he died, he was only a few years older than she was now. The thought amazed her. He was still 'older' to her, despite that.

But he would understand why she had to do this now, she knew.

'How much did the jewellery fetch?' Isaak asked, when she got back.

'Nine thousand. Sorry, it's all he could give me. So you're still three thousand short.'

He closed his eyes as if he no longer wanted to look at the world.

Sara hurried away, returning with her piggy bank. 'Here Pappa, let's count what's in here.'

'Good, darling, that's a big help.' Isaak emptied the few copper coins on the table.

'Is it enough?' Sara asked.

'It's made all the difference,' he said, hugging her tight. 'We've got nearly enough now.'

Astrid's eyes met his despairing ones. 'It's all right. I'll make it up. I'm going to sell my father's stamp albums.'

'Are you sure?' Isaak followed her, watching her pull the albums from under her bed and bundle them up in brown paper. She tried not to look at them too hard. 'I can see it's hurting you.'

'It's only stamps,' she said. 'Pappa would be proud they're being used for this. He would detest what the Nazis are doing to Norway.'

Nonetheless, she had to hurry the two blocks to Rask's place before she changed her mind, because much as her father might have hated the Nazis, had he lived to see them, he definitely had no time for Rask, whom he thought of as a man with no moral fibre whatsoever.

Rask, a quisling, whose house smelt of old urine and cats, was surprised to see her, but could barely keep his hands off

213

the albums. 'The 1871 Posthorn Blue, and the seven skilling red brown, are they still there?'

'I don't know. I believe so,' she said. 'But I'd want two thousand kroner each for them, plus extra for the three albums.' She knew she had to have more money in reserve for when they got to Sweden.

'What made you change your mind? Why are you selling now?' he asked suspiciously, breathing over the paper, his nose close as he peeled back the layers of tissue paper protecting the stamps.

'Now my teaching's stopped, I need a little extra income.' The excuse rolled off her tongue.

'I'll give you eight hundred and fifty a book.'

She shook her head. 'Then I'll go elsewhere, Mr Rask. I only offered you first refusal because you'd shown an interest.'

'The stamps with the traitor King Haakon would have to be removed if they are to have any resale value.' His hand pawed the page. His chipped, yellowing fingernails repulsed her.

She snatched the book from under his nose. 'Two thousand each, Mr Rask, and the rare stamps are yours. Otherwise, I'll go elsewhere.' She stood and prepared to go out, brushing the cat hair from her skirt.

She'd made it half out of the door before he called. 'Naturally albums like this should be forfeit to the state,' he said. 'You would be obliged to hand it over, should I report you for owning an unpatriotic book.'

She brought the book back inside. Damn the man. She couldn't risk it. She was in trouble enough.

Mr Rask took the money out of an old red biscuit tin that was kept under his chair, presumably so nobody could steal it. She caught a glimpse of an obscene amount of money in that tin, and yet this man lived like a pauper in his run-down house that stank of damp and cats.

Reluctantly she counted the notes there, on the stained tablecloth. Half the amount she'd asked for. Just three thousand and fifty altogether. Even handling the money made her vaguely nauseous.

'Where is the rest?' she asked.

'You have a fair price for no questions asked,' he said, his hand on the pile of albums.

Sorry Pappa, she thought. She tidied the money into a pile and folded it. He came to the door as she walked away, but she didn't look back. All the same, she felt his eyes on the back of her neck all the way down the street.

CHAPTER 23

Astrid kept her head down and walked close to the shelter of the buildings. It felt like walking on ice, going down the street carrying that much cash, and it made her tense every time anyone passed. What if there was someone following? She looked right and left, relieved to finally get to the toyshop, and to hand over the down-payment to Grieg. In return, she was given a set of false papers, and a small notebook, the contents of which they must memorize.

When she got home, Isaak's gaunt face was enough to remind her why she was doing this. 'Are we set?' he asked.

'Not quite enough,' Astrid said. 'My bank account was closed by the Nazis too.' Before he could reply, she stalled him. 'Don't ask. I can't raise any more. Not a single shilling. We'll just have to hope when we get there they'll take us anyway. We're only a little short, but I've paid the down payment and got our papers. We'll have to take the gamble.'

Isaak, who had been reading aloud to Sara, put the book down and rocked his head a moment in his hands. When he looked up his eyes were glassy. 'Thank you. I don't know what we'd have done without you.' He took a deep breath. 'I hated it, asking you to do this. I should have been out there taking these risks, not you.'

She shook her head. 'The risk was greater for you. And what would Sara do without you? Anyway, you'll not thank me when you see what we've to memorize. Look, here are our papers.'

She laid them out on the kitchen table. Isaak and Sara left the book and came to see.

'Oh. But there's only two passes. Am I supposed to be this Aksel Dahl?' Isaak asked. 'But it says I'm your husband, and there's no sign of Sara on this pass.' He raised his eyes in concern.

'Don't worry, I have Sara on mine. They thought it safer if I was your wife, and so they added her to mine.' Her face grew hot with embarrassment. 'They say to show mine first, if possible, as yours is not the best forgery. We're to be a family travelling with one child.'

'Let me look.' He grabbed the passes and hurriedly opened them.

'Astrid Dahl. Age 32 … daughter, Inga 13. It says you're the mother of this Inga. That must be Sara, but they've got her age wrong. She's ten, not thirteen.' He pushed them away in disgust, and stood up, eyes on fire. 'Oh, I get it. You're using my Sara as a shield for your own escape. That can't be right. What if we were to get separated, what if they only let two of us go —?'

'Isaak, it's not for my sake. It's for the safety of us all. It will look less suspicious if we're more like a family group.'

'*We* are a family. Sara and I. She should be on my pass. It is you, who are not family.' His bitter words struck home.

Astrid swallowed. 'The child is usually on the mother's pass. If the worst comes to the worst you and Sara must go. She needs you. But very well, if you want to go alone, then go.' She threw the rest of the money on the table. 'Your jewellery fetched only nine thousand kroner. Enough for you alone, not Sara. The rest of the money that will get us all out of Norway is from my father's rare stamp album. You can go back to my contact and tell him to change the papers. And then choose which of us will go.'

'Stop it!' Sara's voice broke over them both. 'Just stop it, will you. I don't mind travelling with Miss Dahl.' Her face was white with rage.

'I'm not giving you up, even on paper,' Isaak said.

'Don't, Pappa. We'd be going nowhere without the help of Miss Dahl. Nowhere except where the others went.' Two red spots of colour appeared on Sara's cheeks.

Isaak pulled her over to comfort her, throwing Astrid a look of shame.

Astrid bit back a retort. Isaak was just under strain; that was all. She made an effort to calm her rising temper. 'Are we travelling together tomorrow or not?' Astrid asked. 'Because if so, there's a lot to do, and we'd be better getting on with it than arguing.'

'Yes,' Sara said. 'Tell us what we need.'

Isaak didn't answer, but stood and paced the floor like a caged lion in a zoo.

Sara took hold of Astrid's arm. 'It's the shop. He misses it. He was so busy, and now ... well, now it hurts him that there is nothing he can do. That all his books are gone, except my picture books.' She took a deep breath. 'Do we need to pack?'

Astrid patted her sleeve. 'Yes. You haven't much, so just your warmest clothes. Take the small blankets from the airing cupboard, if they'll fit. Warm socks and gloves. And there are some tins of oily fish under the sink, get those out and any other tinned food that's not too heavy to carry. Can you pack for your father as well? I need to talk to him.'

Sara nodded and hurried off into the kitchen.

Astrid gave Isaak a wide berth as she continued her preparations. When was the right moment? She could tell he wasn't ready to engage with her because the atmosphere was still so tense and full of mistrust. So she sat at the other end of the table to write a letter to Mrs Bakke thanking her for loan of the apartment and explaining it would soon be empty again. Of course she gave her no clue where she was going.

She couldn't quite believe she was doing this, giving up her life. She'd been naive to think she could go against the Nazis and they would just forget about it. She thought of Ulf, being taken to some icy camp, and of the chain-smoking Herman being interrogated in a cell. She couldn't bear to think of what they might do to him. Or to her, if they caught her. She was suddenly anxious to be on the move, and rushed to collect all her belongings together.

Isaak was still staring morosely at an unopened book. She glared at his back. Why was she doing this; for these people who didn't even thank her? It was all so hard. She thought of Jørgen. Before, she'd thought the Resistance was all guns and bravado, not sitting here deciding how many cans of sardines to pack, or whether Sara had clean underthings.

She walked past Isaak, stretched out an arm and took up the pass for her and Sara, now renamed Inga Dahl.

She was about to put them in her pack when Isaak stood and stopped her, a hand on her shoulder. 'I don't like it,' he said. 'It feels like I'm losing a child. I promised my father we'd stick together no matter what. But if it's the only way for us to get out, then I'll do it for Sara's sake.' Isaak's expression was contrite, but he wouldn't back down by making an apology. He was as stubborn as she was, she realised.

Bearing a grudge wouldn't get them out though, would it? She pointed to her bags. 'Put your pass where it's easy to reach,' she said. 'And you'd better learn your new name and who you're supposed to be. Don't forget to drill it into Sara that her name's Inga, and if you call her that, she should answer.'

The next morning the three of them headed downstairs and Astrid was about to step out when she spotted a car on the corner of the street. She'd swear it was the same car that used to wait at her previous house. She shut the door hard.

'Quick! Back upstairs! There's a car watching the house.'

'Are you sure?' Isaak asked.

'No. But do you want to take any chances?' she whispered. 'We'll have to go out the back.'

Back upstairs. Out of the fire door and onto the rickety iron fire escape.

It was icy and slippery, and now that they were carrying their packs, pretty lethal. Astrid kept a firm grip in the rusting handrail on the way down, afraid that at any moment a Nazi soldier would come around the corner.

They hurried across the yard and round the corner. It was a brisk fifteen minute walk, during which time she kept her eyes almost on stalks looking for Nazi patrols.

No car came after them, but that didn't ease the tension as they waited anxiously outside the pharmacy. Sara was bundled in two layers of jumpers and a knitted hat, with her plaits sticking out beneath it. Isaak wore a woollen flat cap that made him appear strangely youthful, like a costermonger's boy, but his forehead was creased with worry.

Ten o'clock came and went, and there was still no sign of any car or transport. Their presence had drawn attention from a passing German patrol who had seen them standing there an hour ago, and were now about to pass again. Astrid could feel Isaak's nerves as the Germans approached by the way he kept licking his lips and shifting from foot to foot. He gripped Sara's hand tightly whenever she made any slight movement away from him.

When the patrol got closer, about two blocks away, an open-sided flat-bed truck, marked with the name of a hardware firm, its charcoal chimney steaming, suddenly drew up. The driver leaned out of the side window and gestured at them. 'In the back,' he yelled.

'Have you got any cabbages left?' she shouted the phrase she'd been given.

'No, only turnips.'

'Yes!' she shouted gleefully to Isaak. It was the correct password. He unpinned the tailgate and let it drop with a clang, and threw in the bags in under the tarpaulin before giving Sara a leg up.

'Hey, you!' The two-man patrol was nearly upon them.

Isaak bundled himself into the truck and reached out his hand to Astrid who grabbed it and clambered on, the icy metal floor bruising her knees. Sara shunted up under the tarpaulin to make space just as the truck took off, tailgate swinging. Astrid clutched at Sara's arm, fearing she'd slide out.

The men from the patrol called 'Halt!' in German, but the van didn't stop.

Astrid dived flat on the bed of the truck, fearing they would be shot at. The bitter dry wind blowing under the tarpaulin where it flapped loose took her breath. The tailgate clattered and banged as they went, lurching around corners. From here, she could see little under the green canvas, but could hear the roar of traffic and the parp of horns.

Once they had to stop at an intersection, Sara raised her head to look under the edge of the tarpaulin where it was hooked to the side of the truck with eyelets.

'Keep down,' Astrid said. 'There are German soldiers at the lights.'

Isaak pulled her down and they pressed themselves flat until the truck trundled on again.

Astrid's stomach began to heave as they drove for more than two hours, screeching round hairpin bends and up and down mountainous passes. The roads were rutted and the truck jerked under them. Sara gripped the edge of the truck, face white as paper, her eyes wide and terrified.

Finally the road surface grew even more bumpy and the truck slowed. When it came to a halt, none of them could move. They were all too cold and stiff.

The tarpaulin was yanked to one side and they emerged blinking into the pale morning sunlight. They were at the end of a dirt track in some sort of forest clearing.

'Off!' a man's voice shouted.

They were surrounded by men. Rough-looking men, like lumberjacks, with guns pointing at them.

'Shit, they've got a kid,' one of the men said.

Astrid knew immediately something wasn't right, but Isaak helped Sara jump down, and stretched out a hand to Astrid, but she waved it away and awkwardly slithered down. When she hit solid ground, her legs were shaking with cold and fear.

'You have the money?' one of the men asked, a big man with thick lips and hair cropped as if it had been sheared.

'Yes,' Isaak said, fumbling for the cloth bag in the haversack. 'For me and the child.'

The man took it from Isaak's hand without thanks, and counted out the money, whilst the rest of the men smoked, hands on their guns. 'You?' He fixed his eyes on Astrid.

Astrid handed it over, though by now she knew there was something uncomfortable about this whole business.

'What shall we do with them?' one of the other men said, a man in a worn leather coat with a matted fur collar. 'We can't shoot kids.'

At these words Isaak put an arm around Sara's shoulders. 'You've got the money, so you'll take us to the Swedish border like you promised,' Isaak said.

One of them laughed, but then the men went into a huddle, arguing amongst themselves. They seemed to be dividing the money. Finally the big blond man emerged from the group. He and another of the men, a shorter darker man with a cigarette stuck to his lower lip, folded back the tarpaulin on the truck.

By this time, Astrid's stomach felt like an empty cavern. Perhaps they were going to take them after all.

But before she realised what was happening, the men lobbed all their bags off the truck, into the dirt, and leapt on it themselves. The truck screeched off, with the other wood-fired car following it with the rest of the men. A screech of tyres and slush on the wet track.

'Wait!' Isaak let go of Sara and sprinted after them, but they'd soon gone in a stink of charcoal fumes.

Astrid stood for a moment, staring down the track. They'd taken the money. In a sudden sickening realisation, she knew they'd been had. The men had never had any intention of taking them anywhere. They were just after making quick money. The amount had never really mattered.

With a shudder so visceral it made her want to vomit, she understood that they had done this many times. But the other times the Jews had ended up dead. It was only the presence of Sara that saved them from the same fate.

She crouched down where she was in the road, hugging herself.

At length, she stood up stiffly and looked around, but could see no obvious landmarks. She should have made a note of the route, she realised, but now it was too late. She heard footsteps approaching.

'They're not coming back, are they?' Isaak asked.

Numbly, Astrid shook her head.

'Bastards.' He picked up a rock and hurled it as far as he could until it hit a tree. 'D'you know what the worst thing is?' he said. 'Not being able to do a bloody thing about it. Looking like I'm too weak to fight. I'm afraid if I fight back and punch out their lights then they'll take out their hatred of me on her.' He indicated Sara who was scuffing at the gravel with a foot, her face grey with misery.

'They were armed, Isaak. You couldn't have done anything.'

'I'm hungry, Pappa,' Sara said.

'I know. We'll walk a bit, then we'll have a picnic, yes?'

Astrid shouldered her pack and scanned the horizon. Nothing. Forest in front of them with no definite path. Resolutely she started to walk back up the track. They'd given up everything to get out of Norway, and now they were deeper in than they'd ever been, and without shelter in the depths of winter.

She looked back to see the others following her, two dark figures against the grey of the track. Things didn't look good for her, but for them it was so much worse.

CHAPTER 24

Jørgen was readying himself for another journey to Norway. He'd made two trips as crew, and now the Shetland Bus had got some kind of official recognition and was known by the fancy title of the Norwegian Naval Independent Unit, or NNIU. The official title did nothing to ease the tension behind his ribs every time they put to sea. The sea was an unpredictable beast, and the north wind a monster. Each time his heart almost jumped out of his chest at the thought of it; though once he was aboard, he was too busy to think about anything else but the job in hand. Fingers crossed, so far, apart from the mountainous seas, they'd been lucky and entered Norwegian waters without detection. But now winter had truly come, and the weather was worsening. Gales and snow, and pitch-black nights. His fear rose up in his throat as if to strangle him.

Karl had not been assigned a sortie yet, and Jørgen wondered if Harcourt had kept them apart on purpose. He often saw Harcourt drinking with Karl in Cooper's Tavern, and they seemed to be very chummy, often retreating to the Catholic Mission to practice billiards at all hours of the night.

Today he observed Karl and Harcourt with wry interest as he took a swig of beer from his bottle. They were laughing together at some in-joke. Karl used to call Harcourt 'Captain Hard-core', a barbed joke which caused them all guilty amusement, but not anymore. He supposed Harcourt must trust Karl as he often left him to lock up now, after they'd finished their billiard game. Today he saw them exchanging good-humoured banter together, before Harcourt put down his tankard and strode out of the bar, car keys in hand. To be truthful, it annoyed him the way Karl had become Harcourt's sidekick.

'I thought you were desperate to get back to Norway,' Jørgen said, as Karl sauntered back to their table.

'I am,' Karl said, 'but no point in pushing. Dare say my time will come soon enough.'

'What's up?' joked Dag, an ex-fisherman and another of the crewmen. 'You haven't decided to turn Scots and stay in Shetland, have you?'

'No, who'd want to stay in this dead end hole of a place? I just think Harcourt probably knows best.'

So why didn't Karl want to go out with the Bus? Was he afraid? No, impossible. Karl had no fear. Not of snow or water or weather, so what exactly was going on?

A few moments later they were joined by three women from the catering department. Elsie, a big blowsy brunette with a gap between her teeth jostled her way in between Jørgen and Karl, and cadged a cigarette. Karl moved over and gave her his full attention. With some relief Jørgen saw this happen and wondered if Karl had ever asked Morag out. If he had, she'd never mentioned it. The thought still preyed on his mind.

The next day, Jørgen was sitting on the harbour wall taking his lunchtime break when Morag stopped by the paint shed. Instantly, Karl leapt up from his painting job to go and talk to her. A moment later she'd lifted her hand in goodbye to Karl and walked over to join Jørgen.

'I think you made a conquest there,' he said.

She made a face. 'Along with every other woman on the island.'

'A while ago, he told me he was going to ask you out.'

'He did,' she said. 'But I turned him down. There's someone else I'm hoping might ask.' She looked sideways at him, her cheeks growing pink.

Now was his moment.

'Hey, Nystrøm, we need you!'

Jørgen turned and stood up to look. It was Jacobsen calling him over to help get the boat out of dry dock. He hesitated, on the balls of his feet, torn between what he wanted to say, and his duty.

'Nystrøm! Stop gossiping! Give us a hand will you,' Jacobsen yelled.

'Better go,' Morag said.

In the end Jørgen held up his hands in a shrug, downed his tea and hurried back to work. He could cheerfully have killed Jacobsen, but inside, his heart lifted. If ever there was a hint from a girl; that was it. And Morag was lovely.

But the thought of Astrid needled him all afternoon. Somehow, Astrid and Norway were tied together and faithfulness to one implied faithfulness to the other.

In Oslo, Falk was feeling the pressure. He slammed down the telephone receiver and rubbed his jowly face. That was Reichskommissar Terboven, and he wasn't happy. The day before yesterday he'd suddenly sent orders all Jews were to be deported. Not just the men, but women and children too. Falk had until 25th November to do it. His department were supposed to have rounded up every Jew in Oslo, but there were still some who were unaccounted for, despite his men running ragged trying to catch them all. How did Terboven expect him to do it at such short notice? Two days! And he must enforce the death penalty for anyone caught helping Jews escape. Of course, it was always his men who then had the unpleasant task of implementing these orders. Terboven and Fehlis never got their hands dirty.

So yesterday was chaos. Word must have got out to the Resistance, and it was like rats fleeing a burning building. They went by bicycle, taxi, horse, any way they could get out. He put all his men onto it, and they were like lads on a hunting party, but it still wasn't enough.

He hated this part of his job. He was squeamish about blood, and much happier behind his desk. Last night he'd had to witness three Jews, young boys who'd been hiding in a disused cellar, shot as they tried to run away. Schmitt had got rather too enthusiastic with the gun. Falk looked down at his feet. Blood had ended up on his shoes. Good thing his wife had cleaned them up. And worse, despite deploying his whole task force, hundreds of Jews from Oslo had somehow got out of the city. Terboven was on his back and the blame was being laid firmly at his door.

Now he looked down at the paper in front of him. Another message from agent Brevik, who was still on Shetland. He wanted to know when he would be ordered to come back. His reluctance to serve on the boats was raising suspicions. Over the last months he'd kept him there, but now Brevik had begun to realize something was amiss and was demanding they gave him protection on the boat that was to bring him back, and a guarantee that they'd not send planes or patrols after it.

He'd done enough, Brevik said. It was risky getting to the transmitter in Harcourt's office, and he'd supplied them with most of the contacts in Norway and the routes out. Now he wanted to get back to Norway, and claim his cash.

Trouble was, with this Jewish expulsion, only Nazi-approved individuals were granted border zone permits, or were allowed to travel close to the borders with Sweden or Finland. So it would be hard to get him out of the country on false papers. And Brevik knew far too much about German espionage.

Fehlis was right, he'd have to go. He couldn't have a security risk on his watch, not now Terboven had an eye on him.

He toyed with the paper a few moments longer, before telling Selma to send Brevik a coded message; *Get next boat back. Will withhold fire. Will meet you. Advise date, time and landing destination.*

Once they had the landing destination they would make sure to meet him all right. He'd contact the coast patrols and get a warship put in the area to sink the boat and ensure there would be no survivors. Brevik was right; he'd done enough. It would give Falk great pleasure to sink boat and crew. He thought of Nystrøm for a moment. He'd rather hoped to hand him to the Stapo for interrogation, take him down a peg or two. Maybe he'd be on that next boat too.

He shrugged. He didn't care so much now. Not now he was friends with big Nazis like Fehlis and Terboven, and in control of the whole of Oslo's Nazi police force. If Nystrøm was lost, so what? He was just collateral damage.

CHAPTER 25

In the gravel clearing in the woods, snow began to drift downwards in tiny spots as Astrid picked her way back up the track. Isaak followed, silently gripping Sara by the hand. Since the men had abandoned them, they decided they had to try to find a main road and get some bearings. Astrid was quiet. They had no skis and neither she nor Isaak had any idea where they were. All she knew, was that they were in the countryside, a long way from the nearest town. At least there'd be no danger of German checkpoints.

No traffic, no noise of any human habitation. Even the birds were silent. But the gloom was ominous, with a sky so heavy and grey that after the initial flakes, she feared a full fall of snow. They trudged up the track, carrying their bags, their boots crunching the ice puddles. Isaak had to piggyback Sara after a while when she began to slow, so Astrid carried his pack a while as well as her own. She had no answers, no plan, other than to just walk, and hope they'd find a way to get their bearings. At length, the road bore hard right and a junction was ahead, flanked by pine trees.

Isaak was forced to put Sara down, she was too heavy for carrying really, but the break had given her renewed energy. The sight of the junction cheered them all and she ran ahead to the road; a proper tarmacked road, so it must lead somewhere.

'Which way, Pappa?' Sara asked, face suddenly alive with hope.

'I don't know,' Isaak said, 'but I vote we go downhill.'

'Good idea,' Astrid said.

Isaak gave a wary smile. 'One good thing,' he said, 'we're still alive. They could easily have killed us.'

The first few flakes from the leaden sky began to fall as they walked downwards, slipping and sliding on the icy road. Twenty minutes later and they were caught in the sort of blizzard that means you can't see a foot before your face.

'Shall we shelter?' Isaak called out.

Astrid squinted, seeing nothing but the mountains looming behind, and the sparse pines to either side. 'There's nowhere. Let's keep going. Maybe we'll come to a village soon.'

They laboured on, keeping the hard surface of the road under their feet, even though they could see little except a white swirl.

'Look. There! Houses,' Sara yelled. Astrid peered through the snow, until below, faint outlines of roofs were visible.

They stopped. 'What shall we do?' Isaak asked.

'We have to hope they're supporters of King Haakon, and not quislings, and that they'll help us. At least give us a place to shelter.'

'Which house?' Isaak asked.

'That one.' Sara pointed. The house had two dun horses in the paddock; hardy Norse ponies with striped legs and their backs to the wind. 'It can't be that bad if they've got horses.' She began to skid and slide down the hill.

Isaak shrugged. 'I suppose it's as good as any other,' he said. 'And it's away from the rest of the village.'

'Isaak, if this should go wrong ... I'm sorry,' Astrid said. 'I thought Herman could be trusted.'

'Maybe he knew nothing about it. And maybe we're the only people left who can tell him what happens to the people he sends to Sweden.'

'If he's still alive,' she said.

The house had a light showing in the crack of the shutters.

'Here goes,' Isaak said, stamping snow off his shoes. 'Fingers crossed.' He knocked hard on the door.

A voice came from behind it; a quavering woman's voice. 'Who is it?'

'You don't know us, but we're lost and we need your help.'

Silence.

'Please. We've got a little girl here and we've walked for miles,' Astrid said. 'She can't go much further. We just need to know where we are, that's all.'

'I'm not a little girl,' Sara protested. 'And I want to know the names of your ponies, please.'

The door creaked open a little and a small, grey-haired woman in traditional black peered out at them. 'Lost, you say?'

'We were trying to get to Sweden, but...' Astrid shook her head. 'It's a long story.'

'Sweden?' The woman frowned. 'Are you in a car?'

'No. Well, we were, but the car abandoned us up the road there...'

The woman's face grew suspicious, and she began to close the door again.

'Please,' Isaak said, taking off his hat in a sort of gesture of politeness. 'We don't mean any harm. Just tell us where we are and how we can get to a railway station.'

'I don't want to get involved. I can see it's some kind of trouble.'

'All right,' he said. 'We're sorry we bothered you. We'll go somewhere else. But is there some kind of shelter anywhere, a barn or a shed where we can stay until the morning?'

'If there's a stable, I can sleep with the ponies,' Sara said. 'Like Jesus in the Bible.'

The woman hesitated. There was a long pause, as her expression shifted between fear and guilt. Finally she opened the door wider. 'I can give you a map I suppose. You'd better come in out of the snow, anyway. We can't talk out here. Take off your wet things. That's right, hang them up there. Boots too.' She fussed around Sara before leading her into a cosy sitting room with a wood fire blazing. 'If you wait there a moment, I'll be back.'

They heard the whirring noise of the telephone being dialled and her urgent voice asking the operator for a number. Then, 'Einar? It's me. I've got a bit of a situation. Can you come?'

Astrid caught Isaak's eye.

'Shall we leave?' Isaak whispered.

The woman continued on the telephone. 'What? No. Now.' A pause. 'I don't know. I just need you to come over right away.' Then; 'Yes, yes. See you soon.'

Astrid's heart sank. Whoever Einar was, would he be sympathetic, or would he hand them over to the quisling police?

'My son's coming over. He has a car. He'll drive you to the station. Sit down all of you, and I'll make some hot milk.' She turned to Sara. 'Goat milk. I have goats as well as ponies.' She pulled a large flat book from the shelf. 'Have a look at that, and then I'll show you where we are in the Atlas in a moment. Where are you from?'

She must have heard Sara had an accent. Isaak gave a warning shake of his head.

'Oslo,' Sara said.

Astrid breathed a sigh of relief. The right answer.

Sara settled herself on the rug before the hearth engrossed in the Atlas, and after a few minutes the woman brought hot milk and the traditional butter biscuits. Sara pounced on the biscuits and had devoured several before her father's wagging finger persuaded her to stop.

The woman introduced herself as Mrs Follestad. After a little deliberation Astrid decided to risk telling her the truth. She gave her a potted version of their journey, but leaving out the names of their contacts in Oslo.

'And these were Norwegian men who took your money? Not Germans?' Mrs Follestad was astounded.

'The men had guns,' Sara said. 'But I don't think they wanted to shoot children. At least that's what they said.'

Mrs Follestad's eyes grew even wider. 'This is all a bit out of my league. It's so quiet here. But Einar'll know what to do. My son. He's a dentist in the next town, that's why he's allowed a car. And look.' She picked up the map. 'We're here.' She pointed to the village which was just a dot in the vast hinterland of fjords and mountains. 'Sweden's there. It's too far to walk; I don't know why you could even think of it, to walk that far with a child.' She shook her head with disapproval.

'We didn't intend to walk,' Isaak said tersely.

Astrid wished he wasn't quite so volatile. She gave him a helpless look. They'd no option after all; they'd have to trust Mrs Follestad and her son. They had no money and no other means of transport.

Sara provided the distraction they all needed by asking about the ponies they'd seen by the gate.

'Ah, they don't do much now,' Mrs Follestad said. 'Used to carry the churns down to the village, and bring back the potatoes. But they're old now, spend most of their time scratching the paint off my gate.'

Sara continued to listen to Mrs Follestad talk of the ponies' history until the unmistakeable growl of a car arriving sent a shiver of unease up Astrid's spine. She gave Isaak what was supposed to be a reassuring smile. Isaak reached for Sara and drew her into a protective embrace.

When the car engine died, and they heard the bang of the car door, Mrs Follestad rushed out and spoke to her son in urgent whispers in the hall. A draught, as a large man in a thick felted coat entered. He wore a fur cap with earflaps, and the snow had already settled in an icy layer on his shoulders. Despite the advance warning he still seemed surprised to see them huddled there in the steamy warmth.

'Mother says somebody dumped you in the hills and you've no way of getting home.'

'We were duped,' Isaak said. 'We were trying to get out of Norway. We just need directions. We won't be any trouble, we just need you to turn a blind eye.'

'Nobody's handing anyone in.' Einar held up his hands. 'But it's clear something odd has happened, and I need to know the truth before I can agree help you.'

'Tell him,' Astrid said. 'We might as well. Tell him how we paid for passage and were robbed.'

Mrs Follestad repeated the story, with Isaak adding the details. Einar listened, standing by the hearth, shoulders steaming, kneading his fur cap in his big hands.

'I've heard of this route,' he said. 'Usually further south. But to cheat people like that; to cheat people who are fleeing for their lives? That's disgusting. These are not the Norwegian people we know.' He turned to his mother. 'We have to help them.'

'But how? Where can you take them? They're Jews, aren't they? You know we can't; it will only bring trouble on your head.' She took hold of him by the sleeve.

'There's already trouble on my head, Ma. There's been trouble ever since the damn Nazis came.' He turned to Isaak. 'You're in luck,' he said. 'I don't know how this has happened, but you've arrived at the one man in the whole of Vestland that can help. We can get you out of Norway. But if you want to avoid being picked up by the Germans or the quislings it won't be through Sweden. That border's impassable now since the Jewish order. Too many checkpoints and guards. Too many caught that way. But there's another route; less well-known, but effective. I have friends who can help.'

'Wait! Einar? What are you saying?' Mrs Follestad's expression was one of outrage.

'Sorry Ma. I never wanted you to know. I wanted to keep you out of it all. But I've been in the Milorg for twelve months now. You must know I had to do something.'

'But we discussed it! You said you wouldn't do anything risky! They kill people who go against them.'

'But Ma —'

'You promised me. After Kristian Jepson was shot, you promised me you'd keep out of it.'

He was sheepish. 'Ma, it was because Kristian was shot that I had to do something. Don't you see?' He turned to Isaak. 'I can telephone someone and they can get a message to the islands off Ålesund. There are boats that go from there to Shetland in Scotland. They call it the Shetland Bus. We can take you to close to the coast, and give you the name of a boatman who'll take you to the pick-up point. He's a doctor, a man called Moen. After that, you'll have to wait until there's an arms or agent drop.'

'I understand,' Astrid said. 'Any help you can give us is more than we hoped.'

'It's for the girl,' he said. 'I've two of my own. They're seven and four. Elise and Halle.'

'And you'd put Elise and Halle at risk for some people you don't even know?' Mrs Follestad interrupted. 'Does Lilli know?'

'Of course she does. And yes, she worries. But imagine the boot on the other foot. Wouldn't you want someone to do this for ours, in their situation?'

Mrs Follestad was silent then, her arms folded across her chest, but her eyes were full of fear. 'Be careful, won't you?'

'It's all right, Ma. I know what I'm doing. I'm still here, aren't I?' He went and hugged her, a big bear of a man squashing her diminutive frame to his chest. After a few moments he released her. 'I suggest we all get some sleep. I'll stay here tonight. No-one will question a son staying with his mother. But we'll need to get going before it's light. Good job I've plenty of fuel.' He turned to Astrid. 'I'll need to see your papers, please. And Ma, I need to use your phone.'

In the frosty morning air, they piled into Einar's car, a saloon that smelt of old leather and rubber gumboots. He was allowed to keep a car because he was on call to the Nazi barracks in the next town. When they were ready to go, Mrs Follestad, looking tired and fraught, stood at the window, the shutter half-open, to watch Isaak help Sara into the back seat.

Astrid clapped Isaak on the shoulder as she passed. 'Better luck this time, eh?' she said.

'At least we haven't had to pay,' he said, ruefully. He climbed in the back with Sara, whilst Astrid got in the front.

As the engine sputtered into life, she waved to Mrs Follestad, but then fixed her eyes firmly on the road and the passing landscape. She had learnt her lesson — it was vital to know where you were, in case anything should go wrong.

'I had two calls with the Milorg last night,' Einar said, as they drove through the still-dark village. 'From what I can understand, from our brief but coded messages, you must get to Ålesund, and from there a boat to a small island called Radøy. It has only one harbour where the pick-up and drop-off will happen. The only thing is; the boat won't wait. If you're not on time, they can't wait for you, and then you'd be on your own. You've got five days to get there, and you'll need to be on Radøy for the evening tide on November 8th. It's risky, because it's a lot of cross-country, and since the round-ups, the Germans will be looking out for straggling Jews. You don't need me to tell you what will happen if they catch you.'

'We understand,' said Isaak.

Once out of the village Einar pulled up in a layby, and got out a map. He pointed out the route. 'You must go to these safe houses, here and here. Your first night contact is a farmer called Thoresen. He will have further maps and instructions for you, and will supply you with skis for the onward journey.'

Astrid tried to take it in, but her mind was too occupied with the fact they were going to Shetland. Jørgen would be there, and unwittingly, she had ended up following him. Would she be able to find him? And if she did, what would he make of it? He might think she'd done it on purpose. Would he be pleased, or would it make him uncomfortable? She was aware of a slight sense of guilt to be travelling with another man, and wondered what Jørgen would think.

'Astrid,' Einar said, tapping his thick forefinger on the map for emphasis, 'just there, outside Ålesund, there is a checkpoint, so you will need to go around it. You must head for Sæbø out past the fjords. The boat cannot risk coming further inland. They are disguised as Norwegian fishermen, you see.'

She could just picture Jørgen as a fisherman. His father had taken him fishing, she knew, and he had the same practical ease on the water as he did on skis.

Einar paused, until he had her full attention. 'Understand; they are risking their lives.'

Men like Jørgen were risking their lives to get her and the Feinbergs out. She suddenly understood. She looked at the route with clearer eyes. Now the sight of the mountains and rivers, of the sheer expanse of countryside daunted her. 'I'm not sure Sara can manage that distance,' she said.

'Let me see,' Isaak said, reaching forward for the map. 'I can piggyback her if I have to.'

'That far?' Astrid said, turning. 'You struggled to do it just a few yards before. Maybe if we had a sledge, or a pony, we might manage. But not just walking or on skis. I know the danger of our mountains. I've lived here all my life.' She turned to Einar. 'Mr Feinberg only arrived from Frankfurt a few years ago, when he saw how it was going with Hitler.'

'Have you no mountain skills at all?' he asked Isaak.

A shake of the head. 'I was a bookseller, in a city. I had no use for it. And now we have war, I wish I had learned to fight or handle a gun.' He gave a bitter laugh. 'But no, I can only repair spines and stack shelves.'

'Can you ski?'

'I've never tried, but it can't be that hard, can it? I can learn.'

Einar looked to Astrid. 'What do you think?'

'I think it's crazy,' she said. 'But these are crazy times.'

'You don't have to come with us, Astrid. But Sara and I have no choice,' Isaak said. 'We can die in a camp, or die trying for freedom. Which would you choose?'

The car was suddenly icy. She shivered, rubbed her hands together.

'Pappa?' Sara said. 'I can walk. I'm very strong.'

'I know you are, darling,' Isaak embraced Sara and planted a kiss on her cheek.

'Are you sure you want to try this?' Einar asked, fixing Astrid with a serious expression. 'After all, unlike the others, he's right, you do have a choice.'

'No, I don't. I'm a teacher. One who set the teacher's strike in motion and organised Milorg leaflet drops, and the Nazis know. I didn't turn up for my trial. They'll arrest me if I stay in Norway.'

'I didn't know that,' Isaak said accusingly.

'There wasn't time to tell you.'

Einar turned the key in the ignition and the car coughed into life. 'On your own head be it; never say we didn't try to dissuade you.' He pressed his foot on the accelerator and revved up.

'Will there be any Germans on the island we're going to?' Isaak asked.

'No,' Einar said, letting out the clutch. 'But there are patrols up and down the coast all the time.' He paused to round a bend, changed gear. 'Ålesund is overrun with them; they know we are getting agents out from there, but they can't catch us. We use Norwegians to run the boats to Shetland — men who speak Norwegian and who just look like regular fishermen. We sent a wireless telegraph to our man on the coast that you will be going there and will need a boat to get you to the rendezvous with Dr Moen. I gave him the names and details on the papers so they know who to expect, but you won't know any of the rest of the passengers or the names of the crew who come to rescue you.'

Night came unnoticed and they slept fitfully as Einar drove on. Several times they had to drive through small villages to avoid the patrols in the towns. As light grew and the landscape grew brighter they had to stop and fill the burner with more charcoal from a bag in the boot of the car. After another day's driving they finally pulled up at an isolated farmhouse where Thoresen, the farmer, greeted them warmly.

Astrid let her shoulders relax. So far, so good. Yet the thought of the walking tomorrow weighed on her mind. What if they got lost? What if the next farm turned them away? By Isaak's face she knew the self-same thoughts must be going through his mind.

He leaned forward to talk to her. 'Don't worry,' he said. 'We'll make it. Three days from now we'll be on a boat to Shetland.'

'What's Shetland like, Pappa?' Sara asked.

'Oh, I don't know. They're Scots, so I suppose they wear kilts and eat porridge.'

'What are kilts?'

'Skirts that men wear.'

That made Sara giggle so much that Astrid couldn't help but turn to smile back.

CHAPTER 26

On Jørgen's one day off Morag had volunteered to take him to the Loch of Girlsta — one of Shetland's biggest deepest lochs, and very popular with the local fishermen. He eyed the thick dark cloud over the hills and the bands of rain coming in off the sea and hoped for a glimmer of sunshine.

The battered Morris soon rattled into view and he climbed in.

'New gloves?' he asked.

'Yes. Cold this morning. Should have sold these really and got some winter clothing coupons for them.'

'You knit those yourself?'

'Yes, all the girls do,' she said, pulling out into the road. 'They pay us too, a pair of Fair Isle mittens fetches three and six on the mainland. But my hands were cold, and they were such a lot of work I decided to keep this pair.'

'You know I'm going out on the Bus again tomorrow.' The fact he might not survive it was always the unspoken dialogue in both their thoughts.

'Yes. You got your instructions?'

'Larsen's a stickler, but he generally just lets us get on with it. He's not stuffy at all, is he?'

'He's learnt that letting Norwegians save their country their way, is by far the best policy.'

The drive took a while, and they drove without speaking. It was as if his imminent departure had made all other conversation irrelevant. He looked down at Morag's legs and her feet on the brake and the accelerator, and thought how much he'd like to put a hand on her knee. Did he dare?

In the end he didn't. He just watched as the squall of rain got nearer and the rain battered the windows. When they got to the loch, the sideways wind and rain that Shetland was so famous for had truly arrived, and they were reduced to sitting in the car watching grey runnels of rain obscure the view.

'D'you want to hear the legend of the loch?' she said.

'Is it cheerful?'

'Not particularly. But it's got a Norwegian girl in it.'

'Go on then, I'll risk it.'

'It's named after a Norwegian girl called Geirhilda. She drowned here whilst ice skating on the loch, in 870 AD. Her father was a legendary raven master, Floki of the Ravens. She was buried on that holm over there.'

He peered through the rain. 'What holm?'

'Sorry. This wasn't quite what I planned. I imagined it would be frosty and sunny and we'd have a lovely picnic in a scenic spot. I wanted you to have a glorious view on your last day, in case...' She paused. 'Guess Shetland had other ideas.'

'It doesn't matter. I like the company here just fine.' She smiled, and did he imagine the blush? 'And I like our outings. I really look forward to them,' he said.

'Me too.' She was looking studiously away, but now he did put a hand on her thigh, just gently. She didn't move away. Instead, her Fair Isle-gloved hand moved to rest softly on top of his.

She turned to look at him, 'Jørgen, I —'

But it was too late. His other arm reached for her and he kissed her slowly on the lips. The kiss lasted a long time and she didn't pull away. The last time he'd kissed anyone, it had been Astrid. At the thought of her he drew back, feeling immediately guilty. 'Sorry,' he said. 'I got carried away.'

'No, don't apologize,' she said, flustered. 'I can't bear it.'

What couldn't she bear? But she had pulled open the door and run over to the side of the loch, where she was staring out in the rain, her hair whipping around her face.

Should he go after her? He didn't know. In the end he just climbed out of the car, and stood in the rain waiting. After a few moments she came back.

'What terrible weather,' she said, smiling. Though he could see she was tearful.

'Morag!'

But she was already jumping into the car and starting the engine. 'I tell you what,' she said, not meeting his eye, 'we'll go back to the Mission, get a nice hot cup of tea, and eat our sandwiches there.'

'Good idea,' he said, though really he thought it a terrible idea. The Mission was always full of other people coming and going and he'd wanted time with her alone, especially if he was to go on another trip to Norway.

As they drove back, Morag didn't speak, except to point out a sheep that had strayed, and to call out when there was a pothole in the track. He could feel unspoken words as if they were solid inside the car, so that when they got out at the Mission, it was actually a relief.

Morag seemed to feel it too, for after stripping off her wet coat and gloves, she hurried on ahead and busied herself with tea. Seeing her doing that made up his mind. He definitely wanted more with Morag. It was only after they'd sat down that he decided to get it out in the open and broach the subject of Astrid, and tell Morag that he would write to Astrid and tell her he'd met someone else.

He was about to speak when a familiar voice interrupted them. 'Wet out there, was it?' Karl asked. 'You look like drowned rats.'

Blast the man. Karl sat down next to Morag, who smiled politely at him. 'How's the painting going?' she asked. 'Is the waterline finished?'

'No, but I went to see Harcourt about getting on the next run. All this waiting about is getting to me.'

Jørgen raised his eyebrows. 'But only the other day you said you weren't bothered.'

'Well, I changed my mind.'

'What did Captain Harcourt say?' Morag asked.

'He'll think about it. Doesn't want to change the rota. Went on about getting the right people in teams, where we were best suited, blah blah blah.' Karl's foot was tapping up and down as if he couldn't sit still.

'I thought you and Harcourt were friends?'

'Old Hard-core? He's a bit of a bore. If I have to listen to him telling me how to play billiards again, I'll shove the cue where it hurts.'

Morag raised her eyebrows.

Karl turned to Jørgen. 'Don't see why you've got on the next run and I haven't. We arrived at the same time, after all.'

'What's the hurry? There'll be plenty of other boats going out after this one. You going back for any particular reason?'

'I'm bored kicking my heels here. I've never been one for sitting still, you know that. I like a bit of adventure. Can't stand to fill another box of ammo, knowing it will go on a boat back to Norway, when I can't. Put in a word for me, will you?'

'Won't do much good; I have no say in it. It's up to Larsen, or Harcourt, who crews which boat.'

'But a word from you might help. They seem to like you.'

That was rich, coming from him.

'Don't worry, we need every man we can get. Your time will come soon enough,' Morag said, obviously trying to smooth things over. 'Meanwhile, I'd just treat it as a holiday.'

Karl looked rattled, then stood up. 'I don't want a holiday. Are you driving back to Scalloway, Morag? Can I cadge a lift? I persuaded Haraldsen to bring me on the back of his motorbike, but he's gone back already, and I promised Larsen I'd only be gone an hour.'

'Of course,' Morag said, putting her cup back in the saucer, and starting to pick up her things.

Just then, Harcourt came out of his office. 'Ah, Nystrøm. Just the man. I was going to ask you to come in. Some last minute instructions. Can you come in now?'

Jørgen hesitated. What last minute instructions? He didn't want to let Morag go without talking to her again, and he wanted even less to let her drive away with Karl Brevik. But Harcourt was waiting, and he was his superior, so he just said, 'Right,' and tried to catch Morag's eye.

Morag had started to put her coat back on. With annoyance Jørgen saw Karl hold it out for her to help her get her arm into the sleeve. He cursed his luck. Karl's smug face was the last thing Jørgen saw before he was obliged to follow Harcourt into his office.

CHAPTER 27

'We've had advance warning from a contact in the Milorg,' Harcourt said. 'Another agent needs picking up urgently. You'll have some sympathy for him, he's another W/T op. Got into some sort of trouble. Shot in the foot and needs to get out and get to medical treatment as soon as possible. We thought you might like to skipper this one.'

'Thank you very much, sir.' Jørgen was flabbergasted. Harcourt must trust him after all.

'The other news is; Nazis are deporting all the Jews from Norway. Most of them have been taken to Berg and Falstad concentration camps. From there, we think they'll probably transport them by ship to camps in Nazi-occupied territories.' He paused, sucked on his empty pipe. 'The routes to Sweden are clogged, so some are trying the Northern route. There's a woman refugee with a child, escorting a Jew who'd had to leave in a hurry. They're on their way to Ålesund. One of the Milorg has dropped them off within fifty miles of Ålesund, and they're going by foot the rest of the way.'

'So what do you want me to do?'

'Better prepare the boat for extra passengers. Larsen suggested we could cut through the bulkhead and into the fish store to make extra room. But there's something else...' He smiled. 'Another reason we thought you might like to skipper this one. The woman comes from your part of the world. She's from Oslo. Intelligence says you might know her. Papers say she's teacher called Astrid Dahl.'

'What?' Jørgen was so shocked he felt the blood drain to his feet.

'She and her daughter have been escorted via the Milorg to the coast and they need to get out urgently. She's on her way now. She was part of some sort of teacher protest.'

'A daughter?' Now he was flummoxed. 'Is this the Astrid Dahl that was a teacher at Ullsborg Elementary School?'

'I believe so, if our information is correct.'

It could be a false name. But what were the chances of two Astrid Dahls, both teachers from Oslo? 'There can't be a daughter, if it's the same woman.'

'Maybe the daughter belongs to the man. He could be on false papers. A Jew under threat of being transported to Poland. Maybe he thinks the girl might do better without the J on her papers.'

That would be just like Astrid, to think of the child. Jørgen was sheepish a moment. 'Thanks for letting me know about the new passengers. If it is the Astrid I know, you're right, I'd like to be there to meet her myself.'

Harcourt smiled. 'That's what I thought. We discussed it, Larsen and I. He wasn't keen. Thought it might compromise the safety of the crew if you had too much vested interest in the passengers. I spoke up for you though, said you'd been out on a few, that you weren't a risk-taker, and I knew you'd keep your head. So you mustn't let me down, okay?'

'Thank you. I won't.'

'I've got the list here of what Milorg and Sivorg want us to take over to Norway this time. It's quite a list.' Harcourt held out a piece of lined paper torn from a notebook.

Jørgen took it, and stared at the scrawled pencil list, but he wasn't really reading it.

'Best get loaded tonight. You'll have to leave at first light. It sounds like they're in a pretty dangerous fix. Larsen's got it sorted — the civilians will be radio-ing them tonight, via their contact in Ålesund, at 21.45. They'll tell them exactly where the pick-up is, and how to get to Radøy. If it makes you feel better, you could listen in, make sure everything's in order?'

'I will, thank you.' Jørgen suddenly remembered Karl. 'Oh, and Brevik asked if I could put in a word for him. He's keen to get on a run.'

Harcourt rubbed his chin. 'So you two have finally resolved your differences.'

'We never had any differences,' Jørgen said.

Harcourt sucked on his empty pipe, and paced. 'We did take you seriously, you know,' he said eventually. 'We've maybe been too hard on Brevik, though. He seems to be completely above-board and he hasn't pushed to get on a boat until now, so it could be, we were just being over-cautious. And I have to say, we rather liked him being around the base, good for morale.'

He liked to play billiards with him, he meant. 'Anyway, he seems very keen to get on a sortie now,' Jørgen said.

'Yes, he asked me if he could crew on the next boat, but I'd already made the list. Maybe I can take Opheim off. And if you want Brevik on your crew, it's fine by me.'

'I think I've just got used to him, sir.' Jørgen wasn't thinking of Karl any more, his thoughts had sprung back to Astrid.

'I'll put him down for it then, you can leave it with me.'

Afterwards, Jørgen walked in a daze. Astrid was coming to Shetland. She'd actually be here on this shore in less than a week. But what was he to do about Morag?

Of course Morag had always known about Astrid, but neither of them ever thought she'd come here. Now he felt as if he was being torn in two. He'd have to choose, and he didn't know how. His stomach was churning at the thought of letting one of them down. But obviously he had to make sure Astrid got out of Norway. He'd heard of the teachers' strike on the World Service. It didn't seem like Astrid to get involved in any kind of protest, though.

He walked down to Moore's Stores, near the pier and the new slipway. He usually enjoyed browsing the shelves for what he needed — the rope cordage, the screws and nails, the paraffin for lamps, the tin mugs and tinned foodstuffs, wire and crystals for radios.

Today he walked aimlessly, seeing nothing, only Morag's face and then Astrid's face in his mind's eye. If Astrid was bringing Jews out, it would be dangerous. He was surprised at how he felt after all this time; that the tight knot in his chest still pulled when he pictured her face. Or was it the thought of what Astrid's sudden appearance would do to Morag?

He coped with the uncomfortable feelings inside by getting busy. He itched to set off right that minute, but Milorg's operations all demanded different things — sometimes grenades, or explosives for sabotage, sometimes transport, like a canoe, or a bicycle. Different orders, all for different agents or different operations. He pulled the list out of his pocket again.

Ammo was kept in another building, and this was where he went now. He'd intended to sort out the stores for the next run; the explosives in their special containers disguised to be like fish crates, and the paint drums filled with a secret compartment to hold guns. The fact that a woman and child would be on board the same boat that carried all of this weaponry seemed crazy.

Karl was already there packing oil drums with rifles.

'You owe me a pint,' Jørgen said to him. 'You've got yourself a run.'

Karl's face seemed to sag with relief. 'When?'

'Tomorrow, soon as it's dark.'

'God, that's quick. Where?'

'Ålesund. We're picking up an injured Milorg agent.'

Just at that moment the door opened and Morag came in.

'It's on then?' she asked, her eyes flicking to Jørgen's face. 'I saw them prepping the *Vidar* with a radio transmitter, so I guessed you'd be going out soon.'

'Tomorrow. We're picking up an agent from Ålesund,' Karl said. He turned to Jørgen. 'What did you say his name was?'

'You know they won't tell us,' Jørgen said. 'It'll be false, like always.' He felt his face heat up just at the thought of Astrid. To cover his embarrassment he passed Karl one of the new steel inserts they must fit in the oil drums.

Karl pulled down his welding mask but the blue light of the welding torch and the smell of burning metal was still not enough to distract Jørgen from the thought of Astrid, waiting somewhere in Norway, and Morag's searching expression.

'I just came to wish you luck,' Morag said shyly to him, over the roaring of the blow-torch.

'Thanks,' he said. He knew he should take her somewhere quiet, have chance for a kiss before he went, but the thought of Astrid meant he found himself frozen to the spot.

Morag stood a moment, disappointment etched into her face, before she took a deep breath. 'Safe journey, then,' she said, and waved, before turning sharply and going back out into the bluster.

He wanted to run after her, but he didn't. Instead, he turned back to his work, feeling like a complete heel.

Reaching for a welding mask, he pulled down the visor to shut out the world. He had to focus on the mission and on Astrid. It took a lot of effort to fit these false tubes inside the drums, load them, and then to seal them so the remainder could be filled with paint in case they were searched. When the day's chores were done, he and Karl got a lift back to the Mission and sought out Harris, the lieutenant that acted as Harcourt's aide and was the W/T officer.

Karl leaned casually against the door jamb to listen as the messages were put out. Harris the W/T officer removed his headphones, and turned to Jørgen. 'We intercepted one from the Germans early last week. It seems they were pursuing the agent, Nils, and managed to shoot him in the foot. That's why he wants out. You'd better take first aid stuff; bandages and morphine.'

Harris drew his notebook towards him. 'The other three might not make it to the rendezvous point in time. They're coming across country.'

'What other three?' Karl asked.

'The Sivorg teacher and the Jewish man. There's a child too,' Harris said.

Karl frowned and glared at Jørgen. 'A child? Did you know about this?'

Harris tapped his pencil on the desk. 'If the other three are not there by the time the boat lands, Harcourt says you'll have to return without them. We just can't risk the Nazis getting our agent. Too much sensitive information.'

Karl immediately headed out.

As Jørgen came out of the W/T office Karl was waiting for him. 'When were you going to tell me?' he said. 'I thought it was just a weapon drop. Everyone treats me as a second-class citizen just because I haven't trained at Drumintoul Lodge like the rest of you.'

'That's nonsense. You only decided you wanted to crew a few days ago. Harcourt's not like the Nazis; he doesn't force people to do things they don't want to do.'

Karl frowned. 'So who are we picking up?'

'A W/T op and three civilians, like Harris said.' He didn't tell him it was Astrid, or that knowing Astrid would be on board changed everything for him.

'Where will we be landing?' Karl asked.

'A small island called Radøy, off Saebo.'

Karl nodded, took out a notebook and wrote it down.

CHAPTER 28

Astrid slept well but woke early worrying about the distance they had to travel. After a meagre meal of rye bread with a sliver of yellow cheese, the farmer gave them maps, and supplied them with old wooden skis for Isaak and Sara. At first it was just cross-country skiing on the flat, and with a few mishaps they managed pretty well.

Isaak was amazed by the efficiency of skis, as opposed to walking. 'If it wasn't for the fact of the Nazis,' he said, his face pink and his eyes bright, 'I'd be quite enjoying this.'

'Look Pappa!' Sara shouted as she hurtled on ahead, arms going like windmills.

'Tell her to slow down,' Astrid said. 'She'll wear herself out!'

True enough, the initial euphoria soon wore off, and compared to Astrid the Feinbergs were slow movers. After a whole day on skis, their energy began to wane, and they grew breathless and tired.

At night they reached their contact, and could do nothing but collapse into the sleep.

The next day they passed through a network of isolated farm-houses and farming communes. The weather held out with only the occasional squall but it was still bitter, and their food rations were meagre for such hard work. Their new contact escorted them on skis to the next farmhouse in the chain. It was hard going, especially for Sara and Isaak who were unused to skiing.

'I've got muscles on my muscles,' Isaak said.

Mostly Astrid led, but sometimes Isaak got ahead, and she was moved to see him doggedly tramping on, head down to the wind, with Sara struggling after, still carrying her bump of a pack, close on his heels. The winter conditions were exhausting, and more than once they had to seek respite from the driving blizzards in a goatherd's hut.

That third night it was more than minus twenty in the mountains, so they skied onwards to keep warm; and slept the next day in a hut when they were less in danger of freezing to death. On a couple of occasions, well-meaning farmers who felt sorry for Sara would take them a few miles further by car or cart. Without Sara, they would have been left to just get on with it.

Having a child with them actually speeded, rather than slowed their progress, though Astrid was still counting the days.

'I'm worried Isaak,' she said. 'The boat will be setting off now and heading for Norway. It's a two day journey, and we've still got so far to go.'

'Let's look at that map again.'

They looked over the distance they had to cover. There were more hills and mountain passes to navigate. Isaak refolded the map without a word, but she saw his face. He thought it was impossible too, but like her he was too stubborn to give up.

'Let's get going,' he said.

Astrid grew more on edge as the time ticked away. They had only made up a half hour in the whole day, and she had a headache like a vice with the thought they might miss their passage to England. 'Four o'clock,' she said, prompting Isaak and Sara to ski on, when they were tiring.

'Don't keep telling us. I'll break that watch into pieces,' Isaak said. 'We're going as fast as we can.'

At one point Sara stumbled and he stopped, and he and Sara just slumped down where they were, in the snow, unpacking the last of their rations from the previous farm.

'Please, don't stop now,' Astrid said. 'We're behind, and we need to find our next contact before dark. We can't risk getting lost.'

'Just fifteen minutes. Sara needs to eat, and my legs need a break. That last uphill stretch was a killer.'

'Einar said we need to make Ålesund today by nightfall.'

'Fifteen minutes won't make any difference. Don't forget you've got much longer legs than Sara.'

'We can rest when we get there. We have to push on.'

'What were you? Some sort of a slave master in a previous life? No. You go on without us if you must.'

Astrid bit her lip, looked up the trail where it led uphill between pine and juniper. Of course she couldn't go without them, and he knew it. 'Sorry Isaak, it's just —'

'I know, I know. We have to make the boat.'

He unpacked the last of the bread and gave it to Sara who leaned up against him and stared at it listlessly. 'How much further, Pappa?'

'A bit more walking today, and then a bit more the next day,' Astrid said, trying to lighten the mood.

'I'm tired of it,' Sara said, voice trembling. 'I want to go home.'

Isaak put his arm around Sara, and a haunted look came into his eyes. Astrid guessed he was thinking the same. They all wanted to go home, but they couldn't. They were on this journey and had to stick it out to the end, wherever that was.

Astrid did not sit, but kept on her feet anxious to be moving again. After Sara had finished eating they trudged onwards, until finally they saw the spires of Ålesund in the distance.

Thank God. They'd make it to Ålesund before nightfall and they could spend a night with their contact there. Isaak consulted the map. Now they just had to go a few miles down a road instead of on the trail. She glanced up and down the road, her senses on high alert. Roads were a danger because of German traffic that might see them and stop them. She remembered Einar's warning to go around the checkpoint. It must be close now.

She looked at her watch again for the hundredth time, as an icy rain began to fall. Another half mile before they could turn off to the track heading for a small commune of farms lying on the outskirts of the town. From there their new contact would be able to take them down the fjord by boat.

They pressed on as the weather worsened and they had to bend their heads against a freezing shower of icy hail. The clatter of the hail was so penetrating none of them heard the sound of the engine until it was too late.

Astrid turned at the noise. A German truck was coming down the road towards them.

'Keep going,' Isaak said to Sara. To run would have looked more suspicious.

The truck drew up alongside and two men jumped down from the back. The tallest one, a man with red-rimmed eyes and a nose that looked chapped with cold, waved a pistol at Isaak. 'Where are you going?' he asked in Norwegian.

Isaak hesitated only a fraction before answering, 'My brother's in the town. He's a boatbuilder.'

'Papers?'

It was the moment they dreaded. Astrid slipped her hand into Sara's and squeezed it tight though the woollen mitten. Isaak gestured at her to get her Reisepass out, as they had arranged. Then he put the two passes together, hers on top, and handed them over. 'We weren't expecting such weather,' Isaak said. 'The train to Ålesund was cancelled.'

The man was looking at the papers whilst his friend stamped his feet and blew on his hands. 'You've walked from Oslo?'

'No.' Isaak laughed. 'From there to Dombås station, then to Andalsnes.'

'Why you ski, if you were travel by train?'

Astrid stepped forward, pretending to be aggrieved. 'His brother's farmstead is in the middle of nowhere, isn't it? And even with the train we would still have thirty miles to cover on foot. No-one has cars any more. I told Ove it was a stupid idea, this visit, and now look, the train won't go, and the weather's turned against us.'

'Where is this farm?' the German asked, narrowing his eyes.

'Volda,' Astrid said scathingly. 'A dead-end place if ever there was one.'

'Don't argue, Mamma,' Sara said. 'Please. You know I hate it.'

The German tilted his head down to Sara. 'Do you like your uncle? Are you looking forward to visiting him?'

'He's all right. But Aunt Hilde always bakes a cake when we come visit. And she lets me feed the chickens, and she's got a dog called Runa.'

A horn blast from the man in the truck. The other man waiting put a hand on his friend's arm. 'Come on, Norbert, it's foul out here. Let's not stand in the wet. They seem all right.'

The other man glanced at the papers again before handing them back and took out a notebook where he scribbled something down. 'All right, Herr Dahl. I've made a note of your names. Report to the Kommandant at Command Headquarters in Ålesund when you arrive and give him your address. He'll keep your papers during your stay. We need to know your place of residence. I'll make a note of the fact we've spoken to you. Heil Hitler.'

'Heil Hitler!' Sara replied with rather too much enthusiasm.

They men climbed back in the truck and drove away.

'A dog called Runa? And Aunt Hilde?' Isaak said to Sara accusingly. 'You don't have an Aunt Hilde.' He lifted her up and swung her around in a hug.

Astrid grinned. She'd underestimated Sara and her ability to read a situation even at ten years old. 'She was a star. Let's hope our contact has a cake and chickens, hey?'

'I just said the first thing that came into my head,' Sara said.

'Who knew I'd bred such a little liar?' Isaak replied. 'But don't try it on with me, will you?' He grinned and gave her a mock punch.

After a few minutes of studying the map again, they set off, into the bluster. Their tread was lighter now, they were giddy with the thrill of getting away with it.

Isaak hurried to catch up, and stopped Astrid with a hand on her shoulder. 'You were right, Astrid. I'm sorry. Having Sara on your pass was a good idea. I was just pig-headed before. Without you, we would have been much more suspicious, a man and a little girl, with no woman with them.'

'It's all right. You were worried, that's all.'

After another two hours walking they passed a small church where they stopped to drink some meltwater, before turning into a farm track deep in snow. There were compressions where a tractor must have gone, and it made it easier walking, though by now even Astrid was tiring, and dusk was upon them.

When the collection of farm buildings farm came into view Sara whooped.

'Let's find those chickens!' Astrid said.

'And the dog!' Sara said, excited.

Their exultation was short lived. When they reached the farm they found it deserted. Their knocking brought no-one. Astrid peered through the farmhouse window but there was no sign of life. 'But I saw tracks, from a tractor or a truck,' Astrid said. 'Maybe they've just gone out.' Her disappointment at their lack of welcome was a sharp ache in her chest. How would they get down the fjord now? The contact was supposed to take them by boat.

'Why don't you and Sara take shelter in that barn, and I'll take a recce?' Isaak said. He pushed on the door handle and it opened. 'Stay here.' With a warning glance, he disappeared into the blackness.

After about five minutes, he was outside again. 'The place has been thoroughly ransacked. Like a burglary. I don't like the look of it.' He set off again across the muddy yard towards the other outbuildings. She heard him call out, 'Hello?' but obviously he got no answer, because he continued to the second shed about fifty yards away.

Astrid took Sara under the dripping eaves of the barn which was a corrugated iron roof over a stack of hay bales and a half-used pile of wood. An axe was stuck in a big stump as if it had been recently used, but there was no sign of any animals. She could hear lowing in the distance though, and the frenzied bleating of goats.

About ten minutes later he was back, his face white and drawn. 'Bad news,' he said.

'Isn't there anyone there either?' Sara asked.

'Let me just talk to Miss Dahl a moment,' he said, drawing her out of Sara's earshot.

'What's the matter? Won't they let us stay?' Astrid asked.

'It's worse,' he whispered. 'He's dead.'

'Dead? How do you know?'

'His body is there, by the cowshed. He's been deliberately executed. You can see the bullet-holes in the wall. The blood. Everything.'

'My God. What shall we do?'

'We can't stay here. They might come back. It can only be the Germans. No Norwegian would do that.' He turned so Sara could not hear him whisper, 'They've left the body there to rot, not even given him a burial. The cows and goats are still in the barn over there. I threw in some hay and opened the door so they could get out to forage and get water.'

'What shall we do? Shall we tell someone?' As soon as she'd said the words she knew they were stupid words. There was no-one they could tell. No-one they could trust.

Isaak's face was grim. 'It could be because they found out about him sheltering people like us, in which case...'

'Pappa? What's happening?'

'We need to move on again,' he said.

'They killed him, didn't they?' Sara said. 'I heard you.'

'It's all right, darling,' he said, shushing her. 'It was a long time ago.'

'I don't want to stay here!'

He sighed. 'We can't go far tonight, we need shelter. The weather's turned against us and darkness is already setting in. Nothing's going to happen. We'll just get a few hours' sleep and move on in the morning when its light.'

Astrid agreed with Sara, though she could see they had few options now the wind and rain were battering on the roof. 'I don't know. This place gives me the creeps. But I suppose so, as long as one of us listens out for the sound of a car. Is there a fireplace? Wood?'

'Yes, but I don't think we should light a fire,' Isaak said. 'Someone might see it.'

Astrid sighed. 'Guess it's here in the barn then.'

'I'll take the flashlight and go and see if there's anything useful left in the house.'

Astrid helped to bed Sara down amongst the hay, and made up a story to help her sleep. That whispered conversation with her father was enough to give any child nightmares.

When Isaak returned he sat down close to her. 'I found this,' he said in a low voice. He opened his hand, and there was a pistol lying in it.

The sight of it startled her. 'Is it loaded?'

'Not yet. But I found bullets in the same place. Stuffed right down under the cushion of the sofa.'

'Whatever made you look there?' Astrid asked.

'I was looking for money,' he said sheepishly. 'My grandma used to keep her money there. She was scared of the Nazis taking it so she literally sat on it.'

'Is she still alive?'

'No. She died before they started sanctions against us in Germany. Before the beatings and the smashing of shops. Good thing, she would have been horrified.'

Astrid looked down at the gun. He was holding it gingerly as if it might bite. 'Have you ever fired a gun?'

'No. I'm going to load it though, so I'm just warning you I have it. I wouldn't use it unless it was desperate. It's just like … like insurance.'

'Is it supposed to make me feel safer, that you have a loaded gun? Because somehow it doesn't.'

'It's only in case they come back. And I don't know if I could use it. I'm probably a lousy shot.'

CHAPTER 29

Jørgen inhaled the salt breeze of the open sea. Out from Scalloway the wind was about thirty-five knots and there was a heavy swell. They were a crew of six, which included him and Karl, and experienced crew members, Lars, Johan, Dag and Sven. Two of them, Lars and Johan, had done this trip before, but Dag and Sven, bearded brothers from Bergen, were new to this particular route. They were all dressed in British naval uniform under their overalls. Supposedly this might help them, if captured by the Nazis.

He glanced over to where Karl was tying off a rope. He had his usual devil-may-care expression, but Jørgen was grateful for his muscle; he seemed to relish hauling the rear sail that gave the boat stability in the rough seas, and made the heavy work of loading barrels full of weapons look easy.

When a storm blew up, Jørgen had no more time to worry about Karl; he was too busy keeping control, and it took all his grit to contain his fear, and to give orders through the lash of salt-spray and wind. The pitching and rolling, though uncomfortable, didn't put him off course and the previous sorties had made him used to sailing without lights in the pitch black. They all knew that as they neared the Norwegian coast, any lights would draw the Nazi patrols like moths to a flame.

It wasn't until dusk on the third day, when the sea had finally settled to some sort of calm, that they approached Norway.

Two dark dots in the sky. At first he thought it was birds, but then realised it was two German planes in the distance. Henshels. 'Look,' he said to Karl.

Karl looked up, shielding his eyes as they came close and circled. He was remarkably unconcerned. 'Nothing to worry about. We'll just look like a fishing boat that's got a bit far out from the coast.'

Jørgen glanced around the deck. It did look just like a fishing boat. All the weapons were well out of sight, and they continued to chug in a north east direction, pushing along at about seven knots. Although Karl brushed it off, planes were a bad sign, and made Jørgen nervous. It must be obvious they hadn't come from the Nazi side of the ocean. He checked his gun, sealed in its waterproof pouch, and felt for his papers in his specially-made waterproof inside pocket. Couldn't be too careful. He repeated the telephone number of his contact, Dr Moen, in his head. Best try to remember it.

He ordered Lars to steer for the sound, as the darkness fell, keeping the engine tonking at low speed. The Norwegian coast, like a thin black line, seeped into view. They wouldn't land until full dark, though.

He took out a torch and squinted at the map for the co-ordinates of the small island of Radøy where they were to pick up the injured agent, Nils. He hoped Astrid would be waiting there too. What would it be like to see her again? His stomach lurched as he remembered Morag, and her disappointed expression when he left without searching her out. Below them the water poured by, deep and slick like black oil.

Karl suddenly appeared at his side. 'What's that?' he pointed.

'Where?'

'That! Looks like Germans.' He seemed genuinely shocked.

Damn. The grey silhouette of a German patrol boat. Right in their path. Jørgen ran to the bow for a better look, with Karl staggering after him as the boat pitched and rolled. Those planes must have been reconnaissance planes after all.

They couldn't risk sailing past the German boat in case the Nazis decided to search them. Jørgen glanced down at the crates on the deck. If the Germans searched under the fish, they'd find enough gelignite to blow up a town. Not to mention priming charges, fuses and grenades. 'We'll have to make landfall somewhere else,' he said, peering at the patrol boat through his binoculars.

'No,' Karl said, his tone brooking no argument. 'We have to keep to our course. To the landing point we agreed.'

The landing point. Astrid. Jørgen weighed it up. He suddenly realised what changing course would mean. It would be a disaster for Astrid if they changed the pick-up point. Not only had she already made her way more than fifty miles across country, and then more from Ålesund, but now they'd be asking her to go even further.

'What's up?' Lars shouted from the wheelhouse, seeing them both staring into the murky distance.

'Patrol boat,' Jørgen said.

'Shall I turn about?' Lars asked.

'No,' Karl insisted. 'We're just a fishing boat. They won't bother us, I'm sure.'

'A fishing boat full of arms and explosives,' Lars said, coming over to join them. 'Too risky. I vote we put out to sea again.'

'Don't be stupid. We have to land where we agreed,' Karl argued. His jaw was clenched, and he looked like he might punch Lars.

Jørgen baulked. But he didn't see an alternative. It would be madness to risk the lives of the men on board. Harcourt had trusted him to do the right thing.

'Skipper?' Lars had backed away from Karl who was glaring openly at him.

'Yes. Too big a risk. Turn about.' Jørgen forced the answer from his lips.

Lars hurried away and the boat veered sharpish, making a flume of wash. Karl let out an expletive. Within a few minutes the coast faded from sight.

Jørgen shook his head in frustration. Astrid was over there somewhere waiting, and now they were going past. A sick feeling made him lean over the rails and stare glumly into the heaving water. She'd have many more miles to walk, and he pitied the poor child caught up in all this. He took a deep breath. 'We'll have to try further up the coast,' he said, aiming for briskness. 'Karl, go to the cabin, tell Dag to try pick up a signal and radio a message to Milorg.'

Karl was staring back towards the patrol ship, his mouth in a hard line, but finally he went.

Jørgen went over to the wheelhouse to plot new co-ordinates. Lars brought the map over and they pored over it together, looking for somewhere not too far off course. 'Here,' Lars said, pointing. 'It's a small community, fishermen mostly. I've heard talk of it. Let's hope Dag gets through on the radio, or they have a post office where we can send a message.'

They spent another hour out of sight of land, before attempting to head to shore, but as the *Vidar* drew closer to the coast again, the grey hulk and antennae of an enormous German warship stiffened the hairs on the back of Jørgen's neck. This was unlike anything he'd seen on previous trips; every time they tried to land they were stymied. The Germans had certainly stepped up the defences since he last came over.

He was forced to turn the boat westwards, back out to sea, giving the warship a wide berth. Several hours later they steered for a small bay, Stortlfjord, where they hoped there were no German boats. Thank goodness Karl was still below, and nowhere in sight to object. He looked like he was about to punch Lars the last time they'd changed course.

Mountains rose behind the small collection of log houses gathered round the bay as they cut the engine so they could drift slowly in. Near the jetty more fishing boats like their own bobbed on the water.

Arriving well before dawn, their appearance brought out the local fishermen, who were unused to seeing strange boats in their waters and gathered on the shore in the gloom.

'Where's Karl got to?' Lars said, seeing his sleeping place empty.

'Don't know,' Jørgen said. 'Still below, I think. I'll go tell him to get ready to disembark.' He found him in the cabin, head down over the wireless operating equipment, tapping away. 'Where's Dag? What the hell are you doing?'

Karl's eyes flared in surprise. 'Keep your hair on. Thought I'd see if we could pick up a signal from Milorg to tell them we've changed landing point.'

'Where's Dag? You know no-one but Dag's allowed to use the radio. You're only allowed to make radio contact except under specific conditions; that's what the regulations are for. It's risky unless you know what you're doing.'

'Dag wasn't here, so I thought I'd better try. Relax. I couldn't get through, anyway.'

'Crap. Don't try it on with me, Karl. I saw you tapping in morse. The Germans could pick up our signal and intercept it.'

'Testing, that's all.' Karl kept his cool eyes on him, until Jørgen was forced to look away.

'Leave it to Dag, okay?' Jørgen had the uncomfortable feeling he'd lost some kind of battle, but he had no time to ponder it because Lars burst in through the door.

'That war boat. It's onto us!' he said.

267

'War boat?' Karl said. 'What war boat?'

Jørgen didn't reply. He shot to his feet and leapt to the door. Lars must be mistaken.

Karl was right behind him. 'Shit,' he said, plunging back inside the cabin.

Jørgen let him go, he'd got too many other things to worry about. Towards the harbour mouth, children were running excitedly towards the end of the spit. He squinted into the grey mist of the early morning light. The lumbering warship he'd seen by the coast was just coming in, manoeuvring slowly in the narrow channel. They hadn't escaped the notice of the patrol boat after all.

There was no way out. They'd probably search them, and the minute they did, they'd find the cargo, know who they were, and they'd all be dead meat. There'd be troops on that ship too. What should he do?

'Get the dinghy ready,' he yelled to Lars and Johan who were staring transfixed at the hulk that was even now blocking their escape, and moving inexorably closer. Where was Dag? He couldn't see him anywhere.

No time. Jørgen grabbed the plans and their papers and began stuffing them in the boiler. They'd have to destroy everything, or it would put the agent they were rescuing and the whole operation at risk, not to mention Astrid and her refugees. 'Johan, search the cabin, see if you can find Dag. And get anything that might be useful to the Germans and burn it.' Johan's vacant-eyed panic glued him to the deck. 'Go on, man!'

A quick glance to the stern. As he did, his fingers caught a flame in the boiler and he withdrew his hand with a gasp. The warship was growing closer. There wasn't time. Soon they'd be overrun by the German navy. He was going to lose the *Vidar*.

He had to get the men off. But there was no way he'd let their ammunition go to the Germans.

Better to give the enemy something else to think about. An idea was forming.

He ran to the bow to find Lars preparing the dinghy. 'It's no use. We'll have to blow her,' Jørgen said. 'Get the others and get them ready. If we time it right, we'll blast a hole in the warship, and sink her.'

He grabbed more packs of ammunition in their watertight skins and thrust them into his pockets, and zipped them. Everywhere men were running, passing on the plan. With fumbling fingers, Jørgen helped Lars to lay a fuse. Others were doing the same. Every second the warship grew larger and more ominous until now they could see men on deck.

'Where the hell's Karl?' Lars yelled.

'Still below,' Jørgen said. The minute he said it, he knew. Something was very wrong. A million possibilities fled through his mind. The image of him tapping away in morse. The way he'd appeared first of all in the mountain hut. And Dag was still missing.

'Leave him!' Jørgen yelled. 'There's no time.'

But just at that moment Karl appeared out of the cabin, and Johan grabbed him by the arm. Before Jørgen could stop him, Johan was garbling hurried instructions at Karl, 'Get off! The boat's going to blow!'

Karl's face drained of colour. 'Stop!' He ran over to where Jørgen and Lars were finishing laying the second fuse. 'No.' Karl grabbed his sleeve to yank him away.

Jørgen tried to shake him off, but Karl's face held a cold determination.

'First fuse is lit!' Johan yelled. 'Launch the dinghy.'

'Run!' Lars shouted.

Karl ran towards the dinghy. Jørgen lit the fuse and scurried after him, in a half-crouch.

A blast of machine gun fire from the warship. It came directly at them. There was no doubt at all that they were the target and the Germans meant business.

Jørgen dived for the ground. The first round caught Johan in its crossfire. He fell immediately. Sven followed in the next burst, toppling over into the icy water.

Karl stared back at the warship as if he couldn't believe it. Then his face seemed to clear and he scrambled to free the dinghy from its moorings. With one accord Jørgen, Karl and Lars heaved the dinghy over the side and almost fell into it. They began to row like crazy towards the shore, Jørgen and Karl rowing, Lars baling. A voice shouted in German through a loudhailer, but the gunfire kept coming and they kept on rowing.

The dinghy suddenly bucked as a huge wave swamped them, followed by a deep rumble then an ear-splitting bang. Jørgen ducked; covered his head. A splatter of debris rained down — chunks of engine, shards of the wheelhouse, lantern glass and twisted metal. Behind him, burning hatch covers and flaming oil barrels lit up the black water like torches. He glanced back.

Damn. The warship was still intact. Their boat, the *Vidar*, listed, engulfed in flames.

She'd blown too early. His plan had failed. The disappointment hit him like a punch.

'Bloody hell,' Lars said, cowering, his hands over his head as more splinters of wood rained down.

'Row,' shouted Jørgen, coming to his senses.

Panic mismatched their strokes and the water had a thin skin of ice. It made it hard going. The warship meanwhile had spotted the dinghy, and renewed its attack, a burst of staccato machine gun fire. The water seethed and jumped as if full of angry fish.

Water poured into the bottom of the dinghy. Lars slumped and fell, one arm flopping into the water.

'No use,' Karl shouted. 'Lars's been hit.'

They rowed on but it was obvious the boat would soon be underwater.

'Jump!' Karl yelled. With one accord, they leapt into the water, just as another burst of fire strafed the boat.

Jørgen couldn't think, just swam for all he was worth towards the nearest shore. He and Karl were towing the dinghy with Lars inside. The water was so cold his arms would hardly move, and he splashed frantically, feet churning as soon as they hit the stony bottom. He pushed ice floes aside with his bare hands, desperate to get to shore.

Another burst of fire peppered them with spray. Lars and the dinghy disappeared under the water in a cascade of water and blood. Jørgen floundered after him, but when he tried to drag the dinghy it was sinking fast.

'He's dead. You have to leave him,' Karl shouted.

Jørgen stood a moment in the shallows, looking at Lars, who was slumped back in the floating remains of the dinghy, arms dangling. He was absolutely still, eyes staring, his chest a mass of sodden red. Jørgen let the rope go. He hadn't the strength to pull the boat up anyway. He emerged panting and gasping for breath, but managed to stagger, slipping and sliding to the shelter of some rocks.

Karl was shouting at him, 'Come on!'

A few more rounds of fire spattered into the shore, but the warship couldn't get close enough through the shallow water and the shots fell short.

'They'll not get into the harbour; their draft's too deep,' Karl said, hauling Jørgen by one arm. 'Move, whilst we've got a start.'

'I can't feel my feet.'

'Come on, or we'll bloody freeze to death,' Karl said. 'Which way?'

'Up,' Jørgen gasped. 'Towards those trees.'

They scrambled up the slope, wet boots skidding on the snow and ice. Everything ached with cold. He couldn't think. Couldn't process any of it. He just needed to get dry, and soon. They'd die of hypothermia out here. He glanced back. His heart jerked. 'We've got company.'

Somehow the Germans had managed to launch a tender and get men off the ship and they were heading up the hill behind them. About eight men in uniform. The sight made Jørgen light-headed. He paused, breathless, near the summit to try get his pistol from its waterproof pouch, but his fingers were too cold to unzip the pouch.

One of the men aimed a rifle at them but the shot went wide.

'They don't seem to want to take prisoners,' Karl said through gritted teeth. He'd got his gun loaded and tried to pick off the first man of the first group of five that were gaining on them, but his hands were so unsteady it missed.

'No!' Jørgen yelled. 'Keep moving. Our only chance is to outrun them, if they gain distance on us, we're goners.'

They floundered from one hill to the next. Jørgen had no real idea of where they were going, he was just hoping to lose the men on their tail. A quick look back. The German warship was a huge grey island in the shallow water, the sky above it a haze of smoke. Debris and a slick of burning engine oil was all that was left of the *Vidar*.

Men were still climbing after them, like black flies against the white.

Uphill, they got ahead, until the Germans dropped back to just dots in the landscape. The next time they looked they were gone, but already the gloom was bringing cold and flurries of snow.

They stopped for a few moments to slap each other to try to bring the blood back to their frozen legs. Both were too cold to string together a coherent sentence. They staggered through the worsening weather, grateful it was covering their tracks. After a half hour they crested a hill in a blizzard and almost tumbled down hill until they saw another cove, where the dim silhouette of a group of farmhouses hugged the shore.

Without speaking, they held each other up whilst they tottered to the nearest and hammered on the door. A woman in a pinafore and cardigan opened the door and backed away.

'Norwegian,' Jørgen managed, almost falling indoors. 'Help us.'

She hurried away to fetch her husband who from the sound of splashing water, was in the back having a wash.

'You can't stay here,' he said, rubbing his arms with a towel. 'We heard the explosion, and shots from across the bay. If the Germans find you here we'll all be finished. I've a daughter to think of.'

'Please,' Karl said, his charm exhausted. 'Just a few hours, to get warm and dry, then we'll be on our way.'

The woman looked pleadingly at her husband. 'We have to, Thom. Or who will we be? Nazis like *them*.'

The last word was said with such venom, that the man sighed. 'You can have some of my clothes, and my son's. Then you must go, okay? I can't risk you here. The Germans have already been here once before, a few days ago, looking for someone. They searched every house. Marte, get them some dry things.'

The woman disappeared through another door while Jørgen and Karl crowded to the fire and slumped before it. The fire was small and smoky, and hardly made any difference to his frozen limbs. His feet were so cold he couldn't feel them at all.

'Telephone,' Karl stuttered. 'Have you a telephone?'

'No. The nearest is in Stortlefjord, a box down on the corner by the post office.'

The blonde daughter of about twelve appeared from her room, curious to see what was going on. But she was shy, and soon followed her mother into the bedroom, where he could hear them talking in low voices.

After a few minutes, Marte gestured them into a room where there were clothes laid out on the quilt; vests and shirts, two worn felted pullovers. She threw Karl the towel her husband had been using a few moments ago. 'There's no trousers; we can't spare them,' she said, 'but there are dry socks. Give me your trousers and boots, and I'll put them by the fire.'

'No, we'll keep them on,' Jørgen said. Nothing would be worse than the Nazis catching him with his trousers down. He peeled off his sodden overalls and uniform jacket and towelled himself vigorously before putting on the dry warm clothes. He took off his boots and chafed his feet, relieved to find they stung with pain. 'Feet okay, Karl?'

Karl was still rubbing at his with the towel. 'Blistered as hell.' He paused. 'God, we were lucky.'

'Lucky?' Jørgen kept his tone even. 'Yes, I suppose we were. Considering someone told the Germans exactly where to find us.'

Karl paused in his towelling.

'You told them where we were, didn't you?' Jørgen said. 'When you were using the radio. Bastard. Lars and the others would be alive, if it wasn't for you.'

'The Nazis double-crossed me. They promised there'd be someone to meet me, get me off safe.'

Jørgen went and stood over him. 'What happened to Dag?'

No answer.

Jorgen persisted. 'We lost five crew and a fortune's worth of explosives. It'll put the Milorg back months. And now every German in the country's on our tail.'

'So we're in the same situation then.'

'No. I'm fighting for Norway. Who the hell are you fighting for?'

'Put it this way, I'm not partisan,' Karl said. 'I have skills, and I'll supply them to the highest bidder.'

'You work with the Nazis for money?'

'Well why not? I can't think of any other reason I'd want to work with the bastards.' Karl smiled ruefully.

The sight of his smile filled Jørgen with anger. 'Five men are dead and you can still smile?' The gun in his pocket weighed heavy in his fingers.

'You going to shoot me?' Karl's eyes held a challenge.

Jørgen held his gaze. Why was it so difficult? He should do it. Karl was a traitor to Norway. He knew what was supposed to happen. But could he do it here, in cold blood? With Karl stripping off his wet clothes like that? 'No,' he said, grasping for practicalities. 'Firing a shot would be suicide. It would draw attention to us. Have the Nazis here in a heartbeat. Besides, it wouldn't be fair on these folk.'

Karl nodded. 'Not easy, is it? To kill in cold blood.' His tone was cool, conversational. 'What I wouldn't give for a smoke. D'you think these people have any cigarettes?'

'Wouldn't know.' Jørgen turned away from him, irritated that he was taking it so casually. 'I have to hand you in, Karl, you know that.'

'Why? Who to? You going to ring the police? There's nobody here. Besides, I can be useful to you. I know all about the operation at Falk's office, all about how they intercept your transmissions. I could be useful to you and those people in England — Harcourt, Larsen. You could convince them they all need my intelligence, they just don't know it yet. It's pretty obvious to me the Nazis round here aren't going to distinguish between one agent and the next. As far as they're concerned, we're both expendable.'

'Just like that. You'd change sides just like that?'

'If needs be. To be able to change is the ultimate freedom.'

'You're despicable.'

'No. Practical.' Karl slid on a dry sock. 'First law of survival. Keep yourself armed. The second law? Be prepared. But be prepared to change. Being married to any ideology leads to tyranny in the end.' He fixed Jørgen with pale unflinching eyes. 'You were going to kill me for yours.'

Jørgen felt the sting of those words. 'There's a third law.' Karl raised an eyebrow at him. 'Be careful what company you keep.'

'The company's your choice. Don't suppose either of us want to be best pals with the Nazis right now.'

Jørgen paced the room. Karl made him uncomfortable. He always had. He could never quite trust him. He was ruthless, hard to get a fix on. The combination of brutal honesty and hiddenness disturbing. He pulled a warm jersey on over his head. He'd get time to think of it once they were out of this mess. Once they'd found a way back to Shetland. He took a deep breath. First thing was to get as far away from the Nazis as possible. He threw Karl a look. 'You decent enough for female company now?'

'Yep. Except I look like I've wet myself in these sodden pants.' Karl's grin, with his perfect white teeth, was back now, but Jørgen knew him well enough now to be wary.

They returned to the fire to find Marte had made a hot drink of chicory coffee. Jørgen handed her the bundle of wet clothes. 'You'll have to burn these,' he said, 'once they're dry.'

She looked taken aback, and holding them gingerly, as if they might bite, she dropped them into the basket near the fire.

'Papa's jumper's too tight for that man.' The girl pointed at him, and giggled. She went to the tray and passed over the hot cups, before going to sit near the window where she could watch them from afar, like watching two animals in a zoo.

Jørgen was grateful for the heat of the cup on his fingers even if it was excruciating. He asked the fisherman to give them some sense of the best way to Radøy without going the way they'd come.

Karl frowned and whispered, 'There's no point in going there. We've got no boat, and if the injured agent's got any sense at all, he'll have gone into hiding by now.'

'We need to get out, and our best hope's someone from Shetland. If we can get a message to them. Besides, there's the civilians.'

'You're crazy. Everyone in bloody Norway must have heard that explosion. They probably think we're dead.' Karl gave Jørgen a long hard look. 'You'd risk your life for some random Jews?'

'It's not just them. Astrid's with them.'

'Astrid? Not the woman you were seeing?'

His silence was enough of an answer.

277

'So that's it. You bloody fool.' Karl sighed. 'Even if we get there, we couldn't do anything, with no boat. She might have been caught by now. Anything could have happened. And you want to risk your life for her? My vote is we go as far away from this area as we can, find a safe house, then try to get out via Sweden.'

The fisherman, Thom, who'd been looking at this exchange with discomfort, said to Marte, 'Fetch me the map, would you?'

They spread out the map out on the table and Jørgen pointed to the place they were to meet Astrid. At the same time, Karl pointed to the border to Sweden. The fisherman, obviously sensing he'd never get rid of them unless he came up with something stabbed a gnarled finger down on a dot about thirty miles inland.

'There,' he said, tapping another building. 'My brother's farm, *Hallstad*. He has two houses. One is not used … here. Go there, tell him I sent you. Thom Fredriksen.'

'Father! There's someone coming.' The girl was peering out from behind the blackout curtain.

Jørgen lurched to the window. Yes, men were coming up the valley.

Marte grabbed the basket of clothes and thrust everything in it into the fire. She prodded and poked at it, releasing clouds of black smoke.

'Hit me,' Thom said. Jørgen shook his head, not understanding. 'Punch me! It's the only way. You might save my life.'

Karl drew back his fist and hit him square in the nose. Blood began to pour.

'Now go, quick, get out. The back way!' Thom shouted, through dripping fingers.

Out through the door, back into the freeze. Jørgen slithered down the slope towards the water with Karl skidding and sliding after him. They had no skis, no proper snowshoes for this kind of weather, but he knew from instinct that he was too tired to go back up towards the peaks. Their only hope was to go down to the shore, skirt the edge where they'd leave no tracks, then head across country to the safe house, *Hallestad*, that the family had suggested.

Urgent shouts in German. A quick look back to the farm showed the shadows of men moving. He realised now why Thom had wanted it to look like they'd hit him and forced him to help, rather than collaborated. It would go better for the family that way.

He stumbled on until they were at the shore where Karl waded in and headed inland up the fjord. Jørgen followed quelling the gasp as he went in. The water soon deepened and the banks got steeper, but Karl moved doggedly forward. When they were up to their thighs there was a sudden shot. It echoed around the valley. It was followed by an ominous silence.

Karl turned and shook his head. They both knew what it meant. He'd punched the farmer for nothing.

One more shot followed.

'Bastards,' Jørgen said.

'Only two,' Karl said. 'One of them lives.'

Perhaps the girl. Though what life she'd have now, he didn't know. Jørgen gritted his teeth and ploughed on.

On the hill above them they caught glimpses of the helmets and silhouettes of men searching, until after about a quarter mile, they hauled themselves out and headed for a forest where their tracks would be less visible. For the second time, they were soaked, but thank goodness, though they had no coats, the upper parts of the body were dry.

The forest was thickly-wooded and gloomy as a tale from a Norse saga. They weaved their way between the trees until they were in deep darkness. Only the clouds of their breath stood out white against the trees.

'We lost them,' Karl said, teeth chattering.

'Best dry ourselves off and keep warm. They'll still be after us tomorrow, so I think we should rest if we can.'

They rubbed themselves dry with pine needles and debris from the forest floor.

'Agh. We look like tramps,' Karl said.

He was right. Unshaven, in the old farmer's clothes and with trousers covered in filth they would stand out anywhere as on the run. 'Best stay undercover as long as possible then,' Jørgen said. 'And I've been thinking; the farmer could've told them where we were going. We'd best make another plan.'

'We haven't got another plan,' Karl said.

'We do. You just don't want to look at it. I vote we try to get off the coast and get a boat back to Scotland. Here, we can't go anywhere. Every Nazi in the area will be looking for us.'

'No. If you won't vouch for me they'll give me a hard time in Scotland. It'll be a hanging trial.'

Jørgen turned and Karl's unblinking gaze met his own. He was right. The debt to Karl for his own life weighed on his shoulders. He sat down, and took off his boots again to dry his feet. 'Why the hell did you dig me out of that avalanche? If you're on the Nazi side you could have left me to die.'

'Instinct. I was digging before I knew what I was doing.' Karl sat down next to him. 'And without you I knew I'd have no mission.'

'What mission? Who set you up?'

'Falk of the Nazi Police. He offered ten thousand kroner for information from you about the Shetland Bus, if I could catch you up.'

'Sheesh.' Jørgen paused in tending his feet. 'I didn't know I was worth that much.'

'The Nazis ruined my prospects, so it was only right they should pay. Without the Olympics, my skills were worthless. No cigarette company would want me in a magazine smoking their brand now, would they? And I didn't want to go back to police work. What fool would continue to risk their life for a pat on the back and a commendation?'

'It didn't matter then that you were a traitor to Norway?'

'In sport you get used to it. Especially high-level sport, where fractions of a second make a difference. You get on the team most likely to win, and have to be hard-headed about not letting the other man beat you, even if it's a team mate. You get in the mind set where you're prepared to kill to be number one; that you'll do whatever it takes. It's ruthless. You can't be sentimental.'

'And you think loving your country is sentimental?'

'When it doesn't serve your interests, yes. Like you thinking about that girl, instead of how we'll get to Sweden.'

Jørgen shook his head. For when Karl had said 'that girl,' it wasn't Astrid's face that came immediately to mind, but Morag's. 'I'm not,' he said, thrusting the disturbing thoughts away. 'But going to a hideout that might have been compromised is not the brightest idea.'

'What then?'

Jørgen felt bad about Astrid, about leaving her to try to get off the islands herself. He didn't want to let her down. 'We try to get across to the other side of the fjord and make our way to the coast from there. Even if we got to *Hallstad*, we couldn't stay there for ever, we'd have to make a move to get out of Norway. Why go inland, just to come out again?'

'And how are we supposed to cross the fjord? Swim? It's a half-mile across. You felt the temperature of that water. We'd freeze to death before we got there. Which is why we'd better share some body warmth if we're not going to die out here tonight.' Karl shuffled over to Jørgen and began to rub his back with vigorous strokes. 'Go on, do mine.'

Jørgen rubbed at Karl's arms and back, trying to get some heat through friction. All talk ceased as they tried to get warm. Later, he put his boots back on and found some dry branches for them to lie on as a sort of bed. They huddled together, Karl's chest against Jørgen's back. He was so quiet, Jørgen wondered if he'd fallen asleep. 'Karl?'

'I've been thinking. I've had a better idea.' Karl's voice was close to his ear. 'We go back to the village. Try to use the phone. I'll contact my man in Oslo. Sveitfører Falk.' Jørgen sat up. 'Maybe something went wrong. We were in the wrong place after all, weren't we? Maybe they didn't know I was on the boat. He owes me, and I'm going to make sure I get paid.'

'Go back there? You can't be serious. It's crawling with Germans.'

'They're searching for us out here, they won't think we'd go back. Here's the deal. We cover each other whilst we make the calls. I'll contact my quisling friends in the police, you can contact your friends in the Milorg. Neither of us tells on the other.'

'No. You're nuts.' Was Karl serious? Could they be on opposite sides of the war, but still co-operate? He'd never trusted Karl Brevik, and yet they had a kind of uneasy alliance, born of shared experience and narrow escapes from death. And only two minutes ago they'd been lying side by side.

Karl was staring at him in that half-amused way he often had. 'Well, I'm going to head for the phone as soon as there's enough light to move, so it looks like we'll be going separately from now on.'

Morag was standing back from the harbour wall at Scalloway, looking out to sea. The *Vidar* had failed to make contact last night, and there'd been no word from them. It often happened, she knew, but she had never felt this way about any of the crew before.

What was it about Jørgen Nystrøm that she found so fascinating? Partly it was the fact that he said so little. He was not a man to wear his heart on his sleeve, and yet she felt some sort of inner connection with him. She had from the start, to be honest. The awkwardness between them was because it was something so fragile, she feared it could be easily broken, and she didn't want to risk that.

She watched the waves crash in, in billows of spray. A rough sea. That too made her anxious. How many other Shetland women had stood right here, shawls wrapped around their shoulders? All through the generations, women with this same fear in their bones, staring out to sea, unable to do anything but pray and wait for their men to return.

Only now at least, there was radio. She drove up to the Mission and knocked on the door of Harcourt's office. Harris was in there smoking a cigarette and reading a newspaper. She wondered how he could be so calm. 'Any news of the *Vidar*?'

'No. Expect they've been caught in a storm. Bad news for the agent and the civilian refugees though. They'll be waiting a bit longer. And Harcourt just told me that Nystrøm knows one of the refugees personally. A woman teacher.'

'Oh?' Her mouth was instantly dry. She hardly dare ask. 'What's her name?'

'Astrid Dahl. She's travelling with a Jewish refugee and a child.'

But Morag wasn't listening. Her heart felt as if it was being squeezed like a bellows. 'Let me know if you hear anything,' she said, and strode out.

Of course she'd known he had a girl in Norway. He'd never hidden it. But she hoped … well, she hoped his feelings for the other girl might wane. But now he was bringing her here, to Shetland. It stung, and the thought that maybe she'd made a fool of herself, hanging around waiting for him to kiss her goodbye.

She hurried out and jumped into the car. She set off, hardly caring where she was going. She pulled up in a lay-by, only to realise it was one of the places she'd stopped with Jørgen.

'Damn you to hell!' she shouted, thumping the steering wheel.

But the only answer was the keening of the seabirds on the cliffs.

CHAPTER 30

At the deserted farmhouse, Astrid was woken by howling wind and everything in the barn rattling or moving about. Gates clanged, buckets rolled around the yard, dirt and dust stung their eyes. The wind had whipped up from nowhere, and even Sara woke up.

'Let's get out of the wind!' Isaak shouted.

They were forced to venture inside the house to get out of the gale. The house smelt fetid and she heard the scurry of mice. Astrid tucked Sara up on the sofa whilst outside, the wind howled. She had never felt so low. What was she doing out here?

Isaak seemed to feel her mood. 'It's a foul place,' he said, 'but it's only one night. We'll survive it. Think of what lies ahead, on the other side of the sea.'

'I'm scared of the sea,' she said. 'I lost both my parents in a boat accident on the flat water of a fjord. What will it be like on moving water?'

He came to sit on the arm of the chair where she was hunched up, her knees pressed to her chest.

'I think of them often,' she said, 'of how it must feel to drown.'

'How old were you when they died?'

'Sara's age. My aunt brought me up after that. But I never really felt I belonged. They had two other children, and I was just ... well, different. I don't know any other Norwegian that's afraid of water.'

'Don't worry, the men who crew the boats will be experts,' he said. 'They wouldn't do it otherwise. For them it will be just another ride.' He put a comforting hand on her shoulder. 'And we will both be there with you. If Sara can do it, so can you. If I can learn to ski, then you getting on that boat should be a walk in the park.'

She looked up at him, at his concerned face, so thin and worried. She managed a smile. 'I'm just tired. I'll be all right. Finding the man dead like that, well, it just made me realise how expendable we all are. And how will we get to the meeting place? He was supposed to take us. We'll never get there in time now.'

'We will. Somehow. Don't give up now.'

Astrid woke when a hand shook her by the shoulder. 'Let's get out of here,' Isaak said. 'Now it's light, I can see the fjord.'

They emerged into a new world. The storm had passed and a sliver of sun sparkled on the fjord below. Astrid inhaled the freshness of the air as they hurried towards the water, giving the cowshed and its grisly scene a wide berth.

'Look! Our boat.' Sara ran ahead.

There was a small rowing boat moored there after all. Astrid eyed it with trepidation. The boat looked sound enough, despite the storm, and rocked on the water which was still slapping against the shore after yesterday's wind.

'Doesn't look so dangerous, does it?' Isaak said, searching her face. It looked very small, and the water very big. She swallowed her apprehension.

Sara was full of energy after a night's sleep and tried to skim stones across the rippling surface.

Astrid took a few moments to wash in the icy water at the fjord's edge, and Isaak shaved. Being unshaven was like a warning bell to the Nazis, so he had to make sure to do it every day.

'I'm glad you came with us,' Isaak said, wiping his razor on a cloth. 'It would have been much harder on my own. And Sara likes you. She always used to talk about Miss Dahl when she came home from school.'

'I like her too. She's a stalwart, isn't she? And cheeky with it. That business of Aunt Hilde and the dog. She's certainly got a vivid imagination.'

He grinned, and it lit up his face, and gave her a warm feeling in the pit of her stomach. She couldn't imagine doing this without him. His wiry toughness through the mountains had been impressive; for someone who wasn't Norwegian, he'd learned to ski quickly. And he was a good father, always thinking of Sara. But more than that, she felt she could trust him.

Together they loaded their packs and their skis onto the boat, and Isaak held her arm firmly as she climbed in. The feeling of being on unstable ground made her grip the seat tight as Isaak took up the oars. Sara had no qualms about the boat, and her confidence made Astrid relax a little.

The early morning sky was palest blue, with a thin veiling of cloud. Astrid was relieved to be leaving the farm, though guilty they could not do more for the corpse of the farmer they'd left behind. After last night's violent wind, today was such a contrast. Nothing stirred around them on the Hjørundfjord except the plash of the oars as they slid past the low-lying farms. By mid-morning, the water had settled to a smooth ripple as they glided between the rearing mountain peaks of the Sunnmøre Alps.

'The world is so beautiful,' she said.

'Until us humans come and mess it up,' he replied. 'Sitting here, it's hard to think such things as Nazis even exist.'

'What will we do if we don't get there in time for the boat?' She was still worrying.

He paused in his rowing. 'I don't know. I'm just going day by day. In one way, I'd just like to sit in this rowing boat forever and not have to think about tomorrow. The other half of me is telling me to row quicker.'

'Maybe I should shout to you like the Romans did to their galley slaves,' she said.

'Or you could take one oar,' he said wryly, 'instead of sitting there giving me advice.'

She made a face at him, but plucking up courage, moved gingerly to sit next to him on the bench.

'We'll make a sailor of you yet,' he said. 'Heave ho!'

Within a few minutes they had a rhythm going and were making better speed. He turned to her and smiled.

'How far?' she asked.

'I don't know; guess about five hours? According to the papers, our contact is in Sæbø, and we need to find Moen, the local doctor.'

And so the morning passed, in the splash of oars and occasional jump of a fish. The nearer they got to the end of the fjord, the more boats they saw. Both of them kept an eye open for anything that looked like a German boat, but at first they saw only lone fishermen. Sara put her head down on the bags and slept again, the rocking boat lulling her to sleep.

'Pappa,' Sara said, when she woke up, 'I need to pee.'

After another ten minutes or so, they saw a small pebbly shore with a rickety jetty. The place looked deserted.

'Five minutes then, just to stretch our legs,' Isaak said.

They pulled the boat ashore and Sara ran off into the brake of birch trees behind. When she came back she was calling,

'Look, Miss Dahl! I've found some bottles and tins. Someone's had a picnic!'

Astrid went over. 'Don't touch them, they could be dirty.'

The litter consisted of a few beer bottles, along with some German chocolate wrappers and cigarette packets. The thought of Germans nearby made Astrid uneasy, but even as she was thinking this the 'phut phut' of an engine made her hurry to Isaak's side.

'A patrol boat,' he said, grimly. 'And it looks like it's heading for here.'

'What shall we do?'

'Behave normally, like we've every right to be here.' He turned. 'Sara!' he said sharply. She came running. 'Get in the boat. But nice and slow, like we are just leaving after a day out.'

'Will I need to do acting again, Pappa?'

'Maybe. But I'd rather you just kept quiet, okay?'

The motorboat had turned in towards land. It was just two men, both in German uniform.

Astrid helped Sara climb into the boat whilst Isaak untied it from the large stone he'd used as an anchor. She clambered in after him and they took up the oars to take a few strokes.

The motorboat cut its engine. They pulled again on the oars.

'Hey!' called one of the Germans from the boat.

Isaak ignored it and continued to row.

'Halt! Or we shoot,' one of them said in Norwegian.

Isaak fixed Astrid with a look that clearly said they could do nothing, but she knew the safest way was to try to brazen it out.

They let the oars rest. 'Just do what we say,' she whispered to Sara.

Sara gave a frightened nod.

The boat cut its engine and drifted in towards them. It sat taller in the water than them, and one of the men leaned out to talk down to them.

'Can I help you?' Isaak asked in Norwegian.

The Germans raked their eyes over them, taking everything in. Astrid found she was gripping the seat so hard her nails dug into the wood.

'Sailing permit?' asked one of them.

'It's only a rowing boat,' Astrid said, smiling in what she hoped was a disarming way. 'We didn't think we needed one.'

'What are you doing here? Why is the child not at school?'

'She's been ill,' Astrid improvised. 'We thought a day out on the fjord in the fresh air might help her get better.'

'What's the matter with her?'

'Polio.' It was the first thing that came into her head. She saw Isaak's eyes flash in surprise. Sara took on a hang-dog expression.

The conversation between the two men continued in German. She was able to translate it, though Isaak obviously understood every word. 'What are they doing in "our place"?' asked the one who was behind the wheel. 'It's a long way from town.'

'Don't know, better look at their papers I suppose.'

The Germans told them to get out of the boat and have their papers ready. They did what was asked, wading back to shore through freezing water up to their knees. Sara's hand held onto hers in a tight grip.

When they were back on the beach, the taller of the two Germans, who had a small pinched mouth and receding chin, looked over their papers. It was only when the other shouted that they realised he'd dragged the boat ashore and had been going through their luggage.

The two Germans huddled over their belongings, obviously thinking it suspicious they had so much luggage for just a day out.

'You lied to us,' the taller one said. 'You don't need underwear for a day out.'

'What shall we do?' the shorter man asked.

The taller man was still pulling things from Astrid's bag. He pulled out a pair of panties and waved them. 'Hey, Kurt! Take a look at these. Fancy, eh?' He tossed them to his smaller friend, who let them fall on the ground. Astrid didn't like the way things were going. She started to move towards Sara, thinking to shield her from it.

'Leave off,' the short man said. 'Think I want to touch these from a dirty bitch like her?'

'She's not!' Sara's voice piped up in perfect German. 'Don't say those things about her!'

The tall man turned to her. '*Was?*'

Sara clammed up. She must have realised she shouldn't have spoken in German. Astrid put herself between the tall, thin-lipped man and Sara.

'So you speak German, eh?'

'No,' Astrid said in Norwegian. 'I mean ... a little. She learned it in school. *In der Schule.*'

'Out of the way.' He shoved her roughly aside.

'Look at this. Maps of the coast,' the short man waved the map aloft.

'All right, little girl. Tell me what you learnt in school.' The tall man loomed over Sara, but Sara said nothing. Her lips were pressed together. He suddenly swung around to Astrid and punched her hard in the face. She saw the fist coming but couldn't move in time. The shock was such that she crumpled instantly. Instinctively Sara crouched down, her hands over her head.

'Don't hit her!' Isaak shouted in Norwegian.

'Shall I hit your Mama again?' the man said to Sara in German, looming over her. 'Tell us where you came from this morning and where you're going.'

Sara was frozen where she was, huddled on the ground. She didn't answer. Isaak tried to move towards her but the smaller man brought out a gun and levelled it to Isaak's chest. 'One more move and you're dead.' He shouted to his friend, 'It's hopeless. She's not going to speak. What shall we do with them?'

'We'll have to take them in. They're refugees from somewhere. Could be Jews.'

'But there's no room in the boat, and then the Kommandant'll know we've been skiving.'

'We could fit two. One of them and the child.'

'And let one go?'

'Not much choice, have we? We should take the man and the woman. Someone would soon pick up the child.'

'No!' Isaak said in German. 'I'm not leaving without Sara. You could tow our boat. We'd come quietly.'

Sara leapt to her feet and rushed to her father's side. At the same time, face throbbing, Astrid stepped forward, 'I'll stay,' she begged. 'Let them go together.'

The taller man pushed her hard in the chest. 'Don't you tell us what to do.' She staggered back and tripped, landing heavily on her hip on the stony beach. 'You want to stay here, do you?' The man crouched over her. 'In that case, you'd better give me a good time.'

His eyes were mocking, enjoying the power he had over her. She tried to stand but he pressed her down thumping a heavy hand into her sternum. He said something in German she couldn't make out, but his expression told her it was a threat. A cold hand tugged up her skirt. This couldn't be happening.

Isaak's voice in German, 'Leave her alone!'

But the man's heavy weight was on top of her now, his belt buckle grinding her hip bone as he fumbled with his fly. Stones dug into her back, his breath stank of beer. Over his shoulder she saw Isaak, still as a statue, and the other German still pointing his gun at him.

Nothing she could do. Lie quiet. Pray it would soon be over. Cold, sharp fingers probed between her legs.

Isaak suddenly swung himself to face the German.

A deafening bang and the German staggered and fell.

Another loud crack. The man on top of her slumped and rolled.

What was happening?

She scrambled to her feet in time to see the other German clutching his stomach. His rifle had fallen from his grip. Hardly knowing what she was doing, Astrid ran and swept it up away from his reaching fingers. The weight of it in her hands felt cold and alien.

She swung it towards where her attacker had been, but he lay still, eyes open.

'It hit him in the back of the head,' Isaak said. His voice seemed strange; far away. 'He's dead.'

It was then she looked at Isaak's overcoat. There was a big blast hole in the front of it. The gun. It had been in his pocket.

'I shouldn't have done that,' he said, leaning over, vomiting onto the shingle.

She dropped the rifle down as she struggled to take hold of Sara who leapt up to cling to her like a monkey, legs wrapped around her waist, burying her head in her shoulder. The man on the ground was still groaning, clutching his stomach.

'Let's get out of here,' Isaak said.

'And leave him?' She was still in a world where you didn't leave injured people to fend for themselves.

'We haven't a choice. We certainly can't turn up at the local hospital with him in tow,' Isaak said.

'It seems…' She began to weep.

'Don't cry. I know it seems terrible. But we have to do it. For Sara's sake. For her future.'

Astrid let Sara down to the ground, and stifled her tears.

'Come on,' Isaak said again.

Astrid grasped Sara by the hand and pulled her towards the water.

'Not that way,' Isaak said. 'We'll take their motorboat. We've got more chance of making the rendezvous and if you keep low, people will just ignore it. It's a patrol boat, after all.'

'What about our luggage?'

'Grab what you can, but be quick. Someone might have heard the shots.'

A few moments later Astrid hoisted Sara into the motorboat. There was no time to think. Isaak took the wheel, pulled on the cord, and the motor sprang to life.

Once they were away from the shore another shot rang out. She looked back. The German with the injured stomach had crawled to the rifle and was now firing at them.

'Down!' She pulled Sara down into her seat as the boat sped off.

Nobody spoke for a long while. Isaak was concentrating on driving. From here, his head and shoulders were rigid, his white hands gripping the wheel. Astrid leaned forward to place a hand on his shoulder and he nearly jumped out of his skin.

'Only me,' she said. He slowed a little then, and seemed to exhale.

'Miss Dahl!' Sara said. She held out a packet. 'Food!'

Astrid turned back to see what she'd found. 'Looks like it's the Germans' lunch,' she said. 'They must have been going to eat it on the shore where we stopped.'

'Ugh.' Sara threw it overboard. 'I don't want anything they've touched.' Her lower lip quivered. 'Will they come after us?'

'I don't know.' She decided to be honest. 'When they don't turn up where they're supposed to be, I expect they'll send out a search party. But I hope we'll be long gone by then.'

Sara snuggled up to her and put her hands around her neck for a hug. Astrid put a hand on her head to stroke her hair. 'Your face looks funny,' Sara said, leaning back to look. 'Like you've got the mumps.'

They kept to the middle of the fjord, like the Germans did, and hoped no-one would stop them. They passed another German motorboat, but it paid them no attention, and after a brief moment of heart-stopping tension, they were able to continue down the fjord undetected.

Astrid glanced at her watch. Damn, it was broken. The glass had gone. She wondered when that had happened but couldn't be sure, and she didn't want to dwell on the day's events. The motorboat's engine ruled their speed, and she was grateful for its monotonous hum, which seemed to echo the numbness she felt. Her cheek throbbed. She reached up a hand to feel it, and felt the swelling's heat.

No-one stopped them and by the late afternoon they'd reached Sæbø. There was no-one about as they pulled up at a small jetty opposite a few turf-roofed wooden houses and a clinker-built general store. In the distance the spire of a white-painted church, by far the largest building in the village, jutted up over the houses. It was a picture of normality.

They went in the general store and there was a calendar hanging up behind the counter. November the 8th. They'd made it. But they still needed to get out to Radøy before the evening tide, and the sky was darkening and time was getting short. She wished her watch still worked.

'We are meeting Dr Moen's boat here,' she said.

The wrinkled store-keeper in his woollen hat looked at her swollen face and shook his head.

'The boat to Shetland?' she asked.

'No,' he said. 'No boat.'

Tears sprang to her eyes. 'We're too late?'

He must have realised her distress. 'You are refugees?'

'We need to get to Radøy, for the boat to England,' Isaak said. 'And it will leave without us if we don't get there by the evening tide.'

'Dr Moen telephoned earlier to say there's been trouble. Too many German patrol boats. He's delayed.'

'What time is it?' she asked.

'Half after six. He should have been here at four.'

She exchanged a look with Isaak. They were already late, but not by much. 'D'you think it will wait?'

'I don't know,' Isaak said. 'I don't know anything about tides.' His shoulders drooped, the scorch mark and hole in his coat reminded her of what this journey had already cost him. Like her, he was probably thinking it was a bitter blow to get this far, but fail at the last hurdle, through no fault of their own.

'Listen,' Sara said. 'An engine!' She ran to the door of the store.

'No! Come back,' Astrid shouted. 'It could be Germans.' She dived after her and dragged her back, hugging her hard against her chest.

The shopkeeper went to the door and a few minutes later he was back. 'It's the Doctor,' he said.

Dr Moen was weather-beaten and bearded, and an old sou'wester shadowed his face. He looked nothing like Astrid expected a doctor to look. The relay boat was a small fishing coble with a diesel engine but a mast and sail too. Nils, the agent who was to be picked up, was on board already. He had a bullet wound in his foot, well-bandaged. Like them, he'd obviously been in some sort of trouble with the Germans. He eyed them sympathetically but didn't speak. His foot was obviously causing pain as he kept wincing if he had to move.

As they loaded the bags aboard, Astrid overheard the doctor talking in whispers with one of the other fishermen. She tried to make out what he was saying. She heard whispers of 'Shetland' and 'explosion'.

She hurried over. 'What's happened to the boat?'

Moen sighed. 'We don't know yet. There's talk of a warship, and the *Vidar* being sunk, but we never know anything for certain. We've heard nothing from Jørgen Nystrøm, the skipper. It could be a different boat that sank, or anything.'

'Nystrøm?' Her heart had begun to thud hard in her chest. 'You don't mean Jørgen Nystrøm from Oslo? Has a scar on one eyebrow?'

'You know him?'

'I'm from Oslo too. We were…' she hesitated, 'friends.'

'Oh.' Dr Moen frowned in an embarrassed way, uncertain what to say.

Isaak came over to see what was going on.

'The boat's been in some sort of trouble,' she said, agitated. 'Nobody's sure what's happened yet, they're waiting for news.'

'Oh no. What will we do until we hear?' Isaak asked.

'Stay calm, sail to the island rendezvous at Radøy and wait for more instructions,' Dr Moen said. 'They'll be keen to get Nils off, and to hospital with that foot. We don't want gangrene to set in, and besides, he's a security risk.' He clapped Isaak on the shoulder. 'Fetch your lass aboard now, we'll be off again soon.'

Isaak went to fetch Sara, who was petting one of the skinny grey cats that lurked on the quay looking for scraps.

Dr Moen helped Sara aboard the fishing vessel and within the half-hour they set sail for the tiny island where they were to be picked up. Astrid couldn't stop thinking about Jørgen. It didn't seem possible that he'd actually come to fetch her. But the boat had had to go further up the coast for some reason. Now it was missing. She hoped he was all right.

'Astrid?' Isaak reached out a hand to press hers where it rested on the wooden crates where they were sitting.

'Sorry. Yes, I was miles away. I'm worried about the boat. I just found out a friend of mine was on it. They said there was an explosion.'

'A friend? From Scotland?'

'No. A Norwegian. Just a man I knew in Oslo.' His question made her feel immediately guilty.

Isaak was silent a moment. 'Sorry to hear about your friend. Let's hope it's all rumours and we'll know more soon. It's not unusual for people to go missing in action, and for them to turn up later.'

It was what people always said when they wanted to be a comfort.

CHAPTER 31

Dr Moen sailed them out to the island of Radøy, a tiny, rocky nub sticking out of the sea, and uninhabited except for two croft-like cottages. To Astrid's surprise, they weren't the first to arrive there. The little harbour bobbed with small craft, and one of the cottages was already full of people, the men who'd come to meet the Shetland Bus and take the weapons and armaments to distribution points all over Norway. They rushed out to see who was arriving and seemed disappointed it was only the doctor's small boat and not the boat from Scotland.

After Dr Moen left, Astrid, Isaak and Sara crowded into one of the cottages with the rest. Built from wood planks the house had a selection of benches and no other furniture. It was clearly not lived in, but only used as a staging post. Astrid asked one of the other men what had happened to the relief boat that was to take them to England. He shrugged and carried on smoking his pipe. He had no more news than the doctor. Her neck was so tight with tension, her head ached. She feared they'd be stuck on this tiny island now until the Germans caught up with them.

They were dozing when a boat finally did arrive. The men all started rushing about, getting their small craft ready.

They staggered out into the dark. Thank God, the boat was here at last, the sinking of it must have been just a rumour after all. They all hurried out in the wind to greet it. It was a fishing trawler, about seventy feet, like a huge black hulk. No lights on it, and it looked like it was built a hundred years ago.

When the crew came ashore, she searched their faces, but Jørgen wasn't there.

'Was Jørgen Nystrøm with you?' she asked one of them, a swarthy engineer called Nesse.

'Nystrøm? No. This is the *Bergholt*. He was on the *Vidar*. We're waiting for news of them.' He looked exhausted, and she didn't want to press him. One by one, the men came ashore, all bedraggled, unshaven and haggard.

'Bit of a rough night,' she overheard one of them say. 'One bastard of a storm. Wouldn't mind a drink if someone could find one.'

A fisherman from one of the small craft brought a bottle ashore and the men were soon passing it round.

'We've missed the evening tide, so we won't leave until the morning; when the tide turns,' the skipper said. Clausen, his name was; a rather well-spoken man with a clipped moustache. 'Suggest you go aboard and have a look around,' he said to Isaak. 'Take the kiddie, you'll find a berth for the three of you below.'

Astrid had the impression they wanted them out of the way, but she could think of no objection, so they went down to the jetty.

'I think they'll make a night of it,' Isaak said. 'Get roaring drunk.'

'In that case I'm glad we'll be somewhere else. Come on, Sara.'

But one look at the boat close to brought up all Astrid's old fear of the water. It was a wreck of a fishing boat, filthy, and stinking of fish. It didn't look as if it could go five yards, let alone right across the North Sea. Isaak's face showed he shared her opinion.

'We can't go on that,' she said. 'It doesn't look safe.'

'It came here from Shetland, so I suppose it must be seaworthy,' he said doubtfully. 'Anyway, we don't have a choice. It's big enough.' He turned to her with softness in his eyes. 'We can stay here, and be fodder for the German army, or take our chances. No other boat has come for us.'

A grizzled old fisherman who was standing nearby overheard, and said, 'She's a fine sturdy boat that one. She has to look that way. The worse she looks, the less likely the Germans are to think she can make her way to Shetland. If I were you, I'd thank your lucky stars there's men willing to risk their lives to get you out.'

'I dare say you're right,' Astrid said. 'We're just tired and anxious.'

'Not as tired and anxious as those men who've just been out in a force ten gale,' he said, and strode off.

'Come on, it might not be as bad as it looks,' Isaak said, climbing aboard, helping Sara up, and then holding out a hand to her.

She took his hand, and the warmth of his grip helped the cramping feeling in her heart ease a little. Once aboard, they found a lantern and matches and groped their way down into a cabin that had been partitioned off from what looked like a store room. Portholes gave small pinholes to the dark outside.

Sara screwed up her nose. 'Stinks.'

'It's only for a few nights,' Astrid said, lighting the lamp, and turning it low. 'Let's make our own little den here. Like trolls underground.'

'Trolls are for babies,' Sara said.

But fortunately, someone on Shetland had sawn a hole in the bulkhead, and made a hole through to the fish hold, and there were some hammocks hanging there. Sara was soon thrilled by this exciting discovery, though Astrid suspected these were for the men and not for them.

Sara was soon swinging there in a string hammock, as Isaak unpacked some blankets and set out their bags as pillows in the cabin. It was the first time she'd slept so close to Isaak and it made her feel a little awkward. It didn't seem to bother him though, and he was soon asleep. After a while, Sara tired of swinging and came to snuggle in between them.

Despite her ever-present anxiety, Isaak's proximity was comforting and she managed a little sleep, but she woke imagining Jørgen, somewhere out at sea. The ferocity of the wind on the dead man's farm made her wonder if he'd been caught in it, wherever he was. She kept hoping his boat would appear, that his familiar face would appear at the door. By the morning there was no sign of the *Vidar* still, and the crew were getting ready to depart in a big hurry.

'Why the sudden rush?' she asked Nesse.

'The Germans are onto us,' he said. 'Some bastard has told the quisling police they saw a limping man go into one of the houses in Bremnes. That was probably Nils. Bloody informers. And to make it worse, someone shot two German patrolmen on the fjord. So now they're sending German patrols to the coast to look for places the perpetrators might get away.'

Blood pounded in her head. The Nazis were after them. 'Will they catch up with us?'

'Not if we can help it. Their boats are only an hour or two away. We need to be gone by the time they arrive.'

Nils, the agent was helped to board, though by the reek of him, he needed help because he had a hangover, rather than because of his injury. She wanted to scream at them to hurry, but she could see they were going as quick as they could.

Clausen, very stiff and correct despite his fisherman's jersey, came down to brief them all. It irritated her that most of his instructions were conveyed to the agent Nils, rather than to them, but she listened anyway. Isaak likewise was giving him his whole attention. Their lives might depend on it.

'You must stay indoors at all times,' Clausen said. 'We are a fishing vessel, and that pretence has to continue. If anyone sees a woman or a child on deck, there will immediately be suspicion. Most Norwegian sailors are for the King, but some are not, and the last thing we want is some quisling alerting the Germans. The weather forecast is for gales, and the journey may be uncomfortable, but I ask you still, remain out of sight.'

'Okay,' Nils said, wincing with pain, 'we get it.'

A crewman called Mathison, a burly Shetlander was in charge of stores, and he supervised the loading of the cabin with empty oil drums and crates. The cramped space was soon filled with the stench of paint and tar. They crammed themselves in around it as best they could.

'Talk about sardines,' Isaak said.

Sara huddled under a shelf holding tight to Astrid, and endearingly, Isaak positioned himself close by, on the outside, to shield them.

'Don't worry,' he said. 'We've got this far. Soon we'll be in Scotland. And we'll be safe.'

'But if we're in Scotland, how will Mamma find us?' Sara asked.

'I expect she'll come and find us later if he can.' He looked to Astrid with a resigned expression, and she suddenly grasped how hard it must have been for him. His whole journey, the rejection of him by his wife, his country, and now even his adopted home. It didn't seem fair. And now Sara was asking for her mother, who had done nothing to keep her safe at all these last five years.

They finally set to sea from Radøy just before midnight. The sky was dark, but roiling clouds obscured any stars. Already the wind was stinging, and they hadn't gone very far from land when the boat began to pitch and things inside the cabin started to slide and shift about. Nils struggled to lash everything down as best he could.

Sara was sick over Isaak's shirt, and as Astrid was trying to comfort her and clean up, the door opened, banging hard as the boat pitched.

'Take these,' Clausen yelled over the noise of the increasing wind, and he began to thrust piles of weapons down through the hatch — rifles, machine guns. Nils grabbed them as they came in and he and Isaak tied them in bundles to stop them moving about. Salt water slashed in through the door in icy sheets. From the tiny square windows all Astrid could see were heaving mountains of water.

The howl of the wind and the crash of the sea were deafening.

'Here, tie these down,' Nils shouted. 'Decks are flooded … don't want to lose anything overboard.' His instruction kept a lid on Astrid's terror, but only just.

Night passed. The boat heaved on the waves. Icy water washed in every time the door to the deck opened. Astrid was too sick to do anything except cling to the nearest beam and pray for it to end. When the sea finally settled into just a rock, and a pale grey dawn lit the porthole windows, Nils hauled himself up the few stairs and stuck his head up out onto deck.

'Are we nearly there, yet?' Sara whimpered, her face blueish-white.

Nils ducked his head back inside. 'Bad news, I'm afraid. Gundersen in the charthouse says the storm blew us off course back towards the coast. We've covered less than fifty miles, and we're only just out of Norwegian waters.'

Isaak groaned. The sound was the one Astrid wanted to make, had she been able to speak without vomiting.

A low drone. 'I'll go and see,' Nils said, hobbling to the door and throwing it open to reveal a view of grey sky.

The plane came from nowhere. A black shape. A burst of gunfire.

Astrid ducked down and covered her head with her hands.

'Pass the rifles!' Mathison yelled.

She and Isaak scrambled to untie them. So the Germans hadn't given up trying to find them. They were sitting ducks for planes, this small dot on the open sea. And worse, the storm had left them unprepared. Unprepared and unarmed.

As the drone of the aircraft engine faded, the crew dashed in and out of the cabin as they dragged out rifles.

'The Brens!' Clausen yelled. 'Get the Brens!'

The door was open, so Astrid could see Mathison bolting a machine gun onto detachable mountings on deck. Despite his injuries, Nils was half-crouched, holding something steady in the spray as the boat turned hard to starboard.

In the distance the speck of black in the sky turned. My God, it was coming back. The door was still yawning open. 'Get down,' Astrid screeched to Sara.

Isaak huddled over Sara, and dragged Astrid in beside him, cowering into the small space left by the luggage. The plane's engine drew nearer, a horrible rattling hum.

There was another deafening splatter of machine gun fire, but this time from on board. Nesse the engineer was manning the gun but in the confusion it blasted holes in their own mast, not the enemy.

Unscathed, the plane banked and turned. Through the small square of window, Astrid couldn't take her eyes off it as it dived low, bearing down like a wasp. Flashes spat from it, as the boat juddered and heeled. Splinters of wood flew from the door and bullets embedded themselves in the bulwark behind.

'*Scheiss!*' Isaak cried, dragging them both further into the darkest corner, out of range of the door. The German word. He was being shot at by his own people.

The plane veered away, but the next time it came around the rat-a-tat of bullets was insistent, an assault on the eardrums, needles spattering the deck. They gripped each other, praying for it to end.

Then silence, as the plane engine drew away.

No sound from the deck above. What if the skipper had died? What if there was nobody left alive on deck? They'd be floating there with no idea how to get anywhere. Where was Nils?

Astrid scrambled out, to see the deck riddled with holes and the wheelhouse splintered into matchwood.

Nils was flat out on deck, his shoulders and back of his head torn by bullets and shrapnel. Water sloshed back and forth around him as if he'd drowned and been washed up.

'You okay?' Clausen appeared.

She nodded dumbly, then burst into tears. She was so relieved there was someone left alive who could steer the boat.

'The others?' He put a firm hand on her shoulder.

'All okay,' she said, sniffing and wiping her wet face.

'Then go back below. We've a lot of mess to sort out, and we don't know if they'll come back with reinforcements.'

She stumbled back inside. Isaak's face asked a silent question.

'Nils got hit,' she said. 'He's...' She shook her head and he seemed to understand.

A few moments later and Clausen and Nesse staggered inside, carrying another of the crew, Mathison, who'd been hit on the right side of the chest and had shrapnel wounds to his legs. His trousers were in shreds, torn by splinters of wood.

Astrid shifted their bags to make space for him to lie down. Isaak had a shirt in his, and got Sara, who was silent and white-faced, to tear it up to make cloths to staunch the wounds. It was hopeless, for the boat was still rolling, and trying to pick out the shrapnel caused Mathison too much pain. Astrid took hold of Sara's hand, which was icy cold, and squeezed it.

'How much blood does a man have inside him?' Sara asked, in a whisper.

'Oh, I don't know ... lots,' Astrid answered, looking to Isaak for help.

'How much of it has come out?' Sara asked, wide-eyed.

'Not too much,' Isaak said. 'But we have to look after him until we get to Scotland.'

'Will they take him to hospital in Scotland?'

'I expect so,' Astrid said. Actually, she had no idea if there was even a doctor in Shetland, let alone a hospital. And Mathison was pale and sweating now. She must get some pain killers. Surely they had a first aid kit? Something?

She hurried up out of the cabin just in time to see the men heaving a canvas-wrapped bundle over the side. It stopped her in her tracks.

The men had taken off their hats. They were consigning Nils' body to the sea. It made her wonder, with a tearing ache, what had happened to Jørgen. She understood now the peril of his journey across these northern waters, where you were a plaything for German planes.

She glanced at the lifeboat and sent up another prayer. It was full of shell-holes.

When the men had finished, she went up to Clausen. 'Mathison's in a bad way,' she said. 'Haven't you anything in your supplies that will dull the pain?'

'Oh, sorry. That was stupid of me,' he said, as if this was a normal day and a normal request. 'Of course we have. First Aid kit. It's in the chart room. I'll fetch it, I should have thought of it before, it's just...' He gestured round at the wrecked wheelhouse and splintered mast and sails. He hurried away, but she saw he was bleeding, from a wound in the back of his arm, where, judging by the holes in his oilskin, a bullet must have passed through.

She looked up at the sky. It was quiet now, just cloud rolling and unfurling in shades of grey. Behind the boat, darker streaks showed rain. A three hundred and sixty degree view of grey swelling water with no land in sight. She clung to the side-rail which was gritty with salt, and scanned all around for any sign of a returning plane, but none came. Not even a bird was in view. The only sound was the tapping of a hammer. One of the crew nailing something back together.

'Here,' Clausen passed over a wooden case with a big red cross painted on it.

'If you come into the cabin, we can fix up your arm,' she said.

He looked from one arm to the other. 'Have I been hit?' He found the injury, and shrugged. 'Didn't know. Do your best for Mathison. He's a good man, and this is his tenth trip, you know.'

Tenth trip. God. She nodded and headed to the cabin, with new respect for Mathison, and Jørgen, and all these men who risked their lives for Resistance men and refugees like them.

Mathison didn't last the night. Sara was inconsolable. She seemed to think it was her fault, that she hadn't 'nursed' him well enough. The men didn't bury Mathison at sea, because he was a Shetland man, and they knew he'd want to be buried in his native soil. The seas were heavy again as the battered boat limped in towards Sumburgh Head, in the Shetland Islands, two men fewer. In the darkness Astrid could barely see the land but grabbed Isaak by the arm and they all went up on deck to cheer.

Sara was desperate to get off the boat and onto dry land, but Clausen refused to let them go ashore.

'No, we'll heave-to, and put into Lerwick at first light,' he said.

So Astrid had to be content with another uncomfortable night of damp and salt, and cramp and cold, with the body of Mathison under its stone coloured tarpaulin. Sara soon fell asleep, but she and Isaak talked long into the night, reliving the journey, as if they couldn't believe all that had befallen them.

'I can't believe we're here, that no-one will fire at us,' she said. 'Will you try to make a home in Shetland?'

'I don't know,' he said. 'I hadn't thought that far ahead. It always seemed to be tempting fate to even think of making it all the way here. And the Nazis may still invade England.'

She shuddered. 'God forbid.'

'I don't know what we'll do next, but in some ways it doesn't matter as long as Sara and I can be together.' His eyes hooked hers, and something passed between her and Isaak, a tingling, mixed with an ache of the heart. 'What about you?'

She was suddenly tongue-tied. She thought of Jørgen, somewhere out there, trying to fetch her back and it was too hard to contemplate what might have happened to him. And yet here was this man, looking at her with such a clear, open gaze that she could not drag her eyes away. 'Too soon,' she managed. 'It's too soon, I think, to make any firm plans or commitments.'

'You're probably right,' he said. But the light in his eyes dimmed.

She pulled back her sleeve to see her watch, and then remembered anew it was broken. 'Better sleep. We'll be able to actually see where we've ended up tomorrow. I hope they give a good breakfast. My stomach's rattling against my ribs.'

'Mine too.' There was a moment's silence. 'Goodnight Astrid. I hope your face doesn't hurt too much.' His voice was soft, and his hand patted her shoulder, and rested there, light as a butterfly.

The touch broke something inside her, a sort of grief she couldn't explain.

CHAPTER 32

In the morning, the sky was clearer, with a crisp breeze blowing and rays of sunshine spiking through the rushing clouds. They were woken by the movement of the boat, and they all went up on deck to witness the sight of Lerwick coming into view, with its row of stone cottages and smoke already billowing from the chimneys.

'Look! Look!' shouted Sara. It brought tears to Astrid's eyes.

A hand grasped her arm. 'Thank you,' Isaak said, close to her ear. 'We couldn't have got here without you.'

'Nor I without you,' she said, turning. 'You gave me the reason to come.'

He reached out his arms and she fell into them. They hugged silently for a long while, and she gripped him so tight, it was as if he'd always been a part of her.

'Me!' Sara shouted. 'Let me in to the hug!'

They laughed, and opened their arms. When Astrid looked at Isaak's face his eyes were glassy too.

Clausen helped them off, and it was marvellous to feel her feet on solid ground after so many weeks of snow and sea. They had to be taken for debriefing, to have their papers checked, and a health check, before anyone could be allowed to go onwards. A woman called Morag did the honours.

'Astrid Dahl?' she asked, as if she didn't believe her.

'Yes. Is something wrong?'

'No, nothing.'

But Morag's slightly chilly stare made Astrid uncomfortable. She chided herself. She was being silly and imagining the hostility. It was the shock of the last few days, and the fact she was safe hadn't yet registered. Her body hadn't realised yet that no-one would come after her with a machine gun.

After checking their papers and bags, Morag provided tea and bread and jam, in a big old house that used to be a Catholic Mission. She smiled at Sara and handed her a thick slice of bread and jam.

'Jam,' Sara said, gazing at the bread as if it was a hallucination.

Isaak and Sara joined Astrid at a table by the window and the three of them sipped tea. It was so normal, so ordinary. A cup and saucer, a plate. Things they had taken for granted now seemed amazing. 'Gosh, that's good,' Astrid said. 'I don't think I've ever been so grateful for a hot drink in my life.'

Later, Morag came over rattling a set of keys in her hand. 'I'll drive you over to the refugee house now,' Morag said to Isaak in Norwegian. 'You and Sara will have a room there. It's where we put families.' She turned to Sara. 'Look out for our Shetland ponies on the way, won't you, and shout if you see one.'

'Can't Miss Dahl come with us?' Sara asked coming and clinging to Astrid's arm. 'She's family.'

'You'll see her tomorrow,' Morag said. Again, that slight hint of disapproval.

Astrid and Isaak hugged and Sara hurried after Morag.

'Have a nice evening, Astrid,' Isaak said.

Astrid stared at him a moment. It seemed such a banal statement. Her lips began to twitch. The smile spread to him until he began to laugh. Unable to stop herself, she felt the laughter bubbling up in side, until they were both standing there clutching their sides. 'A nice evening!' she echoed, overcome by mirth.

Morag and Sara reappeared, looking at them both as if they were crazy. There were more gales of laughter, until finally Sara scolded him, 'Pappa! Stop laughing. Hurry up, we're going to see the ponies.'

When they'd gone, a man called Harcourt came and showed Astrid the way to the women's barracks, an old fish factory.

'Please, can you tell me if there's any news of Jørgen Nystrøm?' she asked. 'We heard his boat was in trouble, and we were picked up by Clausen in the *Bergholt* instead.'

Harcourt shook his head. 'It's bad news, I'm afraid. They telephoned Milorg from the village. The boat went down in an explosion after a fight with a German warship.'

'But what about Jørgen?'

'Still unaccounted for. But don't hold out too much hope, my dear. I'm afraid we suspect he might have gone down with the boat. We'll wait a month, see if we get more news.'

The women's barracks were empty, and when Harcourt had gone, she spent a long time just staring into space. She wasn't ready yet to think Jørgen was dead. It was complex, her feelings about it. The idea of drowning was all connected with her parents and the thought of another underwater death made all her old grief resurface.

Yet in these last weeks, she'd felt more connected to Isaak than to Jørgen. She'd always thought she needed a hero, someone to admire and look up to. That if she could only be accepted by the people who were popular, she would be popular too. But Isaak wasn't a hero. He'd accepted her just as she was. But more than that, he and Sara needed her, and she'd responded, and the thought of being without them both made her realise how much they meant to her.

Yet she couldn't quite let Jørgen go; he was part of her past, part of the Norway she loved. At the same time, Isaak was part of the new Astrid, the woman who could defy the Nazis and walk hundreds of miles to freedom. The strong woman who was able to survive a storm and a battle at sea. *At sea!* She marvelled at herself.

It was odd to be suddenly so alone after so many weeks, and yet here she was. She went to look out of the window, to find she faced inland, and there was no view of the sea here. But above the hill a kestrel hovered, poised beneath earth and sky.

Two days later, they gathered for the funeral of Mathison, and to hold a Memorial to Nils, the agent they'd buried at sea. Many local people turned out, coat collars turned up against the wind, but it seems Mathison was a well-known crew member, and Nils well-respected by all the rest of the Norwegians who manned the boats for the 'Shetland Bus'.

The small stone church was packed to overflowing. Astrid caught sight of Isaak and Sara ahead of her and hurried to join them. Sara stood to let her pass and she found herself next to Isaak. He placed a hand on hers as the coffin was brought in, and she squeezed his back in return. She could barely understand the service, for it was all in Scottish, and her limited English couldn't understand the accent, but the solemnity of the faces gathered in the cold grey church made a deep impression. As Mathison's body was committed to the ground, a local man lifted his bugle to play the last post, before two of the Norwegian crew members broke into the Norwegian National Anthem.

To hear those words carried on the breeze out to sea made her heart ache with pain for Norway and all those left behind.

Isaak put his arm around her and hugged her.

'Miss Dahl?' Sara said. She silently passed her a handkerchief. Once Astrid had blown her nose, Sara said, 'You can keep it.'

Astrid and Isaak laughed through the tears.

CHAPTER 33

Jørgen was stiff and numb, the bottoms of his trousers frozen into hard creases when he drifted back out of sleep. He and Karl had huddled in each other's arms for warmth and piled pine branches underneath and over them in an effort to conserve warmth. He hadn't slept much. Karl was a traitor and he should shoot him, yet Karl hadn't lifted a finger against him. It made it seem inhumane. And what was he himself fighting against? Nazi inhumanity.

Besides, their situation was pretty bad. When he was simply trying to survive, taking sides seemed irrelevant; it was all he could do to muster the energy to move. He was tired, and running low on resources. His toes were stinging so much with chilblains he could hardly bend them. Or maybe it was frostbite. And if he wanted to get out of Norway alive he knew it would take a superhuman effort.

Maybe some help from Milorg would be a good idea after all. He still remembered the number of the doctor in Radøy. Dr Moen might know what had happened to Astrid and the refugees. But getting to the telephone would be risky. They'd have to travel carefully and wait until dark to call. He was too exhausted to plan another hike.

He prodded Karl's back to wake him. 'Bit of light in the sky now if we're going to get moving.'

Karl slapped him on the shoulder, smiled in silent acknowledgement, and hauled himself to his feet. Inside the forest it was still dark but as they emerged towards the shore a little wan sunlight peeked through the clouds to warm them. In the daylight it was easier to see the terrain.

Jørgen scanned the fjord anxiously for German boats but could see none. No sign of any other boats either. 'We'll walk at the edge of the forest,' he said. 'Can't risk going too near that farm.'

Karl didn't answer him, but set off trudging along the edge of the trees, back again towards the coast, with the forest on their left.

Every snap of a twig, cry of a bird or jump of a fish made Jørgen's heart pound and adrenaline surge through his veins. They saw three patrol boats trawling the edge of the fjord, and had to bolt back under cover. One of the boats stopped a lone guy who was fishing and it looked like they were questioning him. On the ridge opposite, they saw more men, rifles on their shoulders. Heart thumping, he and Karl flattened themselves to the ground until they passed.

As they got nearer habitation, they lay down behind some rocks to look down on the fjord again and the settlement clustered at the shore. An offshore wind had got up, and the water was full of miniature rills. The warship was still there water slapping against its sides, and there were also four German motorbikes that must have been brought in by boat, and two more German patrol boats by the pontoon. There were no civilians to be seen. After the explosion yesterday they were obviously keeping themselves away from the increased number of troops in the town square.

A black Mercedes-Benz was now parked by the harbour — presumably drafted in since the *Vidar* had gone down. The only road in or out seemed to be up over the mountains and a road block had been set up there manned by the Wehrmacht.

The sight of their helmets aroused an inner hatred that fuelled his anger against these interlopers in his land. 'We'll never do it,' Jørgen said. 'Too many Germans.'

Karl didn't look up. His eyes were fixed on the patrol below. Jørgen thought he looked as if he was enjoying himself, his eyes bright with some sort of fervour. 'There's the Post Office and general store,' Karl whispered, pointing his finger at a red-painted clapperboard building. 'And that fisherman was right. There's a telephone. I can see the pole and wires behind it.'

'Let's hope they haven't cut the wires.' Just as Jørgen said that, a woman in a black winter coat and galoshes hurried over from a side-street and stepped inside the Post Office. After a few minutes she emerged again, pushing something into her handbag.

'It's open,' Karl said. 'Now all we have to do is get inside.'

Though it was daytime, the lights were on inside because of the winter gloom. As it grew darker, the activity in the village seemed to shift to what was obviously a tavern. They watched as many soldiers headed indoors out of the cold. All except four by the roadblock. Jørgen had begun to shiver again and his hands were turning numb now that the meagre warmth had gone out of the day.

They inched their way downhill, mostly on their bellies and backs, hiding behind what cover they could find and stopping every time there was movement in the square. It was a long and painful descent, but finally they propped themselves up behind a turf-roofed barn. They could hear the bleat of goats from inside, but fortunately the animals paid them no attention.

Jørgen took out his pistol and loaded it. Karl did the same. Karl's was identical to his; standard naval issue from their waterproof pouches, an old Webley No.1 Automatic. He had a momentary flashback to the long pistol with the silencer, the one he'd first seen in the mountain hut. It seemed years ago.

'We'll go in together,' Jørgen said. He didn't trust Karl an inch.

'Yes, then one of us can cover while the other's on the phone.'

'Who'll call their people first?' Jørgen said.

Karl pulled up a hunk of coarse grass and carefully separated two strands. 'Choose. Short straw calls first.'

Jørgen was unsurprised to find he'd plucked out the short straw. So he was to go first. Silently they nodded to each other. He waited until the men at the road block were walking away from him. 'Now.'

Karl jumped up and they began to walk briskly towards the Post Office.

Every step hurt his feet. Every step seemed to take forever. His neck sunk into his shoulders as he listened for shouts or shots. He could hear Karl's breath just behind him.

Nearly there. Desperate to be out of sight, he fumbled as he pulled open the door.

The elderly white-haired woman behind the counter glanced up with a welcoming smile. It died when Karl aimed the gun towards her chest. 'Lock the door,' Karl said. If you're quiet, I won't shoot. We need to use the telephone.'

She nodded dumbly, her eyes wide behind her spectacles.

'We won't hurt you,' Jørgen said, sorry for her. 'Just lock the door.'

As if galvanized into motion, she fumbled in her pocket and hurried to the door where she pulled down the blackout blind, took out a key and turned it in the lock.

'Is there a back door to this place?' Karl asked, following her.

'No. That's the only door. What is it? What's going on?'

'Give me the key.'

She handed it to Karl as if it was on fire.

'If someone comes, don't answer, okay?' Jørgen said. 'Just keep quiet, and pretend you're not home. And show me your telephone.'

She looked up at him. Her fear had turned into a cold hard expression. 'The Germans'll kill me for this,' she said. 'And the rest of the village. They'll think it's my fault.' She stuck out her chin. 'All you Resistance men are the same; you care nothing for innocent Norwegians. It'll be like the massacre at Telavåg. I hate you. Every last one of you.'

Her words stabbed him where it hurt. Jørgen took out his pistol, anger flaring. 'Just show me the telephone.'

She was cowed then, and that hurt worse. The thought he'd just threatened an innocent woman made him squirm. She showed him where the wooden booth was at the corner of the shop, while Karl kept lookout by the door. Jørgen gestured the woman to sit on a rush-topped stool where people obviously waited to use the phone. He dialled the operator with the booth door open and the gun still pointing at her, the receiver clamped between ear and shoulder. When he got through to Dr Moen, the doctor was amazed.

'Nystrøm?'

He explained that he was the only survivor of the *Vidar*. He didn't mention Karl, though he could clearly see his tall, broad-shouldered figure pacing by the door.

There was silence on the other end, though he could hear the slight buzz of the line.

'Doctor?'

'Sorry, I can't help you. You shouldn't even be calling, the line could be tapped. It's too dangerous to do a pick-up in these circumstances.' Moen gave an audible sigh. 'I have to think of the others I help.'

'I understand.' The disappointment was needle-sharp. He was on his own. He didn't dare think what that meant.

A pause and the line crackled — mumbling in the background. Eventually, another voice, younger, hurried, said, 'I can tell you though, there are three fishing boats moored at the end of the spit, out past the warship. If one of those went missing in the middle of the night, well…'

Jørgen was saying thank you to the unknown man when Moen cut in over him. 'Good luck, Nystrøm.'

The line went dead.

The postmistress was still sitting on the stool, twisting the strings of her overall in her hands. 'All your friends went down on that boat?'

He nodded. A sudden vision of Lars, sinking in the dinghy, made him swallow.

Karl had hooked a finger round the blind and raised the corner. 'Watch out!' he said, dropping the blind. 'Wehrmacht man.' He swivelled his gun on the postmistress. 'Stay out of sight. Don't make a sound, or I'll shoot.'

The door shook and rattled as the German tried to open it. 'You open?' the voice came from outside. A bang, as if he'd kicked the door. The woman scurried away and ducked down behind the counter, obviously expecting trouble.

Another bang. 'Lousy shop. I only want tobacco. Open up.'

Jørgen and Karl kept the gun trained on the door as it rattled and strained against the jamb.

After more expletives in German, there was the sound of footsteps as the soldier walked away. Jørgen let out his breath. 'Thank God. I thought he was going to break the door down.'

'You get through to Milorg?' Karl asked him.

'Yep. Nothing doing. Got to find my own way. There's a boat at the end of the spit. When you've made contact with your man, I'll head for that.'

'Okay. Watch the door in case he comes back with reinforcements. I'll call Falk now, get him to call off the men and arrange a pick up.'

'Hope you have better luck than I did.'

The woman emerged from under the counter to plead with Karl. 'Please, just leave me in peace. We didn't want to be in any battle.'

'Stop whining,' Karl said, pointing his gun. His aggressive tone was enough to silence her. He strode towards the telephone booth and ducked inside, swinging the wooden door shut.

In Oslo, Falk was having his second cup of coffee and his third biscuit. He'd always had a sweet tooth and it showed in his waistline. Whilst he was doing it, he was reading through the papers for the deportation of the Jews. He was to supply two hundred officers for the transportation of prisoners via the SS Donau which would leave Oslo for Stettin on the 26th November. He wiped a crumb from his lips. From there, onwards to the German camp Auschwitz.

When the telephone rang in the outer office it made him jump and knock his coffee cup against his teeth.

A moment later, Selma knocked, put her head round the door. 'Karl Brevik on the telephone, sir. Shall I put him through?'

Brevik? Impossible. His thoughts raced. The ship had blown itself up. A suicide mission as Nystrøm tried to sink the German warship. Two men got away; eyewitnesses said one was Nystrøm, and they were still searching for him. But the other — he'd assumed… He slammed his cup down. 'Put him through.' He grabbed the receiver.

Brevik's voice came through in an intense whisper. 'You messed up. You nearly killed me. Here's the deal. I've got Milorg man Jørgen Nystrøm here with me. The Germans think I'm one of the Milorg men that keep him company. You have a choice. Either you get me out of here, or I leave with Nystrøm and give the English all the information I have.'

'Now wait a minute,' Falk blustered, trying to take in all this information.

'No. No time. You promised me my money. Do you want Nystrøm or not?'

Falk's pulse quickened. The thought of arresting Nystrøm after all this time was sweet. But he didn't want Brevik alive to tell the tale.

Brevik was still talking in a rapid whisper. Falk pressed the receiver to his ear until it hurt.

'You'll need to send a car to fetch us,' Brevik was saying. 'There's a Mercedes parked close to here. A gas-powered thing. Get word to the Germans we want out. But I won't go anywhere without Nystrøm. He's my insurance, and if you mess up again, I'll shoot him. Understand? Once we're in Oslo and I get paid, I'll hand him over.'

'Yes.' Falk managed to get a word in. 'Yes to your terms. Now tell me where you are.'

'Stortlefjord. The Post Office. I want to see the car pull up outside before we come out, or Nystrøm's dead.'

So Brevik was still there by the fjord? Why hadn't the Wehrmacht found them before now? Bloody inefficiency. 'Deal,' Falk said. 'You'll have your car. Stay where you are. I'll get word to German command and the Stapo.'

The line went dead. Falk found his heart thudding uncomfortably loud in his chest. Today was going to be a good day after all. He rubbed his stomach where a twinge of indigestion stabbed in his side. Then he picked up the receiver again and asked Selma to put him through to Fehlis.

Karl was a long time on the phone. Through the glass in the door Jørgen could see him cranking the handle, then talking rapidly, though he had turned his back to them. Finally, he sauntered out, and gave Jørgen a smile. 'They're arranging a pickup. But it won't be until tomorrow. So I guess I'll just have to spend the night here.'

'I don't want you here overnight,' the woman protested. 'Please, I don't live very far away. I just want to go home.'

'Unless you want a bullet through the head, you've no choice,' Karl said. She paled. 'But you could do something useful. Neither of us has eaten. Can you get out some food — bread, meats, cheese?'

Silently, she went to the counter and began to slice up a loaf of black bread.

Jørgen went to the door to check for Germans and see which way the patrol was facing on the road. 'Looks quiet out there,' he said to Karl. 'If you pass me the key, I'm going to get on the road soon as I can. I'm definitely not hanging on for your quisling friends.'

'Aw, come on. A few minutes more whilst you have some food won't make a difference.'

'I'd rather get going. Being cooped up like this makes me jittery. Just give me the key.'

Karl walked over, one hand feeling in his pocket, as Jørgen held out his hand for the key. 'Sorry. No can do.' Karl leapt forward and pressed his gun to Jørgen's neck.

Jørgen's stomach dropped like a stone. 'You wouldn't.' His mouth went dry.

'Best sit down, Jørgen. I'm not playing games.'

'You double-crossing bastard. You're going to hand me over.'

'Don't move,' Karl said. 'Drop the gun.'

Jørgen hesitated, but Karl pressed the muzzle of the gun against the soft flesh of his neck. The woman dived down behind the counter, hands over her head. Jørgen let his gun fall with a clatter.

'Move to the door,' Karl said. 'Nice and slow.'

Jørgen shuffled until he was close to the door with its blind hanging down. Karl lifted the blind with his other hand. 'Karl, can we at least —'

'Shut up. I'm not bluffing.'

Jørgen was still, but his mind raced. What were the probabilities of getting out of this alive? Less than five percent if he made a run for it, and the door would have to be open. If he didn't fight, Karl would hand him over to be questioned by the Stapo. He'd be dead by now if he didn't have some value to Karl and the Germans. But if he bided his time that meant a journey to a cell and probably more guards. Several enemies, instead of one on one.

Karl lifted the blind again, waiting for someone.

Jørgen's thoughts kept churning. Easier to give the Germans the slip if they were on the move. But then again, the more guards, the worse the odds. He hedged his bets. He'd wait until the moment the door opened, then try to make a run. If they shot him, well, it would be better for Larsen's Shetland operation than him giving up their secrets under torture.

They must have waited there for forty-five minutes. Jørgen's legs started to shake. He was tired and tense, and ready to run, but every minute of waiting made his heart race faster. A cold sweat trickled down his back. Finally, he heard it, the noise of a car engine start up, the roar of motorbikes. Karl lifted the blind for the umpteenth time. Jørgen glimpsed a big black car and a motorcycle escort drawing up outside the shop.

The pressure on his neck eased a touch. He risked a look at Karl who was pulling the key from his pocket. *Not yet*, he told himself. *Go easy. Got to wait until the door's open.*

Karl put the key in the lock and pulled up the blind for one more look. There were voices outside and a creak of a car door opening, over the hum of the idling engine.

'Do exactly as I say,' Karl said, pressing the gun to the back of his skull. His hand reached past Jørgen to turn the key and pull open the door.

A push from behind and Jørgen was out. Cold wind battered his face. A voice in his head screamed 'Run!' but there was no time. The car was there, but there was no space to move. Karl pushed him in through the car's open door, and was about to follow him.

No sooner had Jørgen hit the leather seat than there was a double pistol shot from behind him. Instinctively, he turned.

He was unhurt.

Then he understood. They'd gunned Karl down right inside the car door.

Karl was clinging to the car roof, an expression of bewilderment on his face. He was slipping, and he tried to haul himself up by grasping the sill. His eyes looked into Jørgen's with disbelief, his mouth opened to speak, but no sound came.

The German nearest the car had levelled his gun again, and now pulled the trigger at point black range. A dull crack and Karl fell.

Jørgen stared in horror at the crumpled shape at his feet, before anger surged inside him. Almost immediately his body hit panic mode. He saw his chance and shot across the seat to where the guard on the other side had his door half open. He thrust his whole weight behind the door and gave the man an almighty push. With a cry, the German staggered before he was knocked off his feet. Jørgen scrambled over him and began to run down the street, dodging side to side to the path by the fjord. Chance of escape, three percent. He leapt over a hay-drying fence, almost stumbled and ploughed onwards into the dark. Shots rang out after him — the strafe of a machine gun, flashes in the dark. A motorcycle started up and roared behind him, but the machine couldn't get over the fence.

Men shouting to each other.

Mustn't stop. Across fields. Over a gate. Into the dark, his chest like a dry husk, his side in a spasm of cramp. He pelted past the lights of the warship on his right, which was sounding a klaxon alarm. He was vaguely aware of men like ants gathering on the deck.

Head down, he saw the end of the land and the glimmer of open sea.

Frantically he rushed up and down the rocky promontory searching for the boats.

He glanced back. They were gaining on him.

Another burst of fire.

There! A sudden rush of euphoria. He rushed down the rocks to the pebbly shallows and unhooked the nearest boat from its moorings. It was an *Oselvar*, a sailing boat like the ones he'd seen in Shetland.

He pushed the boat hard and leapt in. He barely thought, just hoisted the sail and to his relief, it filled like a great pale balloon. The wind was stiff and he grabbed the rudder and turned it into the breeze.

Another spate of fire missed him by a bare inch but tore a hole in the bottom of the sail. It wasn't enough to stop him bearing away. He kept heading out to sea, out over the waves with Shetland firmly in his sights.

CHAPTER 34

At the harbourmaster's stores, a large hangar with a tin roof, Astrid spoke to the harbourmaster about Jørgen Nystrøm and the *Vidar* to see if more news had come.

'I know no more'n you. He was well-liked, Nystrøm. Never took to his friend though, Karl Brevik. He was a bit stand-offish with the fishermen, like we weren't good enough for him.' He paused in packing up some fishing weights. 'Sorry, it's bad to speak ill... I mean, when we don't know what's happened yet. But I hope Nystrøm's safe somewhere. And I'm not the only one. Morag Airdrie's been mooning after him for months.'

'Morag?' She stepped back in surprise.

'Aye. She thinks no-one knows, but it's as plain to see as the nose on my face.'

Astrid wandered out of the hangar, her gaze straying out to sea for the umpteenth time. There was nothing in view on the horizon, merely gulls shrieking round the mouth of the harbour as a fisherman mended his nets by the harbour wall. Did Morag know she'd been Jørgen's girlfriend? Was that why she was so strange with her?

'Miss Dahl!'

She turned to see Sara running towards her. She was wearing a brightly flowered frock and a blue cardigan. Her shoes shone with polish. Behind her, Isaak hurried along by the cottages. He was wearing a different coat, old but good quality.

'Hello smarty-pants,' Astrid said, swinging Sara up for a hug.

'We're leaving this afternoon,' Sara said, breathless. 'We're going by boat then a train. I'm a bit scared of the boat, but

Pappa says there won't be any Nazis or guns. There are no Nazis in Scotland, he says.' Her excited face was rosier than Astrid had seen it for months.

Astrid bent down to put Sara on the ground. 'So soon?' she said. 'You were a very brave girl. We couldn't have done it, couldn't have got here at all, without your clever acting.'

'Oh, Miss Dahl,' Sara said, and suddenly reached her hands around Astrid's neck for a hug. 'I'll miss you.'

'And I'll miss you.' Astrid hugged her back, fiercely. 'You take care,' she said. 'And write to me, care of Captain Harcourt. Tell me what you're doing in school.'

'What will you do?' Isaak had arrived, and was standing watching. 'You can't go back to Norway.'

'I'll stay on here a while. They need more women to do domestic stuff, get things ready for the Norwegian agents that come in and out from this place, mend clothes, you know…'

'You're still waiting for Nystrøm, aren't you?'

She flushed. 'It feels like I'd be letting him down if I didn't wait. He knew I was waiting and he risked his life to get us out, but we still don't know what happened to him. I can't rest easy until I know.'

He shook his head, but his eyes were soft. 'He's a very lucky man. I thought … well, I thought we made rather a good family.'

His words winded her. She looked up into his face and saw how he looked at her with a light in his eyes she'd tried to push away. 'I —'

'No, no need to say anything,' he said. 'I wish you well, I truly do. I hope he comes home safe.' Now he was hurrying on, glossing over what had probably been the most important thing anyone had ever said to her. 'We'll keep in touch and there'll always be a place for you wherever we go. London seems so far away, but I hope we'll get resettled there, and I can begin my book business again. I'll write, and I'll make Sara write and tell you all her news, just as soon as we have an address.'

'I can't believe you're going,' Astrid said, her voice choked.

He held out his arms and they hugged tight, until Astrid pulled away.

'Don't miss your lift,' she said, through eyes brimming with tears.

Watching them walk away was like watching half her life disappear.

'Good luck!' Her wave was a desperate gesture.

Isaak strode away, upright and unbowed, with Sara hopping along beside him. And for the first time she really understood what it was like to be a refugee. They had been half-way across Europe already, built a new life, and now they were travelling again to some unknown place where they must do it all over again with only one small suitcase between them.

Out on the sea, Jørgen's euphoria was short-lived. The Germans would be after him soon enough. He couldn't go far in this. Little boats like this weren't built for open water. And the whole coast was riddled with Nazi patrol boats. Again, he weighed his options. There were few. He was about two miles out now and still heading for Shetland in the dark. Could he try to sail to Shetland in what amounted to a dinghy? Impossible. And planes or motorboats would soon pick him off. It left only one option. To sail up the coast and hope to get on a bigger boat. He was just thinking this when he heard the 'tonk tonk' of an engine. Hastily, he lowered sail. No point in advertising his presence. But when the boat heaved into view, he made out the dim outline of an old Norwegian fishing boat, a big one, not a German patrol. No lights.

Please let them be sympathisers.

'Hey!' he yelled. He stood and waved, hoisted the sail again.

The boat turned and came towards him. He watched it approach with trepidation. They could be quislings, and then it really would be the end.

'Jørgen Nystom?' a voice came out of the dark.

'Yes, Nystrøm,' he called.

'Dr Moen.' Jørgen sagged. It was friends. He could have wept. 'Want to come aboard?'

'You bet. What about the *Oselvar*?'

'Leave her drifting. Someone will pick her up. Some fishing friends have lent us this boat. We've to get you back to Shetland.'

'What, now?'

A ladder dropped down into the sea. He had a moment's panic trying to climb it, but then a hand extended down to help him up. Suddenly his limbs felt like lead. They hoisted him on deck and someone found him a bottle of beer. The rush of it made him immediately light-headed. The fishing boat plunged through the waves, but Jørgen was too exhausted to feel anything. At some point he was helped into the wheelhouse where he collapsed against a wall. Someone brought him a blanket. He slept.

When he awoke it was to see the sky weirdly aflame. Adrenaline surged, and he leapt up and out of the cabin. But it wasn't enemy fire. The whole horizon was flaring with a swathe of green; a vivid transparent river flowing across the sky. He went to stand on deck.

'*Aurora borealis*,' Moen said. 'The Northern Lights.'

Jørgen watched the sky shift and change, as if playing some great tune no-one could hear. A curtain, swaying across eternity. He thought of Karl, lying on the street where he'd left him, betrayed by the men who were supposed to help him. He wondered what had made Karl the man he was, and who would mourn him. He had been far luckier, to have friends who would risk themselves to save his life, just to keep him on this beautiful earth. He was humbled by it.

And as the colours eddied and danced, his thoughts turned to Shetland. Could they see this there? He wished Morag was here with him, out here on the ocean, under the emerald sky.

'I had to leave some refugees behind,' he said to Dr Moen. 'A woman escorting a Jewish child and her father. I failed them.'

'No,' Dr Moen said. 'They made it. I dropped them with Clausen. God willing, they'll be in Shetland by now. We're following in the same wind.'

CHAPTER 35

Astrid slit open the letter and pulled out the thin piece of paper. It was written in Norwegian, with colourful crayon drawings in the margins. Isaak's signature and his neat bookish hand set off a breathless feeling in her chest.

Dear Astrid,

We have been lucky and have temporary lodgings right in the East End of London where there are many other Jewish people with similar stories to ours. Such a relief. Of course we had just got settled when they found out we are German Jews, so we are to be transferred again to a camp for 'aliens' in the countryside. I begged them to let us stay together, and after all my explaining, they finally agreed. So we are to go to Sussex to a camp for families there. Another journey. I'll write again when we arrive. Sara is well, but she misses you, and she is so longing for a place to put down roots and be a child with playmates again.

She has drawn the dog on the top of this paper. She is determined we will have one, one day. I think the business when she made up the imaginary dog must have been a long-held wish! I hope you are well. We are so surprised at how much food there is in England and how green the land is.

When I said Sara misses you, I mean I do too.

Do write, a letter would give me so much joy.

Until we meet again, and I hope we will soon,

Isaak

The ache in her heart was quickly replaced by frustration. Even in England they were being treated as enemies. And he was a good man, Isaak, not deserving of it.

She tucked the letter in her pocket as she walked to the laundry. She would write later when she had some quiet time, and as soon as she had his new address she would send a letter. He missed her, he said. The thought echoed inside her as if around an empty room, painful but consoling. She had not known missing someone could be this sore.

The laundry room was steamy, with big metal tubs on trestle tables where the sheets were being laundered or wound through the two mangles near the doors. One of the other women, an English woman called Eileen, who was also labouring over the wash tub, looked up and smiled.

'News just come in,' she said, rubbing red hands on her pinafore. 'Another boat from Norway's due today. Landed last night near Sandwick, so they say. They should arrive here mid-morning. Daresay they'd like a welcome. Will you go out to meet it?'

So after hanging out the sheets, she walked down to the harbour. Already there was a crowd. Captain Harcourt, his pipe hanging out of his mouth, was chatting to the head of operations, Larsen. On the new slipway the skipper Clausen, who had brought her over, was staring out at the waves.

Further down, standing on her own was Morag Airdrie, her brown hair blown sideways in the gusts. Astrid watched one of the fishermen go down to talk to her.

The wind dropped. She felt something in the air, a quiet tension, broken only by the swoosh and slap of waves. Then the familiar 'tonk tonk' of an engine.

They crowded to the landing stage. There it was, the bow cresting the waves. And right at the front, a man with his hand lifted.

She stood back, half-afraid. Was it him?

She looked again, her eyes fixed on the man near the prow. There was no mistaking the set of his shoulders. It was Jørgen Nystrøm. The word ran round the men quickly and they let out a cheer. Astrid cheered with them, a wild whoop of joy.

It took a few moments to secure the boat and for the men to get ashore. He was thinner — worn-looking and weather-beaten, a scruffy beard — but unhurt. Harcourt was slapping him on the back, but his eyes were restless, searching the crowd.

Jørgen's gaze passed over Astrid as if she didn't exist, and then he caught sight of Morag. His face seemed to lose its tension. Morag gave a half wave and he broke away from the others and rushed towards her. She gave a huge smile and within a few seconds he had swept her up and swung her round. They hugged for a long time, tightly folded in each other's arms.

Astrid let out a long breath as if a weight had fallen away.

She watched as Jørgen bent down to listen to what Morag was saying. Then they both looked over to her, and she guessed from that, that Morag was pointing her out.

They came over together, Jørgen limping, but holding Morag's arm tight in the crook of his elbow.

'You made it,' he said to her. His smile was open and friendly.

'No thanks to you,' Astrid said, grinning. 'What held you up?'

'A few Germans,' he said. 'They seemed to want to kill me.'

Morag turned to him. 'What about your friend, Karl?'

Jørgen pressed his lips together and his eyes clouded. 'He saved my life,' he said. 'But he didn't make it.' There was a kind of finality to his words.

Morag squeezed his arm.

Jørgen glanced down into Morag's face as if to reassure her, before returning his gaze to Astrid. 'Your refugees? Are they safe? When they said Astrid Dahl, I couldn't believe it could be you.'

'Another long story, but they're both well. I got rather close to them actually and I'm going to visit them as soon as I can, maybe stay awhile.' She hoped he read the message in her expression. *I'm letting you go.*

He smiled, the understanding soft in his eyes.

She had barely time to register it before they were swept up by Harcourt and Larsen and all the crew of the Shetland Bus, all wanting to share stories and welcome home their lost sailor. She recognised Dr Moen, who she'd last seen in Norway, but she didn't rush to greet him.

She stood aside as the crowd walked up towards the village, away from the harbour, and she didn't hurry after them. Instead, she sat on the harbour wall and watched the boat shift on the undulating tide. She was glad Jørgen was safe, and she had a good feeling about him and Morag. It felt natural, inevitable even.

A feeling of deep peace settled over her, as if all the jarring parts of her had resolved into harmony. She put her hands deep into her pockets and as her fingers touched something cold, she remembered, and drew out her father's compass.

It seemed to be a message from him, a confirmation that she had survived this particular journey, and even if there were others, he'd somehow still be with her.

She'd always keep it. It would be something to remind her of Jørgen, the man who came to rescue her from her beloved Norway, the man she had to miss meeting, in order to find Isaak, the man who moved her heart. And Sara, who needed family the same way she did.

She gazed at the water and let the rolling motion of the swell soothe her as she weighed the compass from palm to palm. In her imagination she took a train to Sussex, to rolling green fields and sunshine glinting on a sandy shore. Soon she'd go there, take hold of Isaak's and Sara's hands, and away in the distance, a dog called Runa would romp ahead of them, tail wagging in joy, as he bounded into the sea.

HISTORICAL NOTES

The Shetland Bus

In the year 1940 more than fifty fishing boats made the perilous journey between Norway and Shetland, known to Norwegians as 'England', although in fact Shetland is an island in the North Sea closer to Scotland. In 1941, 2,388 people were carried by the small army of boats that made up the Shetland Bus, and this continued until late 1942 when an increase in German Forces around Norway's coastline, and the Nazi's determination to stop the traffic to England, and infiltration of their contacts, made it too dangerous for fishing boats to take the risk.

During its time of operation the Shetland Bus took not only escapees, but also equipment such as radio transmitters with their trained operators. Hundreds of tons of arms, weaponry and military equipment were shipped to the Resistance in Norway, and in return naval intelligence on the location of German troops, positions of warships, and the German military plans for the Baltic made the journey back.

Operating mainly in the winter months where cover of darkness made it possible to go in and out of the small inlets and fjords of the Norwegian coast, the Shetland Bus was lashed by the worst weather at sea that any boat could be expected to survive. This, and the fact that the boats were vulnerable to attack by German planes and submarines, made the journeys especially hazardous.

After the Shetland Bus operation was infiltrated by the Germans, many of the Milorg (Norwegian Resistance) were arrested and tortured, and the support network for the Shetland Bus broken apart. Realising how essential the flow of traffic was between occupied Norway and the British Isles, the United States sent three subchasers which were more effectively armed and better able to survive Nazi attacks from air and sea. However, Norway still honours those countrymen who made the perilous journeys across the North Sea in their wooden fishing boats, and there is a museum for The Shetland Bus in Scalloway where visitors to Shetland can learn the real story.

The Norwegian Teacher's Strike

The Nazis wanted Norwegian schools to follow a fascist curriculum, and with this aim, Nazi sympathiser Minister President Quisling disbanded the existing teachers' union and ordered all teachers to register with the new Nazi Norwegian Teachers' Union. Three quarters of Norway's 12,000 teachers signed a letter refusing to cooperate. In response, the government closed the schools, sending the children home to their parents, and more than 200,000 annoyed parents then wrote letters to protest.

Classes were then held in secret, and teachers did their best to provide non-partisan education through any means possible. When it became apparent the teachers weren't caving in, the government ordered the arrest of 1000 teachers, 500 of whom were sent to a prison camp near Kirkenes in the Arctic.

As the teachers were shipped north, students and families gathered along the railway tracks, singing Norwegian songs and offering food and warm clothing to the teachers as they passed. Intimidation continued, but the strike continued in solidarity with teachers refusing to join the Nazi union.

Realising they could not continue with a school system that no longer functioned, on November 4th, 1942, the quisling government released all the teachers and abandoned their earlier plans. Ulf in my story would have been one of these men. During their time at Kirkenes, one teacher died and several were injured in the course of the back-breaking work they had to do. In times of war there are always compassionate people, and a German soldier secretly helped the teachers create beds out of hay to improve the spartan conditions.

The Norwegian teacher's strike is often used in schools now as an example of an occasion where non-violent resistance proved effective. Thanks to the courage and determination of the Norwegian teachers, their young people were protected from Nazi indoctrination, and Norway was prevented from becoming a fascist state.

SELECTED FURTHER READING

The Shetland Bus by David Howarth

Our Escape from Nazi-Occupied Norway by Leif Terdal

Shetland Bus Man by Kaare Iveson

Defiant Courage: A WWII Epic of Escape and Endurance by Astrid Karlsen

Hitler's Arctic War by Christer Jørgensen and Chris Mann

The Teachers' Protest Film

An Analysis of Norwegian Resistance during The Second World War

A NOTE TO THE READER

Thank you for choosing this book and I hope you enjoyed *THE LIFELINE*. All the characters in the novel are fictitious, and so are their stories. There was no such boat as the *Vidar*. However, *The Lifeline* is based on research and the real events that took place between Norway and Shetland in WW2. The difficulties that Norwegians faced in using the lifeline of the Shetland Bus were real. You will find some explanatory historical notes at the end of the book.

If you've enjoyed *The Lifeline*, I would really appreciate an online review on **Goodreads** or **Amazon**, which will help other readers to discover it. I love to chat to other readers about what I'm reading too, so do look me up on my Facebook page: **AuthorDeborahSwift** or on Twitter: **@swiftstory**.

Deborah Swift

www.deborahswift.com

Sapere Books is an exciting new publisher of brilliant fiction and popular history.

To find out more about our latest releases and our monthly bargain books visit our website:
saperebooks.com

Printed in Great Britain
by Amazon